Gift Made Possible by
Medford Friends
of the Library

JACKSON COUNTY
Library Services

DATE DUE

GAYLORD

PRINTED IN U.S.A.

DRAGON HOUSE

**Center Point
Large Print**

**This Large Print Book carries the
Seal of Approval of N.A.V.H.**

DRAGON HOUSE

JOHN SHORS

CENTER POINT PUBLISHING
THORNDIKE, MAINE

ISBN: 978-1-60285-656-1

Library of Congress Cataloging-in-Publication Data

Shors, John, 1969-
   Dragon house / John Shors.
      p. cm.
   ISBN 978-1-60285-656-1 (library binding : alk. paper)
   1. Americans--Vietnam--Fiction. 2. Street children--Fiction.
   3. Self-realization--Fiction. 4. Vietnam--Fiction. 5. Large type books. I. Title.

PS3619.H668D73 2010
813'.6--dc22

2009035006

For Mom and Dad

Whose child is this
Who walks the streets
Who cries alone
Who fears the night?

Whose child is this
Who was never a child
Who has not known the touch
Of a loving hand?

Whose child is this
Who dreams of warmth, of bread,
    of simple things
Who aspires only to survive?

This child is ours.

—ANONYMOUS

AUTHOR'S NOTE

In 1965, the United States sent combat troops into Vietnam to thwart a communist takeover of the southern half of the country. Fighting alongside their allies, the South Vietnamese, American forces waged a conventional war against the North Vietnamese, who received substantial logistical support from China and the Soviet Union. In 1975, Saigon fell, and the few remaining American troops were evacuated. During the course of the conflict, about five million soldiers and civilians were killed.

In 1986, the Vietnamese government launched free-market reforms, which led to substantial economic growth. The United States established diplomatic relations with the Socialist Republic of Vietnam in 1995.

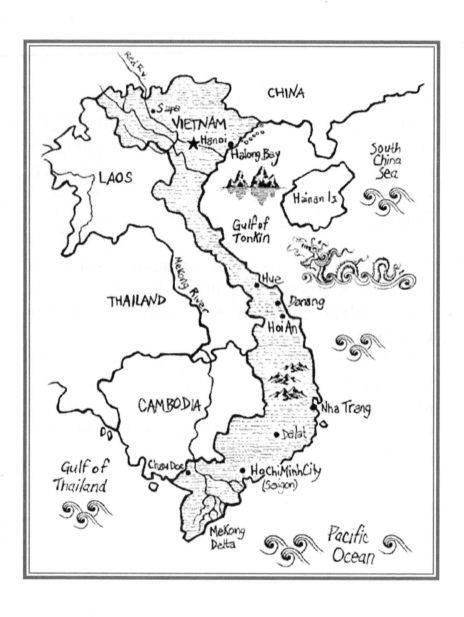

The Dreams of Another

The hospital room looked as ill as the patient it housed. Though everything was the color of fresh snow, the room's walls, ceiling, floor, and linens seemed tainted—as if the stains of misery and death had been scrubbed from them too many times. The room smelled not of life, but of chemicals and atrophy. Several bouquets of once-proud flowers leaned limply. Balloons that no longer tugged against their moorings hung in the stale air.

A man who looked older than his sixty-one years lay atop the room's only bed. He had been a large man, but now only the length of his frame hinted of the shadow he'd once cast. Clear tubes darted into his nose, the back of his hands. A razor hadn't slid over his face in more than a week, and a gray-and-white beard obscured the blemishes of time that dotted his skin.

His daughter sat beside his bed. She was taller than an average-size man, though her shoulders and waist were slender. Her eyes were as dark as walnuts. Her hair, a comparable color, was unkempt and rife with wide curls. Her face was thin like the rest of her. After thirty-one years of wear, the contours of her forehead and cheeks had been infiltrated by faint wrinkles. At first glance

11

she might have appeared awkward, but when she leaned forward to adjust his blankets, her movements were graceful.

"Are you still cold?" she asked, looking at a bag of clear fluid that hung from a steel post beside him. Her gaze followed a tube that ran from the bag into his flesh. "I could ask for another blanket," she added, wishing that he weren't so emaciated, that cancer hadn't already claimed so much of him.

He tried with little success to shake his head. His forefinger rose and her hand found his. "Do you remember," he asked faintly, "why I . . . why we chose your name?"

Iris had heard the story and nodded. "But tell me again."

"I wanted a reminder of the good in the world."

"Was I?"

"You are . . . the good in the world."

She smiled, wiping a tear from her cheek with her free hand. "Can I get you anything? Anything at all?"

He closed his eyes, appearing to fall asleep. He soon began to mumble and groan. He continued conversing with someone, though she wasn't sure whom. She sensed him fading away from her, falling into a distant world, and she leaned closer to him, squeezing his hand. Her grip seemed to bring him back. He opened his eyes. He studied her, recognizing her once again. "I'm sorry. . . . I failed you. Sorry I didn't . . . give you what I wanted to."

"Don't be—"

"My baby girl. My sweet baby girl. I made . . . such a mess of things."

She brought his hand to her lips, kissing it. "I don't want you to be sorry. You did your best. That's what matters."

"I thought . . . I could leave the war. Be good to your mother. To you. And I tried so hard . . . to leave it." His eyes glistened. His lips quivered.

She leaned over him, kissing his brow. "I love you."

He moaned faintly. She'd been told that the painkillers had numbed him to suffering, but still, she worried.

"We had some good times . . . didn't we?" he asked, his voice no stronger than the rustle of wind passing through leafless limbs.

"Of course we did."

He nodded.

She realized that he needed to hear about such times, needed to be reminded of what he'd done right. "I remember sitting on your shoulders," she said, "and walking to Cubs games. Listening to the crowd. Looking at all that grass. I loved those games. Do you know how special I felt? How lucky? I never wanted those afternoons to end."

A smile, feeble yet poignant, lit his face. "What else?"

She adjusted his pillow, stroked his hair to one side. "I loved it when you picked me up from school. When you took my hand and we walked to the ice-cream store. And you taught me how to ride a bike, and how to put a worm on a hook." She recalled a photo of the two of them holding a basket of bass, and her eyes began to tear again.

"Don't cry, my sweet Iris."

"I don't want you to go. I'm just not ready for that."

"I'm so proud of you. Proud that you escaped . . . the world I made for you. Proud of the . . . of the woman you've become."

She started to respond but stopped, aware that he wanted to say something else.

His lungs filled and emptied. "Two things in my life . . . I've been proud of. You . . . and my center in Saigon. You're both so wonderful."

Iris stroked the back of his hand, careful to avoid the bruises that covered most of his flesh, the wounds left by needles. "I've been thinking a lot about your center," she replied, trying to hide her apprehension. "I'm going to go, Dad. I'm going to finish what you started. What you almost finished."

"What?"

"I'll go to Saigon and see that it's opened."

"No."

"I've already decided."

"But . . . but your reviews. And your novel."

"I can take everything with me."

"Iris . . . don't go for—"

"I want to go. I need to."

"Why?"

"Because I love you. Because it will make you happy. And because you'll . . . rest better knowing that you helped those children. The beautiful children you've told me so much about."

Tears welled in his eyes. "Come here," he whispered.

She leaned against him, wrapping her arms around him, shuddering when she felt him kiss her head. "I want to go," she whispered. "I want to see the good that you've done."

"Are you sure? It's so far from home. From your mother."

"She understands. She thinks I should go."

"She does?"

"Yes."

"And you . . . really want to?"

"I want to do it for you. And those children."

He licked his cracked lips and she placed a piece of chipped ice in his mouth. "I love you more . . . more than anything else . . . in this world," he said. "I don't . . . deserve you. I never have."

Her tears dropped to his chest, and she stroked his brow. "Please don't go. I'm not ready. I want more time with you. I need more time with you."

"I went . . . a long time ago. Except for you. I tried . . . and tried and tried . . . never to leave you."

"You didn't," she replied, fighting the shudders that threatened to consume her. "I promise that you didn't. I missed you . . . when you left. But I knew you still loved me."

He tilted his head so that his flesh pressed more firmly against her palm. "Someday . . . if you have a child . . . will you take her to a ball game and tell her about our afternoons . . . and about how her grandpa wanted to take her? I would have taken her. And we'd have done . . . the same things. Eaten peanuts. Cheered with the crowd."

"I'll tell her everything. And I'll take her. I'll show her where we sat."

He nodded, searching her face, longing to bring it with him on his journey. "I love you," he said. "I love you . . . so much, Iris. More than words . . . can say. And I'll find you in Saigon."

"You will?"

"I'll listen for children's laughter. And I'll follow . . . I'll follow it to you."

"Promise?"

"I do."

She kissed his brow, aware that he was between worlds, drifting from one to the other. Weeping silently, she carefully climbed into his bed and lay beside him, comforting him as he'd done for her when nightmares had left her shaking.

"My baby girl," he whispered. "You shine . . . such a light on me."

$\mathcal{D}$usk and $\mathcal{D}$awn

The small apartment that Iris had rented for two years resembled the office of a college professor. In the living room, on wooden tables and shelves, piles of books were stacked like cords of firewood. The books were old and new, worn and untouched. Hundreds of hardcovers comprised the bases of these piles, while paperbacks teetered on top of them. Several of the piles had tumbled, and books were strewn in odd places.

The rest of her home was unremarkable in every way. The kitchen, bathroom, and bedroom could have housed a monk. No luxuries abounded. No family photographs gathered dust. Twenty stories below, the pulse of Chicago drifted up to her closed windows. Horns, sirens, the rumble of a passing elevated train seeped into her room—though she'd long ago learned to block out such sounds.

Though Iris would have normally kept her books in perfect order, since her father's death five weeks earlier she'd been far less inclined to complete such tasks. Her thoughts had dwelled on her memories of their time together. She tended to think about their best moments—of renting a canoe and paddling to an island, where they camped for two nights, of him teaching her how to throw and catch a baseball. She tried to ignore painful recollections—times when he'd unexpectedly gone away or broken his promises to be by her side. As a young girl, she'd hated such occurrences. They'd made her feel unloved and unwanted and, most of all, confused. She didn't understand why he needed to be away from his family. How could he love her, yet leave her so easily? The misery and bewilderment that this question created had lasted for years.

As a teenager, Iris had resented her father. It wasn't until after finishing college that she began to grasp why he'd so often been gone. He had never told her of his demons, but she'd read several books about the war and realized that his maladies weren't unusual. He'd been wounded deep inside, where light never reached and couldn't help him heal.

Iris wasn't sure exactly why she was going to Vietnam. Of course, she'd wanted to put her father at ease during his last days, and her words about traveling to Saigon had done just that—resonating within him. But a part of her also needed to complete his dream. Over the past two years, he'd spoken to her about this dream, about his longing to do something good. And she had seen beauty in what he was trying to accomplish. Her love for him had grown then—because he'd confided in her about his hopes and fears. And when he had taken trips to Saigon, they'd been with her blessing. He'd returned with pictures and stories, and they had eaten pizza in her apartment while he told her about the children he was trying to save. During these conversations, which often lasted long into the night, she had never felt closer to him.

Though her father had often been gone during her childhood, her mother had tried valiantly to fill the holes in Iris's life. Because of her mother's unending support, Iris couldn't imagine growing up alone on the streets, with no one to care for her. And upon hearing her father's stories of such children, she had instinctively wanted to do something to help. Of course, she'd never expected to try to finish what he'd started, but as his death had loomed, she knew that she couldn't walk away from the children. She couldn't leave them alone, not when she might be able to make their lives better.

Now, as Iris lay on her futon, she tried to suppress her nervousness about what she'd promised her father. Propped up on her chest was a battered copy of *Heart of Darkness*. The book had long been one of her favorites, and with thoughts of her trip to Saigon dominating her day, she thought it apt to read about Marlow's journey through the Congo and through himself.

Iris laid the book down on her chest and closed her eyes. The lone window in her room was darkening, as dusk unfolded in the city below. Though she had eaten only a premade salad for dinner, and though her stomach was in want of more food, she was ready for sleep. She'd spent the afternoon packing and e-mailing her contacts in Saigon about her visit. After turning off the evening news she had showered, brushed her teeth, put on light-weight pajamas, and crept into bed.

She rolled to her left and glanced at the urn containing her father's cremated remains. One of his last wishes was to be cremated, and she'd done as he asked, sobbing when she had first opened the silver container and seen his remains. She'd touched him, surprised that the urn didn't contain ashes but rather tiny pieces of bone. How she longed to somehow fashion those pieces back into the man she had glimpsed on and off through the years—a man who loved her, who was able to temporarily place his sorrows aside and push his little girl high on a swing.

A soft but abrupt knock on her door caused her heart to skip. Iris had few visitors and couldn't imagine who'd stop by without calling first. She stood up, buttoned her top higher, and walked toward the entryway. Peering through the peep-hole, she saw a woman's familiar face. Iris opened the door and leaned toward her former neighbor. "Mrs. Woods?"

An ample woman dressed in a gray sweater and jeans nodded. "Hello, Iris. Sorry to . . . drop by like this. May I come in?"

"Oh," Iris replied, opening the door wider and stepping backward. "Of course."

Mrs. Woods stepped inside and glanced around. Iris noticed that her visitor's face seemed haggard, that she looked to have been crying. "Here," Iris said, lifting a pile of books from a cracked leather chair. "Please sit down."

"Thank you."

"May I bring you something to drink? I don't have much. But I could put on a pot of tea."

"There's no need to trouble yourself." When Iris nodded but made no reply, her visitor shifted on her seat and finally made eye contact. "Locust Street seems like a long time ago, doesn't it?"

"It was a long time ago."

"I heard that our house is for sale again. We should never have left."

Iris remembered watching from across the street as men filled a moving truck. "We were all sad to see you go," she replied, clearing off another chair.

Mrs. Woods leaned forward. "I'm so sorry about your father. I didn't know him well, but he must have been a good man to have such a daughter."

"He was wonderful."

"How's your mother doing? I called her yesterday, and we caught up, but some things don't always get said on the phone."

"Oh, she's fine, thanks. Busier than you might expect—traveling with friends, still playing bridge."

"And you?"

"I'm okay. I miss him."

Mrs. Woods looked at the piles of books. "You know, we're all really proud of you. You're famous around here. At least, to those of us who read book reviews."

Iris pushed a tendril of her long hair from her face. "Thanks, but I don't think there are many of you left."

"You might be surprised."

"Well, that would be nice. But with the Internet and iPods and everything else, sometimes I feel like I'm only writing for myself."

"Trust me, Iris, your words have meaning. If they didn't . . . publishers wouldn't send you so many books."

Iris smiled faintly, wondering why she was entertaining Mrs. Woods, whom she hadn't seen in several years, but not wanting to ask. "How's Noah?"

The older woman's demeanor immediately changed. Her body seemed to sag, her lips pressed together, and she shook her head. "He's not good," she replied, easing her hands beneath her thighs.

"Why not?"

"Did you know he was in Iraq?"

"No. No one's told me anything. Did something happen to him?"

Mrs. Woods pursed her lips. She closed her eyes for a moment. "His Humvee hit a roadside bomb. And he . . . he lost part of a leg. And the side of his forehead . . . Oh, Iris, they had to stitch him all back together."

Iris moved toward her visitor and, kneeling, took Mrs. Woods's hands in her own. "I don't know what to say," she confessed, her eyes, lately so accustomed to tears, glistening once again. "I'm so terribly sorry."

"He's been home for five months. He's so depressed. So angry. I hardly recognize him. It's just terrible . . . for us all."

Iris shook her head, as if she could deny what she was hearing. Noah, three years her junior, had always been such a happy boy. She remembered him following her home from elementary school, stepping in her tracks in the snow. Years later, she had been aware that he'd had a crush on her, and had pretended not to notice his awkward advances. He'd been much shorter than she, and older boys had often teased him about his misplaced affections. But Noah had never seemed bothered by their antics.

"He was always so active," Iris said softly. "Running around, dribbling his basketball. I can't imagine him . . . without a leg."

Mrs. Woods wiped her eyes. "He has a prosthesis, of course. But it hurts him. And he hardly moves. He sleeps until noon. He drinks too much and too often. He doesn't listen to me, though I don't blame him for that. I don't know what to say to him. How could I?"

23

"Has he been to see a—"

"Sometimes I worry that he wants to die. It's so awful, Iris. He doesn't smile. Doesn't call his sisters." Mrs. Woods closed her eyes, shaking her head. Iris handed her a tissue, which she blew into and held tight. "I just don't know what to do. I've tried everything. And I mean everything in the world. But he won't . . . he won't do anything. He's so miserable. So lost."

"What about—"

"Will you take him with you? Will you please take him with you?"

"Take him with me?"

"I heard about your trip. About how you're spending a month in Vietnam to open your father's center. Can you take Noah? Take him there and give him something good to do. Give his life some meaning."

Iris pushed her hair aside. Though she wanted to help Noah, she couldn't imagine having to watch over him on top of everything else. How would she ever open her father's center if she also had to worry about Noah? "I don't know," she replied, twisting a ring. "I just don't think I could take him. I've already got more than I can handle. And he's probably better off here, with you. Wouldn't he be better off with his family?"

Mrs. Woods reached for Iris's hands. "He's alone . . . and in so much pain," she said, tears streaming down her face, her voice cracking. "He'll go with you. I'm sure he will. He's always looked up to you. And yesterday, after I spoke with your mother, he asked about you. And when I told him what you were doing, he actually asked me another question. He seemed . . . interested. Not like the old Noah, but at least . . . at least he spoke more than three words."

"But I just don't think—"

"Please, Iris. Please don't let me watch my boy die. Please don't. He's dying now, and watching him die is killing me as well." Mrs. Woods shuddered, drawing Iris closer. "Please, please, please take him. If it doesn't work, I'll come for him. I'll bring him home. But please try. He's a beautiful soul and watching him suffer is just . . . It's too much."

"And you really think he'd like to go?"

Mrs. Woods nodded, her eyes bloodshot. "A mother . . . knows her children, Iris. And I know Noah. He used to speak about you so often. I think he loved you . . . in his own way."

"That was a long time ago."

"And he loves children. He always has. What you're doing . . . what your father was doing . . . he'll respond to it. I just know he will. He wants to go back to who he was. But he doesn't know how."

Iris took another tissue and wiped Mrs. Woods's face. "I'm leaving so soon. In four days."

"That doesn't matter. The sooner, the better."

Iris thought about her father, about how he also came home shattered from a war that wasn't of his making. A marriage and a daughter hadn't saved him from his demons. Why would Saigon save Noah? Though Iris was unsure, she knew what her father would say, knew he'd want her to bring Noah. "I'll take him," she finally replied. "If he wants to go. If he really wants to go."

Mrs. Woods leaned against Iris, hugging her tight. "Thank you, thank you, Iris. You don't know what this means to me. To my family."

Iris stroked the older woman's back, wondering how Noah's presence would change things, wondering what the future held for them both. In four days she'd be on a plane with Noah, and they'd arrive in a country that had both destroyed and redeemed her father. How could a place have such power? Such influence?

As Mrs. Woods continued to thank her, Iris wondered what Noah would find in Vietnam. What would she find? Would her father come to her, as he'd promised? Would she somehow manage to fulfill the dream that had occupied his last years of life? Or would she fail him? Or watch Noah die?

Anxious about her trip and what she might discover, Iris glanced atop a pile of books to where her plane ticket rested. She suddenly wanted to hold the ticket, to feel one more connection to her father. She wanted to leave.

AT THE MOMENT THAT IRIS GLANCED at her plane ticket, a new day was unfolding in Vietnam, a country of a thousand faces, a thousand voices.

To the south, immense wooden barges plowed through the muddy waters of the Mekong Delta. The barges were often blue with red trim and were curved like bananas. Though their profiles were almost majestic—with brightly painted wheel-houses and rigging—the barges fought the currents like slugs making their way up a brown leaf. A pair of owlish yellow-and-black eyes was painted below each bow. These eyes warned countless smaller vessels that behemoths approached. Despite the size of the owl-eyed barges, the Mekong Delta was several miles wide and dwarfed everything atop it. The murky waters contrasted powerfully with the vibrant foliage on either shore. Flowering water lilies bobbed against the current. Children swam in the shallows. Ancient house-boats filled with tourists journeyed toward Cambodia. And perhaps most prominent, floating markets drew buyers toward canoelike vessels filled with vegetables, fruits, and fish.

North of the delta, narrow roads led toward Saigon or, as it was known these days, Ho Chi Minh City. The roads thrived with life, carrying commerce the way a vein moves blood. They brimmed with countless motor scooters, trucks, and ox-driven carts. Most of the roads were lined with stalls—rusty shelters that sold axles, bricks, food, lamp-posts, refrigerators, and everything else that the mind could conceive. Occasionally, the stalls would vanish into the jungle, within which hundreds of hammocks hung from slender trees. The hammocks held travelers who, for a nominal fee, could park their vehicles in the shade, drink something sweet, and then sleep for as long as they'd like.

Even though the day was young, Ho Chi Minh City pulsated like a hive containing every insect species on Earth. The city was a kaleidoscope of old versus new, memories versus ideas, stone versus chrome. Dilapidated bicycle taxis mingled with customized SUVs. Sparkling hotels rose like rays of sunlight above squalor and sin. Red flags bearing a yellow star fluttered in a dirty wind. College students sat drinking lattes and text messaging friends, while crippled veterans of the American War begged on street corners. And two children—a brother and sister by all accounts other than blood—awoke beneath a bridge and wondered when they would eat and if they'd be beaten that night.

Farther to the north, the country rose and fell. Mountains resembling green waves were rife with ancient shrines, underground tunnels, scents of flowers and decay. Stonesmiths cut white and black marble from deforested foothills, while more distant rises were almost untouched by human hands. Snaking around the mountains, scores of rivers created a seemingly infinite network of waterways. Villages hewn out of the jungle thrived beside the rivers. To the east, salt-encrusted towns bordered the South China Sea. As in the rest of Vietnam, the weather in Hanoi was already damp and hot, infused with the breath of people, machines, and creatures both seen and undiscovered. The new capital moved slower than its counterpart to the south. Women in conical hats sat in open-air markets and sold dried shrimp, rice, natural medicines, vegetables, eels, and flowers. At the city's center sprawled Hoan Kiem Lake, one of Hanoi's most famous sights. Massive willow trees surrounded the large body of water. On a tree-lined path strode students and lovers. In small courtyards women practiced tai chi.

Beyond Hanoi, farmers labored in secret fields, growing poppies that they refined into opium. Indigenous tribes traveled by elephant through rain forests. Malaria-ridden mosquitoes attacked nursing babies. Traders ferried goods to Laos and China. Children sat in classrooms, hunted giant catfish, and worked in fields and factories.

Though the day was just unfolding, Vietnam was already changing. People had died. Mothers had ushered new life into the world. A cloud was being painted on a ceiling of the Iris Rhodes Center for Street Children. A cancer-stricken girl named Tam clung to her grandmother's back and was carried to a market where they'd spend the day begging. A nearly blind policeman tried to catch criminals. And the bones of lost Americans were overturned by a plow.

Vietnam, a country that had known little but war for many generations, was strangely peaceful, as if the spirits of the slain had somehow infiltrated the prejudices of the living. Hope abounded across the land. Hope often obscured by shanties and brothels and misery but, nonetheless, the collective aspiration for a better tomorrow.

⁓ TWO

Steps to Nowhere

Making her way back to her seat, Iris glanced at Noah, who stared into the blackness beyond his window. She saw the unmarred side of his face, which was defined by a thin, almost delicate nose and jaw. His blond hair was short and ungoverned by gel or spray. It was almost accidentally stylish, as if he'd come from a movie set. His eyes were turned away from her, but she knew they were a light blue—to her the color of the oceans on a world map. Though his scar faced the window and not her—which she assumed was no accident—she'd seen where his skin had been pulled together. The forced fusion of torn flesh started above his right eye and curved back into his hairline. It looked like a trail of purple lipstick.

Though he was not a large man, Noah's knees pressed into the seat in front of him, and as soon as Iris sat beside him their elbows touched. She looked at his tray table, which bore two Heineken cans that the stewardess hadn't bothered to remove. A third can was in his right hand. Though Iris had tried to initiate conversations during the long trip to Asia, he hadn't seemed eager to talk. During their school years he'd always been the first to speak, and she found herself repeatedly surprised by his silence.

"Why did you come?" she asked quietly, finally voicing what she'd wondered for the past few days.

Noah didn't turn to her but continued to stare at the blackness that would soon become Ho Chi Minh City. He raised the beer to his lips and drank. When he set the can on his tray table and shifted in his seat, Iris followed his movements and saw the outline of his prosthesis beneath his pant leg. "Because of my mother," he replied, his voice smooth and soft, so unlike the wound on his forehead.

"Your mother?"

"She needed me to go."

Iris watched him open a small container and place two pills in his hand. He took a gulp of beer and swallowed the pills simultaneously. "How much does it hurt?" she asked, unsure if the medicine was for his forehead or his leg.

He pointed to his knee. "Do you know what the army calls my stump?"

"No."

"A residual limb. That's what everyone calls them. Sounds kind of cool, doesn't it? A residual limb. But to me it's just a stump. A stump that hurts."

She looked away from his leg. "I'm sorry."

"Don't be. It's not your fault."

"Do you want to talk about any of it?"

Noah took another drink, then pointed to his can as a stewardess came by. She nodded and he set his beer aside. "I don't remember much about your father," he said.

"He was a vet like you."

"Was he wounded?"

"A doctor would have said no. But I'd say yes."

Noah nodded, wondering how many companions her father had seen die, if he'd killed, if he'd been lied to. Noah thought of his friend Wesley. He thought of the Iraqi man who'd run toward their checkpoint, trying to get their attention. They had shouted at him to stop, and when he didn't, Wesley had opened fire, killing him. Later, when they'd learned that he'd been in a traffic accident, and that his baby girl had been bleeding to death, Wesley had spoken of taking his own life. Noah had saved him that night, but it hadn't mattered. Two days later, still awash in his sorrow, Wesley had failed to hear Noah's warning and had driven their Humvee past a discarded backpack. The bomb made the world explode. Everything turned a bright and brilliant orange. Noah's leg wasn't found. Wesley was pieced back together but never regained consciousness.

Their plane was suddenly buffeted by turbulence, and Noah instinctively cringed. His heartbeat quickened. His neck perspired. He felt as if the walls were closing in on him. He swore silently, reaching for his beer, drinking what remained in the can. Closing his eyes, he asked himself if he'd care if the plane's wings fell off. At least then his pain would be gone, his hatred gone. For he hurt and hated so much. The hurt radiated outward from his lower back and his stump. The hatred stemmed from lies—deceptions told to prompt a war that had cost him a leg and a friend.

The stewardess gave Noah a fresh beer, which he quickly opened and consumed. "We should get a do-over," he said, noting lights in the distance.

Iris set her Vietnam guidebook down. "What?"

"One do-over in life. Is that too much to ask?"

"No, I don't think so."

"I'd give everything I have for that chance."

She saw the bitterness of his expression and wondered if her father had experienced the same thought. "It isn't right . . . what happened to you."

He drank deeply. "I used to love you. Imagine that."

"We were kids. And I—"

"Don't worry about it. It doesn't matter anyway."

"If you'd been older, things might have been different."

He shrugged, then awkwardly repositioned him-self in the seat. "I won't get in your way."

"I want your help, Noah. I could really use your help."

Despite the beer and the painkillers, his stump ached and he continued to shift in his seat, glancing away from her. Ho Chi Minh City was coming to life below. Lights flickered like stars, as if the world had been turned upside down. "Do you still believe in good?" he asked.

She nodded. "My father was doing something good. He spent the last two years of his life doing it. He believed in it. And I'm here because I believe in it."

"I believed in the tooth fairy. In Santa Claus. In going to war. Shouldn't we know, instead of believe?"

Iris didn't begrudge Noah his bitterness, because as a girl she'd shared it on many occasions. Still, her eyes found his and she said, "I know that I love my father and my mother. I know we're going to land soon, and that I'm scared to death about what I'll find. And I believe in good. Because if there wasn't any good in the world . . . well . . . then there wouldn't be any music, or books, or children. And to me, at least, sometimes those things . . . they . . . they pull me through the pain."

Noah mused over her words, finishing the last of his beer. To him, pain was impenetrable—an ocean that he couldn't swim across, a mountain that he could never summit. "We're here," he said, watching the runway rise toward him, wishing that he were like Iris, who had only lakes and hills before her.

FROM THE ROOFTOP BAR OF THE Rex Hotel, Ho Chi Minh City resembled some sort of carnival ride. Neon signs flickered. The headlights of countless motor scooters illuminated French-colonial buildings and treelined boulevards. Women—clad in everything from traditional full-length dresses to Donna Karan knockoffs to tank tops—strode down sidewalks bordering art galleries, massage parlors, sushi restaurants, and nondescript government buildings.

The symphony of the city—a combination of horns and screeches and beeps—rose to mingle with the sounds of a band that played in the bar. The lead singer did his best rendition of "Hotel California," his Vietnamese accent giving the song a surreal quality never heard on a Western radio. Seven Rex Hotel employees attended to a handful of occupied tables. Near the edge of the balcony, a young Australian couple sat with a pair of Vietnamese street children. The children's tattered clothing—short-sleeved shirts, shorts, and san-dals—would have looked at home on a scarecrow. The boy's features were as disheveled as his clothes. His dark hair jutted out in odd directions. His eyebrows were thick and nearly touched. His face was wide and dirty, his teeth crooked and stained. Most prominent, his left forearm ended in an ugly stump. The girl, ten and a half years old and slightly older than the boy, wore her hair in short pigtails. Her face was the opposite of her companion's—narrow and delicate. Her smile was balanced, her nose rounded with slightly flaring nostrils. Both children were small for their ages, the result of lifelong malnutrition.

The girl, Mai, studied the game before her. It was Connect Four, which featured a yellow, upright board designed to accommodate falling checker-like pieces. The black and red pieces were dropped by opposing players until someone managed to connect four of their pieces in a row, winning the game. Mai was worried, because her friend, Minh, seemed to be losing to the visitor from Sydney. And the fate of an American dollar rested on the outcome of the match.

"Don't be a twit," the Australian woman said to her companion as he prepared to drop his black piece. "He's got too bloody much happening on the other side. You'd best put a stop to it right away."

The traveler pondered his move.

Minh hoped that he wouldn't listen to the woman, for she was right. Scratching a bug bite with his good hand, Minh tried to slow his breath, to hide his anxiety. To the Australians, the game was a way of passing time; to Mai and Minh a win would feed them for a full day. Better yet, a win would almost ensure that Loc wouldn't beat Minh for his failure.

"What you going to do, mister?" Mai asked in broken English, twisting a plastic ring that she'd found earlier in the day, not used to the feel of it on her finger. "Maybe I fall asleep before you make next move. Same, same as last game."

The Australian glanced at his watch. "Christ, it is getting a wee bit late. If we're going to find a pub, we'd better leave." He dropped his piece into a slot far away from where Minh had done most of his work.

"You're a bloody idiot," the woman griped, shaking her head.

Five moves later, Minh was victorious. He nodded to the foreigner and, unsmiling, took the greenback.

Mai emptied the game board of pieces. "One more game, mister? I bet you lucky this time."

"Against that little bugger? Not a chance."

"He lose already two time today. You can beat him. Sure, sure."

The Australian stood up. "I reckon we'd best be off. Maybe tomorrow we'll have at it again."

Minh and Mai watched the foreigners depart. The woman had consumed several soft drinks, and Mai handed Minh a half-empty glass of Coke. "He was good, wasn't he?" she asked in Vietnamese. "Except for that last game. He was way too frustrated to win that one. I've seen policemen with more patience."

Minh nodded, sipping the sweet drink, savoring the taste of sugar.

"Another dollar and we can quit," Mai said, tapping her foot against a chair leg. "Should we wait outside the Sheraton? Or Reunification Palace? Or Q Bar? Remember the last time we were there? Was that just two nights ago? You won seven dollars. Remember that? The night was perfect and everyone came outside. I sold four fans and you . . . you, Minh the Conqueror, won almost every game. What a night that was. Let's go back there. Maybe we can find a game with someone who wants revenge. They should all be nice and drunk by now."

Minh finished the Coke, pleased that Mai was happy with his winnings. He nodded again and then began to put away his game.

A waitress strode over to their table. "Was he good tonight?"

"When isn't he good?" Mai replied, leafing through her thin stack of bills and handing the woman two dollars. She'd have preferred to give her an equal amount of Vietnamese dong, but everyone coveted American dollars, which were more stable.

"Huy wants three," the waitress said, gesturing toward a uniformed man standing behind the bar. "He says if you can't pay that, you need to find somewhere else to play."

Mai started to reply angrily but realized that the woman's eyes contained sympathy, not greed. And so Mai handed over an additional greenback. "Maybe if Huy paid as much attention to his customers as he does to us, he wouldn't need another dollar," she replied, knowing that after Loc took his cut, only a dollar would remain for Minh and her.

The woman shrugged, pocketed the money, and left. Mai muttered to herself, checking her bag to ensure that none of her fans had fallen out. "Let's go," she said, "before the tourists spend all their money."

Minh took a final glance at the bustling city below. He then lifted the battered box that contained his game and followed Mai. As she weaved around tables, he listened to her say good night to the staff and the few remaining patrons. Though his stomach was empty and called for attention, he paid it little heed. At least they would eat tomorrow. Assuming he didn't lose a game, that was. Watching Mai's thin frame, and knowing that he earned most of their money, Minh walked faster, nervously trying to recall the games of two nights before. Whom had he played and how had he won? How would they try to beat him tonight?

On the narrow sidewalk that separated hundreds of passing motor scooters and a few cars from nearby shops, Mai and Minh walked toward the opera house, the basement of which contained the popular Q Bar. Large trees, whose trunks had been painted white, jutted from square holes in the cement. Bordering the sidewalk were stalls that sold *pho*—a traditional soup usually containing rice noodles, beef, green onions, and bean sprouts. Other shops sold snacks, silk ties and blouses, original artwork, antiques, war relics, and airline tickets. The sidewalk was populated with children who hawked packs of postcards, disheveled men who carried passengers via bicycle taxi to distant parts of the city, and attractive women who handed out brochures touting nearby restaurants, clubs, and stores. Some women wore the *ao dai*—a traditional, long-sleeved dress that was often silk and had buttons that ran from the front of the collar down to the underside of the shoulder to the waist. The tight-fitting *ao dai* covered most of the wearer's pants, which were usually an identical fabric and color.

Mai knew many of those they passed and offered smiles and greetings. The same men, women, and children tended to work in particular areas of downtown, selling their wares to wealthy Vietnamese and tourists. "Are you hungry?" she asked Minh, taking the stub of his forearm in her hand.

He shook his head, stepping over a sleeping dog.

"Me neither," she replied, though it was untrue. An immense, Russian-built truck rumbled past, shouldering dozens of motor scooters aside. "Want me to tell you a story?" she asked, for he enjoyed her tales.

Minh looked at her and nodded, eager to take his mind off the looming matches.

"Remember that little boy . . . the one who came from the jungle and shivered all the time?" Mai asked. "He slept under the bridge with us the afternoon it rained so hard? You won eleven games that night, Minh the Great, and after Loc left us, we got three ice-cream cones. That little boy had never eaten ice cream. Remember?"

Smiling, Minh unconsciously licked his lips.

Mai squeezed her friend's stump. "And even though that ice cream made him colder, he laughed at the taste of it. He tried yours and mine, and he couldn't stop laughing. He thought ice cream was the funniest thing he'd ever seen."

Minh walked closer to Mai, remembering how they'd giggled, how they'd ended up giving the boy all their ice cream. Where had the boy gone? Did he still like ice cream so much?

"He was a sweet boy," Mai said. "In some ways, he reminded me of you. He didn't talk much. Maybe all that shivering made him tired." She squeezed Minh's stump again. "Do you think you'll win tonight? I hope so. Too many kids are selling fans. And we've all got the same ones. I'm so tired of selling stupid fans. And Loc takes too much of our money. Someday, Minh, someday we have to leave him."

Minh glanced anxiously about, worried that Mai would be overheard.

"Oh, he's not around here," she said. "He's in an opium den, spending our money. He probably couldn't find his own ears right now."

Minh nodded, slowing to watch a barber who attended to a boy perched atop a bucket. The barber had hung a cracked mirror from a building and meticulously snipped at his customer's locks. Sitting nearby on an old-fashioned bicycle was a woman, presumably the boy's mother. Minh studied the woman as he passed, studied the boy as well. What would it be like to have a mother who sat and waited for him, who liked looking at his face?

"I'll find a drunk one for you tonight," Mai said, leading him across a street, walking erratically so as to avoid the looming headlights of scooters and taxis.

Minh shook his head. He didn't like playing the drunks, for they could be cruel to Mai. And they always seemed to ask about his hand and why he never spoke.

"I wish you'd play them," she countered. "Their money's so easy to take. They toss it about like trash. Ah, you can be stubborn, Minh the Powerful. As stubborn as that old water buffalo we saw the other day. If only I could play like you. I'd beat every drunk tourist in the city and we'd be rich."

Mai turned toward Minh and saw that he was

watching boys kick a soccer ball in a park. "Did you hear anything I said?" she asked, knowing that he did, but understanding that his thoughts were with the boys, that he was somehow in their company.

Mai understood because she also knew how to place herself in the company of others, to pretend that she inhabited different worlds. Minh was better at the game, of course. But she still played, still imagined that she walked among schoolgirls, ate *pho* on the street with her father, read a book while waiting for her mother at the market. Mai, like Minh, played the game because it transported her from a place of hunger and pain, weariness and fear. In the pretend worlds she didn't have to worry whether or not Minh would win, whether Loc would beat them, whether she'd have to someday sell herself to survive. In these worlds she went to school, Minh was her brother, and she was loved and protected by those who had given her life.

BEN THANH MARKET HAD BEEN IN existence for about a hundred years—since the time of the French occupation. In the muted darkness, the entrance to Ben Thanh resembled an old schoolhouse or country church. The yellow, rectangular structure boasted an arched entry, above which rose a square face that bore an immense black-and-white clock. Inside this entry, the market opened into a sprawling labyrinth of stalls and passageways. At a height of some thirty feet, a vaulted ceiling was supported by yellow girders and protected merchants and shoppers from the city's unpredictable weather.

Hundreds, perhaps thousands, of locals and tourists populated Ben Thanh, browsing for bargains in Ho Chi Minh City's most famous and popular market. Closet-size stalls offered eel, pig stomach, skinned oxtail, sea snails, lemongrass, dried shrimp, coffee beans, dragon fruit, and loaves of fresh bread. Beyond the food stalls, vendors sold lacquer platters, teak chopsticks, traditional Vietnamese clothes, tea sets, bronze animals, sunglasses, T-shirts, and about anything else imaginable.

Gathered outside the entry to Ben Thanh were the Vietnamese who made a livelihood from pleasing tourists. Drivers leaned against dozens of cyclos, or bicycle taxis. Entrepreneurial tour guides scanned the area for confused travelers. Women moved quickly about, selling bottled water, bags of potato chips, and candy bars.

Sitting near the entry, atop an old bench, a hunched woman who looked two decades older than her fifty-one years held a child on her lap. The woman wore a traditional conical hat, which was made by sewing palm leaves onto a peaked bamboo frame. Her clothes were simple blue pants and a shirt—an outfit that Westerners might think to be pajamas. The woman's face was thin and sunspotted and bore ripples of wrinkles. Several of her front teeth were missing. Those that remained were stained and crooked, jutting from her gums like the rocks at Stonehenge.

The child was seven years old. She wore shorts and a tank top, revealing legs and arms as thin as the handle of a tennis racket. Her elbows and knees were much wider, inflamed by a disease beyond her understanding. Short and parted in the middle, her hair was held fast by rusty pins. Her face, narrow and pleasant, was dominated by large, almost oversize eyes. Half of a coconut shell sat on her lap. Several gold-colored Vietnamese coins occupied the bottom of the coconut. Beneath the coconut was a worn blanket, which was flowered and full of patches.

"We'll get going soon, Tam," the woman, Qui, whispered, stroking Tam's cheek. "The river misses you."

Tam nodded absently. "A pretty sky."

Qui glanced above. At first she saw streetlights that drew countless insects. But higher, several stars managed to penetrate the glow of the city. "Yes," she replied, "but not as pretty as you."

"Or you, Little Bird."

A bearded foreigner walked past, and Qui tried to capture his attention. Switching to English, she said, "You want good book? *The Quiet American*? *Lonely Planet Vietnam*?"

The man paused, his eyes darting from an

orderly pile of books at Qui's feet to the sickly form of Tam. "My money's gone," he replied, lifting full plastic bags. "Too many souvenirs."

Qui stroked Tam's arm. "Please. Maybe you have few Vietnamese dong left? Or U.S. dollar? My granddaughter so sick. Please help me."

The foreigner looked more closely at Tam. He saw how her body was wasting away, how her eyes didn't seem to fix upon him, but drifted about. He wondered what was wrong with her. "I don't think I have anything left," he said, avoiding Qui's gaze.

"Please, please look in your pocket," Qui replied, placing her hands together as if praying. "I must buy more medicine for granddaughter. Please help her. Please, kind sir."

Setting his bags down, the man unzipped his fanny pack and groped inside it. He produced several nearly worthless Vietnamese coins, and placed them into Tam's coconut. "I'm sorry. It's all I have."

"Thank you," Qui replied. "You are good man. You have good heart. Maybe tomorrow you come back and buy book?"

"Maybe."

Qui took her hands, placed them outside Tam's, and again appeared to pray. "May Buddha smile on you."

The man said good night and disappeared into the chaos that was Ho Chi Minh City. Tam groaned and instinctively reached for her blanket. The coconut fell to the ground, coins scattering. Knowing that she'd stayed too late, Qui carefully lifted Tam from her lap, set her granddaughter on the bench, and began to gather the coins. Qui then placed two straps around her shoulders and tossed a baglike canvas device over her head. The contraption rested against the middle of her back. After setting her books and the coconut in a pouch that she wore against her belly, she nodded to a nearby cyclo driver and the man stepped toward Tam. He lifted her gently, positioning her within the bag, so that her legs encircled Qui's waist and her arms draped down upon Qui's chest. Tam's blanket, held tight in a small fist, swung to and fro.

Qui thanked the driver, drew a deep breath, and began to walk. The night was humid, but not too hot. Along the wide road near Ben Thanh Market, buses—either sleek havens for tourists or ancient contraptions for locals—belched fumes as they lumbered past scooters and cyclos. Many pedestrians and scooter drivers wore cotton masks so as to spare their lungs from the soot that permeated the air. Qui had once tried placing one over Tam's face, but Tam hadn't liked breathing through the fabric. And if Tam wouldn't use a mask, neither would Qui.

After a few blocks, Tam's weight—nominal as it was—caused Qui's back and knees to ache. Though the pain slowed her down considerably,

Qui was accustomed to it. In some ways, she welcomed the pain, for Tam suffered so much, and it was better that her precious granddaughter not be alone in her misery.

Thinking of this misery, Qui asked Tam how she felt.

"My front hurts," Tam replied.

Qui knew that Tam's belly and chest were aching, that she was finding it difficult to breathe. Two weeks earlier, Qui had used every bill and coin she possessed to take Tam to a hospital. Several doctors had spent hours with them, and many tests had been run. Qui had left the hospital with Tam on her back and had cried, just as she did now. Soon Tam would be taken from her. No matter how much she loved her, treasured her, and wanted to protect her, Tam would be taken. Stolen forever.

Her tears dropping like rain from a statue's face, Qui continued onward.

"Will Momma kiss me tonight?" Tam asked, as she did every day.

Qui sniffed, pretending that something was lodged in her throat. "She's . . . still in Thailand. Working hard so we can buy your medicine. She loves you so much, Tam. She and I love you so very much."

Tam didn't respond, and Qui wondered what she was thinking. Was her sweet, innocent mind able to guess that her own mother had abandoned her, and probably would never come back?

As she did many times each day, Qui prayed that her daughter would return. She begged Buddha to be compassionate, to send her daughter home so that Tam could hold her again before she died.

Qui turned toward the canal that stretched below their home. She tried to quiet her despair, for soon Tam would look upon her face, and her grand-daughter could never see such tears. Qui had told Tam that someday she'd fall into a sleep that would magically take her into a different world, into a realm where children weren't sick, where they swam in warm seas, where they awoke each morning nestled between their mother and father. Tam believed in this realm, and Qui could never destroy this belief. So she could cry only when Tam's eyes couldn't find hers.

The buildings of modern-day Ho Chi Minh City disappeared. Tin shanties soon encroached upon narrow passages, and Qui tried to ignore a variety of ever-present sounds—a baby's wail, children laughing, moans of pleasure. Tam asked about these noises, and Qui told her stories that had been repeated scores of times. After a few more blocks, just as Qui felt she could go no farther, her feet fell on planks that lay perched above brown water. She followed these planks until arriving at a vinyl tarp that covered the entrance to their room, which sat on stilts above the canal.

Perhaps seven paces wide as well as long, the room was mostly empty. Bamboo mats covered the tin floor. Plastic garbage bags full of crumpled balls of newspaper comprised a bed. Stacked neatly in the corner were metal plates, an iron pot, and a pan. A tiny, wood-burning stove was also present, as was a trio of potted plants. Hanging below the room's lone window were two sheets, an extra set of clothes for Qui and Tam, some pajamas, and a small towel. A square hole in the floor served as a toilet. Near the hole was a plastic bucket with a rope attached to its handle.

Qui carefully knelt on the bamboo mat and removed Tam from the sling. Tam groaned at the pain that movement brought. Moving as swiftly as she was able, Qui plucked a sheet from the wall and placed it over the garbage bags. She then lowered the bucket into the canal below, hauled the bucket up, and dipped a corner of the towel into the murky water. She lifted Tam, setting her on the far side of the makeshift bed.

"Let me clean the day from you," Qui said, kneeling next to Tam, using the damp towel to wipe soot from her forehead. Tam smiled faintly, and Qui leaned closer. "You like that, don't you?"

"Rub my back, Little Bird."

"I have to clean you first, sweet child. I can't let you go to sleep so dirty."

"My blanket?"

"Oh, sorry about that. Here it is." Qui started to clean Tam once more but quickly stopped. "My wits have left me," she muttered, reaching into her pocket to produce a plastic bottle with several pills in it. She set a pill aside and stood up, dipping a cup into a wide bowl in which she collected rainwater. After Tam had swallowed her medicine, Qui wiped her closed eyes with the damp cloth.

"I love you," Tam said tiredly, holding her blanket against her cheek.

"I know, sweet child. And do you know how much I love you?"

"How much?"

Qui continued to clean Tam's face, thinking of tonight's response. "Remember the gecko that lived with us?"

"He was green."

"Remember how he'd wait in that corner of the ceiling? Wait for a bug to come crawling toward him?"

"Yes."

"Well, I love you like that gecko loved his corner."

"That much? Really, Little Bird?"

Qui fought back a sudden shudder, glad that Tam's eyes were closed. "Yes, that much, my precious child." Setting the towel aside, she lay down next to Tam, drawing her close, so that Tam's last memory of the day would be of shared warmth.

AS SHE STRODE TOWARD THE BAGGAGE claim area of Ho Chi Minh City's new international airport, Iris felt as if she were inside a giant white shoe

51

box. Almost everything seemed colorless. The lone exception was a row of potted flowers that stretched down the long corridor. Thousands of pots held bright flowers, and Iris couldn't imagine how they were all watered.

After having her passport stamped for the first time and passing through customs, Iris waited for Noah, and the unlikely traveling companions descended toward the baggage area. It was late, almost eleven o'clock local time, and most of the airport's shops and stalls were closed. Scores of Vietnamese waited next to her as she eyed the conveyor belt for her two bags. Most of the luggage on the belt came in the form of cardboard boxes. The boxes glistened with clear packing tape and were often covered in Chinese markings.

Iris and Noah found their bags, and she followed him outside, trying not to notice how he limped. Beyond the orderly confines of the airport, chaos unfolded. Hundreds of people stood in a waiting area, restrained by a chain-link fence. Many eyes fell on the two Americans, and immediately people offered them hotel rooms and taxi services. Iris nodded to a smiling driver, asking how much the fare would be. The price quoted seemed reasonable, and they followed him to a car that looked as if it had just finished competing in a demolition derby. The headlights, doors, and rear bumper had all been smashed.

The car's inside was surprisingly clean and

undamaged. Iris and Noah settled into the backseat and the driver turned the key. The car and its radio jumped to life. A high, almost feminine-sounding male voice seemed to try to keep pace with plucked guitar strings, violins, and the metallic clash of drums and symbols. Iris had studied Spanish in high school and believed that she had a good ear for foreign languages. But the sounds she listened to now totally baffled her. She recognized nothing.

The taxi merged onto a busy road and Iris forgot the music. She'd read about the four million motor scooters on Ho Chi Minh City's streets, and now it felt as if all of them suddenly descended upon her. The scooters were everywhere, darting around their taxi, driving directly toward them, running red lights, crossing roads as if daring the approaching traffic to obliterate them. The scooters carried about anything the mind could conceive. Entire families crammed together on the black seats—often with a baby in the front, a father behind, then an older child, and last a mother. The families laughed and chatted, weaving in and out of trucks and cars, missing other vehicles by less than an inch. Some scooters had reinforced racks behind their seats, and these carried refrigerators, baskets of live pigs, steel girders, televisions, crates of Tiger beer, wedding cakes, pets, and engine parts. Many of the drivers wore masks, though the fabric didn't stop them from talking to one another, from asking directions as they dodged potholes and fallen debris.

Construction work was being done on the street, and sparks flew as boys wielded welding torches. A soldier held an assault rifle at the corner of a busy intersection. Buildings no more than fifteen feet wide rose up almost ten stories. A train rumbled across the street and their taxi stopped. Scores of scooters eased around the taxi, moving so slowly that drivers and passengers were able to reach out and touch the car, using it to balance their overloaded vehicles. The dozens of people who were no more than an arm's length from the taxi were clad in traditional dresses, suits, fashionable club attire, and collared shirts.

After the train lumbered past, the scooters surged forward and a haze of exhaust enveloped the taxi. The grit seeped into the car and Iris instinctively held her breath. She saw Noah flinch as the taxi bounced over the tracks and wondered if he'd forever think about roadside bombs.

As they approached the heart of Ho Chi Minh City, the buildings changed from mold-ridden, teetering piles of concrete to gleaming glass structures and steel high-rises. The streets were wider, the potholes a memory. To Iris's surprise, she saw dozens of uniformed workers hanging strands of Christmas lights on trees and building facades. From her research, she recognized the broad, white building that was Reunification Palace, and she imagined the famous North Vietnamese tank that smashed through its iron gates during the fall of Saigon. Somewhere nearby was the U.S. Embassy, which at the time was inundated with desperate South Vietnamese and Americans who were being rescued by helicopter from its rooftop.

Though Iris had traveled around the world through the thousands of books she'd read, she had never physically been abroad, had never felt her pulse race at the sight of her surroundings. She looked for comforting sights but saw none. Squares and parks were filled with statues of a triumphant Ho Chi Minh. Rivers were lined with shanties and bore what looked to be floating shacks. Nothing made sense, and despite her best efforts, she felt panic rise within her. Was coming to Vietnam a mistake? she wondered. How can I possibly hope to open his center when I've never even been overseas?

Needing to talk, she turned to Noah. "What do you think of it all?"

Noah watched a man chop off the top of a coconut and put a straw into the hole he'd made. Though also surprised by the sights around him, Noah felt numb to this new world. He was tired from the long flight, the seven beers he'd consumed, and a series of near-sleepless nights. A part of him recognized that these streets were vastly different from those of Baghdad, that here people seemed happy, eager to explore the night. But he didn't care. He felt dead, and even though the world around him teemed with life, no sight could pull him from the depths of his own misery. His mother had been wrong to send him here. Nothing could cure his pain.

"Why did your father start the center?" he asked, noting that a glaze of tropical sweat already covered her forehead.

"I don't really know," she replied over the wails of a woman on the radio. "He never talked much about what happened in the war. But I think something bad . . . something terrible happened with some children. I think maybe he saw some die. And . . . as impossible as it sounds . . . he wanted to try to make up for that."

The taxi pulled against the curb and the driver said, "We at Rex Hotel."

Iris paid the man, ensured that a porter found their bags, and followed Noah into the lobby. The walls were covered with intricate bamboo renderings of birds and flowers. Iris had read that the CIA operated out of the Rex during the war and wondered about all that had occurred within its walls. After speaking with the receptionist, she handed over their passports and followed the porter to their room. He opened a door, stuck their key into a specialized slot in the wall, and the lights and air conditioner turned on. The room's interior looked to have been made entirely of thin slices of bamboo. Intricate bamboo lamps and chairs, tables, and bed frames dominated the layout. The porter showed them how to work the shower, radio, telephone, and television. Iris tipped him and he left. Noah walked to the window, peering out. Iris hadn't showered in more than twenty-four hours and could hardly wait to freshen up. "Can I take the first shower?" she asked, feeling awkward about sharing a room with him, but not having much of a choice, as the hotel was completely booked. She'd made her reservation long before she knew he was coming with her, and she didn't want to send him to another hotel.

Noah nodded, relieved when she left him alone. He heard her turn on the water, and steam soon seeped beneath the bathroom door to merge with the room's murky air. Sitting on the edge of one of the two twin beds, he thought about how he'd once loved her. He had dreamed about her, imagined what she might look like naked. Now she was naked and not ten feet from him, and he didn't care. Nothing within him stirred. Not his curiosity. Not his ambitions. Not even a sexual urge.

He strode to the bathroom door, knocking on it softly. "I'm going to get a drink. Want to join me?"

"Thanks, but I'm ready for bed."

"Well, good night, then. I'll be back in an hour or two."

"Good night, Noah."

He took the extra key, closed the door behind him, ensured that it was locked, and awkwardly made his way down a nearby stairwell, wondering if the hotel had a bar. He hoped it did, for he didn't want to venture out into the chaos of unknown streets—too many memories would be sparked to life by such places, memories even harder to face at night, when the earth's darkness mingled with his own.

Back in the room, Iris finished her shower, put on a T-shirt and underwear, and climbed into the bed farthest from the door. Though her muscles felt inordinately tired, her mind raced. In Chicago, the sun had been up for just a few hours, and her body felt the conflicting pull of differing time zones. She lay awake, her eyes open, looking out the window into a country that had shattered and saved her father. She tried to slow her thoughts, the rapid beating of her heart. She tried to feel him, as he promised her she would.

But no matter how much Iris longed to sense his presence, to bring him into her, she felt alone and afraid. The city's noises and scents were so foreign, so troubling. She began to panic, wishing that she hadn't come, that her father had never started his center. He was dead, and perhaps his dream should have died with him.

Iris beseeched her father to find her, not to leave her alone once again. But his presence never entered the room, and she didn't fall asleep until Noah finally returned, until dawn filled the air with its sweet, welcome light.

THREE

Hell and Handbags

Under the bridge, dawn came slowly, as if teasing of warm and pleasant tidings. Muted light seeped through the tin shanties on either side of the space directly under the bridge. The light was unnoticed at first, simply one more intrusion into a world not of Mai and Minh's control. The trucks rumbling above, the giant cockroaches scavenging for food, the stench of urine in the early-morning air were such intrusions—realities impossible to govern or flee.

Minh woke first, as usual. He kept still, not wanting to bother Mai, who lay next to him. The two friends were on their sides, curled with their knees drawn up—a pair of twins still in the womb. Around them, a circular basket rose three feet high. The basket, made of tightly woven bamboo and waterproofed with sealant, was a traditional fishing boat that had one day floated down the river. Mai and Minh had swum out and retrieved it. When no one claimed it, they'd started sleeping in it, bringing pieces of discarded carpet from the city above to make their bed more comfortable.

For more than a year, Mai and Minh had slept in the basket. It comforted them the way a home comforts others. It had walls. It kept rats at bay. It contained a blanket and two extra sets of clothes. On most nights, a dozen or so people slept beneath the bridge. Each had her or his own bed—fashioned from boxes, from old scooter seats, from carefully sculpted sand and mud.

Mai stirred beside him and Minh carefully sat up, raising his head above the rim of the basket. Not far away, a legless veteran of the American War was tying a wooden block to the stumps below his waist. Upon this block, as well as on smaller blocks that he attached to his palms, he'd propel himself along the city sidewalks. The blocks protected him from glass and other debris.

Several children had risen and were bathing in the river. Minh knew them all, knew them to be discarded in some form or another. Thi, whose name meant "poem" and whose body had been poisoned by lingering chemicals from the war, had oversize eyes that looked as if they'd burst from her head. Phuong had run away from the orphanage that had housed him for three years. And Van, who'd been born in a back alley, had known nothing but the streets.

Minh watched the other children for a few minutes, then lay back down in the basket. He reached beneath a piece of carpet and carefully felt the section of bamboo that he'd loosened months earlier. Under this false bottom, under rocks and the silt of distant lands, was a plastic bag containing fourteen dollars. The money was the result of a year's worth of secrecy, of deceptions that could cost him his life. Only Mai and he knew of the stash. Were Loc to find it, he'd beat the flesh from their bones. One day, so went their dream, the two friends would save enough money to flee Loc, to travel to a place where they could go to school and not fear the night.

"You didn't sleep well, did you, Minh the Restless?" Mai asked softly, her eyes still closed.

Minh watched dust drift down from the bridge above as a heavy truck strained the pitted concrete. He wondered who'd be under the bridge when it fell someday.

"You're like a boiling pot of *pho*," she added, rising to survey the morning. "Never resting. Never sitting still for a minute. Are you like the *pho*, afraid that you're going to be eaten?"

Minh smiled, never having been compared to a pot of noodles. He wiggled his head back and forth, pretending that he was being boiled.

She giggled. "Maybe I'll toss some onions and sprouts on you tonight while you're sleeping. I'll prepare you just right, and slurp you up."

Happy that her face carried a smile, Minh pointed to their game of Connect Four.

"You think it's time to go play?" Mai asked. "Ah, I'm so tired of selling fans. Why don't I play? You sell fans and find foreigners for me to play against. I'll just sit and drop checkers. And I'll be Mai the Magnificent."

Minh shook his head and rose to his feet. The

other children had finished bathing in the river, and he wanted to clean himself before the adults entered the water. Mai followed his lead and the two friends carried their extra set of clothes to the water's edge. After carefully setting the clothes aside, they strode into the river. The water, as brown as dirt, gently tugged at their ankles, then legs, then waists. They stripped to their underwear and began to clean their shirts and shorts, wringing the pollution and grit from them. Over the past few months, they'd seen dead snakes, cats, and even a water buffalo float past. But since the rainy season had ended, the river tended to steal much less life.

"We should find a mosquito net," Mai said, scratching at her neck.

Minh shrugged, knowing that if they ever found such a sought-after net it would be promptly stolen. Better just to sleep under their blankets than to worry about mosquito nets. Still, he wished that Mai didn't attract so many flying pests. Maybe he'd try to find her a net after all.

"What should we get today with our dollar?" Mai asked, for one crisp dollar bill was all that remained from the previous day's winnings, and they had to decide whether to buy noodles, bananas, dragon fruit, bread, or rice.

Minh wanted to save the dollar, to add it to their secret stash. But they'd eaten nothing for so long that he felt weak, and so he pretended to slurp up a noodle.

"*Pho* it is," she replied, darting underwater to rinse her hair. She then rubbed her scalp, her gums, her privates. "What about going to the war museum?" she asked. "I bet I could sell some fans there. The new tourists will go there first, like they always do, and they won't have seen too many fans by then. And you might get a quick game or two. We can sit beneath that big tree and it won't be too hot. Well, what do you think, Minh the Teeth Scrubber?"

Minh stopped cleaning his teeth and shook his head. He didn't want to be near the war museum, as he'd seen what was within its walls.

"I don't like it either," Mai replied. "But you can't be so picky, Minh. We need to—"

"She's right," a man said, stepping to the water's edge.

Minh turned toward the raspy voice, instinctively lowering himself deeper, as if the river were a mighty shield that could protect him from every danger. Loc hacked and spat in Minh's direction. Gathering his will, Minh forced himself to look at Loc—a large man who always wore a New York Yankees baseball jersey. Loc's face was prematurely aged from years of smoking opium. His bloodshot eyes wandered slowly. His fingers were burned and battered. A mole on his chin sprouted thick hairs that fell halfway to his neck.

"Get over here," Loc said, pointing at his own chest.

Mai was closer to shore and bravely walked forward, feeling naked in her underwear. Loc reached for her hair and pulled her roughly ahead. She whimpered but made no effort to resist him. Seeing her in pain, Minh stepped faster. Loc's hand swung out with surprising speed, striking Minh on the side of the head. Minh's ear rang. His vision blurred. He felt as if someone had thrust a steel pole into his brain. Still, he didn't fall, for he knew that if he did, Loc would kick him. And kicks hurt even worse than cuffs.

"I need more money," Loc said, speaking loudly, as if addressing everyone under the bridge. His voice, ruined from years of sucking on his pipe, sounded as if it emerged from a hole in his throat. "You need to win more. You hear me, you motherless half boy?"

Minh nodded, his knees weak.

"You two brats want protection?" Loc asked. "A place to sleep? Then win more games and sell more fans. Four dollars a day isn't enough. I want five."

Mai risked a glance into Loc's eyes and saw that he was reeling from a crash, from whatever it felt like to no longer be within a world fashioned from poppy seeds. Before he could strike Minh again, she said, "You can take our only dollar. The dollar we kept after paying you last night. We were going to have some *pho*, but you—"

"Give it to me."

Mai hurried to their basket, removing the dollar from within a fold of their blanket. Loc grabbed the bill, and with a grunt, dumped the basket upside down. The blanket and sections of carpet fell on compressed mud. Loc rifled through the pile, searching for anything they might have stashed away.

"We'll win today," Mai said, trying to distract him, to keep him from finding the loose piece of bamboo.

"Where?"

"What?"

"Where will I find you?"

She thought quickly. "Tonight? At the train station. We'll be with foreigners."

Loc glared at Minh and through the haze in his head remembered finding the abandoned toddler, remembered cutting off his hand so that he'd be a better beggar. Though Minh had almost died, Loc had been careful, and had managed to stop the bleeding and ultimately heal the wound. "I know why she left you, half boy," Loc said, craving his pipe, fueled by the repressed aches of his own childhood. "You weren't good enough for her. But you'd better be good enough for me. You'd better win."

Minh nodded, trying to keep tears from his eyes.

"He'll win," Mai answered. Then, seeing the misery on Minh's face, she added, "And he's as good as anyone."

Loc hacked, spat on their bedding, and then stumbled away from the underpass and into the web of nearby shanties. Mai left Minh alone, knowing that he wouldn't want attention in front of so many eyes. And so she cleaned the befouled bedding, rearranged the interior of their basket, and put on her spare set of clothes.

Soon the two friends were back aboveground, in a realm where sounds and light weren't subdued. They saw uniformed children riding bicycles to school, a beautiful woman in Western clothing getting her photo taken, and a boy selling flowers from a crate on the back of his motor scooter. Shanties disappeared. Hotels and banks rose skyward. Mai gripped the stub of Minh's bad arm. He held his game.

Minh's head still hurt from the blow, and his steps were unsteady. He tried to watch the children on their bicycles, to pretend that he was among them. But his pain was too great, and he squeezed his eyes shut. Mai saw his state and led him to a bench, where they sat and stared. Nearby, government workers wrapped Christmas lights around the bases of hundred-year-old tropical trees.

"Forget about Loc," Mai said, stroking Minh's stump. "What does he know anyway? You're Minh the Marvelous and he's got nothing but opium in his head. He couldn't beat you in a game for all the dollars in the Sheraton. He shouldn't even be in that big, strong body, but on some fisherman's hook."

Minh rubbed his aching ear. Even though he knew Mai was right, he couldn't forget Loc's words, for he often asked himself why his parents had left him. Is it because of my deformity, he wondered, like Loc always says? Is it because I'm stupid and ugly and worthless? Is that why I have no father, no mother, no uniform to wear to school? Why I sometimes want to swim beneath the brown water and never reappear?

Suddenly tears came and Minh could not stop them. They came like waves come to a shore, like birds flock to a branch. They welled from deep within him, bringing pieces of him into the air. As men strung Christmas lights, these pieces of Minh cooled. They fell to the dirty ground. They absorbed dust. And in the heat of the coming day they vanished as if they'd never existed.

THE PLANE WAS SO HIGH THAT to him it was unheard. Its bombs fell toward Earth as if stones dropped from a bridge, silent orbs of hurtling steel that erupted in massive balls of fire and death. The walls of his home exploded around him, light turning to dark, comfort to pain. A monstrous crashing of concrete filled his ears, his every pore. Into the darkness he went, tumbling, striking unseen objects. He tried to escape this darkness, but his arms and legs were quickly pinned, his body becoming immobile.

He heard the cries of several of his siblings and

he called for them. One of his sisters was moaning, the other full of whimpers. His big brother coughed weakly. No words or pleas emerged from his parents or little brothers. They were as silent as the rubble surrounding him. He tasted blood on his lips and shouted for his sisters. Their voices called back to him, but these voices were no longer familiar. They sounded distant and hollow, as if connected to him by thousands of miles of old telephone wire. He knew where his sisters were going and he screamed at them not to leave. They couldn't go to such a place. Not now, when they were so young, when their dreams were unfulfilled. He tried to crawl from the tomb around him, but on all sides he was pinned. The weakening sobs of his siblings prompted him to claw at concrete, to try to move what was unmovable. He shouted for help until his throat ached. Sirens wailed. A dog barked. Voices seeped into the tomb, but they weren't the voices of his loved ones. Those had gone silent, though he still pleaded for them to speak. Light filtered down upon him. Later, in this same light, he saw their faces. Yet now their faces were like fresh paintings that had been cast into the sea, crushed against rocks by uncaring waves.

The light evolved, seeping into him, pulling him from the past. He awoke, stirring on his bamboo mat. Now that his dream was over, he found it hard to recall the faces of his family. So many years had passed. Too many.

Squinting, Sahn searched for his glasses. Even with their aid, the details of his room were unclear. A bright fog seemed to fill the air. This fog stole the clarity from his sight, as if he were looking through a camera that was out of focus.

Sahn ate a breakfast of cold rice and thin slices of mango. He then tidied his room—watering plants, sweeping the floor, hanging his blanket outside a window to bask in the sun. As he worked he thought about his dream, wondering why his unconscious so often reminded him of what he'd for so long tried to forget.

Standing in front of a large mirror, Sahn carefully dressed in his uniform. He'd ironed his olive-colored pants and shirt the previous night. He had also shined his shoes, belt, and the wide, black brim of his cap. A yellow star adorned the red ribbon that encircled the lower part of his cap. Sahn was proud of the star, proud that he wore it. The star had defeated a monster.

Before stepping into the day, Sahn paused in front of his fish tank. Several brown blurs sped about the tank, rising to the surface as he tilted a can of food. He watched the blurs eat, then left his room and locked the door behind him.

Sahn carried no gun. A black baton hung from his belt. He'd swung it twice in thirty years. As always, Sahn did his best to search the streets for criminal activity. He ignored taxis that darted through traffic lights, as well as scooters that drove the wrong way down busy boulevards. Even though more than a thousand people died each month on his country's roads, nothing he could do would change that. And so he made it his mission to seek out those involved with crimes he could stop—offenses such as drug trafficking and child prostitution. Yesterday, his commander had told him about a crate of elephant tusks that was rumored to be in the city. Sahn's beat included Le Cong Kieu Street, which housed scores of antique stores. For years the owners of these stores had paid him a monthly fee, ensuring that he wouldn't report their stashes of ancient treasures that had been smuggled out of China. Still, even though Sahn turned a blind eye to such dealings, he wouldn't stand for certain things. And a crate of elephant tusks was such a thing.

Sahn walked straight and without haste. Soon he was on Le Cong Kieu Street. The power must have gone out, for the antiques stores were unlit. Sahn navigated down the narrow sidewalk. He pretended to peer into the distance, though he could discern only his immediate surroundings. Moving into a darkened shop, he eased his way past piles of silk scrolls and bronze statues. The store's owner, a young man who seemed perpetually afraid of him, strode in his direction.

"I am looking for elephants," Sahn said softly.

"Elephants?"

"What dead elephants would be missing."

"Captain, I haven't heard about any ivory. I swear it."

Sahn wished he could see the man's expression. "If you do hear of these elephants, you'll tell me. You'll tell me and then I won't stop by your store for many months."

"I will. And I'll get word to you as fast as possible."

"Be careful what you do here," Sahn warned, gazing into the gloom ahead.

"Yes, Captain."

Sahn stepped out of the shop. The sun brightened the fog before him. Following the line of the sidewalk's edge, he moved ahead. Most shopkeepers stayed hidden, though several nodded as he passed, looking up from newspapers or antiques that they were repairing. Sahn said hello to no one. But neither did he trouble anyone. These merchants had already paid him for the month. And he wouldn't ask for more than was expected.

A tap on his shoulder served to break his train of thought. He turned, surprised to see two foreigners standing in front of him. The foreigners looked as if they were on safari, dressed in khaki-colored shorts and shirts. The man and woman wore sunglasses and oversize hats. "Excuse me," the man said, pulling a map from his pocket. "But we're looking for Ben Thanh Market. Is it near here?"

Sahn grunted. The market was just a few blocks away. Shrugging, he pretended as if he couldn't speak English. Why would he want to help foreigners, especially ones who sounded like they came from America? Though most of his countrymen were delighted to have Americans back in Vietnam, Sahn didn't share that outlook. He knew what these people were capable of.

"He can't speak English," the woman said, taking the map from her companion. "Let's just hop on a cyclo and tell the driver to take us there."

"How can he stand the heat in that outfit?" the man asked.

"He's used to it. They all are."

Sahn watched the couple depart. Soon they were blurs like everyone else. Soon they were gone. But the memory of what their people had done was not. Sahn scratched at an old scar on his arm. He thought of his sisters, recalling their whimpers in the darkness. The memory weakened him, as it always did. He leaned against a streetlight, no longer concerned with elephants. Instead he wondered where his siblings had traveled to, and what they might have become. He still missed them, even after so many long years. Whoever said that time heals all wounds was a fool, he thought. Time has no such curative powers. Neither does revenge or victory. I've tasted both and they meant nothing to me.

No, Sahn thought, such wounds are forever open, like the side of a mountain that's been stripped of lumber and minerals. This mountain will never be the same, no matter how proud and noble it had once been. Nothing can change the ugliness of the past, and nothing can replace the beauty that's been stolen from the world. Time doesn't have the power to do either. Wounds don't heal. They just fester and rot until the end.

To IRIS, HO CHI MINH CITY in the daylight was almost as incomprehensible as it was at night. She found it hard to believe that Chicago and Ho Chi Minh City were on the same planet. She'd once thought Chicago to be hectic, even frenzied. But Chicago's streets were nothing like what she looked upon now. Every inch before her seemed to be defined by movement. The scooters were everywhere, swirling like snowflakes in a storm. They darted. They moved as one. They avoided one another in last-second swerves that were somehow almost graceful. Mingling with the scooters were tractors, trucks, and bicycles—hundreds of bicycles, often ridden by pairs of uniformed schoolchildren.

Holding the directions her father had given her, Iris navigated the obstacles of the sidewalk. He'd often told her of the peace and sanctuary found at his center, but Iris found it hard to believe that anywhere in the city could be quiet. Too much of everything existed. Too many sights. Too many sounds. Even the immense tropical trees seemed to twist and lock branches, as if they too were trying to step through the crowds.

Ten feet behind Iris was Noah, his eyes instinctively looking for danger. The torn and buckled sidewalk presented a myriad of problems for his prosthesis. Made of a steel spring that connected an artificial foot with a sleeve that fit around his stump, Noah's prosthesis enabled him to walk but made doing so difficult. When he planted his injured leg, it felt as if it were pushing into the pavement instead of away from it. The result was an uneven, ungainly gait that gave him chronic and severe back pain.

A flower market appeared beside them. The open-air market was comprised of scores of individual stalls that offered flowers rarely seen in the West. Many of the flowers sprang from branches, opening wide to the sky so their vibrant petals could gather as much sunlight as possible. Though they rose out of bamboo baskets that looked to have been woven at the dawn of time, the flowers were immaculately organized and presented. Brown or wilted petals weren't in sight.

Soon Iris passed Ben Thanh Market. She glanced inside the vaulted entry but didn't stray from her path. An old woman with a girl on her lap managed to catch Iris's eye. The woman held out a book and asked if Iris would buy it. She didn't want the book, but seeing the girl's thin legs and swollen joints, she placed thirty thousand dong—about two American dollars—into a coconut that the girl weakly held out. She would have liked to give more, but the operating budget for her father's center was moderate at best, and she'd have to be careful with her resources.

Continuing to follow her father's directions, Iris turned down an alley. There was no sidewalk here, and, practically hugging the nearby buildings, she stayed as far from traffic as possible. Battered cars built by older generations rumbled by, often hitting potholes and sending brown water into the air. Aware of Noah struggling behind her, Iris walked slowly, pretending to study her surroundings.

He tried to focus on the path before him but watched the locals watch him. Their eyes inevitably were drawn to his forehead and crippled leg, and he felt their stares as if they were hands pressing against his flesh.

Iris turned left, stepping into a small courtyard. Behind this empty space rose a white, three-story building. The lower front of the building was open, resembling a two-car garage that one would find in the West. Above this entry, large, red letters spelled, THE IRIS RHODES CENTER FOR STREET CHILDREN. Having had no idea that her father named his center after her, Iris stood still. Her eyes immediately welled with tears. How long had the building carried her name? What other surprises were in store for her?

"Let's go in," she heard herself say, her eyes still on the sign.

Inside the open-air entry, a sizable room

stretched toward the middle of the building. The room's floor was checkered with green and white tiles. Its walls were also green, though the painted outlines of children dominated every surface. Some of the figures were playing soccer. Others were standing in a circle and holding hands. Iris couldn't tell for sure, but it looked as if the children were meant to be dressed differently, as if they came from many countries.

"Hello?" she called out, unsure what to do.

His back aching, Noah sat awkwardly on a plastic chair. "Maybe we should—"

"Miss Iris?" an unseen woman replied. "Miss Iris Rhodes? From Chicago?"

Iris glanced up, for the first time noticing a stairwell at the side of the room. A young woman came down the stairs. She appeared to be in her early twenties. Her black pants and yellow button-down shirt were covered in smears and drops of blue and white paint. She wore a black baseball cap with a pink koala bear on the front. A long ponytail emerged from the hole in the back of the cap. The woman's face seemed out of place when compared with her untidy attire. Large, oval-shaped eyes complemented dark, arched eyebrows. Her nose was sculpted and pleasing, her lips full and bent into a half smile. Though her baggy clothes hid much, she appeared to have a lean, almost girlish figure.

"I am Thien," she said in a soft but confident

voice, bowing slightly. "Your father's assistant and cook."

Iris had heard all about Thien, about how she was indispensable and almost unfailingly upbeat. Iris's father had been served by her at a hotel and had later hired her to help him. By his account, she nearly ran his fledgling center—buying supplies, dealing with the local bureaucracy, helping him renovate rooms, and spreading the word among street children about the center's looming opening. He'd rewarded her as best as he could, and every month she sent money to her parents, who lived in the countryside.

Iris stepped closer to Thien. "I'm Iris. It's wonderful to meet you. I've heard so much about you."

Thien smiled, revealing a row of bright teeth. "You are so tall. Just as your father told me. I wish I could be so tall. That would help with the painting." Thien scratched the side of her face, leaving a smudge of white paint on her smooth skin. "Is this your boyfriend?" she asked, glancing at Noah.

"Oh, I'm sorry," Iris replied. "This is my friend Noah. He came here to help us."

Again Thien smiled. "It is nice to meet you, Mr. Noah."

Noah said hello, aware that her stare didn't linger on his forehead.

A few heartbeats of silence passed; then Thien asked, "Would you like to see your center?"

Iris pocketed her directions. "Very much."

Thien took Iris's hand. "This way," she said, leading the American to the back of the room. They stepped through a doorway and an immense kitchen confronted them. Tile countertops stretched to stoves that bore empty, woklike cauldrons. Steel utensils hung from a wall. A new refrigerator dominated a break between countertops. The kitchen smelled of garlic and lemongrass.

Most of the second floor was occupied by a classroom. Several large, battered tables stole much of the space. Wooden chairs surrounded the tables. On one wall was an unfinished painting of a world map. Shelves were piled high with books, art supplies, empty crates, old cameras, and rolled-up scrolls. Two ceiling fans spun listlessly, as if gathering their strength for the coming day.

An office sat adjacent to the classroom. The office was almost as cluttered as Iris's apartment. Tables held thick notebooks and two computers. An immense, old-fashioned safe supported a variety of potted plants and flowers. Ten feet outside the room's only window, a dilapidated yellow building reached skyward.

The children's dormitory encompassed the top floor. Five sets of metal bunk beds spanned opposite walls. Between the beds ran a row of chests. Though a nearby bathroom featuring four showers sparkled with fresh tiles, the main floor in the dormitory was covered with newspapers, for paint cans were everywhere. Even with the room's windows open and the ceiling fans twirling, the smell of fresh paint permeated the air.

Thien pointed to the ceiling, which was blue and bore the white outlines of clouds. "Your father asked me to paint while he was gone," she said. "So I have been painting. He thought the children would enjoy some clouds."

Iris bit her lip, wishing that her father were standing beside her, that they could help Thien finish the clouds. "He'd like what you've done. It's going to be beautiful."

Nodding, Thien again took Iris's hand. "I am so happy you came."

Iris looked from the clouds to Thien. "Thank you."

"You remind me of your father. Your eyes are the same."

"They are?"

"Oh, very much so."

"Did you know him well?"

"Yes."

"Really?" Iris said, surprised at Thien's grip, but not minding it. "Then . . . may I ask you something?"

"Of course, Miss Iris."

"Do you think he was happy here?"

Thien glanced at Noah, then returned her gaze to Iris. "Not always. But sometimes, yes, sometimes he was very happy."

"When?"

"When he was able to do something nice for the children."

Iris smiled faintly, remembering how her father's face had sometimes seemed to blossom when he spoke about his center. "Maybe later you can tell me some stories."

"I would love to."

"Thank you . . . Thien."

"Come, I have something to show you," Thien said, guiding Iris toward the stairs.

Noah watched the smaller woman lead Iris forward. Though his back ached, and he wanted nothing more than to find a quiet place to have a drink, he followed them down the stairwell, which had been painted so as to make one feel as if he or she were climbing or descending a tree. As Noah studied a beautifully rendered green parrot, his prosthesis slipped from the edge of a step and he almost toppled into the women below. They glanced up at him, and he looked away, hiding his scar, his shame, his misery.

Thien walked through the kitchen and a doorway that led outside. A large open space bordered this side of the center, which was opposite the main entrance. The square area was perhaps fifty feet across. The soil was hard and covered in tiny cement chips. A wooden fence had been erected around the area and painted so that it resembled distant rice fields. Propped against one side of the fence were scores of immense clay jars, which ran from one side of the area to the other.

Thien lowered the bill of her baseball cap, shielding her eyes from the sun. "Your father, he enjoyed being out here."

"Is this the playground?" Iris asked, for she'd heard about his dream to add a park to the center.

"Children used to work here, Miss Iris," Thien replied. "In a shop where bicycles were repaired. The children were young. Sometimes less than ten years of age. One day your father bought the shop. And then he tore it down." Thien led Iris to the clay jars, still holding her hand. "And another day he took three men and a truck, and we drove into the countryside. We filled all these jars with dirt." Thien reached into her pocket, producing what looked to be a tangerine. "Are you hungry?"

"You went with him?"

Thien began to peel the fruit. "It was near my village, so far from here. A bomb from the war was there, not far from where children often played. Your father destroyed this bomb. Everyone was so happy. They helped us clean the dirt and fill the jars." Thien looked into the distance, a smile dawning on her full lips. "Your father was a hero that day. I felt very lucky to be his assistant."

Iris reached into one of the jars and watched soil fall through her fingers. "He never got the chance to lay this dirt down, did he?"

"He was so sick," Thien said, shaking her head. "He went back to America to get better. But he never returned to Vietnam. He e-mailed me many times, telling me what to do next, what to work on. But he never came back. Even though he promised that he would."

Iris now understood why her father, on his deathbed, had asked her to scatter his ashes here, to bury him where children would someday play. She'd brought the urn with her, and thinking of scattering him over this soil, over the grass upon which children would run, brought tears to her eyes. He would be happy here. He'd hear the laughter of young voices, the patter of small feet, and maybe then he'd find her as he had promised.

Not bothering to wipe her eyes, Iris continued to feel the dirt. Though the world around her remained foreign and incomprehensible, she felt powerfully connected to the earth that she now touched. Her father had failed her so many times. He'd broken her heart and her family. But she missed him, and he'd also touched this soil.

"Your father, Miss Iris, he loved you so much," Thien said, a gust of wind causing her ponytail to rise and fall. "He told me that. Many times. He showed me all of your newspaper stories, about books. He was so proud of you. And I am so, so happy that you are here."

"Why?"

"Because his dream was good. And he tried so

hard to make it real. And we can be friends. I can be your Vietnamese sister. Your little sister."

Iris stepped toward Thien. "Will you help me? Will you please help me?"

Thien took Iris's hands within her own. "Of course, Miss Iris. We will paint every wall, plant every seed. And your father, and the children, they will all be so very happy."

QUI CLOSED HER EYES AND LEANED backward on the bench, gently holding Tam against her chest. For Tam, some days were worse than others, and today was one of the bad days. A profound weariness enveloped her. Even breathing seemed hard, as if the air were too thick and heavy to pull into her lungs. She had no appetite. Her head hurt. And her joints ached terribly.

Aware that her granddaughter was suffering, Qui prayed that their fortunes would change, that someone would take pity on them and give them the money to buy more painkillers. So far, only one tall foreigner had placed thirty thousand dong in Tam's coconut—enough for a pill or two. But nothing would be left over for food. And Qui knew that she needed to feed Tam something, even if only bananas and rice.

Stroking Tam's face, Qui asked, "How are you feeling, my sweet child?"

Tam groaned faintly, pulling her tattered blanket up against her face. "I'm tired."

"I know, my love. I know. Is there anything I can do for you?"

"Call Momma."

A tourist passed and Qui held out a book, trying to make a quick sale. The man avoided her eyes. "One book, please, mister?" she asked in English. The man walked onward, as if she didn't exist. Perhaps we don't exist, Qui thought bitterly. At least not to him. To most people. To them we're no more than minnows in a river.

Tam shifted atop her lap, bony hips pressing on Qui's legs. Weakly rubbing her blanket against her face, Tam moaned. "Little Bird . . . will you sleep with me now?"

Qui knew that Tam wanted to go home, but the medicine was almost gone. Home might mean temporary comfort, but tomorrow would be worse. Without enough pills Tam would writhe in misery. "Soon, I promise," Qui replied, continuing to stroke Tam's brow.

"Is Thailand beautiful, Little Bird?"

Once again Qui wished that her daughter would come home, that Tam would no longer have to ask about her whereabouts. "Thailand is known as 'the Land of Smiles,' " Qui replied. "So your mother must be happy, though of course she misses you terribly."

"Do children get sick in Thailand?"

"Yes, unfortunately."

"Maybe Momma is taking care of one of them."

A group of travelers passed, and again Qui pleaded with them to buy a book. She said that her granddaughter needed medicine, that she was in pain. No one seemed to hear her.

Tam moaned, rubbing her blanket against her aching knee. "Why . . . why do I call you Little Bird?"

"Because I carry you on my back. We fly together and see so many things."

"I like to fly."

Qui heard the weakness in Tam's voice and suddenly felt trapped. They'd been at Ben Thanh Market for six hours and had only about two dollars to show for it. If they didn't make more money, Tam's suffering would soon be much worse. Qui stood up, adjusted the bag that would hold her granddaughter, and asked a nearby cyclo driver for help.

Before long Tam was in the sling, the sides of her knees pressing against Qui's back. Qui slowly moved down the congested sidewalk, grunting from the exertion. She begged as she walked, beseeching tourists to buy a book. Tam moaned more frequently, and Qui longed to take her home. But they couldn't go home just yet. Not when daylight existed and tourists were abundant.

"I love you," Tam said. "I love you . . . when you fly with me."

"I'd never fly with anyone else," Qui replied, stepping around a sleeping dog.

"Will you still fly with me when I go to the new world? After I wake up with all the other children?"

"Of course, my love."

"Will I like it there?"

Qui reached backward, feeling Tam's brow, caressing the contours of her face. "Your knees won't hurt there. And you'll be able to run. You won't even need me to carry you."

"But you will . . . if I ask?"

"As often as you like."

Tam dropped her blanket and, grunting with effort, Qui managed to pick it up. They were now in the heart of downtown, the wealthiest area of Ho Chi Minh City. Tourists were everywhere, walking along tree-lined boulevards toward Reunification Palace, Notre Dame Cathedral, and Tao Dan Park. Galleries, banks, travel agencies, restaurants, and hotels sprouted like polished mountains from the pavement. Qui's heart began to quicken its pace, for she wasn't welcome here. Nevertheless she had no choice but to walk these streets.

At a busy intersection stood a Louis Vuitton store, a glass-and-steel creation that might have been a diamond set on a giant's ring. Inside was a quiet and open space, so unlike the nearby environs. Qui, of course, had never been inside the store. But she'd seen well-dressed men and women emerge from it carrying beautiful purses and bags. The purses, she knew, sometimes sold for vast amounts of money—more money than she'd ever held in her life, more money than was necessary to buy Tam's painkillers for many months.

Though leery about being harassed by the police or someone else, Qui walked to the store and stepped beneath the sweeping glass-and-steel canopy that rose above her. Believing that she'd invite less trouble if she stood, Qui forced her tired body to stay straight. She peered into the store and saw an unknown world that she'd never touch or understand.

For a few minutes no one entered or emerged from the store. Qui's back began to ache. Her legs trembled. Her breath tumbled through the gaps between her remaining teeth. Tam started to moan again. Hearing her granddaughter suffer, Qui turned around, looking for someone who might help.

Before long a white-haired couple emerged from the glass doors. They each held a crisp shopping bag. Qui stepped toward them, holding out a book. "Hello," she said in English. "Do you like book? Will you please buy book? I have good one for you."

"We have enough bloody books already," the man replied, taking his companion's arm and leading her away.

"My granddaughter sick. I need money for medicine. Just little money. Please, kind sir. Please help us."

"If she's ill, fetch a cyclo and take her to a hospital."

Qui watched the couple depart. Her back throbbed, and she longed to sit and rest. But she stood, politely asking other shoppers to buy her books. People tended to look at her with pity or disdain, sometimes acting as if they didn't hear or see her. They walked away, clutching their full bags, and didn't glance back. With each disappearance, Qui's sense of despondency increased. Did she and Tam appear as animals to these people? Was Tam's life of so little meaning?

Despite her best efforts, Qui began to cry. She balled her fists and wiped her weary eyes. Why is Tam dying? she asked herself, looking skyward. Why does no one care? And why . . . why, sweet Buddha, does this world let a little girl suffer so much? Suffering should only be for the old. We're ready for it. We know it's coming. But not Tam. She shouldn't hurt so much.

Qui's knees buckled. She struggled to stand. Suddenly a security guard was beside her, pulling her arm, taking her away from the storefront. She asked him to leave her be, to help her granddaughter, but the man only pulled harder. He must have scared Tam, for she started to cry. And Tam's tears caused the walls to fall down around Qui. She'd built these walls to protect herself, to protect Tam. But now the walls were falling, smothering her. She shuddered and wept and pleaded. She told the man that her granddaughter was dying, that she was in pain, that a little pill could take the pain away. The guard only tugged with more determination, his fingers biting into Qui's flesh.

And then, seeming to appear from nowhere, a dark-skinned woman from a foreign land stood beside her. This woman reached into a pocket and withdrew a twenty-dollar bill. The bill was placed in Qui's hands. Qui bowed so low that she almost fell over. The woman helped her up. Still weeping, Qui grasped the woman's fingers tightly, squeezing the flesh of Tam's savior. Qui repeatedly thanked the stranger, handing her a book. The woman smiled and said good-bye.

Once again Qui could breathe. The walls were quickly rebuilt around her. Tam would not suffer so horribly tomorrow, or the next day or the next. Qui wiped tears from her cheeks, and then her hands found Tam's face, and she told her they were going home, how they would fly like birds to a nest of their making.

—FOUR

A Smaller World

Iris awoke early, her internal clock still unadjusted to the time change. Dawn had just stretched its radiant body across the sky. Roosters had screeching contests in the distance. The beeps of unseen scooters sounded as often as the ticks of an old clock. Raising her head from the futon that she'd laid down in the office, she looked appreciatively at the cluttered room. On a nearby desk she'd placed several prepublication copies of novels that she was supposed to review. Her notebook was also present, within it a collection of thoughts and musings that she was trying to assemble into a novel. Though she'd worked on it for six months, she still hadn't finished her first draft. To her disgust, she knew that her characters were as deep as the paper upon which she wrote. She still didn't understand them, which made it impossible to bring them to life.

Aware that the income generated from her book reviews was important, but suddenly unwilling to do what she'd done so many times, Iris ignored the stack of review copies and her deadlines. Instead she dressed quickly, putting on jeans and a blue T-shirt. She left the office, peeping into the classroom, where Noah slept. She counted nine beer cans sitting under his cot. His prosthesis also rested on the floor. How odd it looked—a rod of sorts connecting a shoe to a hard plastic sleeve that fit over his stump and thigh.

Iris wished that she could help Noah, that she had training in such matters. She wished that nine beer cans didn't litter the floor of her father's classroom. The cans seemed sacrilegious, as if casting sins in all directions. Impulsively, she walked in, quietly collected the cans, and disposed of them. Noah continued to sleep on his belly, not stirring. The skin of his stump was puckered and scarred.

In the stairwell, Iris heard noises coming from the kitchen. She was surprised to find Thien cutting up a pineapple. Thien wore an apron over her paint-splattered clothes. The same baseball cap was perched atop her head.

"Good morning, Miss Iris," Thien said, smiling.

"You can call me Iris. If you'd like to."

"I am preparing breakfast for you. If you are going to work, you must have a full belly."

Iris nodded, watching Thien's quick fingers. Thien began to sing quietly, her voice melodious. The Vietnamese words were still foreign to Iris, but she was no longer afraid of them. On the contrary, Thien's voice put her at ease. "Do you mind," Iris asked, "if we paint a little first? I'd like to work some, then have breakfast."

Thien removed her apron and placed the pineapple in the refrigerator. "Will you help me paint the clouds? They are so hard to get right."

"I think what you've done is wonderful," Iris replied, following the smaller woman upstairs. "If you don't mind my asking, how did you learn English so well?"

"Oh, my vocabulary needs improvement. But I tried hard to learn in school. And for three years I worked in a hotel, behind the concierge desk. I was very lucky to have this job."

"I bet you were good at it."

"I worked hard, Miss Iris. I was happy to help the guests. They had come so far, and I wanted them to enjoy their time in Vietnam."

Iris and Thien walked into the dormitory. Thien used a screwdriver to open a can of white paint. She dipped a wooden spoon into the paint, swirling it around. She then handed a balled-up piece of newspaper to Iris and proceeded to a far corner of the room, where a table had been covered with an old sheet. Thien eyed the outline of the cloud above. After gently dipping her own ball of newspaper into the paint, she stepped onto the table and dabbed at the interior of the outline. Several drops of paint fell atop her shoulder, but she paid them no heed. "You must be gentle," she said.

Iris watched Thien dab at the surface. Thien was quite good, and Iris shook her head. "I think you should do this. I don't want to mess it all up."

"It is only paint, Miss Iris," Thien replied. "It can always be covered over. Now please try."

Hesitating, Iris continued to watch Thien work. Soon Thien began to sing softly, as if unaware that Iris was so close. Her voice, high and haunting, breathed life into long notes, into a song that Iris didn't know whether was sad or joyous. Still, the song soothed her. Thien's voice was beautiful, rising and falling as if carried by winds.

After a few minutes, Iris began to work, carefully dipping her newspaper into the paint and then dabbing the area within the cloud that Thien was fashioning. Thien continued to sing. At first Iris applied as little paint as possible, but she quickly grew more confident, putting greater pressure against the ceiling. The cloud billowed outward.

"See, Miss Iris, you can do it," Thien said, wiping her nose, covering its tip with paint. "Did you ever think that you would make clouds?"

"No, I didn't."

"These are good Vietnamese clouds. Full of rain and dragons."

"Dragons?"

"Dragons are everywhere in Vietnam," Thien replied, continuing to paint. "If a river runs red, a dragon below the water is bleeding. If a breeze blows suddenly across the sky, a dragon must be flying above. And warm rains mean that dragons are crying. We Vietnamese love dragons, which deepen the seas, guard our treasures, and rule the natural world."

Through the countless books she'd read, Iris had come across several stories of dragons. "In the West," she said, "dragons are seen as evil, as creatures to be destroyed."

Thien paused in her work, her full lips tightening together. "To be destroyed?"

"People feared them."

"In Vietnam, dragons are the greatest, the most noble of creatures. They have protected us for thousands of years."

Iris filled in the last part of the cloud. "And you see dragons in these?"

"I see parts of them."

"This cloud . . . it turned out well, didn't it?"

"You are a wonderful painter, Miss Iris."

The two women moved the table and began to create another cloud. "Do you really think we can open the center by Christmas?" Iris asked, for this had been her father's plan, and he'd told local officials as much.

"Christmas is still a month away. We can paint many clouds in a month."

"But what else needs to be done?"

"Painting mostly. And gathering textbooks. And hiring a teacher. And of course, the playground must be built. Maybe your friend can work on it. Such a man should work outside."

Iris nodded but said nothing, wondering what Thien meant. Finally she asked, "Why do you work here and not the hotel? You said it was a good job."

Thien gently pulled apart her ball of newspaper, so that it would leave a different impression. "You should walk with me, Miss Iris."

"Walk with you?"

"Walk the streets. Then you will understand why I am working here. Why it is my honor to work here."

Iris glanced around the room, eager to see it complete. "I'll walk the streets. Today. But still,

I'd like to know why you're here. If that's all right with you."

Thien set her ball of newspaper aside and reached into her pocket and withdrew a small, red fruit that resembled a cross between an apple and a pear. She offered the fruit to Iris, and when Iris shook her head, Thien took a bite. "On the outside, the street children are not beautiful," she said. "Their clothes are dirty. Their hair is uncombed. Sometimes they are crippled in some terrible way. This is often why they have been abandoned."

"My father told me about that."

"But inside, Miss Iris, inside, these children are beautiful. They have such smiles. And such laughs. Nothing could ever be so beautiful." Thien took another bite of the fruit. "But after a time, the children no longer smile or laugh. The streets destroy them. The children begin to steal, to sell drugs, to sell themselves. They have no choice. Your father understood these things. And he wanted to give the children a chance, to bring them into his center where they could learn and be safe. When he asked me to be his assistant, I felt like I was the luckiest person in Ho Chi Minh City. Because I was going to be able to help these beautiful children."

Iris nodded, wondering why she hadn't felt lucky to come here, to finish what her father had started. "Let's go now," she said. "I want to see what you've seen."

Thien finished the fruit. She then stepped from

the table and, taking Iris's hand, helped her down. "Your father told me about your wonderful heart," she said, leading Iris toward the stairway. "And I am most certain that he is smiling on you now."

RISING FROM BED WAS ONE OF the most difficult challenges that Noah faced each day. Asleep, within a womb of oblivion, he was protected from the demons that haunted him during daylight. His mind could rewind time, step backward, and recollect an age when he was happy. His body couldn't remind him of his aches—the fire in his back, the pain of his inflamed stump. And his hatred for those whose lies cost him his friend and his leg was at rest.

When he was awake, the world was not one of light, but of darkness. Noah feared this world, for he lacked the power to save himself from his thoughts, his pain, and his hatred. He looked into mirrors and saw a stranger. He turned on the television and saw a man he wanted to kill. His loved ones were no solace. Despite his best efforts, he was envious of their happiness, their lives free of pain. They didn't understand his sufferings. No one could.

Noah sat upright on his cot. He rubbed his eyes. His detested prosthesis lay on the floor. He looked at the contraption the way a miner dying of lung cancer might observe his pickax. He swore softly, pulling the carbon-fiber sleeve upward until it rose around his thigh and rested against his stump. Most days he placed a gel on his stump, which served to bind the sleeve to his flesh. But in the heat of Vietnam, his stump seemed swollen, and the gel didn't tempt him.

After pulling on loose-fitting travel pants, Noah stood up. To his surprise, he realized that the beer cans he'd scattered about the previous night had disappeared. He walked unsteadily into the office, looking for Iris. He tried to remember the Vietnamese girl's name but couldn't. And so he quietly moved about the building, wondering whom he'd run into.

Despite the clouds, birds, maps, and trees that had been painted on the walls around him, the rooms and halls felt claustrophobic, and he suddenly had to escape. He stepped outside the center and was confronted by sights that reminded him of Baghdad. The buildings were white and stained. Television antennas and rusting air conditioners dotted roofs. The street was patched like an old quilt and was full of potholes. The smell of diesel fuel filled the air.

A scooter passed him, its driver dodging potholes as if a child playing hopscotch. Noah followed the course of the battered street, emerging onto a much larger thoroughfare. The sleeve of his prosthesis chafed against his stump, rubbing it raw. He tried to favor his injured leg, and his graceless gait produced an ache in his back. He swore, bitterness rising within him. An immense truck approached, and he thought about falling in front of it, about how such darkness would feel.

A pair of young women in traditional dresses walked past. Their eyes found the scar on his forehead and he glanced away. The sidewalk was thick with pedestrians. He shuffled past them, needing to flee, but not knowing where to go. Several children soon trailed him, asking for candy and pens. He had neither, and they left him, their voices replaced by those of the city. These noises assaulted Noah, reminding him of the sounds of war. A motorcycle engine became a jet, a thumping jackhammer a machine gun. The siren of a police car pulled him back to roadside bombings. He closed his eyes, leaning against a lamppost. He tried to remember what Iris had said, that good things still existed in the world. But his stump and back ached. His will to endure was gone. And goodness was but a word.

Noah passed a streetside vendor who sold clothes from a stainless-steel cart. Money was exchanged and soon an olive-colored baseball cap hung low on Noah's brow. Though the fabric hid his scar, he felt no less naked. And so he hurried into the lobby of a nearby hotel. A Western-style bar was present and he sat down and ordered a Tiger beer, which descended his throat as if water. He couldn't get the alcohol into his system fast enough. A second and a third beer were finished as quickly as the first.

The terror of the street began to fade. The pain within his mind and body diminished. A stillness emerged. In this stillness he was able to temporarily detach himself from his sufferings.

"Where you from?" the bartender asked in broken English.

Noah eyed the older man, who was constantly cleaning glasses or the countertop. "America," he replied, avoiding the man's stare.

"Why you come to Vietnam?"

"I don't know."

"Your first time here?"

"Yeah."

The bartender nodded. "It good to have Americans back in Vietnam. When I was boy, here in Saigon, I saw many Americans. We South Vietnamese fight with you, against the north. We fight and die together. And then, when we lose, Americans left. One day they all gone, thousands of them. And for many years they no come back. Those times very hard. No jobs. No food. No reason to—" The man stopped speaking when the power abruptly went out. He smiled. "Some things always stay the same, as you see."

"Does that happen often?"

"As often as it wish," the bartender replied, opening another Tiger beer for Noah. "As I already say, it good to have Americans back in Vietnam."

"Why?"

"Why not? I friends with Americans before. It

good to be friends again. Maybe you no welcome everywhere in world, but you welcome here in Saigon."

Noah looked through a nearby window. "I thought people called it Ho Chi Minh City."

"Ah, only young people and government people say Ho Chi Minh City. To me, Saigon is Saigon. If people told you to say George Bush City instead of New York City, would you?"

"No."

"You see?" The bartender sighed when the power came back on. "There. Now I must go and reset the air conditioner. You please excuse me for a moment?"

"Sure."

"If you want another Tiger, take one. I trust you. And as I say before, I am so happy that Americans come back. Your country, my country, we are good countries. Good peoples. We have great futures ahead of us. Better to go into this future together, yes, than to go ahead alone?"

Noah watched the man depart, envious of his outlook on life, wanting to also be a cheerful bartender in Saigon.

Tao Dan Cultural Park was an idyllic span of green in the heart of the city. Beneath the shade of more than a thousand towering trees, people walked, read, and practiced tai chi. The park was a haven, the groans and cries of the surrounding city muted by the thick foliage. Birds sang in lofty branches. The wind could be heard. The laughter of children rose and fell.

Holding Minh's stump, Mai walked along an old, concrete path. Her eyes darted to nearby benches, looking for foreigners who might be interested in a game of Connect Four. Mai liked coming to the park, for tourists could be found and easily engaged. And while Minh played she could watch the trees.

"The Shaq was something else, wasn't he?" she asked.

Minh smiled and nodded. The two friends had just come from an electronics store. Several times a week they stood outside the store and, staring through a glass wall, watched the televisions inside. On this particular morning, they'd seen an NBA game.

"No one can dunk shoot like the Shaq," Mai continued. "Do you remember the video of when he broke the backboard? What strength!"

Minh recalled that day. It had been raining, and they'd stood beneath the store's awning for hours. Thinking of how the Shaq had broken the backboard, Minh raised his Connect Four box, pretending to throw it down as if it were a basketball being jammed through a hoop.

Mai laughed. "That's right, Minh the Dunk Shooter. You look just like the Shaq. I think that maybe you could even beat him. It's too bad that he can't come to Ho Chi Minh City and play you for a thousand dollars. We'd be rich. We'd eat ice cream every day for the rest of our lives."

Licking his lips at the thought of so much ice cream, Minh watched a group of older women practicing tai chi. The women moved as if they were in slow motion, their arms and legs as graceful as anything he'd seen. He wondered what they thought about when moving so slowly. Do their thoughts move at the same speed as their arms? Do they hear and see things that I can't?

Mai and Minh continued to walk, looking for foreigners. The path curved deeper into the park. A large banner portraying Ho Chi Minh fluttered in the breeze. Minh thought that their great leader looked happy, as always.

"I need to cut your hair, Minh the Monster," Mai said, touching his locks with a folded-up fan. "You look like some kind of jungle creature. We'd better tidy you up or children will scream and run away. I'm afraid of you, and if . . ." Mai paused, glanced at her feet, and then said, "Loc's here. Don't look, but he's following us."

Minh bit his lip. He lowered his shoulders, no longer feeling like the Shaq. Gripping his game tightly, he increased his pace.

"We should find someone to play," Mai said. "He's probably spent all our money and we'd better get him some more."

Minh saw a grasshopper on the ground, thought about stepping on it, but didn't.

"We have to leave him," Mai said softly. "But fourteen dollars isn't enough. Oh, how will we ever get more?"

Minh looked away from her. He didn't want to talk about leaving Loc, not with him so close.

"He can't hear us, Minh. So stop worrying your dirty little head. Besides, he's probably so full of opium by now that he thinks he's a deer, or invisible or something."

Continuing his fast pace, Minh scanned his environs. Not far ahead, a blond-haired man sat on a bench. Minh headed in the man's direction.

"Good spot," Mai said. "He looks bored. Maybe you can play him a few games." Mai let go of Minh's stump and waved to the foreigner. Switching to English, she said, "Hello, mister. We can sit with you?"

The man glanced at her briefly. "Sure," he said, pulling an olive-colored baseball cap lower on his brow.

"Why you here all alone?" Mai asked, as she and Minh sat on the opposite side of the bench. "You lose your girlfriend?"

"No."

"You no lose her or you no have?"

"No have."

Mai smiled. "That too bad. Anyway, you look bored. Maybe you play my friend a game? It good way to pass the time. If you win, we give you one dollar. If he win, you give us one dollar."

Noah rubbed his brow. He'd been on the bench for almost an hour, and his aches had returned. After leaving the bar, he had again struggled with the chaos of the city and had sought refuge within the park. He'd wanted to lie down on the grass and sleep, but thought such a spectacle might draw too many eyes. Squinting against rays of sunlight that seeped through the foliage to reach him, he studied the boy and girl. Both were dressed in tattered clothes. One of the boy's hands was missing, and thinking of his own self-consciousness about his leg, Noah pretended not to notice. "I'll play a game," he finally replied.

Minh opened up the box and began to set the game up on the bench.

"You know how to play?" Mai asked.

"I think so."

"You must get four pieces in a row. Down, across, or diagonal works same, same."

Noah motioned for Minh to make the first move. The boy placed his black piece in the center. Thinking that he'd start filling up one of the sides, Noah dropped his red piece into the slot farthest from him. Minh's next piece went beside his first. And Noah's next piece went atop his first.

"No, no, silly man," Mai said, laughing. "Now Minh put third piece next to his other two. And you cannot win, because he then have three in a row with a space on both sides. No matter where you go next, he get four in a row."

Noah looked at the board. She was right. The boy had already beaten him. "I guess I owe you a dollar."

"You sure you play this game before?" she asked, giggling.

"Yeah."

"Must have been a long, long time ago."

"It was."

"You want to play again? You play better this time. Sure, sure."

Noah's stump itched, but he didn't reach down. "What's your name?" he asked, placing his first red piece in the board.

"Mai. In English, it sound like the month after April. My friend is Minh. He no speak, so I speak for two of us. I like to talk, so it good deal for he and me."

Minh dropped his piece, wondering why the foreigner was sitting alone on a park bench.

"Speaking is overrated," Noah replied, watching the boy.

Mai shrugged. "Why you no have girlfriend?"

"Girlfriends are overrated too."

"Then you no have right girlfriend," Mai said, opening one of her fans and then cooling herself. "I think when you have right girlfriend you no sit alone on park bench."

"I wouldn't know."

"How much you pay for your hat? My friend sell this same hat."

"Seven dollars."

"Seven dollar? Are you crazy? Next time you come to me. I get for you cheaper. Sure, sure. Or I can sell you fan if you like. Very good to keep you cool."

The board was filling with black and red pieces. Noah studied it carefully, aware that the boy rarely took his eyes from it. "Why aren't you in school?" he asked, glancing at Mai.

Her smile faded. "We must make money. If we go to school, we no make money. Then we no eat. So I sell fans and Minh play games. Maybe someday we can go to school. Then we can learn more English, two plus two, capitals of Europe, and so on."

Noah held a game piece, debating his next move. The board was almost full, and he was being forced to go where he didn't want to. "Does he ever lose?" Noah asked, dropping his piece.

"Oh, yes. Many time. Maybe you even beat him next game."

"Next game?"

"Oh, this game you lose. Sure, sure."

After a few more moves Noah lost. He watched the boy empty the game. Minh's stump was just as active as his hand, separating the black and red pieces. Noah's eyes found his and Minh nodded, clearly wanting to play again.

"Just one more," Noah said, wishing that he were still a child, that he could go back in time and then make different choices. His childhood had been the best part of his life. He'd cared only about sports and comic books and his family. He hadn't yet pulled a trigger and watched a man crumple. He hadn't looked into a mirror and seen a stranger. "Tonight," he asked, "if I wanted a drink in a quiet place, where would I go?"

Mai pursed her lips. "A quiet place in Ho Chi Minh City? Easier to find a hundred-dollar bill on Ham Nghi Street."

"There must be somewhere."

"Go to big riverboat. You can have dinner and a drink, and riverboat take you up and down Saigon River. You see many beautiful things. Maybe you even find lovely girlfriend. You look like you could use lovely girlfriend. If I find one for you, you give me five dollar? My friend, she sell noodles near Park Hyatt hotel. She very, very beautiful. And so nice."

"I'll never beat him," Noah said, dropping another piece.

"Where you stay anyway? Sheraton? Omni? Sofitel?"

"Do I look rich?"

"No five-star hotel for you? Maybe three-star? What about Continental? Empress? Metropole?"

"I'm helping a friend open a center for street children. I sleep there."

Mai looked from the game to Noah's face. "The Iris Rhodes Center?"

"You've heard of it?"

"Sure, sure. Everyone on street hear such things. Is Mr. Rhodes your friend?"

Noah thought about telling her that he'd died. But instead, he replied, "I'm here with his daughter, Iris."

"Wow. Then you like a famous man in Vietnam. Maybe you give me autograph."

"I won't be here long."

Mai started to fan Noah after noticing beads of sweat on his face. "Why not? You no like it here? Maybe it too hot?"

Suddenly tired of the conversation, Noah lost the game on purpose. "That's three dollars I owe you," he said. "What if I give you five and take that fan?"

"Good idea," Mai replied, handing him the fan.

Noah watched the boy put away his game. "You're smart. I don't think I could beat you if we played ten games."

Minh nodded, wishing that he could sit and play with the man for the remainder of the day.

When the children didn't rise from the bench, Noah knew that he'd have to leave. And so he rose awkwardly. "Good-bye," he said, looking from face to face.

"You break your leg, mister?" Mai asked.

Noah locked eyes with Minh. Impulsively, he pulled up his pant leg, exposing his prosthesis. "Good luck," he said, for the first time openly staring at Minh's stump. Then he turned and limped away.

• • •

THE KITCHEN SIMMERED WITH THE SCENTS of dinner. Thien held the handle of a large pan and used an oversize bamboo spoon to stir a concoction of garlic, pepper, bok choy, and prawns. Occasionally she added a few squirts of fish oil to the dish. At the counter, Iris peeled rambutan fruits. Once she'd peeled a score of the lime-size fruits, she cleaned the firm, white flesh that remained. "I've never seen these," she said, glancing at the discarded skins, which were red and hairy.

"Try one," Thien replied. "They are as sweet as candy. But bite gently, as a seed is inside each."

Iris sampled the fruit, which, once torn by her teeth, seemed to cast sugary juices into her mouth. "Wow," she said, surprised by the taste. "That is sweet."

Thien nodded, starting to sing softly as she continued to stir the dish. By now Iris was used to her singing. Thien's voice had the remarkable ability to relax Iris, almost as if it were classical music emanating from a speaker. "Why do you love to sing so much?" Iris asked, cleaning up her cuttings.

"I sing of happy things, Miss Iris. And that makes me happy."

Iris heard a noise behind her and, expecting Noah, turned. Her heart skipped when she saw a policeman standing nearby. His uniform was an olive green, and a yellow star sat prominently on his cap. His face was stern and unfriendly. He began to speak in Vietnamese, and though Iris couldn't understand what he said, his words seemed harsh. Thien lowered the heat on the stove and set her bamboo spoon aside. She didn't appear intimidated by him and spoke much faster than Iris had ever heard her.

When their conversation paused, Iris looked to Thien. "What does he want?"

"I speak English," the policeman replied. "So ask your question to me."

Iris wiped a small piece of rambutan from her lips. "Oh. I'm sorry. Why . . . why are you here?"

Sahn scrutinized the American, her features muddled by the haze that perpetually dominated his sight. He wondered why he hadn't been told that she'd be arriving. His informers were getting sloppy. That would have to change. "I responsible for this area," he finally replied. "Why you come here?"

"I am sure, Captain, that you know the answer," Thien answered in English, a trace of defiance in her voice. "She came to finish what her father started."

"Your father, the American war criminal?"

"The what?" Iris asked, stepping back.

"You Americans think you understand everything. That you can save or destroy world when and where you want." Sahn's fists clenched as he remembered meeting the big American, the man who'd once fought in Vietnam. He had hated the

110

man immediately. "Where is war criminal?" he asked, glaring at the foreigner.

Thien walked to Iris's side. "Do not listen to him," she said, taking her hand.

"Where is he?"

"He is dead," Thien replied. "And he was no more a criminal than you or I."

Sahn heard the American sniff but didn't think she was crying. "Again, why you here?"

Iris shook her head. "To open the center. That's all."

"To right a wrong?"

"No. But to . . . but to do a right."

Sahn wondered if he should demand to see the center's licenses and official letters. But he knew that Thien would have everything in perfect order. He'd already asked to see the papers several times, and she'd always been ready. And she'd bribed him so that he'd go away. "You think you save children?" he asked, looking at Iris.

"I don't know."

Grunting, Sahn peered about, pretending to scrutinize his surroundings when they were really nothing more than a collection of blurred images. He'd return later and demand another payment, he decided. Better to ask then, at which point Thien would expect to hand out a new bribe. "You no wanted here," he said to the American. He then turned and strode out the front entrance.

Iris watched him leave, feeling small and beaten. She looked to Thien. "Why did he say those things?"

Thien squeezed her hand. "I do not know, Miss Iris. But there is no need to fear him. We have official permission to open our center and have the blessing of high-ranking officials. He knows this. And I give him a few dollars every week just so that he will not make trouble for us."

"You . . . bribe him?"

Thien nodded, her ponytail bobbing through the back of her hat. "Pay no attention to what he said about your father. Your father made many, many people happy here."

"That was awful . . . to hear. Just awful."

Thien saw the sadness in Iris's face and wanted it to depart. "Do you want to do something good tonight?"

"Now?"

Thien took a steel bowl from a nearby shelf. She then scooped some of the meal that she'd prepared into the bowl. She placed two spoons in her pocket. Opening a chest in the corner of the kitchen that Iris had assumed contained utensils, Thien removed an old Polaroid camera. She hung it about her neck. "Come, Miss Iris," she said. "Follow me."

Soon Iris and Thien were outside. In one hand Thien held the bowl. In the other she gripped Iris's fingers. She led Iris forward, singing softly as they entered the chaos of the night. Iris tried not to think about the policeman's words, instead gazing at her surroundings. Earlier that day, Thien had taken her

112

down a seemingly countless number of streets and alleys. At first Iris had been afraid of the strange sights, sounds, and smells. But as the day had progressed she'd seen scores of people smile and wave at her, as if they knew her, as if they'd missed her. Iris had waved back, saying hello in Vietnamese, the way Thien had taught her.

Now, as Thien led her along once again, Iris wondered where they were headed. Who's Thien bringing the food to? she asked herself. What good is she going to create, and why did that awful man say those things to me? As she thought about the last question in particular, Iris watched Thien interact with some of the merchants and vendors they passed. Clearly, she had walked this path many times before.

Thien guided Iris across a boulevard, moving in a start-and-stop fashion to avoid hundreds of approaching scooters. The air here was so thick with pollution that Iris held her breath for as long as possible. When she finally needed to draw air, she placed her T-shirt over her face and inhaled through the thin cotton.

After crossing the boulevard, Thien seemed to walk away from the city's biggest and most beautiful buildings. Soon she passed people who appeared to live on the street. She dropped Iris's hand when they came upon a one-armed man who begged in front of a travel agency. Handing Iris the bowl of food, Thien greeted the man. They spoke for a moment and he grinned. Thien lifted her Polaroid, capturing his face and smile. The photo emerged from her camera, and after blowing on it for a moment, she showed it to Iris.

Iris saw that Thien was skilled. She'd shot the picture so that the man's head was in front of a store light, so that this light created a halo effect around the man's features. His wrinkled face struck Iris as having seen more tragedies than triumphs, yet at the moment Thien had captured him, he seemed to be pleasantly surprised, as if life suddenly weren't all that terrible.

Thien handed him the photo. He chuckled, showing it to a nearby soft-drink vendor. The two men laughed and spoke with Thien. She soon waved good-bye and moved ahead, stopping every block or so to take someone else's photo. "We are going to Ben Thanh Market," she finally said. "Someone there is very hungry."

"Who?"

"A sick girl. Her grandmother tells me that she likes my cooking."

Iris walked behind Thien, amazed by the sudden notion that she'd follow this stranger anywhere. Soon she recognized the market, the front of which was crammed with cyclos and scooters. Drivers asked foreigners and locals if rides were needed, dusting off cracked seats. Thien zigzagged through the mayhem, soon approaching an old woman who sat with a child on her lap. The woman smiled, her tongue visible between gaps made by missing teeth.

Thien dropped to her knees before the woman, handing the girl on her lap the bowl of food. Iris's gaze didn't leave the girl, whose legs and arms were impossibly thin, whose eyes wandered about as if unable to focus on anything. Remembering the girl from their earlier encounter, Iris watched Thien and the woman converse, watched the woman gently and patiently guide food into the girl's unresponsive mouth.

"These are my friends," Thien said in English, nodding toward the pair. "This is Qui, and this is her granddaughter, Tam."

Iris nodded, feeling ridiculously tall, wanting to be at the same height as these strangers. "Hello," she said. "I'm Iris. It's nice to meet you."

The woman motioned for Iris to crouch beside her and then asked, "What you think about Vietnam?"

Iris watched the spoon rise slowly, depositing half of a prawn into the girl's mouth. "It's not what I expected."

Thien took a photo as Iris responded to the question. The photo soon emerged, and Thien handed it to Iris, who held it carefully and watched colors and shapes materialize. Soon she saw herself, saw how she contrasted so mightily with the girl and her grandmother. Iris had never felt so different from anyone, and yet she also felt connected to these strangers. She felt connected to them because she knew she could help them. She could give them food. She could buy them clothes. She had the power to take their hands in hers and make their lives better.

Iris was tempted to ask Thien about the girl, about her condition. But not wanting to appear rude or to make some social blunder, she simply sat and watched Tam eat. Several times Tam looked at her, and Iris tried to smile. But it was hard to smile when staring at such a sick child. Iris couldn't imagine what it would be like to be ill and young and on the streets. Tam must be lonely, and, thinking of her own experiences with feeling abandoned, Iris wanted to sit beside Tam and do something to make her smile. Iris thought about reading her a story, about combing her hair, about doing so many things that might lessen the burdens that she carried.

Iris watched the woman continue to feed Tam, the process seeming to occur in slow motion. As she ate, Tam often moaned softly, and these moans somehow penetrated Iris's skin, seeping through her flesh, past her rib cage, and into her heart. These moans dampened her eyes. They stirred her soul. They caused her fingers to move out, to rest upon Tam's swollen knee.

At that moment Iris realized that she didn't know where she was going, but that she wasn't going back.

FIVE

Bridges

Breakfast was a hurried affair of coffee, French baguettes, and sliced papaya. Iris wasn't hungry but forced herself to eat. A full day awaited her. The previous night, as they had walked back to the center from the market, she'd asked Thien if they might explore more today, perhaps even venturing outside the city. Thien had seemed pleased by this request and had promised to arrange such an excursion.

Iris had decided that she'd be best able to help street children if she better understood their plight. And that meant understanding their country as intimately as possible. She needed to know how people lived, what made them succeed and struggle. Though in the past she might have read dozens of books in an effort to learn such things, she wanted to experience life in Vietnam firsthand.

Finishing the last of her baguette, she strode upstairs and into the classroom. Noah lay asleep on his cot, his arm over his eyes, a T-shirt and shorts covering his torso. Unlike the previous morning, beer cans weren't present. But she suspected that he'd drunk late into the night, for she had heard him moving about long after she'd first dreamed. "Noah," she said, standing respectfully distant.

He stirred, moving his arm from his face. Blinking repeatedly, he pulled the sheet over his stump. "Yes?"

"I've rented a car and driver. Thien and I are going out to the countryside, to the Mekong Delta. I want to do some exploring. I think it'd be good, really good, to see how people live. And I think you should join us."

He rubbed his aching brow. "I'd slow you down."

"We're not in a race."

"No, you go. I'll stay."

She crossed her arms. "If you're going to stay here . . . you need to work. All right? Would you please do that? I won't ask anything else of you as long as you do that."

"Sure."

"I wish you'd come with us."

"Not today. But thanks."

Iris said good-bye and hurried downstairs. Thien was waiting outside, dressed in white trousers and a collared blue shirt. Her baseball cap had been somewhat cleaned of paint. She spoke with a small man who leaned against a battered car. "This is Danh," she said to Iris. "He will be our driver."

After introducing herself, Iris climbed into the back of the car, sitting next to Thien. Soon they were rumbling over the streets of Ho Chi Minh City, listening to the radio, feeling the wind against their faces through the open windows. Thien acted as a tour guide, eagerly pointing out landmarks. They drove past the former U.S. Embassy—a white, forbidding building that looked unchanged since the war. As they followed a treelined boulevard, Iris marveled at impressive displays of French architecture. She'd never been to Europe but for a moment felt as if she looked upon the streets of Paris.

In thirty minutes they made it to the outskirts of the city. Their driver paid a toll and abruptly they were on a new highway. The pavement was smooth, the air almost clean. A blue suspension bridge carried them over a wide river. Alongside the highway flowed a series of canals. Large stretches of water were surrounded by nets, and Thien explained that these areas were fish farms.

Buildings disappeared, replaced by endless rice fields, which were such a bright green that they seemed to sparkle. Men used ancient, seesawlike contraptions to ferry water from narrow canals into the fields. Women in conical hats weeded, ankle deep in water. Behind the fields rose palm trees and a blue sky.

The highway was shared by huge, Russian-built trucks, as well as buses, taxis, countless scooters, and water buffalo that pulled stout carts. At one point traffic stopped as a pair of boys with bamboo poles herded thousands of white ducks across the pavement. The ducks were remarkably orderly, waddling between the bumpers of trucks and buses as if strolling across a meadow. Iris was surprised that not a single vehicle honked. Those riding scooters spoke through their face masks, sent text messages on cell phones, and readjusted children and produce.

"The ducks don't bother anyone?" Iris asked.

Thien removed two tangerines from her pocket. She handed one to Iris and began peeling the other. "We Vietnamese love to eat duck," she said, smiling. "Those boys are just bringing us our food."

Soon the car was once again heading south, toward wide waterways that flowed from Cambodia. Every five or ten miles they passed a small city, which was little more than a collection of stores, schools, and repair shops that bordered the highway. Bulky Christian churches dominated many horizons, crosses of cement or steel thrusting high into the air. Temples were also plentiful, their walls covered with dragons, clouds, and pink lotuses. The dragons often wrapped around columns, rising toward the sky.

"Did it look like this before the war?" Iris asked.

Thien smiled. "This superhighway was not here before the war. But, yes, many things are the same. In the countryside, not much has changed."

An immense snake somehow made it halfway across the road before being crushed by a bus. Iris turned from the sight. "How well did you know my father?" she asked.

120

Thien paused from scratching paint off her elbow. "Your father wanted to work," she replied. "I have never seen a man work so hard. But sometimes I would bring him tea and we would talk. He told me many stories about you." Thien pointed out a trio of boys riding an immense water buffalo. "May I ask you something, Miss Iris?"

"Of course."

"Your father . . . he was so proud of you. But he also seemed sad when speaking about his family. I always wondered why."

Iris nodded absently, watching scooters dart around them. "I was born five years after he returned from Vietnam," she replied, trying to resurrect her earliest memories, wanting to let Thien into her life.

"So long after?"

Iris knew that her father had tried to give himself time to heal before bringing her into the world. But five years hadn't been enough. "I didn't know anything was wrong until I was six or seven. Then I started to notice things. The mood swings. The silence. The fighting with my mother. One day he left and didn't return for three weeks. When he finally came home he brought presents. But he soon left again. I thought it was because he didn't love us, that we'd done something wrong." Iris glanced at a rice field, which shimmered in the early light. She remembered crying after a dance recital, how she'd searched for her father in the audience until she ruined her routine. After turning again to Thien, she continued. "As I grew up I spent less and less time with him. I read books and . . . and I stopped looking for him. Later, maybe in high school, I tried to stop loving him, even though I always did. He came back enough for that."

"He loved you. Very much."

"I know."

Their driver turned down a narrow street and suddenly Iris was looking at the Mekong Delta. She'd once crossed the Mississippi River and had never again expected to see anything so wide. But the waterway she saw now was miles across. Their car pulled up to a wharf of sorts—the trunks of decapitated palm trees had been chained together and rose from the shallow water by the shore. A blue boat was tied to this bundle of trees. Their driver led them across a plank to the boat, chatting briefly with a man who'd been sleeping in a hammock that hung from the boat's roof. The shirtless captain introduced himself and then reached into a cooler and withdrew two green coconuts. The tops of the coconuts had been sliced off, and a straw inserted into the white, fleshy hole at the top of each fruit.

Iris sipped the sweet milk, surprised at her thirst. She emptied the entire coconut without pause. The captain pulled the straws out, threw the coconuts overboard, and said something in Vietnamese. He then untied the bow and hurried to the stern of the boat, which was no larger than the back of a pickup truck. The boat's engine powered a propeller that sprang from the end of a long pipe. The captain lowered this pipe, so that it was almost parallel to the water's surface. Once it dropped about a foot beneath the surface, he started the engine and the boat lumbered out into the delta.

"This water is born in the mountains of Tibet," Thien said, pointing to the northwest. "It runs through China, Burma, Thailand, Laos, and Cambodia before it gets to Vietnam. When the Mekong River enters Vietnam, it breaks into two smaller rivers and finally enters the sea as nine rivers. And so we call this area Song Cu'u Long, or the River of Nine Dragons. The Chinese, the Thais, the Burmese, we all have different names for the river. But of course, I like our name the best."

Iris nodded, scanning the immense waterway. In the middle of the river, monstrous barges fought against the current, brown water splashing almost as high as a pair of great, painted eyes below each bow. Scores of much smaller vessels stayed clear of the behemoths, bobbing up and down in their wakes. The barges were wooden, which amazed Iris, for it seemed as if every tree on a mountain-side would have to be cleared to create enough lumber for one such craft.

In the shallows Iris saw children jumping from docks, women attending to large pens of fish, and men sleeping in brightly colored, anchored fishing boats that were rigged with massive lights. The shoreline was rimmed with palm trees and giant ferns that rose twenty or thirty feet into the sky. A floating market came into view—a collection of perhaps a hundred longboats filled high with fresh fruits, vegetables, and fish.

"In Cambodia, there are dolphins in this river," Thien said. "And here, there are giant catfish as long as a truck."

Iris smiled. "You like being my tour guide, don't you?"

"I do. It makes me happy. And I am glad that you are exploring Vietnam. This will help you open the center."

"It is helping me."

"Good."

Iris watched a longboat full of bananas rush forward with the current. "Did my father ever do this?"

"Come to the delta?"

Nodding, Iris replied, "He always liked the water."

"He came here three times, I think. The last time, he rented his own boat and was gone all day."

Iris remembered her father taking her to the shore of Lake Michigan. He'd shown her how to skip rocks, and they had counted splashes together. She wished that she'd traveled with him up and down the Mekong Delta. To do that once would have created one of her most precious memories.

Holding her baseball cap between her knees, Thien ran her hands through her hair and then retied her ponytail. Iris was abruptly conscious of her beauty—how her skin was nearly flawless, her eyes wide and pleasing, and her hair impossibly black. Yet Thien appeared unaware and uncaring of her appeal. She didn't call attention to it. In fact, her clothes almost seemed to hide it.

"Your father was so brave to come back here," Thien said, breaking Iris's train of thought. "I cannot imagine doing such a thing."

Iris watched a man on a small boat carefully unroll and position a fishing net into the dark water. "Do you think I can do both, Thien?"

"Both?"

"Explore the city and open the center?"

Thien nodded. "I think you must do both, Miss Iris. And I think you can do both."

Iris wiped her brow, which glistened even in the shade beneath the boat's canopy. "You have a beautiful country," she said. "I can't describe why, but I don't feel as much like a stranger here any-more. Maybe it's because my father spent so much time in Vietnam. And being here . . . it makes me feel closer to him."

"I am so happy to hear this."

"I think it's also because of you, Thien. You make me feel welcome. And that means so much. You have no idea how much. So thank you for being my friend. And for helping my father."

Thien reached across the space between them, taking Iris's hands within her own. "We will be great friends. Like sisters."

Iris looked closely at Thien, wondering where she came from, who she was, and who she wanted to be. "I don't have many friends," Iris admitted. "I've never been good at that. But I'm glad . . . I'm really glad, Thien, that you're with me now. I don't think I could do this alone. I wouldn't have the courage."

Thien shook her head. "You came here. To Vietnam. I did not help you come here."

One of the gargantuan barges neared, its owlish eyes growing larger. "Why do I feel so alive?" Iris asked. "Is it because everything is so new to me? Like I'm discovering a new world? Or do you think it's something else?"

Thien grinned and, holding Iris's hand, led her forward to the bow, into the sunlight. "We should put our feet into the water."

Iris removed her sandals and sat where Thien pointed, placing a leg on either side of a pole that ran from the boat's deck to its roof. Her feet struck the brown water and she sighed at the warmth of it. The boat rose and fell amid gentle swells, and her feet plunged into and soared above the water. She smiled. For the first time since her father's death, the troubles of the world didn't seem to press on her shoulders.

Thien sat nearby, her shorter legs barely touching the water. She started singing. Her voice was nearly drowned out by the drone of the barge's engines. So she sang louder.

Iris's smile broadened. The warmth of the delta traveled up her feet, into her body, and she no longer felt so alone.

THE LARGE JARS OF DIRT STOOD like rows of tree stumps before him. There were several hundred jars, each filled to the brim with dark, rich soil. Some of the soil had already sprouted grass, weeds, and flowers. Noah lifted his shovel and drove it into the nearest jar. Swinging his arms up, he sent dirt flying, scattering it over the tiny cement chips that covered the empty lot.

It took Noah almost five minutes to empty a single jar. He couldn't work faster, as such labor placed excess weight and strain on his prosthesis. Soon his back ached. The carbon-fiber sleeve of his prosthesis rubbed painfully against his stump. He cursed, thrusting the shovel deeply into the next jar. Pivoting to his right, he swung the heavy shovel high, sending the soil skyward. His body protested the movement, yet he didn't pause. Instead he worked harder, as if intent on putting so much strain on his prosthesis and back that he'd break one or the other. A second jar was emptied, then a third and a fourth.

Soon Noah's body screamed at him to rest, but the pain merely propelled him onward. His rage grew as the pain grew. Jars were chipped by his shovel. His hands blistered. His back ached as if he were being flogged. Still, he moved faster, seeking to hurt himself, wanting the pain to overwhelm him. Within such agony, he couldn't think.

The ground before him darkened with dirt. He moved down the line of jars, emptying a seventh and an eighth. His prosthesis was scraping his stump and thigh raw. Suddenly he hated it beyond anything he'd known. He lifted his pant leg and, hopping on his good foot, yanked his prosthesis from him. He threw it aside and picked up his shovel. Continuing to hop, he attacked the ninth jar. Half the dirt seemed to fall on him as he tried to spread it around. His leg trembled. His back might as well have been on fire. But he didn't stop. The jar was cursed, cracked, and emptied. He hopped toward another, tripped, and then was falling. The fresh dirt rose to strike him, and he rolled from his back to his belly, unwilling to look at anything but darkness. He screamed, smashing the side of his fist onto the soil he'd just cast.

Suffocating in the hell that enveloped him, Noah crawled to where he had left a bottle of Vietnamese whiskey. He drank deeply from it, swallowing several mouthfuls the way he might lemonade on a hot day. He felt the alcohol's presence almost immediately. It warmed him. Holding the bottle in one hand, he crawled until his shoulders were against a nearby jar. His back and stump hurt fiercely and he took another swig of whiskey.

His stump was ugly and he despised the sight of it. For his whole life he'd never even considered his feet. He had taken them for granted. But now that his foot was gone forever, Noah longed to see it again. He wanted to touch his toes, to jump, to run, to kick through clear water. He would give every possession he owned to have his foot back. He'd live in a shack for the rest of his life, walk to work each day, and wouldn't drive a car again. He'd never drink another beer or eat a delicacy or sleep on a bed.

Noah cursed, his thoughts soon moving to Wesley, to their unlikely friendship—the white, middle-class boy from Chicago and the black boy who was raised by his uncle in Detroit's housing projects. Wesley had always believed in the war, and in himself—at least until he'd shot the Iraqi man, until he'd learned that the man's daughter had died because she couldn't get to a hospital. Then everything had changed. Wes had fallen into a bottomless pit that turned him inside out, that stole his soul.

More whiskey traveled to Noah's belly. He thought about the things that conspired to ruin his life—a country led blindly into a war that didn't need to be fought, his reckless decision to enlist, and the traffic accident in Baghdad. Had anything gone differently in this chain of events he'd still have his foot and Wes would still be alive. Life would be good again. He'd laugh, take joy in simple pleasures, and muse over a future that appeared so bright.

Instead of such a life, Noah spent his days in pain. And such chronic pain broke his will as surely as would a stay in prison. He awoke each morning afraid of the agony that would soon dominate him. And this agony, experienced day after day, wore him down until he was unable to think of anything but his own misery. Though painkillers and alcohol provided reprieves, they dulled his mind to the point where his thoughts formed and moved within a dense fog. In this state he couldn't hope for better days. He couldn't laugh. He was no different from a caged lion that lay motionless day and night, crippled by the bleakness of its existence.

Aware that he'd be sick if he drank more whiskey, Noah rolled the bottle away. Still leaning against the jar, he glanced at the open space before him, wondering how he'd ever get it covered in soil. A year ago, he could have finished the work in a day or two. And he'd have enjoyed the labor, knowing that he was doing something good. Listening to music, he'd have imagined children playing on what he was creating, and worked from dawn to dusk.

Tears began to roll down Noah's dirty face as he thought about whom he'd become, about who was gone forever. The best parts of him had vanished as completely as his foot. His laughter, his joy, and his optimism were but memories, recollections that now tormented him. They tormented him because he didn't believe that he'd ever have such feelings again. Those feelings had been stolen from him, taken somewhere distant to be smashed into a thousand pieces. Even worse, those feelings had been replaced by bitterness and misery, hate and pain.

Wishing that the roadside bomb had killed him, Noah lay down on the warm soil, still crying. If the bomb had killed him, he'd have died with honor. He'd never have encountered this world of blackness, of perpetual woe. Perhaps he would be in heaven. Or at the very least, he'd sense nothing, be nothing. And sensing nothing was infinitely more appealing than lying on dirt, wishing he were dead. At least then he'd be at peace.

Noah took a handful of the soil and dropped it on his chest. He looked up, gazing at a slice of blue sky. "Heal me . . . or kill me . . . goddamn you," he whispered, shuddering, his tears leaving trails on his cheeks. "Do you hear me?" The sky remained motionless and Noah moaned, the pain in his back almost unbearable. "Please . . . please help me. I can't . . . I just can't . . . go on like this. Please."

Noah cried until a crushing weariness overcame him, a weariness that he welcomed as if it were his lost lover. His breathing slowed, his pain dissipated, and he fell asleep.

• • •

Minh prodded Mai forward with his hand. She hadn't eaten in two days, and he didn't like how weak she seemed, how she wasn't as talkative as usual. They'd been trying to set aside a little money each night, and Minh also had an empty stomach. The first day without food had been the worst for him—the endless cramps that caused him to double over, the many thoughts of delicious treats. He'd drunk water constantly to try to fool his belly, but this trick didn't work well for long periods of time. Fortunately, the next day had been better. He'd been lethargic, of course, but at least the cramps were gone.

"When we leave Loc, we won't ever be hungry again," Mai said, walking slowly, eyeing the Saigon River below.

Minh glanced around, worried that they'd be overheard.

"He's not here, Minh the Jumpy." She scratched at a bug bite on her arm. "Now that he has our five dollars, he'll have the pipe in his ugly mouth."

Minh recalled awakening to see Loc standing above them. He'd taken five of the six dollars they'd earned the previous night. Though Minh hated to see so much money go, at least Loc hadn't hit them. He'd seemed very tired.

"Are you sure you want *pho*?" Mai asked.

Minh nodded.

The sidewalk ended, dropping into a one-lane

road that was covered by a steel awning. Hundreds of scooters idled on the road, which turned into a ramp that led toward the river. As a ferry pulled into a docking area, people on the scooters watched two televisions that hung from the awning. When the ferry was secured, the ramp lowered and the drivers revved their scooters' throttles. The battered vehicles moved up and over the ramp and onto the ferry. A cloud of exhaust lingered for a few seconds and was then carried away by the wind.

Mai stepped ahead, watching the ferry depart for the other shore. Day and night it traveled across the river, carrying thousands of scooters to and from the city's center. "I wonder what's on the other side," she said, for they'd never crossed the waterway.

Minh shrugged, having asked himself the same question many times.

They rounded a bend and immense riverboats came into view. The riverboats were tied to the paved shoreline and were three-storied vessels about half as long as a city block. Scores of tables, a dance area, and a stage occupied each floor. At night, the riverboats bustled with diners and activity. Most of the boats would leave their moorings and travel up and down the river while people ate and danced.

Mai and Minh were friends with a chef on one of the boats. For a nominal fee he'd cook them *pho* and let them sit at a table nearest to the water, where they could watch the river traffic. This outing was one of their favorite activities. On the boat, eating *pho*, they were temporarily able to forget how they would earn their money that night, or how they'd keep Loc happy.

Holding Minh's stump, Mai guided him across the stainless-steel walkway that led from the shoreline to the riverboat. The friends stepped onto the vessel's linoleum floor and said hello to a waitress they knew well. They proceeded up a stairway that carried them to the top level and moved to a table in the distant corner. Each sat as close to the railing as possible. Below, the wide and lazy Saigon River brimmed with commerce.

After a few minutes the waitress brought them two large bowls of steaming *pho*. The light brown broth was filled with rice noodles, chicken, green onions, and cilantro. Minh's mouth watered. He picked up a spoon and savored a bit of the broth. Mai asked him how it tasted and he smiled.

Like Minh, Mai had learned not to fill her belly quickly when she hadn't eaten for several days. She sipped the broth at first and then sucked in a white noodle. "Ah," she said, licking her lips. "That's some good *pho*."

Mai and Minh continued to eat, watching the river below. Ferries and water taxis sped about, darting around much larger barges and naval vessels. Coconuts and clumps of floating flowers bobbed in the currents. On the opposite shore rose giant electronic billboards amid countless apartment buildings. More than a dozen cranes reached skyward, swinging supplies to the tops of unfinished structures.

Chewing slowly on a piece of chicken, Mai smiled for the first time all day. She could already feel the food fueling her, almost magically replenishing her fatigued body. "Should I tell you a story?" she asked, glad that Minh appeared to also be relishing his food.

He nodded, a noodle dangling from his lips.

"You look like you're trying to kiss that noodle," she said, giggling.

Minh grinned, leaning over his bowl as broth dropped from his lips.

"I should call you Minh the Messy . . . or maybe Minh the Noodle Kisser." She sipped some water, wondering what story he might like to hear. Should she tell him an old fairy tale, or repeat some adventure they'd had together? "Do you remember the story of how the tiger got his stripes?" she asked, suddenly inspired.

Of course Minh did, but he shook his head nonetheless.

"Well, one day," Mai said, "a tiger came to a field. In the field a man and a water buffalo labored. The tiger watched the buffalo hard at work and later said to him, 'You are much stronger and bigger than the man. And yet he makes you work for him. Why don't you crush him and run away?' The buffalo thought and then said, 'I will never escape the man, for he has wisdom, which I do not.' The tiger reflected on this, thinking that if he had wisdom, he'd no longer have to hide in bushes and stalk his prey. He could simply trick them into becoming his dinner.

"And so the tiger said to the man, 'Will you teach me of your wisdom?' The man looked carefully at the tiger, thinking that this was the beast that had been eating so many of his pigs. 'Certainly,' said the man. 'But first I must go home and get my wisdom. And I must tie you up, so that you do not eat my buffalo.' The tiger quickly agreed to this plan, because he knew that with wisdom, he could eat whatever he wanted."

Minh smiled, sucking up more noodles.

"You do remember this story, Minh the Slurper," Mai said, laughing. "So, once the man had tied the tiger to a tree, he began to set branches beneath him. He then lit the branches on fire and said, 'Here is my wisdom!' The tiger snarled, realizing that he'd been tricked. He fought against the ropes, and only escaped when the fire burned through them. After many days his burns healed, but the burning ropes left the stripes that we still see today."

Minh clapped, bringing his good hand together against his stump. He'd always liked the story, because even though the man was weak compared to the tiger, he'd been able to outwit him. And though Minh was terrified of Loc, he hoped to someday trick him just as the man had the tiger.

"You want to be that man, don't you, Minh?" Mai asked, seeing the gleam in her friend's eyes.

A nod confirmed her thoughts.

"But you're already him, don't you see?"

He shook his head, not understanding.

"Every night, Minh, you play your game against people who've traveled around the world, who went to the best schools, who had the best parents, who have both their hands. They look at you, and I know what they think. They feel sorry for you, and they let you win the first game. But soon they try to win. But unless they're very, very lucky, they can't win. You see? You sleep under a bridge. You have a stump for a hand. You never went to school. You don't talk. But every night you tie a tiger to a tree. And I watch you tie him, Minh, and it makes me so happy to watch you do this. Because then I think that someday . . . someday maybe I can tie up a tiger. Maybe I'll be more . . . than a girl who sells fans."

Mai's eyes glistened, and Minh moved beside her. He leaned her head against his shoulder. His fingers went to her hand. He wanted to speak, to tell her that she was his sister, that he loved her. But he couldn't give life to such words. And so he continued to hold her, thinking of how he could help her become all that she wanted to be.

• • •

QUI ADDED SOME WOOD TO THE small fire that fluttered beneath her pot. She dipped a cloth into the water that she was warming. "This will feel good," she said to Tam, who lay in her underwear on their bed. Tam smiled weakly but said nothing, exhausted from their day of begging. Kneeling beside her granddaughter, Qui stroked her brow with the damp cloth. She moved with no sense of haste. Dusk was still an hour or so away, and they had little else to do. More important, Qui knew that Tam enjoyed being bathed.

Qui proceeded to wash Tam's face, softly stroking the contours of her eyes, nose, lips, cheeks, and jaw. She talked as she cleaned, telling Tam how beautiful she looked, how it might rain tomorrow. Tam replied on occasion, though she preferred her grandmother's voice to her own.

After shuffling to the pot and rinsing her cloth, Qui began to wash Tam's shoulders and chest. Cleaning her torso was always the hardest, for she was so much thinner than she ought to be. Glancing at Tam's ribs, which seemed to grow more visible each day, Qui closed her eyes. Tam's hips also protruded from her flesh, as if trying to escape from her body. The sight of Tam's bones made Qui sometimes wish that she were blind.

As she wiped the grime from her granddaughter, Qui remembered bringing her to the hospital and saving their money for six months to make such a visit possible. The doctors had been kind and many tests were taken. And Qui had learned about something called acute lymphoblastic leukemia. She hadn't understood much of what the doctor had told her. But as she'd sat and wept, he had explained that Tam was dying, that it was too late to save her. If Tam had been seen earlier, she probably could have been saved. But not now, not when the cancer was already deep in her bones.

Knowing that she'd failed Tam was the source of endless pain to Qui, as endless as raindrops during the monsoon. It kept her up at night, because night was the only time she could cry. And in the darkness of their room she wept until her body seemed empty of salt and water. At that point Qui would beg Buddha for some sort of miracle, would silently beseech her daughter to come home, and would lie as close as possible to Tam.

Now, as Qui cleaned Tam's emaciated legs, she wondered if she should have stolen so they could have gone to the doctor sooner. If she could step back into time, Qui knew that she'd do just that—perhaps sneak into the market and steal the watches and necklaces that tourists seemed to favor. Qui would have stolen, sold her body, done anything to take Tam to the doctor six months earlier.

Qui pretended to sneeze, allowing her to blow her nose and wipe away a tear. She rinsed the cloth, then helped Tam put on her pajamas. "I've something to show you, my sweet child," she said, doing her best to smile.

Tam's eyes didn't focus for a moment, but she soon found Qui's face. "What?"

"Today, when you were sleeping, I traded books. I gave a foreigner my guidebook for Vietnam, and he gave me his for Thailand."

"For Thailand?"

"Yes," Qui replied, showing Tam the book. "I thought we could see pictures of where your mother is staying."

Tam nodded. "Please show me, Little Bird. Show me where she lives."

Qui opened the book to a section of color photos. The first page depicted a golden temple with a peaked, angular roof. Next was an image of a water taxi making headway down a canal. "Bangkok looks like Saigon, doesn't it?" Qui asked.

"Momma must like it."

"Yes, though she misses you terribly."

The following page showed tourists atop elephants, moving through a rain forest. "They are so pretty," Tam said, eyeing the elephants.

"Maybe in your dreams tonight, you'll ride one."

"With Momma?"

"Imagine that before you go to sleep."

"I'll try."

Qui pointed to a white-sand beach. "I bet your mother has been here. Look how beautiful it is."

"Maybe she'll send me a postcard. Oh, I hope she does."

Biting her lip, Qui turned the page. A photo of smiling Thais graced the paper. "These people look nice, don't they? And happy."

Tam searched the photo. "Is Momma with them?"

Qui wondered if Tam remembered what her mother looked like. It had been so long since she'd left. "I don't see her," Qui replied. "But I see her in you, Tam. Do you want me to describe what I see?"

"Yes."

Qui studied her granddaughter's face. "She has beautiful eyes, round and with long lashes. Her nose is wide and slightly upturned. A nose that you want to pinch. Her skin is as soft as silk. And her smile . . . it's the best part of her. Her smile makes me so happy."

"Are there more pictures, Little Bird?"

A train was revealed. A vegetable market. Ornately dressed dancers. Tam studied each image, wondering if her mother had seen such things. She asked more questions. She looked for a familiar face. In time, weariness overcame her, despite her interest in the book. Moaning softly, she closed her eyes.

Qui gave Tam her medicine. "Good night, my love," she said, stroking Tam's brow.

"I'm . . . thinking about elephants."

"Good."

"You think about them too."

"I will," Qui replied. "And I'll ride with you tonight." She kissed Tam's forehead, continuing to stroke her flesh. Soon Tam was asleep, taking shallow breaths. Qui wished that she'd breathe deeper, fill her lungs with air and power. But her chest barely stirred.

Qui looked above, begging Buddha for a miracle. She prayed for Tam's health, that her mother would return, that she might know the joy of a friend. She beseeched Buddha to take something from her own body and give it to Tam—strength, perhaps, or years left to live.

Her belly aching from a day with no food, Qui carefully placed the guidebook in the corner of their room. She knew that Tam would study the book every morning and night. She'd memorize its pages, search repeatedly for her mother.

"Why don't you come back?" Qui whispered, closing her eyes, remembering Hong's abrupt departure. The death of Hong's husband, and the poverty that dominated all of their lives, had been too much for her. She had withered and blown away before Qui's eyes. She'd disappeared—figuratively and then literally.

"Tam needs you so much," Qui added, looking toward the doorway, toward where Hong had often rested. "Please come back to us. And please hurry. You shouldn't have gone for so long. But I'll forgive you. Just come back. Please, Hong. Please come back."

Qui listened for a reply but heard only distant horns and sirens. Suddenly pain shot from her chest to her side, so powerful that she dropped to the ground, rolling silently on her back. She clutched at her ribs, wondering if Buddha had heard her, if he'd taken some of her strength and given it to Tam. She prayed that he had and begged him to take more.

Finally her chest ceased to throb. She peered outside and saw that somewhere the sun was setting. Once, she had loved sunsets. But now they served merely to remind her that Tam was one day closer to death. Again she prayed for a miracle. Then she lay next to Tam, stroked her cheek, and tried to think of elephants.

~ SIX

The War Museum

In Chicago, with the wind blowing from the lake, Iris had seen plenty of hard rains. But as a storm unfurled in Ho Chi Minh City, and she looked from the window of her office, she realized that she'd never seen streets saturated with rain, never witnessed what rain could do to a city with few sewers. The water filled up streets until they looked like manicured rivers. Scooters sped through these ankle-deep waterways, casting up spray on either side. Most of the drivers wore yellow ponchos, which billowed behind them, flapping like uncertain sails. Children stripped off their shirts and ran through the water, kicking it at one another. Sounds of laughter drifted up to Iris, mesmerizing her. She tried to remember if children in Chicago played in the rain and wasn't sure.

Smiling, Iris continued to watch the children, and how the raindrops left dimples in waterways. Lightning cracked overhead. A gust of wind drove the rain almost horizontally. Reaching out, she felt droplets on her palm, surprised at their warmth. She recalled Thien's words about dragon tears and looked up, as if she might see the mythical creatures weeping among the clouds.

After a few more minutes of gazing at her first tropical rainstorm, Iris dressed for the day. She walked toward the stairwell, heard a noise in the classroom, and entered it impulsively. Noah lay with his hand over his eyes, yet he was clearly awake, his foot tapping against the wall. Beside him on the bed was a half-filled bottle. Iris wondered what it contained. Noah reached for it, pausing when he saw her.

"I'm sorry," she said, feeling like an intruder.

He put his hand on his belly, watching her. "I didn't hear you."

"I just came in."

"Oh."

"Should I go?"

Noah started to speak and then stopped, unsure what to say. "This is your place. You should do whatever you want."

She glanced at the bottle, once again feeling as if it defiled the classroom. "May I ask you something, Noah?"

"I suppose."

"What do you find in that bottle?"

He sat up. His head ached from the previous night, and he rubbed his brow. He glanced at her, remembering that he'd once longed for her. He wished he still did. "Sometimes . . . it takes away the pain."

Iris knew of pain. She'd faced it as a child and a young woman. Her escapes had been books, faraway worlds that she'd gladly stepped into. "Can you tell me about your pain? I'd like to know about it."

"Why?"

"Because I want to understand."

He bit his lower lip. "Can I have a drink first?"

"What?"

"I need to relax . . . to talk about something like that." After Iris nodded, Noah took a gulp from the bottle. The liquid warmed him. "Sorry," he said, screwing the lid back on.

"You don't have anything to be sorry for."

He listened to the rain.

Iris watched him, wondering what was going on inside his head. "Hemingway used rain to signify death," she said, remembering the end of *A Farewell to Arms*. "And war."

Noah set the bottle aside. "He must not have been to Baghdad. It never rained. And there was plenty of death."

She thought more about Hemingway's words. "Why did you enlist anyway?"

"Would you hand me my prosthesis? It doesn't feel right . . . talking like this."

Iris did as he asked. She saw the scars that encircled his stump, and his grimace as he pulled the sleeve over his thigh.

He stood unsteadily and walked toward one of the big wooden tables. They sat opposite each other. "Are you sure you want to hear?" he wondered. "Most people . . . they ask about it . . . but they really don't want to hear about it."

"I want to. Very much."

Noah took a slow and measured breath. He didn't like talking about the past, for bringing it to life was like cutting himself. "After the trade center fell . . . I wanted to do something. Do something for my country."

"So you enlisted?"

"In the marines. I'd been in the city selling cars. And not many of them. So the timing was right." He twisted the sleeve of his prosthesis, trying to get somewhat comfortable. "After my training I was sent to Afghanistan. I'd never been overseas, so I had no idea what to expect."

"What was it like?"

He remembered the voice of a comrade. "A friend told me once that good people died and went to heaven, and that bad people died and went to Kabul."

"Really? Was it that bad?"

"Well, at first it was. Everyone was scared. Really scared. And the city was a mess . . . like some kind of World War Two movie set."

She leaned forward, her chair creaking. "And what happened?"

"A lot of good happened. We did things right. And it felt . . . it felt great." He watched a fly beat itself against a nearby window. "Are you sure you want to hear about this? I feel like I'm talking too much."

"You're not."

He took a sip of whiskey. "We routed the Taliban and had bin Laden cornered in the mountains. Trapped like the rat he is. Our intel said he was there. And I know he was. Because his men fought like they were protecting something priceless. They ran screaming at us and we cut them down."

"You . . . cut them down?"

"When you're scared, it's easy. Later it's hard."

She followed his eyes as he looked away. "And then?"

Noah remembered how a man he'd shot had fallen like a tipped domino. "And then we weren't allowed to finish the job," he replied, shaking his head, still dumbfounded by the decision. "We didn't have the troops, the resources, to get bin Laden because Bush wanted Saddam. So we left that rat in his corner, redeployed, and a few months later I was in Iraq. In the desert. And that seemed good too. Watching them pull statues of Saddam down, watching them dance. I'd never felt better. I was with the bravest, best group of soldiers in the world. And we'd won."

"But you hadn't."

"No. Not by a long shot. We spent months in that desert. Sweating. Searching. Getting shot at. But we couldn't find any weapons of mass destruction. Couldn't find a link to al-Qaeda. It was all a lie. One lie told after another. And I believed them all. Like a fool."

"A lot of people believed them. It wasn't your fault."

Noah glanced at her, wondering if she'd also been duped. "Then I lost my friend. And my foot. On the same goddamn day." He adjusted his prosthesis again, the mere sight of it causing his stump to ache. "And after that . . ."

"What?"

"After that I was so angry. I still am. I sacrificed everything . . . for a lie." He closed his eyes, trying to listen to the rain, to settle his emotions.

"And your pain? Is it more physical or mental?"

"The physical comes first. But the mental is just as bad. Maybe worse. It's like . . . your own mind becomes a prison. Pain does that to you. You can't escape it."

Iris was about to speak when footsteps echoed in the stairwell. Thien entered, a lacquer tray in her hands. The tray bore two cups of tea and two plates of sliced fruit. "Good morning, Miss Iris," she said. "And to you, Mr. Noah."

He glanced at his prosthesis, feeling naked even in his shorts and T-shirt.

"Do you like the Vietnamese rain?" Thien asked, setting the tray down.

"I've never seen streets flood like this," Iris replied, still thinking about Noah's words.

"Oh, wait until the monsoon. Then it will seem as if you have come to Venice."

Iris took a cup of tea. "Thanks for breakfast, Thien."

"It is my pleasure." Thien pulled a paintbrush from her back pocket. "Today will be perfect to finish the clouds. We can look at the sky and . . . be inspired."

"I'll come up in a minute."

Thien nodded, turned, and walked upstairs. She began to sing softly, her voice floating down the stairwell.

"Why don't you ever speak to her?" Iris asked, sipping her tea.

Noah turned from the stairwell. "I . . . I don't know. She seems so happy. Maybe I don't want to interfere with that."

"There's a lot more to her than a smile," Iris replied. Thunder boomed, and she glanced outside. "Can I give you some advice?"

"Feel free. Everyone else does."

Iris lowered her tea. "I guess I'll see you—"

"Sorry. I didn't mean to sound like that."

She nodded, and though not hungry, took a bite of fruit for Thien's sake. "I know that you've . . . lost yourself. Lost who you were. But my father lost himself too, and he somehow found himself."

"After thirty years?"

"Maybe you won't need so long."

Noah shrugged, not believing that he'd be alive in three decades. "I know you're trying to help me," he said. "And I wish I could say and do what you want. But I can't. I live in hell. And for me, every day is just about . . . survival."

Iris tried to imagine his pain. "You're in a whole other war, aren't you?"

"Maybe. Maybe the first one never ended."

She moved toward the door. "All wars end, Noah. Just remember that. Remember where you are and look around."

He watched her disappear. When she had, he moved to the stairwell, listening to her talk with Thien. To his surprise, Thien didn't ask about him, but about the clouds they'd almost finished. The women spoke of the clouds as if they were all that existed in the world. And as Noah listened to them, he realized that they were so much stronger than he. Iris, whose father had just died and who was in a foreign country for the first time, and Thien, who rose to his shoulder and probably couldn't lift fifty pounds—these women were strong and resilient and everything that he was not.

Disgusted with himself, he glanced at the whiskey bottle, longing for a drink. The bottle beckoned to him the way a lover might from an unmade bed. Noah looked at the bottle, unconsciously licking his lips. He stepped toward this temptation but managed to stop himself. Glancing at one of the office computers, he decided to e-mail his mother and tell her that things were better. She'd be waiting for such an e-mail, and its arrival would lift a weight from her shoulders.

Noah knew that he needed to write the e-mail now, before he picked up the bottle again. The bottle might rescue him at times; it might bring him to a warmer place. But it would muddle his thoughts. And then he'd be in no condition to write his mother. With his mind clouded, she'd see through his lies and even more weight would press on her.

The computer flickered to life before him. The rain continued to fill the streets. His body ached as if he'd fallen from a high balcony. Wishing that he possessed the strength of the women above, Noah began to type. His fingers moved quickly as he spoke of worlds that he didn't believe in.

Though he hated the liars, he'd become one.

151

• • •

THE RAIN FELL HARD ON THE roof of Ben Thanh Market, creating an endless drumroll for everyone inside. Normally abuzz with activity, the market seemed eerily empty. Vendors swept their shops until the cement floors glistened. Items were dusted and rearranged. Chipped pieces of lacquer were touched up with carefully blended paints. While such duties were performed, vendors chatted amiably, sipping soft drinks or nibbling on strips of dried squid.

At a plastic table near the rear of the market, Mai and Minh sat and stared. They didn't like rain, for it tended to keep tourists in their hotels and off-limits. Luckily, a few foreigners would brave such weather and head for markets and museums. Depending on the weather and the day, Mai and Minh could often predict where these tourists would venture. Upon awaking under the bridge, the two friends had debated where they might find a good game and sell fans, finally settling on Ben Thanh Market.

Mai and Minh hadn't eaten since the day before, and the smells of grilled shrimp, roasting duck, and simmering lemongrass made their mouths water. Both found it maddening to be hungry with so much food nearby. It was better, they agreed, to be hungry sitting at a busy corner or lying in a park.

"Maybe we should go somewhere else," Mai said, her chin propped up by her elbows. "There's no one here. And everything smells so good."

Minh tugged on his shirt, which was finally dry.

"Oh, would a wet shirt really kill you, Minh the Particular?" Mai asked. "Maybe we could drink the rain. Put some fish sauce on it and drink it down. Anything would be better than sitting here, watching people eat. You'd think they were pigs being fattened for the market."

Shrugging, Minh looked again for tourists. He wondered what it was like to sit in a fancy hotel room and listen to the rain. Still imagining, he slumped when Loc shuffled into sight, heedless of who was in his way. Loc's baseball jersey was filthy. He looked as if he'd rolled down a muddy riverbank.

"Here comes our water buffalo," Mai whispered, pretending she didn't see Loc.

Minh glanced at his game, wishing that he were playing someone.

Loc stopped at a food stand, gave a girl some bills, and then moved toward their table. He sat on a plastic chair, unaware that its legs bent beneath him. Mai risked a glance at his eyes and saw that they were bloodshot. "You brats better make some money today," he said in his hole-in-the-throat voice, his words lacking intonation, but his face hard and unforgiving. "Win it, beg it, steal it. I don't care how. But get my five dollars. Don't get it, and my protection is gone. And everyone will know it."

153

Mai shifted in her seat. "Where should we go? The tourists are all inside."

Loc ignored her. Instead he watched a girl bring him a steaming bowl of *pho*. He was soon slurping up broth and noodles. Minh tried not to look at him, breathing through his mouth to avoid the smells drifting around him. Loc belched. Bits of shrimp and noodles were visible between his teeth. "I'll come tonight, to the bridge. And you better have my money. I'll put your heads in the river if you don't. Hear that, half boy?"

After finishing his *pho*, Loc stood and left.

"He paid for that *pho* with our money," Mai said, pushing the empty bowl away from her. "And he'll come tonight, just as he said. He'll be full of opium and he won't . . . he won't know what he's doing. Oh, Minh, we have to get his five dollars. But how are we going to get them today?"

Though normally Minh feared Loc more than Mai did, he could see that she was terrified of being thrust underwater. And so he picked up his game box and started walking around the immense market. His legs trembled, and he looked about, trying to take his mind off Loc. A nearby vendor bartered back and forth with a foreign woman, each typing figures into an oversize calculator. Ahead, a ladder rose far upward, and a man perched at its peak worked to restart a ceiling fan.

Minh rounded a corner, moving into a quiet part of the market where tourists sometimes sipped fresh coffee. To his surprise, a pair of older Westerners sat at a table. Between them lay a chessboard. Minh had seen chess played two times before and on each occasion had been fascinated by the game. When one of the men looked at them, Mai asked if they could watch.

Soon Minh's chair was near their table. He observed the strange pieces being moved up and down, diagonally, even two spaces up and one across. Minh didn't know the names of the pieces, but soon grasped their powers. The little ones seemed insignificant. The horses could create turmoil. The large, pointed ones appeared all but invincible.

The men, both gray haired, continued to play, paying no attention to the children. Minh wasn't sure what the term "checkmate" meant, but one player said it, and the other nodded and removed his remaining pieces.

Mai pointed to Minh's game. "You want to play Connect Four?" she asked in English. "Why go outside? It raining . . . cats and mice. You only get wet. Maybe catch a cold, and then have no fun tomorrow, when it be a beautiful day."

One of the men smiled. "Play him?"

"Sure, sure. You play for American dollar."

"Not Vietnamese dong?"

"U.S. dollar is better for us. Everyone want them."

The other man looked at his companion. "Fancy

a game, Paul? I reckon it might be a wee bit of fun."

"Of course it fun," Mai replied.

"Can we both play him?"

Mai glanced at Minh, certain that he'd be nervous about trying to beat two chess players. "Sure, sure," she said. "But if he win, he get two dollar. If he lose, you get one dollar."

The men agreed, moving their chairs so they could sit opposite Minh. Mai explained the game as best she could. As she spoke, Minh gathered his red pieces, his heart thumping quickly. He didn't like the prospect of playing two men who'd been so intent on their chess game. Mai had only a single dollar in her pocket, and if he should lose, they'd have to return to the bridge with nothing.

The older man, who wore bifocals and a vest full of pouches, dropped his black piece into the center of the game board. Minh would have preferred to go first but, having been preempted, let his piece fall beside the other. Additional pieces were played while Mai watched anxiously.

As the game board filled, the men took more time to play each piece. They spoke and strategized at length, clearly understanding the nuances of the game. Minh began to scratch his stump, something he did when nervous. Mai might have said that he tied tigers to trees each night, but now, as he debated where to place his next piece, he didn't feel powerful. He felt tired and hungry. He felt afraid. But he played and the game went on.

"Bloody hell, he's trying to force our hand," said the younger of the two men, who relished the challenge before him.

The older man looked at the board, aware that fewer options were available, that most of the slots had been filled. "Clever little bugger, isn't he?"

Thunder crashed outside. The younger man produced a cigarette and began to smoke. "He's dictating things, and you'd best put a stop to it before you get whipped."

Minh listened to them strategize, glad that they made their thoughts known. For a few moves he let them force the action, let them believe they were making him go where they wanted him to. Before they knew what had happened, only two slots remained for them to place a piece in, and either slot would let him connect a fourth piece. Relieved, Minh sat back in his chair, glancing toward a porcelain vendor.

"Checkmate," Mai said happily, extending her hand. "Two dollar, please."

The older man nodded. "Blow me down. That was really something, how he did that."

"Well," said Mai, "you are good players. Very good. I never see him so nervous."

"Is that so? Is that why he doesn't talk?"

Mai shook her head. "No. I think when he lose his hand, he lose his voice."

"How did he lose the hand?"

"Me not know. He lose it when he very little."

The foreigner looked closely at Minh. "You're quite a player."

Mai watched the younger, cigarette-smoking man reach into his pocket. He removed several bills, one of which fell to the ground. He didn't see it fall, and she was tempted not to tell him about it. She could see that it was a ten-dollar bill, as much money as they'd make in two days. Tapping her foot in frustration, she picked up the bill and gave it to the man. "You drop this," she said, wishing that she'd found the money on the street.

The man put his cigarette butt in an empty soda bottle. "Thank you, dear," he said, handing her two dollars.

Mai pocketed the money. "Maybe you play one more game. You win this time. Not same, same as before."

Both men smiled. The younger one rose from the table, walking toward a food stand. The other helped Minh organize the pieces. "You both should be in school," he said kindly. "You're too bloody bright to be here."

"If we go to school, we no have money for food, for clothes," Mai replied. "We must make money during daytime."

"You don't have parents?"

"Maybe once, the day we are born. But not now."

The man was about to respond when his friend returned with two orange Fantas and two bags of potato chips. "For the victors," he said, giving Mai and Minh each a bottle and a bag.

Minh smiled, grasping the bottle with his good hand.

Mai took a sip, melodramatically licking her lips. "Thank you, mister. This very lucky day for us. Sure, sure."

"For us, too. Even though we stuffed up the game." The man looked at his watch. "We'd best be off."

The foreigners said good-bye, waving when Mai called out her thanks. When they disappeared, she turned to Minh. "What a wonderful day this has become, Minh the Victorious. Such nice men. And such good players. I thought for sure that they were going to beat you. But they got impatient at the end, and you tied them to a tree." She laughed at her joke, taking his elbow. "Let's drink these outside."

Minh carefully wrapped his game in a plastic bag. He stood up and followed Mai as she zigzagged her way through the market. Outside, the rain seemed to be falling even harder. Scooters sped by, sending up fountains of spray. Cyclo drivers huddled beneath old umbrellas. Mai and Minh moved under the canopy of a nearby bank, pausing when they spied a beggar. Mai recognized him as Dao, a kind man who'd lost his sight in the American War. He sat motionless, apparently listening to the rain. Though many people who lived on the street preyed on one another, Dao had been generous to Mai and Minh, giving them money when they'd been desperate.

Mai sat next to him. "Hello, Dao," she said, still pleased with winning two dollars and being given the Fantas and chips.

"Mai, sweet Mai. And is that Minh?"

"He's here," she replied, holding her bottle carefully. "He just beat two men at once. And they're expert chess players. They sure were surprised."

Dao smiled, revealing pink gums and a few crooked teeth. "Are you staying dry?"

"Oh, it's a warm rain, Dao. Nothing to be afraid of."

He inhaled deeply. "It smells warm."

Mai studied Dao's leathery face. His body seemed thinner than usual, his legs reminding her of fence posts. "Are you getting enough to eat?" she asked.

"This old body doesn't need much, Mai. All I do is sit."

Minh glanced at Mai, remembering how Dao had saved them. She nodded and Minh carefully placed his Fanta and bag of potato chips on the ground in front of Dao.

"What's that?" Dao asked.

"A treat for you," Mai replied. "From Minh."

"No, no. Minh, you take your treat back."

Mai stood up, knowing that they had to leave or Dao would force them to take back their gift. "It's right in front of you, Dao," she said. "A bottle and a bag. Merry Christmas."

As Dao continued to protest, Mai and Minh walked away. Soon the rain splattered on their backs. Mai led them into a park and moved beneath a massive banyan tree. The tree looked like a giant green insect that towered above them. They sat under a particularly dense section of branches, which protected them from most of the rain.

Minh sipped the Fanta and, smiling, handed the bottle to Mai. She tasted the sweetness, exhaling melodramatically. "I thought you might lose that game, Minh the Mighty."

He nodded, pinning the bag of potato chips between his stump and his hip. He opened the bag with his good hand, took out a few chips, and gave the bag to Mai.

She ate a chip and handed the bottle back to him. "Dao was looking thin, wasn't he?"

The bottle to his lips, Minh nodded.

"Too bad he can't sell fans or play games," she said, wondering what would happen to him.

Minh returned the bottle to his friend.

"Should we go to the train station?" she asked, eating another chip. "People will want to leave the city with this rain. You know foreigners. They have to always be doing something. They'll be getting on a train and heading somewhere sunny."

Minh let her know that he agreed. But he ate and

drank slowly, as he was in no mood to leave the tree so soon. He'd never owned an umbrella, and the tree was like an infinite umbrella, protecting him from the elements. Beneath its canopy, he smiled, sipped more Fanta, and nibbled on a chip. For the moment his hunger had been suppressed, his fears scattered. He was just a boy sipping a sugary drink, happy to watch the rain fall into big brown puddles.

NOAH SAT IN THE KITCHEN, UNAWARE that he'd remained almost motionless for several hours. His whiskey bottle was nearby, next to the uneaten fruit that Thien had prepared for him much earlier. After e-mailing his mother, Noah had moved as far away from the women as possible. He didn't want to hear them talk, or even laugh. Being reminded of happiness was something best left undone.

The whiskey-induced numbness that surrounded him was wearing off. He felt the edges of his emotions starting to sharpen. If it hadn't been raining, he might have tried to spread more soil on the playground. He felt trapped inside, with two sets of such keen eyes on him. Iris had already checked on him twice. And Thien had popped into the kitchen to make a fresh batch of tea. Covered in white paint, she'd squeezed lemon juice and honey into boiling water. She had smiled at him before leaving, and he'd tried to hide his misery.

Noah was tempted to go outside but wasn't sure

how the rain would affect his prosthesis. It wasn't hard to imagine the sleeve slipping on his thigh, further inflaming his stump. Though sometimes Noah sought out pain, today was not such a day. He felt inordinately tired and planned on closing his eyes and listening to the rain. A nap would help pass the time.

He reached for the bottle, intending to carry it to his cot. After taking a few unsteady steps, he heard someone descending the stairwell. Not wanting to meet anyone on the stairs, he leaned against the kitchen counter. Iris emerged, her clothes almost as paint covered as Thien's.

"You've been in here all morning," she said, her eyes not leaving his.

"So?"

"What are you doing here, Noah? Why did you come?"

He glanced outside. "I'm . . . I'm thinking about leaving."

"And doing what?"

"I don't know . . . really. Maybe just traveling . . . from place to place."

Iris stepped toward him, for the first time frustrated by the inertia that seemed to grip him. She handed him a piece of folded paper. He opened the paper and saw that it bore Vietnamese writing. "These are places," she said. "Two places not far from here. I want you to see them."

"Why?"

163

"Please. Go find a cyclo driver, and show him this paper. He'll take you."

"Did Thien write this?"

Iris nodded. "I've been to these places, Noah," she said, her voice softening. "They aren't easy to see. But I think you should go."

"What are they?"

"Would you please go for me?"

"For you?"

"For someone you used to love."

He looked away. "That was a long time ago. I was a boy."

"So?"

"So I'm different now. That boy . . . he's gone. And I don't believe what he believed."

"Just go. Please do that for me. Go see what I saw."

Noah started to respond and stopped. Iris found his eyes again, then turned and walked back up the stairwell. He glanced at the paper. Setting his bottle aside, he left the kitchen and moved through the center's greeting room. A bucket near the doorway held several umbrellas, and he took a black one.

Outside, fat raindrops thumped against the fabric above him. He moved forward slowly, not wanting to slip. After a minute or two, he approached a busy street. Almost immediately a man stepped in his direction. "You want ride?"

Noah showed him the paper. "Here."

"Fifteen thousand dong."

The fare was about a dollar, and Noah nodded, following the man to his cyclo. The driver got on a small seat that rose directly over an old-fashioned bicycle wheel. In front of this seat was a padded cushion positioned above two wheels. Noah sat on the cushion, bending slightly as the man pulled a canopy over his head. Soon the driver was pedaling, steering his cyclo by moving a bar that was connected to the two wheels ahead of him.

The ride was surprisingly pleasant, and Noah watched the wet city pass. Many of the streets were covered ankle deep in water. Tarps fluttered over stalls. People hunched together beneath canopies and ate noodles. Young children pushed sticks along the water, pretending they were boats. Though scores of scooters darted about, there were fewer than usual.

The cyclo driver was talkative, telling Noah how he escaped the Khmer Rouge in Cambodia and fled to Vietnam. He'd been only sixteen at the time and had survived in the jungle for weeks by eating lizards, snails, and even worms. Initially, Noah wasn't sure whether to believe the man, but the way he spoke about eating worms made his story convincing.

Soon they approached a city block that was surrounded by an imposing white wall. A sign on the wall read, WAR REMNANTS MUSEUM.

Noah turned to look at the driver. "This is what the note says?"

The man replied in Vietnamese, then added in English, "That what it say."

After paying the cyclo driver, Noah turned around, wondering why Iris had sent him here. A ticket window was nearby, and he paid a nominal fee and was soon inside the complex. Almost immediately, he saw an impressive collection of Western war instruments. Several immense tanks were to his right. Ahead lay artillery pieces, a colossal seismic bomb, warplanes, and a helicopter. Everything was painted a jungle green, and most items bore a single white star.

Noah had seen such sights a thousand times and didn't need to see them again. He headed toward a square, four-story building that was half white and half black. Inside were a handful of dripping tourists and Vietnamese. Surrounding them, display cases revealed hundreds of black-and-white photos, as well as handheld weapons. Noah moved toward the photos, his steps increasingly unsteady. The first pictures were of warfare—of battles and planes and annihilated forests. Noah saw images of North Vietnamese fighting the French, and then the Americans. He didn't like such images, for they brought back too many memories. But the photos didn't shake him either. He'd seen worse sights.

But then Noah rounded a corner and the pictures changed. His eyes welled immediately, and he had to steady himself. The images before him no longer told the stories of those who fought, but spoke about the victims of the war. He saw piles of lifeless villagers, shrapnel-ridden children screaming as doctors pulled out pieces of steel, mothers wailing over dead sons and daughters. Next came photos of crippled survivors. Dozens of misshapen children, ruined forever by Agent Orange, stared blankly into the camera. A boy of three or four, his ears and nose missing from napalm, reached for his mother. Land mine victims too young to fight lay on bed after bed in a makeshift hospital. Everywhere a new horror seemed to confront Noah, an agonized face frozen forever in time.

He turned from the images, tears streaming down his cheeks. Shuffling forward, he tried to keep from shuddering. But his body didn't respond to his thoughts. He managed to make it outside, into the rain. He hurried toward a distant corner of the museum grounds, collapsing against a wall. Though he closed his eyes, the sights of the screaming, ruined children wouldn't leave him, reminding him of what he'd seen in Baghdad. He started to weep—an uncontrollable sobbing that seemed to turn him inside out.

Noah didn't know enough about the Vietnam War to understand if it was wrong or right. But the photos tore at him. They blistered his soul. The rain mingled with his tears, thunder rumbling somewhere distant. He cursed miserably, haunted by what he'd seen. He thought about one photo he'd turned from—a little girl crying next to her mother's bloody corpse—and suddenly found it hard to get enough air. He gasped, rose unsteadily, and left the grounds.

The same cyclo driver was waiting. Though Noah was tempted to return to the center and his bottle, he showed the paper again to the man. Before long they were drifting through the city, pelted by rain. Noah needed to see where Iris was leading him. He needed to understand.

Their cyclo left the wide streets and proceeded down a series of alleys. Modern-day Ho Chi Minh City disappeared. They rode into a shantytown. Tin rooms sprouted from either side of an alley that was nothing but a sea of mud. The man stopped pedaling. Noah handed him thirty thousand dong and lurched from his seat. The driver was still talking, but Noah wasn't listening.

He moved into the depths of the slum. A part of the alley's floor had been covered in boards, and people slept here, wrapped in old tarps. Noah saw children poking their heads out from within the tarps and he began to cry again. Moving carefully, so as not to step on anyone, he proceeded forward. The tin shanties—rusting and tied together with wire—seemed endless. The rain pounded against their roofs, the noise loud enough to hurt Noah's ears. Many of the shanties had open doors, and he glanced inside the entryways, amazed to see families huddling together in closet-size spaces. Some of the families seemed happy—talking loudly or waving at him. But other doorways revealed the sick and crippled—men, women, and children too besieged by disease and misfortune to even note his passing. One woman had giant, ruptured boils on her face and arms—leprosy, perhaps. A few feet outside her doorway, a dead cat was being eaten by rats. Piles of trash rose along the edges of the alley, as if the residents tried to keep things as tidy as possible.

Noah kept walking, passing a skeleton of a man who was attempting to fix a scooter that looked beyond repair. After a few more steps, Noah came to a shanty that had only three walls. Inside, a woman squatted and sewed. Beside her, a young girl, maybe four or five, sat on a newspaper. She'd wrapped a cloth around a can and acted as if the can were a baby. When her eyes found Noah, she smiled. "Hewwo," she said, waving.

He managed to wave but didn't pause to talk, as she might have liked. He was suddenly consumed with the knowledge that the world would never know she existed, and that she seemed almost destined to a life of misery. She might be happy now, when she could entertain herself with an old rag and a can, but wouldn't such happiness fade?

Thinking of what he'd seen in the alley, Noah knew that the little girl would never have a voice, would never be heard. He knew that she wouldn't dream about birthday presents, warm beaches, or a beautiful wedding. She'd never know such things, never escape the cycle that she was born into. She'd only grow older, and whatever dreams she had would lose their luster. In time her dreams would evoke only bitterness, and within this bitterness she'd walk until she could walk no farther.

Noah's prosthesis hit a slick, unseen object, and he fell awkwardly into the mud. He didn't bother to get up but drew his knees to his chest and wept. He wept not for himself, but for those he'd seen who had no one to weep for them.

BEGGING HAD NOT GONE WELL FOR Qui and Tam. Qui had dragged her bench into Ben Thanh Market, and for the entire morning and early afternoon she'd sat next to a jewelry stall and tried to sell books. She'd sold only one and had given half of the profit to the nearby proprietor, who'd demanded a share of the sale. The rain was keeping tourists away, and Qui had repeatedly wished for the skies to clear.

Off and on throughout the day, when tourists weren't in sight, Qui had shown Tam more pictures from the Thailand guidebook. Tam loved looking at the photos, searching for her mother among the many Thais. She didn't remember the shape of her mother's face but was certain she'd recognize her if given the chance.

Tam needed breaks from gazing at the photos,

because her weariness was more pronounced than usual. She often lingered between consciousness and unconsciousness, a place where the aching of her bones seemed less overwhelming. She didn't understand why she felt so tired today, or why her aches were so intense. Qui had said that the rain was dampening her bones, weighing her down. Tam wished it would stop raining. She didn't like to hurt, to feel as if her elbows and knees were too sore to touch.

Moaning softly, Tam rubbed her blanket against her arm, trying to take the pain away. For as long as she remembered, her blanket had soothed her hurts. Yet today her blanket also seemed tired. It didn't whisper to her as it usually did. Tam wondered if the rain had dampened its spirits as well.

Qui turned, noting the misery on Tam's face. She'd already given her granddaughter a painkiller that morning and didn't know what else to do. Perhaps they should go home. Then at least Tam could stretch out on their bed. And Qui could tell her stories until night fell.

About to leave, Qui saw Sahn approach from the distance. As always, his uniform was immaculate. More impressive, it was dry, as if thousands of raindrops had somehow missed him completely. Qui watched him study his surroundings. She wished she had some tidbit of information that he'd find useful. He paid for such information, and his money would be more welcome now than ever.

Thirty feet away from her, Sahn moved slowly, pretending to scrutinize his environs when in truth he could discern very little. As always, everything in front of him was clouded by a bright fog. Once, Sahn had feared this fog, but he'd learned that wading through it wasn't so difficult. He just needed to move slowly, to rely more on his memories than his sense of sight. Fortunately, no one knew about his condition. If such knowledge were common, he'd be jobless and soon destitute. And so he caught criminals and pretended to see.

Sahn headed in Qui's direction, finally recognizing her. He wasn't surprised that she was indoors. The weather would be terribly hard on Tam. "Grown tired of the rain?" he asked, studying Qui's face.

She shrugged. "How do you stay so dry?"

Sahn raised his folded umbrella. "I'm careful."

"And how is your health?"

"As it was when I was a boy." He glanced around, the fog shifting within his field of vision. "I'm looking for poppy. It shouldn't be this far from the Golden Triangle."

Qui knew about the opium dens, which traveled around the city, usually one step ahead of the law. "I heard that long pipes were being smoked on riverboats."

"We captured those boats. They now belong to the Socialist Republic of Vietnam."

She shook her head. "I have nothing else for you."

"No matter," Sahn replied, reaching into his pocket. He produced a piece of hard candy and set it in Tam's coconut.

Tam smiled, placing her blanket on her shoulder so she could unwrap the candy. "Thank you, Captain," she said softly.

Sahn was proud of Vietnam. His people had defeated the Chinese, the French, and the Americans. They had rebuilt a land destroyed by war. But Vietnam had also failed. Gazing at Tam, Sahn was powerfully aware of this failure. The poverty he saw each day shamed him. And no shame was greater than the sight of Tam, of a sick girl whose fate rested on whether tourists felt charitable or not. Suddenly Sahn wished that he were young again, that he didn't understand such suffering.

"Have you ever been to Hanoi?" he asked Qui, her conical hat a white triangle before him.

"Never."

He remembered watching puppet shows by the lake. How perfect those days had been. "Nothing moves there," he said. "So different from this beehive." Sahn set twenty thousand dong in Tam's coconut. "Keep listening. I need to have ears in this market."

"Thank you, Captain. Bless you. You'll always have four ears right here."

Sahn wished them well and moved slowly forward. He opened his umbrella and stepped into the rain. Qui watched him go, deciding that it was also time for them to leave. She asked the nearby jewelry vendor to help place Tam in her carrier. The woman didn't mind and was careful.

Unfurling her umbrella, Qui held it above Tam and left the market. The rain immediately drenched her, but she was concerned only with keeping Tam dry. Qui moved down the sidewalk without haste, circumventing idle cyclos, white-painted tree trunks, and pedestrians. Her sandals often disappeared beneath the surface of brown puddles.

Normally Qui was able to carry Tam many blocks before growing tired. But now, with the rain soaking her clothes and weighing her down, she quickly faltered. She hadn't eaten or drunk for hours, and she stuck out her tongue, trying to collect as much rainwater as possible. Tam moaned softly, and Qui tried to walk faster. But her knees trembled. Her breaths came in gasps. A truck drove too close to them, sending up a curtain of water. Qui managed to turn so that the water struck her front. This wetness seemed colder than what was falling from the sky. She shivered but kept walking.

Not many traffic lights existed in Ho Chi Minh City, but Qui came to one and paused. Scooters darted past like water bugs. A siren wailed somewhere in the distance. Qui struggled not to fall over. She reached for a lamppost, realizing that a foreigner was gazing at her. He had no umbrella and looked as if he'd just stepped from the sea. An ugly purple scar rose from his brow to his hairline.

The foreigner continued to watch her as the light bled red. "I've . . . I've been following you," he said in English. "She's sick, isn't she?"

The light turned green, but Qui didn't move. "Yes."

His head swung slowly from side to side. "Can I get you a taxi?"

"Taxi no can go where we live. Streets is too little."

"A cyclo?"

"Same problem."

"Then . . . can I carry her?"

Qui started to speak and stopped, unsure what to say. She asked Tam her opinion, and Tam whispered that it would be all right. Qui nodded. "Please keep her dry."

"Use your umbrella."

The foreigner carefully removed Tam from her carrier. He held her against his chest, so that her legs wrapped around him. Qui thought he looked strong, but when he stepped forward he winced. He walked awkwardly, swinging one leg forward as if it were a pole. She worried that he'd drop Tam.

But he didn't drop her, and Qui stood tall, holding the umbrella above her granddaughter. The man didn't speak, only nodding when she told him which way to go. Qui alternated her gaze between Tam and the stranger. To her immense surprise, she realized that he was crying. His lips were pressed together and he seemed to struggle, to clasp Tam against his chest. He stroked her back as he walked. Tam must have sensed something happening, for she wrapped her arms more tightly about his neck. She pulled herself closer to him.

Qui watched Tam's response to the stranger, and her own tears mingled with the rain. Tam had stopped moaning. She seemed asleep. The man continued to walk unsteadily. He now grimaced, as if a thorn were pressing deeper into his foot with each passing step. Qui thought about asking if he needed help but found herself speechless. She kept pace beside him, wondering why he'd followed them.

Before long, Qui led the man into their room. He bent over and carefully laid Tam atop her bed. He helped Qui dry her off and then cover her with the sheet. He studied Tam's face, as if committing it to memory. Qui noticed that his tears still fell.

Tam opened her eyes, gazing around the room and then focusing on the tall stranger. "You so strong," she said tiredly in English, the pounding of the rain against the tin roof nearly drowning out her words. "You sit with me? Please?"

He nodded, positioning himself next to her bed.

Tam reached out to him and their fingers met. "Maybe I call you Big Bird."

"Big Bird?"

Pointing to Qui, Tam said, "My grandmother is Little Bird. She carry me everywhere. We fly together."

"Oh. That's nice."

"You have baby girl? You father?"

"No."

"My father . . . he dead. He wait for me, in new world. I can run there. Go to school. Little Bird and me, we always talk about this."

He closed his eyes. "Is your mother . . . Is she in the new world too?"

"She in Thailand. She make money for medicine. She come home soon." Tam looked at the wound on the stranger's forehead. She coughed, grimacing. "You get hurt?" she asked, trying to pull the sheet up closer to her chin.

He helped her as thunder rumbled. "Yes."

"How?"

"Someone . . . someone hurt me."

"That too bad. I so sorry."

"It's okay."

"I think this person make mistake. I think they no mean to hurt you."

Qui watched the man nod slightly, as if repeating Tam's words. "You're right," he said. "I'm sure it was a mistake."

"You be my friend, mister? Please?"

"I'd love to be your friend."

"That wonderful. I so tired now. Maybe I go asleep. See you again later."

"What's your name?"

"Tam."

"I'll see you later, Tam."

"Good night."

Qui rubbed Tam's brow with her thumb. The stranger didn't move, continuing to hold Tam's hand. A tear fell from his chin, disappearing into his wet shirt. His eyes remained on her face as the rain fell, seeping into a corner of the room and pooling on the floor.

Finally the stranger looked around, appeared to steady himself, and reached into his pocket. He handed Qui a thick wad of dong notes and stood up, careful not to disturb Tam. As he rose, his pant leg lifted, and Qui saw that he walked on a leg of steel. "Why?" she asked, looking from his leg to his face.

He shook his head. "Does she dream?"

"What?"

"Dream about happy things?"

"Oh. Sometimes she do."

"That's good."

Qui followed him to the door. "Thank you, kind sir. Thank you for helping us."

"Can I come back sometime?"

"Yes. Tam like that."

The foreigner looked down. "She's beautiful."

Qui watched him step into the rain. He walked unsteadily over the planks leading away from their room. Then he moved into the alley. Qui said good-bye, but he didn't seem to hear her. His footprints remained in the mud for a moment, but then the water filled them up and he was gone.

SEVEN

Milk Money

Noah lifted the shovel, driving it into the soil-laden jar and then spreading the dirt on the nearby ground. The sky had finally ceased to shudder and cast rain, though clouds were still numerous and thick. The damp soil was hard to move, and Noah paused to wipe his sweaty brow. His back and stump ached. He reached for his bottle, taking his first swig of whiskey for the day. The bottle didn't linger against his lips. He set it down and began working again.

He thought about what he had seen the previous afternoon. The little girl seemed to still cling to him. She'd been so light and frail, so eager to draw her hands tighter around his neck. Watching her fall asleep against him had been one of the most gratifying experiences of his life. She had been in pain, and then she was at peace. And all he'd done was carry her home.

Noah emptied a jar. He pushed it against the fence and picked up his shovel. Grunting, he again began to move soil. His prosthesis slipped on his stump and a searing pain shot through him. He swore, feeling a familiar sense of dread welling within him. He didn't want to think about his pain, but now, like countless times before, he didn't have a choice. That was what people failed to understand about his demons. He couldn't pretend that they didn't exist. He couldn't ignore them. They reminded him of their presence constantly.

"You're up early."

Turning, Noah was surprised to see Iris and Thien standing a few feet away. Both wore their painting gear. Thien stepped forward, carrying a tray laden with croissants, jam, and butter. "You should eat breakfast, Mr. Noah," she said, setting the tray down on one of the jars.

"Oh, I'm not hungry."

Thien picked up a croissant. Noah watched her slender fingers cut the flaky pastry in half and spread butter and jam on each side. Her movements were remarkably graceful for someone who always seemed covered in paint. "We are lucky the French gave us croissants," she said, handing Noah his breakfast. "Such a lovely way to start a day."

Noah thanked her. He took a small bite, watching her prepare and hand a croissant to Iris. "Did you finish the clouds?"

Iris nodded. "Thien finished them. I wasn't much help. We spent more time fixing my mistakes than anything else."

"That is not true," Thien replied, smiling, preparing additional croissants.

Noah had returned late the previous night and hadn't seen Iris or Thien. "Thank you both . . . for

". . . for yesterday," he said, glancing from face to face. "I was glad to see . . . what I saw."

"So was I," Iris responded, aware that she'd never forget the museum or the slums.

Noah set his second croissant aside. "I met someone. A little girl and her grandmother. The grandmother was carrying the girl around on her back."

Thien stopped spreading jam. "Qui and Tam?"

"That's right. Tam was the little girl's name."

Thien's smile, such a permanent fixture, was suddenly gone. "Qui was begging, in the rain?"

"I don't know. She was walking home." Noah again thought about Tam, about how she'd so welcomed his presence and asked him to be her friend. "Is Tam . . . Is she dying?" he asked, his voice barely audible, as if a question unheard would also be unanswered.

Thien bit her lower lip. "Yes."

Iris stepped closer to Thien. "You didn't tell me that."

"You were happy, Miss Iris. You were happy that you came to Vietnam. I did not want to change your mood."

"But . . . she's dying? Really?"

"Tam is very ill."

"She's so young," Iris replied, remembering how Tam had held her tattered blanket. "She's too young."

"I know."

Iris shook her head. "Are you sure? Maybe it's a mistake."

"I am sure. Qui told me—"

"Well, if that's true we need to take her to a doctor," Iris said, the jam on her fingers forgotten. "Right away."

"She already went," Thien replied. "But she went too late. I have spoken with Qui about it. Tam has cancer. And it is already in her bones."

Noah wished he were still walking with her in his arms. "We should bring them here," he said. "I've seen where they live, and I've been thinking about it. She shouldn't be there. Not when we have so much room. Not when she's so sick."

Iris turned to look at the center. She saw her father's dreams and hopes, and knew that they were close to being fulfilled, knew that they'd help many children. "I don't know," she replied. "I want to help her. Of course I do. But our license. We're not supposed to house children until the first of the year. That's the agreement. And they could close us down if we break it."

Thien took Iris's hands. "No one will close the center down, Miss Iris. The government supports what we are doing. We may have to pay a bribe, but that is only money."

"Are you sure?" Iris asked, glancing from Noah to Thien. "We couldn't get into trouble?"

Thien's smile returned. "I think that we are lucky today, because Mr. Noah's idea is a most excellent one. Qui and Tam can be our guests. We will not get into trouble for taking them in. I am sure of that."

Iris felt the need to help someone. She'd been in Vietnam for almost a week and hadn't done anything to aid anyone. She realized then that her father's dream had become her own. She wanted to help Tam. She needed to help Tam. "Can you find them, Thien?" she asked. "Can you find them and explain what we want?"

"Yes."

"Then they'll come," Iris replied, her voice picking up speed. "They can stay in the dormitory. And we'll get a doctor. . . . We'll get a great doctor to visit."

Noah thought once again about the strength of the two women. He mused over this strength as he watched their faces blossom while they discussed the details of bringing Qui and Tam to the center—things like new sheets and toiletries and food.

Though his back and stump still ached, though he wanted a drink and knew that he'd soon reach for the bottle again, Noah felt a flash of happiness as he thought about Tam having a comfortable place to sleep. This feeling wasn't the carefree bliss that consumes a child, but the simple gratitude for a moment of solace. With Tam staying in the center, he could try to do what she asked—to be her friend.

Thien sensed his mood. She reached for his

shovel and stuck it in his hand. "This will be her park, Mr. Noah. And you must make it beautiful. Only you can do that."

He glanced around the barren lot, unsure what to say. "I don't move very fast."

"Why does moving fast matter?" Thien replied, shrugging. "You think that mountains grow fast? But look how tall they are." She smiled. "Now, Miss Iris, we should check on the dormitory. Which beds will they sleep in?"

Noah watched the women depart hand in hand. He then looked at the shovel, imagined Tam visiting their center, and began to dig.

THE SKY THREATENED A REENACTMENT OF the previous day but managed only to shut out the light. Noah worked within this infinite shadow until a thin layer of soil covered his skin and his body begged him to rest. He didn't fight his body and walked into the kitchen, drinking deeply from a liter bottle of water. Iris was upstairs preparing the dormitory for Qui and Tam, and Thien had left to find them. Noah had grown accustomed to Thien's soft singing, and in her absence the center seemed unusually quiet. To his surprise, he didn't like the silence.

A knock at the front gate interrupted his thoughts. Setting the water bottle down, he awkwardly moved toward the entrance. A policeman stood a step or two within the open-air entryway.

He wore an olive-colored uniform and cap. A baton hung from his side. His eyes were not friendly.

Noah watched the policeman inspect him from top to bottom. Unfazed by the sight of the man's uniform, Noah asked, "Can I help you?"

The policeman shook his head. "You in Vietnam. You should speak Vietnamese."

"Sorry. I don't know how."

"Your name?"

"Noah. Noah Woods."

"American?"

"Yes," Noah replied, aware that the policeman's eyes roved around him, lingering on his scar.

"You with American military?"

"I was."

"In Iraq?"

"For eleven months. Until I was wounded."

The policeman grunted. "You Americans should stay home."

Noah resisted the urge to shift his weight away from his prosthesis. "What do you need?"

"The woman in charge. Where is she?"

"I'll show you," Noah said, gesturing toward the stairwell. He led the policeman forward, trying not to hobble. But he struggled with the stairs and was certain that the man's eyes were on his prosthesis.

"Why you limp?" the policeman asked from behind.

"A water buffalo stepped on my toe," Noah

responded, tired of the questions. He increased his pace, leading the policeman into the dormitory, where Iris was making a bed. "This man wants to talk with you."

Iris set down a pillowcase. "All right."

"Are you okay with that?" Noah asked.

"Sure," she replied, though her body told him otherwise.

Noah walked back to the stairwell and leaned against a wall, listening.

"Thien isn't here," Iris said, watching the policeman gaze at the clouds she'd helped paint.

"That good. I no want to talk with her."

"You came to talk with me?"

Sahn glanced at the tall American, wondering what she'd eaten as a child. He walked slowly to the other end of the room. It took him a moment to realize that the ceiling was covered with clouds. At first, he'd thought they were areas that hadn't been painted. He was glad for the ceiling fans that swirled above. The day, though overcast, was already hot and humid.

He reached the window at the far end of the room and turned to the tall woman. "What you teach here?"

Iris brushed a fly from her shoulder. "Well . . . we'll teach reading, writing, and math, for starters. And art. The curriculum's already been approved."

"Do boys or girls stay here?"

She had debated this question for many hours.

Most of the street children were boys, but Thien had told her that girls were at even greater risk. "Girls," she replied. "We'll have twenty girls."

Sahn nodded, pleased. "Then you teach sewing, cooking, cleaning, taking care of babies. You understand? Cooking jobs get them off street. Cleaning jobs get them off street. You can teach math and reading. But you teach cooking and cleaning first. Those skills are most important for their future. Understand?"

"Yes," she said, for the first time not sensing him as a threat. "And we've talked about those things. Of course, we want them to go to universities, to build on what they learn here."

"That fine for some. But for most, they never go to university. You remember that. So you also teach how to cook, how to clean, how to take care of rich family's babies. Then they not ever have to live on street again."

"I—"

"If you buy Western washing machine, and teach them how to use, then you also teach them how to wash clothes by hand. You understand?"

Iris mused over his words. "I'll do what you say."

"Who is that man?"

She looked toward the stairwell and saw that Noah was still there. "He's my friend. My child-hood friend."

"His purpose here?"

"To help me. He's trying to build a playground."

Sahn breathed deeply, his nostrils flaring. "If abuse ever happen here, if children is ever abused, then you go to prison. You hear what I say?"

Iris shook her head, appalled by the thought of a man's hands on a child. "That will never happen. Never."

"You think this no happen in centers? We already close two centers. These criminals take children off street, then send them to center, which is brothel. Boys and girls. So you be careful who you let work here."

Iris leaned against a wall, the clouds above no longer beautiful. "You have my word. I'll never let—"

"I will interview children after you open. One time a month. I make sure everything is fine."

"Good," she replied, nodding. "I think that would be good."

Sahn stared at the blur beyond the window, wishing that Vietnam could look after all of its people. "You must understand, I no like America," he said. "But Vietnam is still poor country, so maybe your help is good." He cleared his throat. "What you do in USA?"

Iris didn't avoid his gaze, as she had several times before. She saw a chance to make an ally and didn't want to waste it. "I write book reviews. For newspapers."

"Reviews?"

"I tell people if I think books are good or bad."

"And you get money doing this?"

"Not much," she replied, smiling faintly. A horn sounded below. "May I ask you something?"

"Depend on what you ask."

"How can I succeed here? I want to succeed. But I'm not sure how."

Sahn gazed at the American, wishing he could properly see her face, pleased by her question. "These children, they no trust anyone. Their mother, their father, everyone leave them. So you must get them to trust you. If you get them to do this, then anything possible."

Iris silently repeated his last words. "Thank you," she said, bowing slightly.

"One day, I hope to thank you," he replied. After glancing once more at the clouds, he stuck out his hand. "One hundred thousand dong, please."

"What?"

"One hundred thousand dong."

"But I thought—"

"You no longer in America. You in Vietnam. Pay money or go home."

Iris didn't know what to think. The man's words were helpful, even insightful. But here he was with his hand out, eager to steal her money. She reached into her pants pocket and counted out one hundred thousand dong, roughly seven dollars. "I hope this lasts for a while," she said, handing him the money.

He took the wad of bills. "You think you pay for nothing, for only bribe. But with me watching this center, nothing bad happen. The children be safe. And you have a chance to save them."

IN THE HEART OF HO CHI Minh City stretched a treelined boulevard that housed dozens of galleries. These shops contained original works of art and countless reproductions. Most of the artwork was done with oil-based paints and depicted traditional Vietnamese scenes—floating markets, dragons, temples, women working in rice fields, cliffs jutting from the sea. Reproductions were also present—nearly flawless re-creations of the most famous works of Monet, Picasso, van Gogh, da Vinci, Matisse, Warhol, and Dalí.

Tourists frequented these galleries, often leaving with rolled-up pieces of canvas that could be easily transported overseas. On occasion, when Minh wasn't in the mood to play Connect Four, Mai sold fans on the sidewalk outside the busiest galleries. She usually couldn't make as much money selling fans as Minh could playing his game, but sometimes she had no choice. Today was such a day. The friends had been asleep in their basket, with dawn still an hour away, when Loc had thrown them out of their bed. His eyes were glazed from opium and his words nearly incomprehensible. He'd asked for more money, even though they'd given him five dollars the previous night. When they'd had none to pass to him, he'd torn through their belongings, certain they were hiding some of their winnings. In the mayhem Mai had fallen to the ground. Minh had moved to protect her, earning himself a cuff on the mouth. Unsatisfied, Loc had thrown Minh into the river.

Now, as tourists browsed in the nearby galleries, Mai eyed Minh's swollen lip and wasn't surprised that he wouldn't play his game. He never would after such an encounter. Mai couldn't tell if he was ashamed of being beaten or was trying to plan his revenge on Loc. In any case, the pressure fell on her to sell as many fans as possible. She had to sell about ten fans to earn five dollars' profit. And selling ten fans, with so many other fan sales-people about, wasn't easy.

Mai glanced from Minh to Tung, who'd been their companion for the past few hours. Tung often worked outside the galleries, and Mai had thought his company might raise Minh's spirits. A boy of eight or nine, Tung wore a sleeveless shirt, shorts, and sandals. He didn't live on the street. But his mother had died a few months earlier during child-birth and he had quit school to help his father earn extra money. Tung sold packages of postcards to tourists. His older brother had also left school and now carried passengers around the city in a cyclo he rented.

A Western couple emerged from a nearby gallery, and Mai and Tung descended on them, asking if they'd like to buy a fan or a pack of post-cards. The woman reached into her bag, removing three fans and two sets of postcards. "Sorry, but you are too late," she said, adding something in a language that Mai didn't know.

Mai watched them leave. "Whose fans were those?" she wondered aloud. "I haven't seen them before. They're prettier than mine."

Tung shrugged. "I don't care."

"What?"

"I'm supposed to bring home formula today. We run out tonight, and Long will have nothing to eat."

Mai sat down next to Minh, who held his game box but wouldn't open it unless she insisted. Tung stood nearby, kicking at a piece of loose concrete. Mai sympathized with him. With his mother dead, his baby sister relied on formula to survive. And formula was extremely expensive. "Will she eat anything else?" Mai asked.

Tung kicked harder. "She'll drink cow milk, but she spits it up an hour later. Father's tried every-thing. He even put a little sugar in it to make it sweet. But she just spits it up."

Mai studied Tung, noticing his thinness. She guessed that he and his brothers hadn't eaten for days. Most of what little money they had was probably used to buy formula, to keep their baby sister alive. "What about another woman?" Mai asked. "Can't you find a woman with a new baby who'll also feed your sister?"

"That costs money too, Mai. And it's difficult to arrange." The hunk of cement was resisting Tung's efforts to dislodge it. Minh rose from the sidewalk and started to kick at it as well.

"You boys think you're going to get formula by kicking that stone?" Mai asked. "Stop kicking that stone."

Tung looked up at her. "I miss my mother, Mai."

"I know."

"I dream about her every night."

Minh managed to finally dislodge the piece of cement. He wasn't sure if Tung wanted it but nonetheless pushed it in his direction. He hoped to help Tung, only he didn't know how. His lip throbbed from the back of Loc's hand, and he still tasted blood.

Mai sighed, fanning herself. A woman stepped from the gallery, and Mai approached her without pause. "You buy something pretty?" she asked in English.

The woman studied the three children before her. "No. Not today."

"That too bad. Next time you buy something, sure, sure."

"I leave tomorrow."

"That even more too bad. I think you miss Vietnam."

The woman wiped her brow. "Well, I'll be back."

Mai fanned the foreigner. "My friends and I, we

193

eat nothing today. We very hungry. Can you buy us three milks? Please?"

After glancing at her watch, the woman replied, "I'll give you three dollars. You can buy yourselves some milk."

Mai shook her head. "We cannot go into store. They think we steal. So we cannot buy milk. You come with us. It only take one minute. Please."

The woman looked from face to face. "Only three dollars? Nothing more?"

"Yes, miss."

"And only a minute?"

"Sure, sure."

"Then let's go."

Mai handed the woman a fan and started walking, her heart beating quickly. She didn't like the idea of misleading the foreigner, but Tung's baby sister was probably starving. Mai had heard stories of motherless babies dying before, and she didn't want Tung to lose his little sister. Mai walked fast, telling the woman about the sights they passed. Soon they came to a large department store. The store was sleek and new, and without a foreign escort Mai would have never been allowed inside. She proceeded to an elevator bank, and the group rode together to the third floor.

The door opened and they emerged into a supermarket. Mai proceeded past a bank of cashiers, her eyes searching. The woman was getting impatient and Mai began to fear the worst. She headed down an aisle that contained baby goods, pausing in front of stacks of powdered formula. Lifting the smallest carton from the shelf, she held it in front of the woman. "Please, miss. My friend's baby sister has no food. Her mother die already. Please buy formula so she can eat tonight."

The woman's jaw dropped. "You . . . you lied to me."

Mai lowered her head, ashamed. "Please, miss. Please help. She only three month old."

"That's about thirteen dollars. You want me to spend thirteen dollars on formula?"

"For baby girl, yes, please help. This not for me. It for her."

The woman angrily thrust Mai's fan into her hand. "I should have known better than to trust you," she said, turning away, walking toward the elevators.

Mai felt her face flush. She held the formula and the fan in her trembling hands. She wondered who'd overheard the exchange, and she wanted to become invisible. She'd been unseen her whole life, and she needed to be unseen at that moment, for her shame was endless. She had always tried to be honest, to rise above what she'd watched so many others become. And the way the woman had looked at her, with such disappointment and scorn in her eyes, had stolen whatever pride Mai had managed to muster over the years. She felt so small and tired. She sniffed. A tear tumbled down her cheek.

Minh watched Mai falter, hating her descent. He saw Tung look around, study his environment. He suddenly knew that Tung was going to try to steal a carton of formula. Minh shook his head, aware that he needed to lead his friends away from danger, from a danger that could destroy them all forever. Tung reached for the formula, but Minh was faster, his good hand grabbing Tung's wrist, his stump easing between Mai's arm and her waist. Almost dropping his game, he pulled them away from the formula, from the mixture that would fill a baby's belly.

As Minh guided Mai toward the elevators, he realized that he was going to have to save her. She had led him for too long. She'd been his voice, his mind, his hope. She'd told him stories at night when he needed to hear, held him close when he needed to feel. Now it was his turn to hold her. He knew that she was close to breaking. She had been that way for several months, sometimes crying when she thought he was asleep. Unless he changed their fate, her laughter would no longer please his ears. The street was slowly killing her, though she pretended otherwise. It was killing her as it killed everyone else—even Loc.

Minh brought Mai and Tung into the light, the real light of day. And since he had no immediate plan to save Mai or to buy Tung some formula, he simply headed toward the giant Western hotels, where the stakes were always the highest.

• • •

THE STREETS WERE DARKENING, MOVING IN concert with Noah's mood. Carrying two plastic bags, one that threatened to burst from the weight of its load, he shuffled forward, trying to ease the burden on his prosthesis. He hadn't taken a painkiller of any sort for several hours and his stump and lower back throbbed like giant toothaches. His pants pocket held several pills, and he was tempted to escape from his misery. Unfortunately, the pills numbed his mind as well as his body. And knowing that Thien had brought Tam and Qui to the center, and that they were awaiting his return, Noah wasn't ready to enter oblivion. After he saw her, gave her his gift, and said good night, he could take his pills, enjoy a drink, and then slip away into a realm where he'd float for a few minutes before falling asleep.

Noah tried to take his mind off his pain by gazing at the strange sights around him. He circumvented an outdoor restaurant, which was really nothing more than three wooden tables encircling the base of a large umbrella. Young soldiers and a family occupied the tables, slurping up big bowls of *pho*. Not five feet from the patrons, a woman wearing a purple blouse chopped vegetables on a wooden block and dropped them into a stainless-steel cauldron. She talked incessantly, provoking laughter from the soldiers, who drank beer and had their arms around one another.

Noah turned toward the street that ran alongside Iris's center. Not far ahead, a group of men were huddled tightly together, many of them crouched or kneeling. Noah had seen several such gatherings, and knew that the men were gambling. But he wasn't sure if they used dice or cards or something else altogether. The men were intent on whatever lay before them, chatting excitedly, getting closer to the ground. A boy on the periphery of the group waved to Noah, who returned the greeting and stepped into the street, dodging scooters.

Soon Noah was in the center. The smell of garlic seeped from the kitchen. The first floor was empty, though voices drifted down from above. Noah ascended the stairs slowly, as if a toddler first learning to walk. He listened to the voices, which switched back and forth between Vietnamese and English. He might have heard Tam once but wasn't sure. He tried to remember her face. She'd been so wet, so light against him. Did she really put her arms around me like that? he wondered. Like I was her father carrying her to bed?

He entered the dormitory, noting that Iris and Thien had moved two bunk beds against each other, so Tam and Qui could sleep together on the bottom beds. Tam lay on one bed but was propped up by some pillows. Qui sat next to her, wearing a new dress. Noah realized that several of his whiskey bottles had been wrapped in colored paper, set on nearby chests, and filled with yellow flowers. He didn't know what kind of flowers they were but was amazed to see these same flowers depicted on the new pajamas that Tam wore. He glanced at Iris and then Thien. His gaze swung back to Tam. "Hello," he said quietly, the sight of her in a soft bed causing his eyes to dampen.

She smiled. "I no want dream tonight."

"Why not?"

Stretching out her arms, she replied, "This better. I want . . . feel this bed all night."

Noah nodded. "It's yours," he said, taking a step toward her, reaching into one of the plastic bags, and removing a Vietnamese doll. The doll wore a traditional Vietnamese dress, an *ao dai*, which was blue and adorned with white bamboo leaves. The doll carried a circular pink purse, and her long hair fell from beneath a conical hat. Noah handed his gift to Tam. "Maybe you'd like to share your new bed with her."

Tam's eyes widened. She'd never touched anything so lovely, and she held the doll with reverence, afraid her fingers might dirty the beautiful silk dress. She looked closer and saw that the doll had white gloves and shoes. Her lips had been painted red. A pearl necklace surrounded the high collar of her dress. Tam touched the doll's hair with her forefinger. The hair moved. It wasn't plastic. It seemed real.

At that moment the pain in Tam's bones seemed to travel somewhere else. She didn't feel hot or cold. She didn't find it hard to breathe. She wasn't even tired. And she didn't wonder where her mother was, or why her mother hadn't come home for so long. At that moment Tam was happy. She made sure that her fingers were clean and then she touched the doll's dress, tracing its contours, pretending that its leaves were blowing in the wind.

Realizing that she needed to thank someone for her good fortune, Tam looked up, forgetting where she was. A tall man stood before her, a Western man. His eyes were kind, and she remembered that he'd given her the doll, remembered how he'd carried her through the rain. "Thank you, mister," she said, gently stroking the doll's hair, careful not to dislodge her hat. "Thank you so much. For everything."

Noah noticed how Qui was beaming, how the lines seemed to have fallen from her face. "What are you going to name her?" he asked.

"Dung," Tam replied.

Thien smiled at Tam, then turned to Noah. "In Vietnamese, 'dung' means 'beautiful.' "

Iris watched Tam kiss her doll's cheek. She wanted to e-mail her mother, to let her know the good that her father's center had already done. "Is it too cold in here?" she asked Qui. "Too hot? Or do you need any more food?"

Qui lowered her head, still not believing their extraordinary change in circumstances. "No, Miss Iris," she replied, wondering if she were dreaming, knowing that waking from such a dream would be more than her heart could handle. "You already do too much for us. Please no worry about us again."

"And you know where the bathroom is?" Iris asked. "And how to work the shower?"

Qui had never used a shower and was sure she'd continue to fill a bowl with water and clean herself with a damp cloth. But the American woman had gone to great lengths to show her how to operate the complex system of faucets. And so Qui nodded. "You too kind, Miss Iris," she said, unused to having someone worry about her, and not knowing what to say. "Please go rest. You must be tired."

Iris looked around the room, wondering if she and Thien had forgotten to tell Qui anything. While Noah had been searching for his welcome gift, they'd spent the better part of an hour showing Qui where everything was. They'd been detailed, perhaps too much so. In any case, Iris worried about her guests' first night. She wanted things to go smoothly. "I'll leave the light on in the hallway," she said. "And I'll check on you later."

"Thank you, Miss Iris," Qui replied, turning her gaze from Iris to Tam, who was pretending to comb her doll's hair. Tam grinned, looking as if she weren't sick and in pain, but happy. Qui's eyes watered. For a thousand nights, she had prayed for miracles. She'd prayed until exhaustion or bitterness had overcome her. Remarkably, just as she had ceased to believe in miracles, when she'd felt betrayed by the mere existence of the word, a miracle had finally befallen her.

Swinging her gaze back to the Americans, to the foreigners she hardly knew, Qui shook her head in wonder. She didn't know whether to laugh or cry or to hold these tall strangers in her arms. All she knew was that she could live a hundred lifetimes and never be able to repay them for what they'd already done. "Thank you, Miss Iris and Mr. Noah," she said softly, her voice threatening to crumble. "What you do for Tam, it beautiful."

Iris saw the tears in Qui's eyes and she smiled. "Sleep well tonight."

Noah and Thien also said good night and followed Iris into the stairwell. Iris was about to head down to the kitchen, but Noah touched her shoulder and pointed to a metal ladder that ran from near their feet to a trapdoor in the ceiling above the stairwell. "Follow me," he said. Clenching the remaining plastic bag in his teeth, he slowly made his way up the ladder. Each step sent a spasm of pain pulsating from his stump to his back, but he didn't change direction. The trapdoor had no lock and he pushed it open, dust drifting on him.

Noah climbed to the rooftop and helped Iris and Thien move up and into the fresh air. Dusk was about to blossom, and the fading sun spread a layer of itself on the faces of buildings and towers. This layer made structures glow as if they'd been painted crimson instead of white.

Traffic, most of which was unseen, hummed without pause—the steady pulse of the city.

The center's rooftop was covered in smooth river stones. Noah nudged a stone with his good foot, wondering what purpose it served. He then withdrew three cans of Tiger beer from the plastic bag and handed a can to both Iris and Thien. The women looked at him expectantly, but he wasn't sure what to say and so said nothing. Thien opened her can and handed it to Iris. She then opened Noah's can and then the last. Forty feet below, scooters beeped and darted.

"I'd like to thank you both . . . for putting up with me," Noah said. "I don't make it easy. And I'm sorry about that."

Thien shrugged, sipping her beer. "My life is easy, Mr. Noah. So please do not worry about me. It is my pleasure to know you."

Iris watched Thien, watched how her eyes seemed to linger on Noah's face. "She's right," Iris said, tasting the beer, savoring its coolness. "It really hasn't been a problem."

Noah nudged another stone. "Why did you send me to those places?"

Iris thought about her answer, not wanting to bring the wrong words to life, aware that the wrong words could turn him away. "Because I wanted your help," she said. "Because I knew your heart was good."

"If I stay for a while . . . I'll still have my bad

days, you know. I'll still drink. I'll still have a lot of anger in me." He glanced toward the setting sun, wondering if any of his friends were dying in Iraq. "Just because I saw something that changed me doesn't mean that . . . that I'm changed."

"It doesn't mean that you're the same either," Iris replied.

He continued to eye the skyline. "I want to help. But don't expect the impossible from me. Because I don't want to disappoint you."

She lowered her beer. "Do you know how much work we have to do, Noah? In about twenty-five days we're supposed to open. Have you thought about that? About the supplies? The teacher? The money? The upkeep? Or finding just the right group of children from the thousands out there?" She shook her head, watching a plane disappear toward the setting sun. "Anything you can do for Thien and me . . . for the center . . . is gravy as far as I'm concerned. So there won't be disappointments. Don't worry about that. Just do what you can, and know that whatever you do will be a blessing for us."

Noah looked up from the stones. "Sorry."

"Don't be sorry. I didn't mean it like that. But I want you to understand that anything you can do is important. Is really important."

Thien saw a piece of glass on the roof and placed it in her pocket. "The girls on the street, Miss Iris, they are starting to talk about your center."

Iris turned to her. "What are they saying?"

Thien took Iris's hand and smiled. "Tomorrow, when you are working, look around. You will see them, walking by, pretending to go places. But they will be observing the center. I have seen them already. And I have heard them talking about the room with the clouds."

"But how could they know about the clouds?"

Thien looked skyward. "Oh, perhaps a little turtle spread the word."

"A little turtle in a baseball cap?" Iris asked, smiling.

Sipping his beer, Noah watched the women. He liked how Thien so often reached for Iris's hand, as if they were a pair of young sisters. He had always heard that Asians were unaffectionate. But he'd found that, at least in Vietnam, nothing could have been further from the truth. "You know, we could build something here," he said, wanting to bring himself into the light that seemed to surround Iris and Thien.

"What?" Iris asked.

"Well, look at all this space," he said, gesturing around them. "This roof is huge. And it's so open. We could . . . I don't know. Maybe we could build a vegetable garden. There's so much sun and rain. The children could learn how to grow their own food. I bet they'd love it."

Thien clapped her hands. "My father is a farmer," she said excitedly. "I can get seeds. We can grow cucumbers and onions and garlic and dragon fruit and even some flowers."

Iris looked at Noah and smiled. "So this means you're staying? At least for a few more weeks?"

He considered his options, knowing that he could return to Chicago, wander around Asia, or remain here. Wherever he was, his demons would still follow him and his pain would rarely leave him in peace. He thought about Tam, about children he'd never met but who were sleeping somewhere on the streets below. If he stayed, he could help them, even if he couldn't help himself, even if his own mind and body were beyond repair.

"I'm going to build the playground," he said, looking from Iris to Thien, aware of the happiness in their eyes. "I'm going to build them a beautiful playground, and we'll see what happens after that."

— EIGHT

A New Day Dawns

The river was higher after the recent rains, evidence that the mountains to the north had also been saturated. Minh sat on a boulder at the water's edge, staring into the murky shallows. He thought about the seven dollars he'd won the previous night, disappointed in himself for the final game of the evening. After winning three straight games against a German student, Minh had lost the fourth game on purpose, expecting that his opponent would agree to play him again for higher stakes. And the foreigner had decided to do just that. But as they'd started to set up the game board, the student's friends had arrived, and he'd left, parting with a triumphant smile.

After Loc had found them and taken his customary five dollars, Mai and Minh had been left with two dollars. They'd spent one on a dinner of rice and eggs. The other they had buried under their basket. Minh had wanted to hide both bills, but they hadn't eaten all day, and he knew that he couldn't play and win so many games while on the verge of starvation.

Turning on the boulder, he saw that Mai was still asleep in their basket. She'd been quieter than usual since her attempt to get the money for formula. Minh didn't like it when she was withdrawn, for her voice was one of his favorite things. It made him smile and sometimes even laugh. He was sad more often than not, and with Mai so gloomy, there was no chance for him to be happy.

Mai had told him once that she wanted to see the mountains, and Minh sometimes thought about her words. He knew that, were they to escape, Loc would follow them to a city. A city of any size would have opium dens. So Hanoi and Da Nang and Hue and Nha Trang were places they could never call home. Loc would find them in such places. The five dollars a day they paid him ensured that he ate and, more important, enjoyed his opium and women. Minh was sure that he and Mai weren't the only children that Loc had working for him, but he believed that no other children provided him with as much money. Minh had overheard enough conversations to know that five dollars a day was more than the average factory worker, teacher, or policeman earned. And so Loc would never let them escape. Not if they went to a city, where he'd have an endless supply of opium and could rely on loose tongues to inform him of their whereabouts.

But if he and Mai were to flee into the mountains, to a small village somewhere remote and unknown, Loc wouldn't have the will to follow them. The problem was that Minh had never been outside Ho Chi Minh City. To him, the city was its own planet, and the countryside beyond it was an entirely different universe. As terrified as he was of Loc, the thought of hopping on a truck and heading off into distant mountains scared him even more. Whom would he play Connect Four with? What if Mai couldn't sell fans? What would they eat? Would another man, perhaps even crueler than Loc, come to control them?

Such questions made Minh feel so very small. He knew that he was short and thin for his age, and with only one hand he'd long ago realized that he could never protect himself or Mai from any physical threat. He could win at games, he knew that much, but beyond this skill, what could he do other than save a few dollars and hope to somehow escape the shadow that seemed to always be one step behind them?

"Still thinking about that last game, aren't you?"

Minh turned, surprised to see Mai standing before him. Her pigtails were slightly askew, as if sleep had rearranged her scalp. He watched her yawn, and then he shrugged.

"Oh, I know you are, Minh the Cheated," she said, sitting nearby on a half-buried truck tire. "Everything was just right. We were going to win, and he'd have been angry, and we'd have won again and again. It might have been one of our best nights ever. As good maybe as the night when you played that opera singer and she bought every one of my fans. Do you remember that? The big lady? With the big laugh? She sang us a song, and I thought that cyclo would break when she sat in it, and then she had us sit right in it with her. Right on her legs. And we were her tour guides that night. I told her everything about the city, and she asked question after question." Mai smiled, glancing above toward the bridge. "That poor cyclo driver. I bet he couldn't walk for weeks after that night. How he sweated. I'm sure he was happy to see us go. Even if she did give him that huge tip."

Minh's brow furrowed.

"Don't look at me like that, Minh the Curious,"

Mai said, wishing that they could meet the opera singer again, having never heard such a beautiful thing as her voice. "Do you expect me to be quiet forever? I'm not like you."

A mosquito drifted between them and Minh struck swiftly.

"I don't think he saw that coming," Mai said, glancing for other such pests. A baby cried somewhere in a nearby shanty, and Mai thought of Tung's little sister. The shields Mai had encircled herself with that morning cracked and started to sway, but she quickly patched them up, forcing thoughts of Tung and her own lies toward a distant place. "I think we should stop by that American's street center," she said, voicing what she'd mused over during the long hours before dawn.

Minh paused from wiping the mosquito from his palm. Mai had spoken of the center several times, but never about visiting it.

"It can't hurt to say hello, can it?" she asked. "We'll be careful, and make sure that Loc's not following us. If he doesn't know about it, he can't hurt us for it."

Instinctively, Minh glanced around, not only to ensure that Loc wasn't nearby, but also to see that they were beyond earshot of anyone else. He thought of Mai's suggestion, wondering about the street center. He had heard about it many times, of course. He'd heard that it was to house girls, though, and so he wasn't sure what he wanted to do. He couldn't imagine being separated from Mai, and she wouldn't be safe there anyway. Loc would track her down.

Minh took his good hand and grabbed Mai's wrist, pretending to drag her away.

"I know he'd find us there," she said, her tone suddenly angry. "But what's the harm in looking? Maybe they can help us, Minh. Did you ever think of that?"

He put a finger to his lips.

"Tung was going to steal that formula, wasn't he?"

Minh looked away, wishing she'd lower her voice.

"And do you know what would have happened then? We'd have been caught. Oh, Minh, we can't keep doing this. I'm getting too old for this, for selling fans and worrying about the police. Do you know what happens to girls like me who stay on the street for too long? Do you know what they start to sell? That's right. They sell themselves . . . until there's nothing left of them." Mai's eyes started to tear as she imagined such a fate.

Moving beside her on the tire, Minh put his arm around her. He saw that she was staring blankly at a bush, which didn't surprise him. Better to look at something green than the ugliness that surrounded them. They both did that in the city above, avoiding the areas where older street girls worked, where the girls beckoned to passersby from dimly lit buildings. Minh knew that Mai hated the sight of such buildings. She'd refused to walk by one once, even after Loc had threatened to beat her. Loc hadn't hit her. But he'd smiled.

"Can we go to the center tomorrow?" Mai asked softly, still staring at the bush, which was draped by several dirty plastic bags from when the river had been even higher.

Minh nodded, wondering how the bush managed to live amid all the filth.

"And can you win today, Minh? Please? I'm too tired to sell fans. If you won a lot today, we could take some time off tomorrow and visit the center. And do you know what? I heard there's a room full of painted clouds." Mai looked up and saw nothing but the stained and pitted bottom of the concrete bridge. "They say you can just sit and look at the clouds. Let's go there. Please. I'll say hello to everyone. You won't have to do anything."

Nodding once again, Minh rose from the tire. He moved along the water for a few paces, coming to the bush. Carefully he removed the plastic bags from where they'd wrapped themselves about weathered branches. He set the bags aside and then followed Mai toward their basket. He'd found a discarded roll of packing tape the previous night and had tried to cover his entire game box with the tape so as to waterproof it. The box glistened in the faint light, and Minh picked it up and placed it under his arm.

Minh watched Mai tidy their bedding. He wanted to tell her that he'd never let her become one of those girls, that despite his fears he also hoped to go to the mountains. He wanted to tell her so many things—that the bush reminded him of her, that sometimes he hated leaving their basket, that he was trying to devise a plan for how to trick Loc. But not having the courage to bring life to such words, he simply pointed to his game box and then held his forefinger in the air.

Mai shrugged. "So, you're going to be number one today?"

Minh pretended to grab a basketball rim and pull it down.

"You're going to be the Shaq?" she asked, smiling.

He set his game down, and pulled even harder at the imaginary rim.

Mai giggled softly. "And the Shaq's going to be even more powerful than usual? Even more dominant?"

He nodded, gesturing for Mai to speak more.

"And he's . . . he's going to stomp on his opponents. And break their feet. And dunk shoot over them. And take the ball and . . . and step back and shoot a three-point shot. And when his opponents try to score . . . well, then . . . the Shaq is going to . . . He's going to grab the ball out of the air and pop it like a balloon."

Minh grinned, pretending to do whatever Mai was saying.

Soon she was laughing. Soon the two friends were walking along the city streets, pretending to play basketball, to do things that their bodies were incapable of doing but their minds were not. As an imaginary ball bounced between them and their sandals rose higher than usual above the cracked cement, they didn't notice that their bellies were empty. And for a while they were like any other children out for a stroll.

IRIS LAY IN BED, STRETCHING. HER body was still somewhat unaccustomed to the time change, and she had worked late the previous night, ensuring all her father's paperwork was in order. Drinking Vietnamese tea and listening to Thien sing in the background, she'd hammered away at an oversize calculator until the tips of her fingers ached. The number six button on the calculator often stuck and then repeated itself, making her start over on whatever problem she had been tackling. Math had never been one of her stronger suits, and she'd rechecked her work time and time again, finding more mistakes as the evening progressed. One thing soon became clear—the center had enough money to sustain itself for about a year. But beyond a year, a budget didn't exist.

Iris rubbed her brow, which was already damp with sweat. She yawned. As tempting as it was to remain in bed, she put her feet on the tiled floor and dressed in light pants and a T-shirt. She pinned her hair up, wanting to keep it off her neck in the coming heat. Slipping her feet into sandals, she walked upstairs to the dormitory, eager to hear how Qui and Tam's first night went.

To her surprise, the room was empty. Qui's and Tam's beds were made and their pajamas were folded neatly and set atop a pillow. Confused, Iris looked around the room. She walked back downstairs. Nothing moved in the office but the overhead fans. The classroom was almost as barren, though Noah slept on his cot. Worried for her guests, Iris hurried back to the stairwell and descended to the ground level, making her way into the kitchen. Thien stood next to a counter, cutting fruit and singing quietly.

"Where are they?" Iris asked, putting out her hands, palms up.

Thien paused, a slice of mango falling slowly onto a chopping block. "Qui and Tam are not upstairs?"

"No, Thien. Their beds are made and they're gone."

Setting down her knife, Thien wiped her hands on a towel. "We should go to the market."

Iris sighed, wishing the day had begun better. She followed Thien out of the center. The city's smells greeted her—a striking combination of diesel fuel, roasting garlic, mildew, bougainvillea, animals, thatch, and a thousand other things. Iris didn't recall it raining the previous night, but the streets were littered with puddles. Scooters dodged the puddles the way fish swim in fast currents, darting from side to side.

Normally Thien stopped and chatted with many people she passed, often taking their photo with her Polaroid. Iris hadn't seen her move with the sense of purpose that she did now and was pleased to watch her sandals kick up so much gravel. "Why would they go back to the market?" Iris asked, wondering if Thien should be heading somewhere else.

Thien circumvented a pair of snarling dogs without a second glance. "It was my mistake, Miss Iris. I was not clear with them. Qui will still think that she needs to earn money for food."

"But we told them they were welcome to live with us. That we'd feed them."

"And Qui will think that she has to pay us for the food. And for everything else. She will worry that if they become a burden to us, we will put them back out on the street."

Iris thought about Qui lifting Tam from her warm bed and carrying her to a distant corner to begin a long day of begging. The image made Iris feel as if she'd failed Tam. Surely she must be miserable. "Let's hurry," Iris said, noticing the market's yellow facade in the distance.

Thien stepped into a broad boulevard. Taking Iris's hand, she zigzagged her way through traffic. When a scooter didn't pause to let her pass, Thien took off her baseball cap and swiped at the driver, muttering something in Vietnamese. Almost immediately upon hitting the sidewalk they spied Qui and Tam, who occupied their usual spot atop the bench in front of the market. Tam appeared to be sleeping, her new doll resting against her chest. Qui held three books and was trying to get the attention of a group of tourists.

Iris walked to Qui and knelt before her. "Qui, you don't have to do this," she said, angry at her-self when she saw how Tam lay asleep on the bench, how two flies were perched near her nose. Iris waved the flies away and took Qui's hands within her own. "You're to live with us now. Do you understand?"

Qui blinked repeatedly, unsure what to say. She'd awoken early, wanting to earn as much money as possible, so that she and Tam could con-tribute to the center. Tam had slept so well in the soft bed. Qui couldn't imagine returning to their little room by the water, where cockroaches and rats were often their bedfellows. "Please, Miss Iris," she said, lowering her head. "Please no make us go back. We work so hard. I make money. One or maybe two dollar each day. It enough for food. I only eat a little. I—"

"Sssh," Iris said, shaking her head. "If you want to work for money, that's fine. You can work at the center. You can clean. I'll pay you. You'll clean the dormitory and Tam can rest where you can see her."

Qui looked from Iris to Thien. She wasn't sure if

she'd heard the tall foreigner correctly. Qui had never held any sort of paying job. The thought of someone giving her money to clean was difficult for her to comprehend. Again she glanced from face to face, seeking some sort of clarification.

Thien sensed Qui's confusion. "We'd be honored to have your help," she said in Vietnamese. "Miss Iris doesn't have time to sweep, to wash the sheets, to keep the spiders from spinning their sneaky little webs. She's been worried about keeping the dormitory clean enough for all those girls." Thien smiled, leaning closer. "Between us, it would be a great relief to me if you'd come and work for her. She'd have one less thing to worry about. And she so worries these days. You should have seen her last night, fluttering around the rooms like a bird looking for its fallen nest."

Qui nodded, the prospect of working next to her sleeping granddaughter nearly too wonderful to imagine. "And Tam?"

"Our center is for girls. For girls to learn. Tam will learn like everyone else."

Qui put her hands together and bowed again. "Then please tell Miss Iris that I'll clean that room as if it were my own home."

Thien smiled, adjusting her cap. "You tell her, honored guest. You should practice your English. And let me say thank you for taking this pressure from Miss Iris's shoulders. As her friend, I'm so relieved that you'll be working with us."

Lowering her head to Iris, Qui proceeded to accept her kind offer, not believing that such miracles continued to befall her. As she spoke, Tam stirred in her sleep, muttering softly. Qui watched her granddaughter, eager to bring her back to the room with the clouds, the quiet fans, and the soft bed.

Relieved that Qui would soon be working for her, but worried about other pressing matters, Iris handed Thien some money and asked that they take a cyclo back to the center as soon as Tam awoke. She then said good-bye.

The previous night Iris had spent several hours online, researching doctors who specialized in treating cancer patients at nearby hospitals. She'd found a French physician who was a renowned expert in childhood leukemia and who also ran a local clinic. She wanted to stop by his office and talk to him about visiting Tam. Thien had written down directions to his clinic, and Iris strode to a nearby cyclo driver and handed him the piece of neatly folded paper. He opened it, pursed his lips, and said, "One hundred thousand dong."

Iris shook her head. "Seventy-five thousand."

The man scowled. "That too little. But for you, okay."

After climbing into the cyclo, Iris waved good-bye to Thien and Qui. The driver put his hand out, signaling traffic that he wished to pedal across the boulevard. Iris thought that taxis and scooters might honk at being forced to stop so abruptly, but no one seemed to mind. The sun already appeared to steam the city, and Iris wished that she hadn't rushed off without her sunglasses or hat. Her face glistened. Her lips tasted of sweat. A bus rumbled past, spewing black exhaust. Iris held her T-shirt over her mouth, breathing through the thin fabric. Eyeing the masks that many of the locals wore, she resolved to buy one at the next opportunity.

It wasn't hard to imagine how riding in a cyclo could be an incredibly romantic or exciting experience. She felt quite worldly, like an explorer from some forgotten era when empires were still discovered and lost, when novels like *A Passage to India* were researched and written. She'd have liked to sit in the cyclo and pretend she was writing such a novel. In a world of her making, she'd have spent the morning doing just that.

But the world wasn't of her making, and she had a hundred things to do, and the cyclo suddenly seemed like a very slow means of transportation. She watched enviously as scooters and even bicycles sped past them as the city drifted by. Glancing behind her, Iris saw that her driver seemed to be in no particular hurry. His sandaled feet pressed leisurely on wooden blocks that comprised his vehicle's pedals. He often chatted with other cyclo drivers, and sometimes seemed to talk to himself.

After about fifteen minutes had passed, her driver pulled in front of a gated shop that looked like all the other shops around it. Only a sign bearing a red cross gave Iris any indication that they were at the right address. Stepping from the cyclo, she pulled out seventy-five thousand dong.

He shook his head. "More far than I think before. Cost you two hundred thousand dong."

"What?"

His face tightened. "Two hundred thousand dong. Very far to go here. You pay two hundred thousand dong."

"But we agreed on seventy-five!"

"Your directions no good," he said, raising his voice. "You pay two hundred thousand."

Iris stuck out the seventy-five thousand, which he ignored. "The directions were fine," she said. "You take this money. It's what we agreed on."

The man stepped from his seat, approaching her, his stained teeth bared. "You pay me two hundred thousand. I have to take you very far. Next time you give good directions and you no have problem."

"I gave you—"

"Those no good! Pay me two hundred thousand!"

Glancing around, Iris saw not a single friendly face. She realized she was shaking. Feeling more defenseless than she had in years, she quickly paid the man. Even after he took her money, he scowled at her, and she hurried to the clinic, afraid that he'd follow her.

Only when her hands were on the clinic's gates did she recognize that it was closed. "No," she muttered, trying to see inside, her heart still thumping wildly. Several handmade signs had been glued to the door. One of the signs was in English and gave the clinic's hours. To Iris's dismay, she saw that the doctor was out on Tuesdays, and it just happened to be a Tuesday. "Damn it," she said, disbelieving her luck, wondering why she hadn't asked Thien to call the clinic. She leaned on the gates for a moment, pressing her head against the iron.

Frustrated by her disagreement with the cyclo driver and her failure to contact the doctor, Iris gave the gates a shake. She then willed herself to turn around and eye the street, which was narrow and by no means catered to tourists. Fortunately, a different cyclo and driver rested nearby beneath the paltry shade of an almost limbless tree. Iris approached the man and asked how much it would cost to go to the Rex Hotel, a landmark not far from her center.

"Ninety thousand dong," he replied in well-spoken English, a toothpick between his teeth. "But if we stop at my friend's silk store, and you go in, then my ride will only cost forty thousand dong."

"What?"

"It is very beautiful silk. And would look lovely on you."

"I don't want to go to a silk store."

"No? What about pearls? Or some paintings? Or maybe a massage?"

Tired of wasting time, Iris shook her head. "Which way?"

"Excuse me?"

"Which way to the Rex Hotel?"

"It is very far."

"Which way?"

The driver pointed into the distance. "Okay, I will take you for only—"

Iris started walking. She guessed it to be almost eleven o'clock and felt that she hadn't accomplished a single thing. Discouraged, she increased her pace, glancing into shops in hopes of seeing some supplies that she could buy: a stack of notebooks, a tin of colored pencils—anything she could take with her to ease the failure of her outing. The shops seemed more foreign than ever, however, and her level of annoyance continued to increase. Her father had promised local officials to have a grand opening at the center by Christmas, which was just over three weeks away. And with some six million Christians in Vietnam, Iris knew that this date wasn't insignificant. Several officials were expected to be present for the grand opening, and if the center wasn't ready, she would have to answer difficult questions.

Wiping sweat from her eyes, Iris walked faster, a sense of panic building within her. Scooters and bicycles continued to dart around her, and she was suddenly envious of the Vietnamese. They could move so much more quickly. They didn't have to deal with a language or cultural barrier. They could get things done. She'd just spent two hundred thousand dong and accomplished nothing more than wasting a huge chunk of time.

I have to do better, she thought, hurrying across a street, avoiding traffic. But how do I act like a local? How's that possible?

A pair of girls on a scooter waved and Iris absently said hello. Her mind twisted and turned, searching for a solution. And then it occurred to her—she'd ask Noah. He'd traveled abroad. He'd been in a war, of course, and had seen what didn't work on a scale never imagined. But surely he had seen some things that had worked well. And maybe he'd have an idea. And then she could put her time to better use, could really help those who so desperately needed it.

A smile dawned on Iris's face for the first time all day. She glimpsed a familiar landmark, dodged a stray rooster, and began to run.

BY NOW NOAH'S HANDS WERE ACCUSTOMED to the shovel. His fingers and palms bore slightly raised calluses. His skin seemed rougher. He was able to thrust and swing the shovel more efficiently, reducing some of the strain on his back and stump. Still, his aches seemed as plentiful as the tiny particles that rose and fell as he cast the soil skyward. As always, the aches prompted emotions of guilt, remorse, anger, and betrayal to course through him. Noah wanted to take his shovel, dig a pit, and bury his rage and misery so deep that they'd never see daylight again. He wanted to be the person he once was, but he didn't know how to be that person. Such evolution seemed impossible.

Noah emptied a jar and moved awkwardly to another. He reached into his pocket and found a painkiller, popping the pill into his mouth and swallowing it with a gulp of warm beer. He didn't like taking such a steady stream of pills, but shoveling hundreds of pounds of soil was impossible without them. And he wanted to finish the playground for Tam as soon as possible. He had already covered more than half of the lot with dirt, and if he worked throughout the day, he'd empty all the jars. Tomorrow he could use the rest of the supplies that Iris's father had already purchased to lay stone trails and to plant grass seed.

Setting his beer down, Noah picked up his shovel and pushed it deeply into the nearby jar. He was about to send soil sailing when he heard a woman singing. He paused, rising from his bent position. Thien emerged from the center, a tray in her hands. As usual, her clothes and baseball cap were splattered with paint. She walked over to Noah, still singing, and set her tray down on one of the big jars. She handed him a porcelain cup.

"I made lemonade for you," she said, smiling. "Can you believe that it took ten lemons to fill only two little glasses?"

He wondered if she knew that she had a smudge of paint on her nose. "Thank you," he said, sipping her drink, which was quite sweet.

"I put cane sugar and a drop of honey in it. What do you think?"

"I like it."

Thien glanced about. "You are going to need a long shower," she said, grinning, her full lips glistening from the lemonade.

Noah nodded, then looked toward the dormitory. "Is everything all right with Tam?"

"She is fine. When I told her that she no longer had to beg, she smiled and whispered to her doll."

"She did?"

"She was so happy, Mr. Noah. And Qui, she picked up a broom and started to sweep the room as if the king of Siam were coming for a visit."

Noah sipped more lemonade. "Good for her."

"I know."

"What about Iris? Is she back?"

"Not yet. She was going to talk with the French doctor. His clinic is rather far away, so I am sure that it will take some time."

Through a gap in the fence, Noah saw a woman pushing a broken scooter down the adjacent street. He glanced from her to Thien, noticing for the first time that her eyes seemed unusually large and open, as if she'd never had to squint from the sun's glare. He quickly finished his drink, setting his cup back on the tray. "Thank you," he said, reaching for his shovel.

"What will it look like?"

"The playground?"

"Yes."

Noah straightened, wincing as his prosthesis rubbed against his stump. "Well, I'm not really sure."

Thien laughed. "Please do not be afraid of talking with me, Mr. Noah. I am so little. And you are so big."

He tried to smile, aware that she acted big while he acted the opposite. "I thought about . . . about putting in simple things," he said. "Like a few trees. And a slide. And maybe a seesaw."

"A seesaw?"

"You know, a long board, with a triangle in the middle, so that when one end of the board goes up, the other end goes down? Kids sit on either end and go up and down and up and down." Noah looked at the ground. "I used to love doing that . . . as a kid."

Thien took his hands. "This is how we used to do it," she said, crouching low and then springing upward.

"Yeah. That's it."

She grinned, pulling a small fruit from her pocket and offering it to him. He declined, so she bit into it with her straight white teeth. At a window above, Qui came into view, dusting with a bundle of feathers. "Tam used to talk more," Thien said, thinking as she often did about the girl upstairs.

"She did?"

"Yes. Before the pain started to come. Before she was so tired every day." Thien finished the fruit, then wrapped a finger around her ponytail and pulled it farther out of the hole in the back of her baseball cap. "She talked about her mother, about how she once saw a falling star. She told me that she wanted to ride an elephant. She had seen a picture of some tourists on one and thought it looked like fun. For many months I wanted to take her to my village, where we still have elephants. But then she got so sick. And she stopped talking about anything."

"She's too young to be so sick."

Thien nodded, wishing that she'd taken Tam to her village, that she'd ridden an elephant through the nearby rain forest. As she imagined Tam atop an elephant, an inspiration struck. "Do you think we could build her one?" Thien asked, once again grasping Noah's hands. "On your seesaw?"

"An elephant?"

"Yes, yes! An elephant on one end and . . . and a water buffalo or something on the other. You could make big elephant ears out of wood, and I could paint them. And we could let Tam sit on her elephant and she could go up and down. Oh, that would make her so happy, Mr. Noah. I know it would. Could we please build it?"

Noah felt the strength of her grip and noticed how she stood on her tiptoes. "Of course we'll build it," he replied, aware that her eyes seemed even more alive than usual. He understood then how much she wanted to make Tam smile, to make the world a better place for a girl who seemed destined not to dwell in it much longer.

As Thien continued to hold his hands, Noah saw so many things in her eyes. He saw hope. He saw heartache. He saw desperation and love and a kind of purity that he didn't think remained in the world. He wanted to somehow touch this purity— to see if it was real. But he didn't know how to touch it, and so he just stood and stared, listening to her talk about plans for the elephant—her ideas for its tusks, how its head might dip into a puddle as if to drink. And as she spoke her voice carried him somewhere distant, into a place in his past where he was still a boy and a seesaw could make him laugh for an afternoon.

IN THE DORMITORY, THE DAY DRIFTED by. Tam slept off and on. Qui cleaned. And Iris, Thien, and Noah made multiple appearances. Dusk momentarily filled the room with muted red light, making it seem as if the clouds on the ceiling were illuminated from a distant sunset. Thien brought up a simple dinner of rice and grilled fish, and everyone ate from wooden bowls while sitting on the floor. Only Noah was absent—still shoveling dirt and spreading it on the ground.

Qui enjoyed dining with Thien and Iris, mainly because Tam delighted in their company. Though Tam wasn't talkative, Qui was aware of how she watched the older women, how her hands often stroked her doll's hair. Of course, she still moaned softly and ate nothing but a few spoonfuls of rice. But she also looked often at her new pajamas, marveled out loud about Iris's height, and didn't seem quite as exhausted as usual.

Later, after Qui washed Tam and then herself, they slipped into bed. The sun had disappeared and their room was dark. In the nearby stairwell a light flickered, casting a forest of shadows from the bunk beds around them. Tam put her head on Qui's chest and Qui stroked her brow. Voices drifted up from a floor below—two light and one heavy. The lighter voices moved quickly and often. The heavy voice rumbled like a bout of distant thunder.

Qui gently pulled Tam tighter against her. "Did you get enough to eat, my sweet child?"

"I'm so full."

"Do you have Dung?"

Tam pressed her doll against Qui's hand. "She's tired too."

Qui turned, kissing the top of Tam's head. "Do you like our new home? Our new bed?"

"It's soft."

"Yes, yes, it is," Qui replied, kissing Tam again as a horn sounded outside. Qui offered a prayer of thanks to Buddha. She felt such relief over not having to beg, to worry about whether Tam would be safe at night. Even though Qui's heart would be forever broken by Tam's illness, she felt blessed that Tam was clean, warm, filled with the priceless medicine, and wasn't on the street. A few days earlier, Qui would have traded away her legs for such a blessing.

"Little Bird?" Tam asked quietly, tugging on Qui's finger.

"What?"

"Tell me a story."

"What kind?"

Tam toyed with Dung's hair, closing her eyes, trying to remember her favorite tale. "The day at the beach."

Qui's body stiffened for the briefest of moments. "With your mother?"

"Yes."

"Well . . . it was a beautiful day," she said, beginning the lie that she had repeated a hundred times, a lie that she'd once told while racked with guilt, but now told readily, as it brought Tam comfort. "Your father, bless him, had died only a few months before. And your mother needed to get out and do something."

"What did she do?"

Qui stroked Tam's cheek. "She put us all on a

train. We had just enough money for the cheapest tickets. The seats were steel, but she didn't mind. She held you for the whole trip, against her chest, just like you hold Dung. It took four hours to get to Phan Thiet. She talked to you the whole way and fed you a banana, piece by piece."

"A banana?"

"Sure, sweet child," Qui replied, remembering feeding Tam many such fruits. "You always loved bananas. Bananas and mangos."

"And at the beach?"

"We'd never been to a beach. None of us. Your mother and I didn't know what to do. So we walked down to the water and just put our feet in it. The ocean went on forever, like the sky at night."

"And me?"

"You might as well have been a little crab. How you loved that sand."

"Was it soft?"

"Like this bed."

"Warm?"

"Like the sun."

The corners of Tam's mouth rose as she remembered her favorite part of the story. "Tell me about the boat."

"Ah, the boat."

"Yes, Little Bird."

"So, just as we were about to leave, a fisherman came in from the deep. His small boat was full of flopping fish, so full that he couldn't drag it into the shallows. When your mother saw his predicament she handed you to me, and she waded out into the water and helped him drag his boat to the shore. And he was so pleased with her help that he let her choose one fish for us to take home for dinner. To my surprise, your mother took your hand and let you point out the fish."

"And what did I get?"

"You picked such a tiny fish, Tam. And how we laughed. We laughed and laughed and laughed. And that night we ate your tiny fish for dinner. And even you had a bite."

A spasm of pain pulsated through the base of Tam's head, and she moaned softly. "Momma is so brave," she said, closing her eyes.

Qui ran her fingers through Tam's hair. "You inherited her bravery. Every last drop of it."

Tam snuggled closer to Qui. "I love you, Little Bird," she said, her voice slow and moving toward sleep.

"And I love you, sweet child."

"Will you stay with me? Always?"

"Of course."

"Even when I go to the new world? Where I'll meet the other children and get to run with them?"

"Yes."

"Promise?"

"I'll run beside you."

Tam smiled at this thought, having never seen her grandmother run and wanting to do so.

NINE

Awakenings

Sahn could see somewhat better in the light of morning, before the sun sought to subjugate the land through its brilliance. Moving slowly down the sidewalk, he peered into stalls and schools, hotels and hair salons. He wanted people to see his face, for the more they saw of him, the less likely they were to end up in prison. And while Sahn was happy to send some people to prison, most he'd rather steer in another direction.

Across the street, the towers of Notre Dame Cathedral rose like twin mountains. To Sahn, the towers were nothing but tapering blurs. But he knew that tourists and locals gawked at them from dawn to dusk. Sahn didn't like that French architecture dominated so much of his country. It was bad enough that the French had occupied Vietnam for a century, and he hated being reminded of that occupation every day of his life. Perhaps his lack of vision wasn't so bad, after all.

Sahn walked deliberately, his hand on his baton. Every block or so, he'd stop and ask questions of an informer. His queries were invariably brief and without preamble. He spoke in such a manner to as many people as possible, so that criminals might not easily determine who was on his payroll.

Beggars, shopkeepers, construction workers, and cyclo drivers all knew to pay attention when Sahn approached. Most were happy to pass a secret his way. If that secret led to an important arrest, at some point they'd be rewarded.

Unlike his beloved Hanoi, at all times of day Ho Chi Minh City seemed busy, and morning was no exception. Sahn walked carefully. Even on the sidewalk a misstep could land him directly in the path of an approaching scooter. And such a misstep would reveal that his eyesight had failed. Then he'd be nothing more than a disabled old man without employment, respect, or a means to make Vietnam a better place. Then he'd be forced to sell rice cakes or sunglasses to live. And Sahn's pride would never permit such a future.

Even after his eyesight had been damaged in the fighting, Sahn had continued to help drive the Americans from his land, and then had battled the Khmer Rouge until the villainous Pol Pot was sent into hiding. Sahn had killed in two wars and had been victorious in two wars. He'd sent murderers to prison and had saved children from unspeakable fates. If confronted with the choice of selling rice cakes or putting a bullet through his head, he'd do his best to die with dignity.

Few men of Sahn's age remained in Vietnam, as most had been killed in the American War. As he pretended to scrutinize the outside of a massage parlor, he was glad that Vietnam was moving on without his generation. Yes, his generation had defeated the greatest power on Earth and unified a country that had been pulled apart by the Americans and the Russians during their epic battle for world domination. But his generation had done nothing but fight. And though Sahn would never forget the rage, power, misery, and euphoria that could be found on a field of battle, he was glad that the young men of today's Vietnam didn't know such feelings. Better to let the poets, writers, and moviemakers try to bring these emotions to life. Better to let such people guess at feelings they could never understand than to see these artists foul themselves when fire fell from the sky.

Sahn stepped off the sidewalk and slowly made his way down an alley. He heard a bird singing. Though he'd have liked to see it, he could never stop and try to locate such a creature and so he simply listened. Clearly, the bird didn't care about his musings. Perhaps its ancestors had sung for the French and the Americans. Perhaps the bird was telling him something.

The alley was littered with potholes. He wished they could be fixed but knew that far more important concerns faced Vietnam. His government was wise to let the potholes grow to the size of sinks. Better to cure a man of his disease, Sahn thought, than to cut away tissue and hope for the best.

He rounded a corner and saw the destination of his walk—the American woman's center for street children. He studied the three-story building as much as his vision allowed. To him, the structure resembled a lifeless stone cube. Thinking of the woman's efforts to create clouds on the ceiling, he wondered if she'd paint the exterior.

Sahn walked around the entire site. He wanted people to know that he was interested in the center, as his interest would make it less likely that twisted minds would seek to exploit the facility's future inhabitants. He knew that children could be lured to their doom by nothing more than the offering of pretty things and promises. But with his shadow often looming, those providing such temptations would be forced to think twice.

His feet hardly stirring the gravel beneath them, Sahn moved to the fence that surrounded the lot behind the facility. Squinting, he looked through a hole and thought he saw the American soldier. The man appeared to be lifting stones and placing them on the ground. Either the work was hard or the man was weak, for he often paused. Sahn realized that the foreigner frequently drank from what might be a beer can. Pursing his lips, Sahn left the fence and proceeded to the front of the building.

The iron gate that could be pulled across the open-air entrance had been partially shut. Sahn stepped past the gate. "Hello?" he called out in Vietnamese.

A shape materialized—the girl beneath a baseball cap whom he'd spoken to before. "Good morning, Captain," she said, her voice not unlike that of the bird. "May I help you?"

"Is the American woman here?"

"Upstairs. In her office. Would you like me to—"

"I'll go," he said, moving toward the stairwell.

"Please let me know if you need anything."

Sahn grunted. He could tell that the walls bore brightly colored paints, but in the confined space, exactly what had been portrayed eluded him. Reaching the second floor, he turned to his right, moving more by memory than sight. He cleared his throat and the American woman rose from in front of a white box that he assumed was a computer monitor.

"I didn't hear you," she said, running her hand through her hair.

Sahn looked around the room, wishing she spoke Vietnamese. "You are busy?"

"Well . . . sort of. What can I help you with?"

He gestured toward the computer. "What do you work on?"

Iris wondered why he was here. She wasn't sure what to make of him—if he was friend or foe. She would ask Thien about him. "I was writing an article," she replied, hoping that he'd sit, that he wouldn't always stand like such a statue. "An article for a magazine."

"I thought you write about books. Not about . . . about maybe what you see in Vietnam. About how poor Vietnam is."

"Would you like something to drink? Some water?"

"Is this article about Vietnam?"

"Yes."

"What it say?"

Iris sighed, tired of being intimidated by the strange man before her. "I've got enough of my father's money to last a year," she said, sitting back down, but facing him. "You understand that? A year. If I don't raise some more money . . . somehow . . . whatever we do here will end in twelve months. And the girls will be back on the streets. So I'm trying to write an article, sell it, and get it published. That might create some awareness about children who don't have homes. And I don't think that's a bad thing. Because an article like that might bring some money our way. It might keep us afloat."

Sahn tended to believe that Americans had mountains of money and chastised himself for not anticipating that the woman might run out of funds. "You could sell this?" he asked, amazed that someone might pay for such a thing.

"I don't know," she replied, glancing at the computer screen, knowing that her story wasn't ready, that she didn't yet understand the subject matter well enough. "But maybe to a big magazine. I think people want to hear about what's happening in the world. And maybe if a million people read the story, a few people would help."

Nodding, Sahn wondered if strangers might send money to help children they'd never met. "In America," he asked, "do children live on streets?"

Iris thought about Chicago, about what she'd rarely seen, but knew existed. "It happens. Unfortunately."

"Even in your rich country?"

"Yes. Even in our rich country."

"Then why you no do something in America? Why come here?"

A jackhammer sprang to life somewhere distant. Iris thought of Noah, as he'd be startled by the noise. "My father started something," she answered, glancing at the urn on a shelf behind Sahn. "And I want to finish it."

He grunted. "Maybe your father, he have a guilty mind."

"So?" she replied, the notion of her father being disparaged in his own office causing her voice to intensify. "Maybe he did. But do you think what happened so long ago somehow takes away from what he was trying to do with this center?"

"I—"

"Maybe you should worry less about the past and more about the present."

Sahn let her words tumble within him, knowing she was right but pretending otherwise. "How you choose them?" he asked, looking about the office, memorizing its blurs.

"Who?"

"The children. There be many who want to come."

"I don't . . . I don't—"

"Start with youngest. And those with no family."

"Why?"

"But be careful who you take them from." He took a half step closer to her. "You understand? You be careful. And if you have problem, then you tell me."

She rose from her chair. "But they're all alone. That's the whole point. They're alone and living on the street."

"No. You mistaken. They need people and people need them. So be careful who you take them from. You take them from wrong kind of people, and someone come looking for you. And not a good person. Understand?"

Her heart quickened its pace. She'd never imagined that she could place herself in danger by opening the center. "But . . . but how can I tell . . . who I might take them from?"

He pursed his lips. "You pick your girls. Then bring them to park. Stay there all day. I will change clothes. And I will see who follows them to park. And if bad person comes, then I will take this person away."

"For how long?"

"One hour. Forever. That be their choice. But either way, they no bother you again."

"Why are you helping me?" she asked, unsettled by how he looked at her. His eyes seemed so lifeless, like a pair of dark stones that had been set within his head.

"I no help you," he said, grunting. "I help children, the future of Vietnam."

She glanced at the clock on her computer. "Well, I should get back to work. I've got a lot to do today."

"Tomorrow I bring something for children."

"You'll what? What do you mean?"

He thought about his fish tank, about the brown blurs that he'd fed for so long. He'd enjoyed feeding the blurs, watching them dart toward his fingers. Perhaps the children would also enjoy such a simple pleasure. He hoped so. "You will read it to me?" he asked, turning to leave.

"Read it?"

"Your article. I may wish to add something."

She shrugged. "You may add whatever you want."

NOAH WANTED TO ENJOY THE MOMENT—the process of laying large, flat stones on the new soil to create a path through the playground. Before Iraq, such a project would have created not only a sense of accomplishment, but a comforting knowledge that something of his making would enjoy a degree of permanence. As a teenager, he'd spent his summers working for the park service and had built several trails and bridges. He had liked fashioning such creations and often carved his initials into unseen spaces, so that he could return later and admire what he'd built with his hands and will.

The making of a trail or a bridge had been strangely cathartic, the process of driving a nail into freshly cut wood a simple pleasure that Noah found hard to replicate. While working outdoors, he'd often whistled or hummed, pleased to be alone in the woods with nothing more than a hammer or shovel in his hands. In the woods he could listen to the birds, feel the sun on his face, or find treasures that only he'd ever truly appreciate.

Now, as Noah leaned over and forced a heavy stone into place, he felt immeasurably saddened by the fact that it no longer felt good to be working outside. Even after he'd popped a pain pill earlier in the morning, his stump and back ached. And these aches bound him to his sorrows, as they reminded him of what his life had become and what it had once been. A year ago, creating a stone trail that children would follow into a playground he made would have brought him profound joy. But now, he could focus only on what he'd lost— the freedom to live without suffering, without regret, bitterness, and anger tainting his thoughts.

The stone fell on Noah's finger, scraping the skin from his knuckle the way a paring knife peeled away a potato's casing. He winced, watching blood fill the wound and drip to the ground. He didn't curse, didn't wipe the blood away. The knuckle hurt, but he knew this hurt would fade. It was nothing, of no consequence whatsoever. Its ability to cause pain would expire and his wound would heal.

But nothing would ever bring back his leg, and this knowledge produced a bitterness in him that he hadn't known he was capable of feeling. He was bitter that he'd been maimed, that he'd so blindly trusted his government, that he hated who he had become. If only he could build a time machine. With a time machine he could go back to his job of selling cars instead of enlisting in the marines. With a time machine he could return to who he once was—the man who laughed and played jokes and enjoyed his own thoughts.

Noah wiped the blood from his knuckle on his sock and kept working. He reached for another stone, a part of him wanting to build the path and another part wanting to bury himself beneath the heavy rocks. The stone fought him for a few heart-beats and he wrestled it into place. He forced his misery aside long enough to imagine the path snaking its way through the playground. He started to work again, glancing up as Thien emerged from the center, carrying two glasses.

"Good morning, Mr. Noah," she said, smiling widely, her sandals leaving prints in the fresh soil.

"Hello."

She studied his path, wondering where it would go. "Are you making a yellow brick road?"

He shrugged. "I would if I could."

Thien saw his whiskey bottle lying nearby and walked over to it. She poured a dash of whiskey into the glass of mango juice that she'd prepared. "Here," she said. "This will lead you to the wizard."

Noah saw warmth and perhaps compassion on her face. He took the drink and sipped it. "Why don't you judge me?" he asked, watching her sip her own drink, moved that she'd so freely pour him whiskey.

"Judge you?" she replied, wiping her brow with paint-stained fingers. "How could I? I have never been in a war. Or hurt like you. Or suffered like you. Maybe if I did not have a leg, I would also drink or do something else to escape."

"I doubt it."

"Whiskey does not make you weak, Mr. Noah. People escape with food, with sports, with power and money. Whiskey is no different than those things."

"But those people . . . they aren't . . . numb. They know how to live. They aren't ruined."

She gestured toward the skyline. "Vietnam was once ruined. Parts of it will always be ruined. But there is also much beauty here. More beauty than ruins."

Noah sipped his drink, wishing that he didn't always feel so alone, didn't have to stand and face his demons with no one beside him. "I'm so . . . tired, Thien. Do you think I'll always be so tired?"

Her hand found his elbow, gripping it lightly. "You are worn down, Mr. Noah. Your body and mind are worn down, and you could sleep for three days and three nights and still feel worn down."

"You're right," he replied, his voice trembling slightly.

"I wish I could take your suffering. I would take it for the rainy season, just to give you a rest."

"You would?"

"Of course," she said, continuing to grip his elbow. "But I cannot take your pain. When you need it, though, I will make you a mango whiskey drink. And if you wish, I will sing a little song for you. And maybe my drink and my song will let you rest."

His eyes grew moist. "Would you . . . sing something now?" he asked, needing to be reminded again of beauty. "Just for a minute?"

Thien set her glass down, adjusted her baseball cap, and then began to sing. At first her voice was little more than a whisper of wind as it tried to squeeze through old walls. But then her voice rose, and the whisper became a living thing that seemed to envelope Noah in a cocoon of purity and strength and loveliness. He didn't understand her words. He'd never heard the song before. But her voice rescued him for a moment, taking his hand and leading him toward a place of light. He let her guide him to this place, and he watched her face as she sang of something that made her smile.

When her lips finally ceased to stir, he found her eyes. "How did you do that?"

"Make you a mango whiskey drink?" she asked, grinning.

He shook his head, wondering how she'd briefly managed to make him feel as if he weren't alone. "I don't know how you did that," he finally said.

"I just sang a song, Mr. Noah. Nothing more. But I was happy to sing it for you. Thank you for listening."

He was about to ask her to sing one more song but saw that two children had walked through the first floor of the center and now stood at the edge of the playground. He recognized them. The boy with the missing hand stood holding his game box. The girl whom he'd been with at the park was next to him. The two children glanced around, and the girl waved, her gesture warm but indecisive.

Thien stepped toward their visitors, speaking in Vietnamese. The girl answered, bowing slightly. Noah set his drink aside and walked toward the trio. He noticed the boy staring at his prosthesis.

"You remember us?" the girl asked Noah, twisting a plastic ring.

"Yes. But not your names."

"How you forget our names? I am Mai, like the month. My friend, his name is Minh. He beat you three times when you play Connect Four. Maybe you do better today."

Thien took Mai's hand. "Is that why you came here? To play another game?"

"Sure, sure," Mai replied. "Minh want to play another game. Maybe for two dollar this time. And when he play, maybe you can take me on tour of center."

"How about for a dollar?" Noah asked. "We can play in the kitchen."

Minh nodded, following Thien, Mai, and Noah inside. Minh watched Noah limp, wondering how it would feel to be missing a leg instead of a hand. Minh had always enjoyed walking and couldn't imagine what it would be like to stumble forward on a leg of steel. After sitting in front of a plastic table, Minh opened his box and began to sort through the pieces. He held up a black and a red piece, offering his opponent the choice of colors.

Noah chose red. His back ached and he wished that he'd finished Thien's drink. "If you win, I'll give you a dollar," he said, gathering all of the red pieces. "If I win, will you help me with those stones for a bit?"

Minh thought about the stones. They were large and looked heavy. He lifted his stump and showed it to the American.

"That's okay," Noah said, dropping his first piece into the game board. "We'll do it together."

Minh smiled and played his piece.

A few feet away, Thien held Mai's hand and led her to the stairwell. Despite her eagerness to see the center, at first Mai worried about leaving Minh alone, for they were almost never apart. She took two steps up and then glanced back toward the kitchen.

"He'll be fine," Thien said in Vietnamese. "We'll just be gone a moment."

Mai looked around, marveling at the nearly finished paintings on the stairwell's walls. She traced a branch with her finger, wondering what it might be like to climb such a tree. The birds and squirrels on the limbs seemed to smile. Mai wished that she could create something as beautiful. She was certain that to create such beauty, the painter must have laughed many times.

Mai traced the tree's contours until they reached the second floor. As Iris was out interviewing a potential teacher, Thien led Mai into the classroom, which was still but for the ceiling fans. Mai looked from the desks to the books to a world map that someone had started to paint on a nearby wall. She had never been inside a classroom and wanted nothing more than to spend the day sifting through the treasures surrounding her. But she couldn't leave Minh for long and glanced at her guide. "Will you be a teacher?" she asked.

"Oh, no. I am only the cook, and Miss Iris's assistant."

Mai wondered what it was like to be such an important person. "Do you sleep here?"

"Sometimes. But not usually. I have a room just

a few blocks away." Thien watched Mai's eyes continue to drift about. "Do you live on a street downtown?" she asked, suspecting that their visitor did, but wanting to gauge her honesty.

"No," Mai replied, feeling somewhat ashamed in front of this beautiful woman who had her own room. "We have a bed under a bridge. It's not so bad. We sleep in a big basket and listen to the traffic."

"You and Minh?"

"Yes."

"That's nice."

Mai saw that the older woman's smile didn't waver, that her face didn't fill with disgust. "I call him Minh the Magnificent," Mai said, her voice gaining confidence. "Do you know that he once won twenty-six straight games of Connect Four? He beat all these smart foreigners who'd gone to universities and were so rich."

"Twenty-six games?" Thien asked, feigning amazement, wondering if Mai knew that their center was only for girls.

"He's only got one hand, but I'm sure that he's got two brains. Of course, you'd never know it unless you watched him play. Then you'd see those two brains at work. Have you ever watched the Shaq play basketball? Well, the Shaq uses his two hands to dunk shoot over everyone. Minh uses his two brains to do the same thing. I'm sure your friend is discovering that right now."

Thien laughed, again taking Mai's hand. "Let me show you some more."

They walked upstairs, their speed increasing. Thien led Mai into the dormitory, where she saw two rows of bunk beds, and a girl and an old woman who occupied the last beds. The girl looked asleep. The old woman sat beside her and held an open book.

Thien moved forward and realized that Tam's eyes were only half closed. "Hello, Tam," she said softly.

"Hello."

"Did you sleep well last night?"

"I dreamed."

"About what?"

"Flowers."

Thien smiled, gesturing toward their visitor. "This is Mai. She and her friend Minh came to look around."

Mai saw that illness gripped the other girl, who was a little younger than she. "I like your doll," she said, watching how Tam stroked her hair.

"Thank you."

Qui started to rise from the bed. "I was about to start working. I know there's so much to be done."

Thien put her hand on the older woman's shoulder. "Please don't get up. There's plenty of time for chasing spiders, and I'd like to show Mai around."

Bowing slightly, Qui offered her thanks and

251

again opened her Thailand guidebook. Tam's gaze drifted back to a photo of turquoise waters and an unbroken sky. Qui had been telling her a story of dolphins that lived in the waters, of how they secretly knew how to fly. By flying only at night, they kept their secret from everyone but the stars.

Taking Mai's hand again, Thien led her to the center of the room. They paused beside a bunk bed, and Mai leaned down to touch the bedding, which was soft and clean and so unlike what she slept upon. She wanted to lie on the bed and wrap herself in its sheets. She'd stay there all day, listening to the city below, protected by the walls around her. Maybe she'd dream about flowers too.

"Did you see our clouds?" Thien asked.

Mai glanced from Thien's face to the ceiling. She gasped as the clouds seemed to billow before her. Smiling, she reached up as if to touch them. Beautiful and wondrous, the clouds made her feel as if she were somewhere very distant, at a place outside the city where clouds were untainted and free to roam about the sky. She laughed, wanting to show Minh. "Who painted these?" she asked, looking from cloud to cloud.

"Miss Iris and I."

"Could you teach me to paint like that? Please? Maybe I could paint one under our bridge. It wouldn't be as pretty there, but I could look at it. And Minh could too."

Thien removed a paintbrush from her back

252

pocket and set it in Mai's hand. "Maybe you could paint one here."

Mai turned to Thien. Had Thien somehow read her mind? For her whole life Mai had longed for things she didn't have—things like a father, a family. She'd longed to go to school, to ride a bicycle with a friend sitting behind her, to fill her belly each night with warm food. She'd pleaded silently for such things and yet they had never fallen before her. Now, as she looked at the clouds and soft sheets, Mai wanted nothing more than to try to paint something within this magical building. She wanted to take a brush and stroke bright colors on a surface that had been dull and lifeless.

Even better, if something like an old ceiling could be turned into a beautiful sky, then perhaps people could be painted too. Perhaps Thien could take her miraculous brush and paint Minh's voice back into his body. Perhaps this same brush could cover up Mai's fears and sorrows.

"Could . . . could we stay?" Mai asked quietly, fearing an answer.

Thien saw the want and desperation in Mai's eyes. She was afraid of breaking Mai with the wrong answer, but she couldn't mislead her. "Only girls . . . will stay here," she replied, once again holding Mai's hand. "So you could stay. But Minh would have to—"

"No," Mai interrupted, the clouds above her suddenly gray, her world once again full of wretched truths. "I won't leave him," she said, her eyes tearing. "He has no one else . . . and . . . and I won't ever leave him. He'd never make it by himself."

Thien felt Mai try to pull away from her, but she wouldn't let the girl step back. Instead she drew Mai closer against her. "Wait, wait, wait," she said, stroking Mai's shoulder.

"Why wait? I won't leave him. Never. So go paint your silly clouds with someone else."

"I want to paint them with you."

"No."

"I do, Mai. I—"

"No, you don't," Mai replied, tears dropping to her cheeks. "You don't care about me."

Thien continued to hold Mai tight, not letting her flee, afraid of what might happen to her. She'd seen too many girls ruined by the streets, and she knew that Mai was close to such misery. "I want you to keep my brush," Thien said, stroking Mai's cheek, needing to stem her desperation. "It's my only one and I have so much more to paint. Flowers for the kitchen. An ocean for the washing room. There's so much to paint, Mai. But I won't paint again until you're beside me and we can work together. That's why I want you to keep my brush. My lucky brush."

"What . . . what about Minh?"

"Did you see the children, Mai, the children painted in the entryway who are holding hands?"

"Yes."

"Do you think that we'd ever pull such children apart? That we'd take you from Minh?"

"I don't know. Maybe."

"Well, we won't. Not today or tomorrow or ever. So don't worry about that. I'll talk with Miss Iris. She's very clever and determined, and I'm sure that she'll think of something. And when she does, you can bring my brush back and we'll paint whatever you want."

Mai rubbed her eyes with her free hand. She wanted to believe the older woman, but she'd been disappointed so many times in her life, and to her a promise was only a series of meaningless words. "I should go."

"Take the brush, Mai. Please take it with you and come back in a few days."

"It's just an old brush."

"No, it's not. Believe me, it's not."

"I don't—"

"When you feel it moving in your hand, Mai, you'll know what I'm talking about."

"How?"

"Because that old brush could paint a beautiful rainbow."

Mai glanced at the brush. She felt its bristles with her fingers, moving them back and forth. "You'll teach me?"

"I'd love to."

"You're sure?"

"I'm here, Mai. And I'll teach you. So you and Minh come back to us. Stay safe and come back to us."

Mai looked at the clouds, wanting to believe the woman's words, wishing that words couldn't cut so deeply, couldn't weaken her knees. She pocketed the brush, pleading silently that words wouldn't once again betray her. She didn't know if she could endure another betrayal. The mere thought of it caused her eyes to again dampen. The clouds blurred. They soon seemed to pulsate with the cadence of her heart.

Mai took a deep breath. She steadied herself. She'd have to hide her hope and fear from Minh. Perhaps she would let him see a sliver of her hope, just to keep him going for the coming days. But beyond this sliver, she'd show him nothing, because betraying him was something she'd never do.

If this woman betrayed her, Mai knew that another piece of her would die. And then, there would likely be too little of her to hold together. The strings that she had tied around herself would sever and she would break apart like a bottle cast on stone. She'd never paint a rainbow or feel a soft bed. She'd never hope or dare or dream. She'd simply walk into blackness and lie down, and whatever happened to her, she wouldn't fight it. She was too tired to fight anymore, and if she found herself in darkness, she'd let its waves wash over her until what little memory she had of light was gone.

∙ ∙ ∙

THOUGH THE PIPE HAD LEFT HIS lips an hour before, Loc's senses were still dominated by opium's heavy hand. The drug simultaneously managed to slow his mind yet heighten his abilities to see and hear and smell. Colors and lights filtered into his brain as if his eyes had been fitted with magical lenses that enriched the hues before him. Sounds permeated his ears the way they might underwater. Scents of diesel fuel, flowers, and spices powerfully infused the air he drew into his lungs. His face and body glistened—his altered environs a womb that kept him warm and free of pain.

For the last eight of his twenty-nine years, Loc had visited opium dens each day. The discovery of these dark and quiet refuges had altered his life. With opium in his system, he no longer feared the streets. Nightmares ceased to torment him. Memories could be pushed away. Food and women became appealing, and he grew to crave each almost as much as his pipe.

Loc spent his days in opium dens, collecting his money, and in the company of women for hire. In the dens he was left alone and would bathe himself in the drug's comforting waters. On the streets he protected a handful of children in exchange for most of their earnings. And in the grasp of women he momentarily became a god.

The children were the key to fulfilling his cravings, and Loc treated them accordingly. He'd beaten each multiple times, but never so badly that they'd been unable to work. Though sometimes he took joy in these beatings, he mainly hurt the children because he needed them to fear him. As important, he needed them to fear a world without him in it. And he often let them know what would befall them without his protection. A child had once run from him, and Loc had made an example of the incident, letting the city's most deviant minds know that the boy was no longer under his protection. Three days later the child was found dead and broken. And in the months since, Loc had muttered the boy's name whenever his children seemed ready to wander.

Loc knew that he was cruel but didn't regret it. His cruelty allowed him to survive, to enjoy his pipe and his women. Without his cruelty, he'd be reduced to a creature on the brink of extinction. He saw such creatures each day—beggars and cripples so battered that they seemed to seek death. And while Loc sought oblivion, he enjoyed its comforts and had no interest in death.

Now, as Loc searched Ben Thanh Market, he wondered where Minh and Mai had gone. Though they'd never missed a payment, he had seen less of them on the streets, and their absence troubled him, as they provided most of his earnings. He tried to remember their favorite sites, but his mind lumbered like an old elephant. Had the girl told him where they'd be today? Had he hit the half boy the previous night?

Loc wandered outside, the sun seeming to penetrate his skull. Uncertain of his steps, he moved toward a group of fair-haired tourists. One foreigner tried to refold a map, a silver watch sparkling on his wrist. Loc used to steal such watches, but those days were distant. Better to let the children worry about his money. If they ended up in prison, he could always find more.

The streets teemed ahead. The opium's grip on him was diminishing, and Loc tiredly continued onward. He'd spent all his money that morning stuffing his pipe and buying a woman, and he needed to refill his pockets so that he could satisfy his hunger. The half boy would have won a game or two by now. Loc needed only to find him.

He took another few hundred steps. The haze that so pleasantly enveloped him began to waver. Soon his mouth and throat felt dry. His head hurt. The city seemed too loud. Needing to return to a den, but lacking the money to do so, Loc kept walking. He cursed the half boy and the girl for being so hard to find.

Opium usually held Loc's temper in check, but he now clenched his hands and teeth tightly. He should be drawing from his pipe, not searching the hot streets for a pair of ungrateful brats. Wiping his face with the top of his Yankees jersey, he spat out the staleness in his mouth and increased his pace.

Tonight, under the cover of the bridge, he'd hold the half boy's face beneath the river's surface until the girl promised to stop disappearing. He would scare them both badly, scare them until they pleaded for forgiveness.

His body craving oblivion, Loc abruptly ceased his search and turned into an alley that housed one of his favorite opium dens. He'd have to scrape the bowl and stem of his pipe to gather residue, which he could then roll into a ball and light and smoke. He didn't enjoy such highs, as they tended to leave him lethargic. But he had no choice.

Loc spied the cracked door that led to a den, and was about to move through it when to his amazement he saw the half boy round a corner. Loc stepped into the shadows. The girl appeared next, her voice moving quickly. It seemed as if she spoke with excitement. The boy grinned—something Loc rarely saw. Holding his game in his good hand, he swung his stump to and fro.

The children passed. Loc started to follow them, eager for their earnings, but stopped. Where had they been? he wondered, knowing no hotels or tourist attractions were nearby. His curiosity growing, he moved in the direction from which they'd first appeared. He walked down the middle of the alley, heedless of the occasional scooter. At first he saw nothing but stained apartment buildings and shops. But then, to his right, his eyes fell on a large sign that was written in English. Like most everyone who lived on the streets, Loc could speak some English, though he couldn't read it well. He wasn't sure what the sign said.

Moving closer to the structure, Loc heard the voices of foreigners. His heart thumping quickly at the thought of the girl and half boy betraying him, he stepped toward a child playing in a puddle and asked what the foreigners were doing. The child told him all that he needed to know, confirming his suspicions, causing his anger to rise like mercury.

Loc moved closer to the building. The foreigners were trying to steal from him, and as he listened to them, he realized that he could never let their center open. He'd have to destroy it or them or perhaps both. He couldn't allow them to succeed, because their success would ensure his demise. The half boy and the girl could never go free. He needed them. They gave him life.

Studying the center, Loc looked for weaknesses, for ideas. After a few minutes, he cursed the foreigners again, stepped into the opium den, and pulled his pipe from where he'd tied it against his calf.

Soon he had scraped the pipe clean and was sucking smoke into his lungs. Soon he was content. His aches were gone, he had a plan, and his future would be secure. The children would never escape him. They were his.

HER FATHER'S DESK HAD BECOME HER own. A half dozen bound, prepublication review copies of forthcoming novels sat atop one another. Index cards bearing various reminders and notes had been taped to the edge of her computer monitor. Résumés, official documents, receipts, bills, and office supplies covered seemingly every millimeter of available space. And a paper-clipped outline of her novel lingered, half buried, beneath this sea of paperwork.

Iris studied the chaos before her, trying to slow a mounting sense of panic. How had her father ever thought that he could manage the center alone? How could he possibly have envisioned housing, clothing, feeding, and educating twenty children? Had he been stronger than she'd imagined?

She rubbed her brow, knowing that her career as a book reviewer was at the very least going to be put on hold. Perhaps she could complete a few reviews to pay some bills. But many of her looming deadlines would soon come and go without being met. She wouldn't get to do what she loved most—share her discoveries.

Iris also had to think about other details, now that her trip to Vietnam was going to be extended. For starters, she needed to break her apartment lease back in Chicago. Her mother would have to pack up all of her books and move her out. Iris had also decided to sell her prized collection of signed, first-edition novels that she'd managed to gather over the years. She didn't want to sell the books but knew that they were worth five or six thousand dollars. Such money would go a long way in Vietnam and would, in fact, pay for a library that she wanted to build in the corner of the classroom. Selling fifteen of her own books, even if they were precious to her, was a sacrifice that she needed to make. Otherwise, she didn't see how she could build a library for the children. And though a library hadn't been in her father's original design, Iris felt that she must build one. How could children learn without rows of wonderful books?

After writing an e-mail to ask her mother about the apartment lease, the first-edition novels, and to let her know that she was well, Iris began to review her father's operating plan. Though he'd never had much success in business, he had obviously labored over his projections. Almost everything seemed to be covered. Still, her father's thoroughness gave her little solace—she had no idea if the practical realities of running the center would stay aligned with his expectations.

Her breath tended to grow shallow when she was anxious, and Iris sought to slowly fill her lungs. The thought of the children's fates in her untested hands threatened to overwhelm her. Suddenly the responsibility of running the center seemed too much. She closed her eyes in an effort to relax, but couldn't as the strange sounds of the city made her long for home. She wanted to call her mother, though the differences in their time zones meant that by doing so, she'd awaken her.

Feeling trapped and alone, Iris stood up. Before she could stop herself, she blamed her father for placing her in this predicament. He'd always left her, and even in death he seemed to have abandoned her.

Iris thought of her childhood, of never knowing whether he'd be home to kiss her good night, and she felt old wounds reopen. She didn't want to feel herself bleed, and so she sat down again, sorting through résumés and notes, trying to determine whom she should hire as their teacher. But no matter how hard she attempted to focus, she couldn't step from the shadows of her past.

Iris was about to leave the room when steps echoed in the stairwell. She turned, surprised to see Noah. His shirt and pants were covered in dirt stains. His scar seemed more livid than usual. But his face bore what might have been the faintest of smiles.

"I've been thinking," he said, shifting his weight to his good leg.

"About what?"

"About what you said to me. How you were frustrated with not being able to get around."

"I am frustrated. Very."

Noah nodded, unused to the edge that her voice now contained. "Let me show you something," he said, turning toward the stairwell.

Iris followed him downstairs, wondering what was on his mind. Thien stood at the bottom of the steps, singing softly. She grinned. "Why are you so happy?" Iris asked.

"What a wonderful surprise Mr. Noah has for you."

"He does?"

Thien took her hand and together they followed Noah, who limped into the tiled entryway. Outside the gate a red scooter was parked. Noah turned, offering Iris a key. "The locals seem to do well on these," he said. "Seems like you might too."

Giggling, Thien reached forward to take the key and place it against Iris's palm. "He bought you a fast one, Miss Iris. A Honda. My brother has one just like it, and you are going to feel like a bird."

Iris looked at the silver key. "But . . . but I've never driven a—"

"Come here," Noah said, sitting down and grasping the handlebars. He maneuvered his prosthesis onto the black platform behind the front wheel. "Anyone can drive these. All you have to do is steer and twist the throttle."

The seat was large enough to accommodate them both and Iris sat behind him. Thien inserted the key and pushed the start button. The scooter instantly hummed to life. "You should name it," she said, stepping back.

Iris gripped a bar behind the seat. "Is it safe? Did you really buy it? For me?"

"We need to purchase a helmet," Thien answered. "But then you will be safe."

Noah twisted the throttle and the scooter edged forward. "Good-bye, Thien."

"Good-bye, Mr. Noah. Watch out for the big trucks."

Iris put her hands around Noah's waist as the scooter moved ahead and he lifted his good leg from the ground. She let out a gasp when he pulled into the alley and their speed increased. She'd never ridden a scooter or motorcycle, and felt as if the contraption might fall to one side or the other. "Have you done this before?" she asked, speaking into his ear.

"Nope. Not before today."

"Really?"

"Just trust me," he replied, approaching a busy street filled with hundreds of scooters. He signaled, slowing down, letting his good foot skip atop the pavement. They turned and merged into traffic, their speed increasing. Suddenly scooters were all around them, some just inches away. "See how everyone moves together?" he asked.

"Kind of."

They approached a roundabout and Noah circled to his right, moving in tandem with everyone about him. He drove a few more blocks and then turned toward her. "I'm going to teach you how to do this."

She loosened her grip on him, feeling slightly more comfortable. "I know. But not yet. You drive first. Take me somewhere and show me something."

He nodded, enjoying the freedom that the wheels gave him. For now, movement didn't bring him pain, and that simple fact caused him to further twist the throttle.

"Noah!" she said, as they seemed to skip forward.

"Hang on."

She laughed as they darted ahead. The city blurred around them, signs and shops and stalls merging into a flowing tapestry of color. In Noah's hands the scooter seemed to dance, to soar down the streets, to glide with a grace that Iris wouldn't have thought possible. Her hair flew behind her and wetness was pulled from the corners of her eyes. The wind whipped past, alive and potent. She held out her left arm and felt like a bird, rising against unseen forces, her body buffeted by billions of tiny fingers.

Noah turned, and the Saigon River was suddenly beside them. He raced along its contours, his shirt flapping against him. The scooter swayed to and fro beneath them as he weaved past slower scooters and cars. Iris laughed, having never felt such movement. She watched the river twist, saw children wave in her direction. She waved back, gripping Noah with her thighs and her right hand. She thought about her father, wondering if he'd ever sped along this same stretch of water. Perhaps he'd done so and remembered her.

Iris squeezed Noah's shoulder. She thanked him,

laughing as he nodded and increased their speed. Though she'd been free her whole life, she had never experienced freedom like this. She'd never flown across a foreign land, never felt as if she were a comet streaking through the heavens. "I'll try it," she said, surprising herself.

Noah slowed, pulling over to the curb, heedless of the chaos around them. "Let's see what you can do."

Soon Iris was driving. Soon she was laughing and soaring and her thousand pressing problems seemed so distant. At that moment all that mattered was that moment. Twisting back on the throttle, she watched the world become a blur and felt Noah's grip on her tighten.

⎯ TEN

A Path Leads Away

As Iris sat on her scooter, the city seemed to have sprouted a new dimension. In the bright light of late morning, she maneuvered down a wide boulevard, trying to mirror the speed and movements of nearby drivers. She'd bought a helmet and a face mask, and with these items in place, her confidence level had risen. Noah had been right—driving the scooter was remarkably easy. All she had to do was be on constant guard for other vehicles, which sometimes moved against the flow of traffic or sought to cross congested thoroughfares. People tended to signal with their arms, and Iris was learning how to anticipate sudden turns and changes in position.

The city seemed more alive than ever as she returned from visiting the French doctor, who had agreed to stop by the center later in the day to examine Tam. Through a pair of oversize sunglasses she watched fellow scooter drivers navigate the chaos with amazing expertise. People drove one-handed while talking on cell phones, holding infants before them, and balancing long rods on their shoulders. Women sometimes sat sidesaddle behind their husbands or boyfriends, their tight skirts making it impossible for them to straddle the seat. Strangers often spoke at stoplights or while driving, their handlebars a few inches apart.

Iris felt as if a unique cultural experience occurred on the back of scooters. She reflected that in America, people drove their cars and rarely even opened their windows. Within cars people tended to be isolated, listening to the radio or maybe talking on the phone to a friend. Cars were people's places of refuge, highly personalized sanctuaries within which Americans often sought escape. Driving a scooter in Vietnam was a completely different experience. In addition to the ease of conversation, the lack of lanes and laws almost mandated that people act in cooperation. Drivers didn't cut one another off or blast their horns. Though they drove quickly, always looking for the fastest route, if an old woman was trying to cross an impossibly busy street, people braked and weaved around her without a second glance. Or if someone was asking directions from another driver and slowing traffic, other scooters simply eased their way past the pair of sluggish vehicles. And amazingly, if a scooter was going the wrong way down the side of a street, no one seemed to get angry. They appeared to accept the fact that the person was trying to get from one place to another and was taking the best route possible.

Though she didn't understand why, Iris liked the combination of lawlessness and courtesy that seemed to permeate the streets. She'd always appreciated rules and rarely broke them, but now, much to her surprise, she liked the feeling that someone wasn't watching over her back, ensuring that she did everything properly. She felt liberated, and this sense of freedom was magnified by the little rocket beneath her. She'd never experienced such a satisfying set of sensations, not even when seeing her name in print.

A bell sounded ahead and a machine lowered a long bamboo pole across the street. Iris braked alongside those around her, moving like everyone else as close to the pole as possible. A horn sounded and a beat-up passenger train rumbled across the street. The engine belched thick black smoke skyward. A series of rusting and battered train cars followed the engine, clanging against one another as if each car were trying to move to the head of a line. Arms hung from open windows. Pieces of paper and other litter tumbled as the train swept past.

A man on a rusty scooter eased next to Iris. He was unusually large and wore a baseball jersey. A mole on his chin sprouted long black hairs. He didn't have a helmet, and his matted locks jutted out in a hundred different directions. Iris nodded to him and returned her gaze to the train, which had almost cleared the street. To her surprise, she felt a tap on her shoulder. She turned and realized that the man was leaning toward her. She wasn't sure what to do and said hello in Vietnamese.

"You go home," he replied in broken English. "Leave Vietnam."

Iris released the grip on her throttle. "What?"

"Children no want your help."

She shook her head. "I don't . . . I don't understand. What are you saying?"

"You go home! You understand?" He revved his engine and his scooter bumped into hers. "You leave Vietnam. If you stay, you get hurt!"

Her heart started to thump wildly, and she looked for a way to escape. But dozens of scooters encircled her. She glanced at him and saw that a drop of saliva hung from his lip. He seemed completely unaware of it. "Why are you telling me this?" she

271

asked, bending away from him, fear causing her voice to crack.

"You like your long hair? Maybe I cut it off next time we meet. Maybe I do more. You leave Vietnam soon and never come back. That safer for you. Very much safer." He revved his scooter again. "I see where you live. Understand? You no safe at your center!"

The bamboo pole began to swing upward and scooters edged forward. Exhaust spewed from behind them, covering Iris. Her hands trembling, she twisted her throttle and angled her scooter away from his. She tried to flee him, but he followed behind her, and she felt his scooter bump into hers. "Leave me alone!" she shouted, seeking to maneuver around those ahead of her.

"Go back to USA!"

Iris crossed the train tracks, her speed increasing. She turned too swiftly and her scooter brushed up against a schoolgirl's. For a terrifying second the scooters locked together. Then the girl managed to veer away. Suddenly the thought of crashing was worse than Iris's fear of the man behind her. She pulled to the curb, shaking violently. Turning around, she looked for her pursuer. But he was nowhere to be found. Somehow he'd disappeared.

She struggled to put down the kickstand and then leaned against a cement telephone pole, shaking uncontrollably. Running her hands through her hair, she imagined him cutting it off. His eyes had seemed to see through her, his body like a shadow covering her. She'd felt his evil as clearly as if it had been smoke that she'd drawn into her lungs. "Why?" she muttered, looking for him, afraid that he'd pop into view. The thought of him watching her in the center made her sick to her stomach.

A boy darted across the nearby street and she was reminded of the policeman's warning. Hadn't he told her that some children should be left alone? That people, bad people, might depend on them? Realizing that the man in the baseball jersey must be such a person, she got back on her scooter, still shaking. At least now she understood why he'd followed her. He was afraid of losing a child to her. Nothing more. Nothing less. But which child? And what could she do about it?

Resolving to talk with Thien, Noah, and the policeman, she glanced around once more, ensuring that he wasn't lurking nearby. With trembling hands, she twisted the throttle. The scooter drifted forward and again she was in the thick of traffic. Wanting to get back to the center as quickly as possible, she turned to the west, away from the river.

As Iris drove she did her best to calm her frayed nerves. She'd been threatened before—held at knifepoint in Chicago until her purse was emptied. She had survived that encounter and told herself that she'd survive this one. She just needed to be more careful, and to get more people invested in the success of her center. The policeman would help her. Noah and Thien would help her. She wasn't alone.

Iris knew that the man in the baseball jersey must have scared children in the exact manner that he'd scared her. And this knowledge made her angry. If he had frightened her so much that she'd almost wrecked her scooter, he must have given children nightmares. He might have even hurt them. And perhaps a child he'd hurt was going to come running through her doors.

"You won't shut me down," she whispered, imagining what such a child might have gone through. A threat wasn't going to make her abandon that child. Not when she had help and wasn't alone. Though Iris had never considered herself brave, she was going to be brave for the children. They needed her. And if she had to risk everything to help them, then that was a risk she was going to take. If she didn't take it, the children would suffer, and she'd have failed them like everyone else. And she wasn't going to fail them, or her father, or herself.

The center came into view and she expertly drove her scooter straight to its gate. As she stepped inside, she felt more connected to the building than ever. It had become her home. And no one was going to be forced from it.

NOAH PAUSED IN HIS WORK, GLANCING around the playground. Earlier that morning he'd sprinkled grass seed everywhere and covered it with a thin layer of dirt. He had also planted two trees deep in the soil beneath the chips of concrete. One was a head-high mango tree that he had positioned near the building. The other was a slightly larger banyan tree that he'd planted near the center of the playground. Thien had picked out the trees at a local market. She'd told him that the mango tree would provide healthy food for the children. And though she wasn't a Buddhist, she'd explained how Buddha was sitting beneath a banyan tree when he received his enlightenment. Surely such a tree would be good for children to seek shade under.

Turning around, Noah watched Thien speak with Mai and Minh as they watered the young trees. The children had returned not long after breakfast. Minh had won two dollars from Noah in Connect Four while Thien and Mai had spread more dirt atop the grass seed. Noah had been surprised to see the children again so soon, but Thien had seemed to expect them. She'd given them each a buttered croissant and fresh orange juice that she had squeezed at dawn.

Now, as Noah stood on his stone path and eyed the trio, he wondered what Thien and Mai were talking about. Each was laughing. Mai gestured animatedly, her hands appearing to speak. The girl had seemed sad the day before, Noah reflected. What had made her so happy?

Thien removed her cap and undid her ponytail. Her hair was much longer than Noah had realized. Straight and almost impossibly dark, it moved like water through her fingers. She fashioned a new ponytail, tied it up with a rubber band, and then inserted her hair through the hole in the back of her cap. She did all of this in a matter of seconds, but to Noah time seemed to move much slower.

Laughing at something Mai said, Thien removed a tangerine from her pocket. She began to peel it and after separating it into slices offered Mai and Minh a treat. Noah saw them accept, noting how Thien's bare arm glowed in the light. She smiled. She bit into the fruit. He watched her eat and he saw her, for the first time, not only as someone who was kind and pure, but as someone who was also beautiful and captivating. He wondered if his back and stump would ache were he to touch her naked body. He tried to imagine her contours, but her loose-fitting, paint-covered clothes covered up whatever curves she possessed.

She glanced in his direction, and he swung his gaze toward a pile of supplies that they'd bought the day before. Leaning against the fence was a long, wide board that he planned on using for the seesaw. Beside the board were two truck tires. Much smaller cuts of wood rested on the tires, as did a hand drill and a bag of nuts and bolts.

Two nights earlier, while he lay awake in bed trying to think of anything but his misery, he had envisioned how he might make a seesaw for Tam. A long board, he'd figured, could be mounted to truck tires, so that one tire went on each side of the board's middle. The tires would roll easily back and forth as children leapt upward. He could build an elephant on one end of the seesaw once it had been fashioned. Plywood would work well for the elephant's profile, which he'd cut carefully, and which would then be brought to life by Thien's paintbrush.

Noah walked to the main board, which was about ten feet long, a foot wide, and two inches thick. Without thinking, he lifted it from where it rested against the fence and tried to lower it to the ground. The board was heavy, and his prosthesis seemed to buckle beneath him. He fell awkwardly to his left, the board banging against the shin of his good leg. Pain was instantaneous, and Noah clenched his teeth, trying to remain silent.

Thien must have seen him fall. She handed the children the last of her slices and hurried toward him. Feeling feebler than ever, Noah struggled to his feet. Though certain that his shin was bleeding, he didn't lift his pant leg to inspect the wound. Instead he wiped a streak of fresh soil from his chin. "It's all right," he said when Thien reached out to him, putting her hand on his shoulder.

"Are you okay?" she asked, her face tight with concern.

"Just great. Never better."

"But, Mr. Noah, your leg, it must be—"

"Please . . . please call me Noah."

"That board is too heavy for you to lift alone. Next time please let me help you."

He studied her small frame, knowing that she was far sturdier than she appeared. He weighed twice as much as she did. He'd been in a war. He'd killed and saved. And yet he knew that she was stronger than he was, even though she was untested. "Next time I'll get you," he finally replied.

She rubbed his shoulder and then turned to Mai and Minh. "Will you help us?" she asked in English, wanting to include them.

Mai hurried over, eager to participate. "Sure, sure. What you making?"

Noah unconsciously rubbed his stump. "A surprise."

"If you no tell me what it is, how can I help?" she asked, frowning.

Minh moved beside Noah, glancing at his fake foot.

"Did you get run over by car?" Mai wondered. "Is that how you lose your leg? Or maybe a snake bite you?"

Noah was about to respond when Thien said something to Mai in Vietnamese. Mai dropped her gaze. "It's all right," Noah said, though he hated talking about the past, about his mistakes. Reliving his mistakes tended to make him despise himself, as if he bore all the blame for his suffering. "I fought in Iraq," he replied, wishing he could have a drink. "And a bomb took my leg."

Mai nodded. "I so sorry about your leg. I wish you still had two."

"Thanks."

"Minh and I watched George Bush's war on the television. Outside a store. We watch every day for a while. We saw so much. We no like war, but we watch. Sure, sure, we did. Anyway, why you no find those weapons of big destruction?"

Because they didn't exist, Noah thought. Because the goddamn war was a lie. The weapons didn't exist and Saddam was no more connected to al-Qaeda than my grandmother is. "We tried our best," he said. "But we shouldn't have gone." He reached again for the board, needing to change the subject.

Thien sought to help him turn the board onto its side. "What should we do with this, Mr. Noah?"

He let her hold the board while he grabbed one of the tires and dragged it over. "We're going to take some more wood and bolt it to this board, and then bolt on the tires." He dropped the tire and then gave the hand drill to Minh, hoping that he'd be able to turn it. "Can you drill a hole for me?" Noah asked, pointing to a spot on the tire's sidewall.

Minh nodded. He leaned forward, using his good hand to grasp the drill. He positioned it properly, then took the handle between his teeth. He bit it hard, placed his hand on the crank, and began to turn. It took only about a dozen turns for the drill to puncture the tire.

"Good work," Noah said. "Do you want to try?" he asked Mai.

Mai would have liked to turn the drill but saw that Minh was smiling. "No, no. Minh the Driller is better."

Minh put the handle between his teeth again. As he started to twist the crank, he glimpsed the shiny metal above Noah's fake foot. He shifted his gaze from the foot to the tire to the foot, wondering if he'd ever have a pretend hand. How wonderful that would be. No one would stare at him. No one would laugh. Wishing for such a hand, Minh continued to twist the crank until the hole was complete.

"That's great," Noah said. "Perfect." He took the drill from Minh, noticing that the boy was smiling.

"What next?" Mai asked. "More holes for Minh? He drill all day if you want. He be your assistant. And maybe I cut something with saw. We both happy to help. Sure, sure."

Despite a desire to wet his lips with whiskey, Noah smiled at her enthusiasm. He could see that she was happy for Minh, that she'd also noticed his grin. "You're good kids," he said, handing her a small block of wood.

"Of course we is," Mai replied. "You think we bad kids?"

"No, I don't," Noah replied, seeing the goodness in each, aware that they wanted to please him, that they wanted to be loved. He handed Mai a saw and told her how the block should be cut. Then he gave the drill back to Minh. Thien started to sing softly as she held the tire for Minh.

Noah looked at the three Vietnamese. He looked at the playground. He saw the two little trees and knew that someday they'd grow to shade most of the area. Children would run beneath the trees. They'd climb up and over worn branches. They'd leap from the grass to his path. And a place that he'd built would help them be exactly who they were meant to be—children who laughed and learned and loved to play.

Whatever happened to him, the playground would flourish, lingering when he no longer did. It would bring happiness to those who deserved it most. Children would smile here. They'd be safe here. And that was something. No matter what became of his life, he'd done something good. Nothing—not pain or lies or sorrow—could ever take that from him. He'd build a playground. It would have swings and slides and the greatest seesaw the world had ever known.

When the playground was complete, Noah would sit outside, close his eyes, and just listen. And the sounds he heard would always remain with him, no matter where he went, no matter what fate had in store. He'd remember the laughter and know that he hadn't failed completely, that his life carried some meaning. And though his misery might ultimately overwhelm him, he'd have left his mark on the world, and could depart it with this one sense of pride.

Ever since Iris had told her that a French doctor would arrive later in the day to examine Tam, Qui had struggled to entertain Tam and clean the dormitory. Qui's mind was as restless as storm-driven clouds. Fear and hope dominated all other emotions. To push away the fear, she prayed incessantly for a miracle. Maybe the last doctor was wrong. Maybe this new doctor would say that Tam could recover. Qui begged Buddha for such news. She promised that she'd give her sight, her very life, for such news.

As Tam slept, Qui mopped the tile floor. Nervousness caused her stomach to ache and cramp, and she often hurried to the toilet. She hated not being near Tam, and she always returned from the bathroom as quickly as possible. Upon seeing Tam, she went back to her mop and her thoughts. The mop moved and stopped in her sunspotted hands as she alternated between work and prayer.

When she finished cleaning the floor, Qui sat beside Tam and watched her chest rise and fall. Tam slept in her new pajamas with her doll held near her face. Her beloved blanket was wrapped around her other hand. Sometimes Tam made soft noises that sounded like the coos of a pigeon. Qui wondered if she was dreaming or if her pains even plagued her sleep. For the ten thousandth time, she wished that she could trade places with her grand-daughter. She wanted to take Tam's pain and make it her own, to take what strength remained in her and somehow infuse it into Tam's dying bones.

Tam moaned softly, prompting Qui's eyes to fill with tears. She felt her stomach clench again but resisted the urge to rush to the toilet. Please, sweet Buddha, she prayed, please let the French doctor say good things. Please give me one more miracle. Give me this miracle and I'll never ask anything of you again. Please.

"Little Bird?" Tam asked, yawning.

"Yes?"

"I like . . . this soft bed."

"Me too. Especially sharing it with you."

"Is Momma here?"

"She's coming, my precious child. She's almost done with her work in Thailand and then she'll come."

"She works hard."

"Too hard, maybe. But that's because she loves you so much."

"How much?"

"Like . . . like boys love a soccer ball."

Tam smiled, stroking her doll's hair. "Dung couldn't sleep. She kept waking me up."

"She did?"

"She was cold."

Qui looked at the ceiling fan, which wobbled as it spun. "Are you cold?"

"Not as cold as Dung."

After pulling up the sheet to Tam's chin, Qui stroked her granddaughter's forehead and then stood. Despite the heat, she turned off the fans and closed the windows. Qui was about to return to Tam when steps and voices echoed in the stairwell. Her stomach rumbled and she bent over, clutching her side. She wanted to remain and greet their visitor, but suddenly had no choice but to hurry to the toilet. She tried not to moan as her body convulsed, her hand pressing against a nearby wall.

After gathering her will and strength, Qui stepped from the bathroom and saw a Western man sitting at the end of Tam's bed. He turned in Qui's direction, rising.

"*Bonjour*," he said quietly.

"Hello," she replied in English.

"Are you Qui?"

"Yes."

The doctor motioned her forward. "The others left us alone. Everyone thought this matter should be private. Is this acceptable to you?"

"Yes."

He turned to Tam, who was now wide-awake. "*Bonjour*, Tam. My name is Henri, and I am a doctor. I would like to look at you. Is that fine?"

Tam glanced at Qui, who nodded. Henri smiled and moved closer to Tam, sitting beside her. He pulled back the sheet until her torso was revealed. For more than a minute he simply sat and gazed at her body. Qui watched his eyes as he studied Tam, her heart thumping wildly. She thought she might faint.

Henri carefully lifted Tam's arm and pulled back her sleeve. The exposed flesh seemed to be little more than fabric that tightly surrounded bone. Tam's elbow was puffy and swollen. Removing a stethoscope from his blue backpack, the doctor listened to her stomach, heart, and lungs. "Can you breathe deeply?" he asked, patting her shoulder. "A deep breath would make me so happy."

Tam tried to do what he asked but started to cough.

"*Merci,*" he said, patting her again, continuing to listen to her lungs.

Seeing the discomfort on Tam's face, Qui slumped unsteadily. She leaned against a nearby bunk bed, praying.

"Does your head hurt?" Henri asked, using a small flashlight to peer into her eyes.

"Yes."

"Where else does it hurt?"

Tam ran her fingers along her arms and legs.

"In your bones?" he asked.

"Yes."

Qui saw a sigh escape his lips and her world began to collapse.

Henri found Tam's spleen and pressed down lightly. "Does this hurt?"

"Ooh."

"I'm sorry," he said, removing his hand, aware that the other doctor's prognosis was correct. This girl is dying, he thought. This beautiful little girl, who might have been saved if her grandmother could have afforded early treatment, is being devoured by leukemia. She seems brave and strong, but she'll soon die all the same.

Henri swore silently. He would take some blood, just to be certain. But he knew what the tests would say. "Does the medicine help?" he asked.

"Medicine?"

"Do the pills make you feel better?"

"Yes."

"Good. Please keep taking them." He looked at her doll. "What is her name?"

"Dung."

"She is lovely. Just like you."

Tam smiled faintly, feeling tired and wanting to sleep again. "Thank you, Mr. Doctor."

"I am going to talk to your grandmother for a minute. And then I will return tomorrow and take a little bit of your blood. Is that all right, Miss Tam?"

"Just a little?"

"*Oui.*"

"*Oui?*"

"I'm sorry. Yes, just a little blood." Henri patted

her shoulder again and stood up. He motioned for Qui to follow him into the stairwell. Though her legs didn't seem to work properly, she did her best to stand tall in case Tam was watching. She followed the Westerner as he entered the stairwell and took a few steps down. When he turned to her, and she saw the bleakness of his stare, she thought that she'd fall.

"May I take her blood?" he asked. "I will return tomorrow."

"That okay."

"I will do some tests." His lips pressed together momentarily. "I'm sorry, but I am most certain that, indeed, she has childhood leukemia. Her spleen and liver are enlarged. I believe she has a mass in her lungs. And the pain in her bones . . . that means the cancer is in her marrow . . . deep inside where we cannot stop it."

Qui reached for the handrail, her eyes like leaking dams, tears racing to be the first down her face. "Please, Mr. Henri. I ask Buddha for miracle. Please give one to me. Please . . . please . . . please give me one. She is too young. Too good. Her mother leave her. Her father is dead. But she so good. Please tell me about miracle. Please, kind sir."

Henri reached into his pocket and removed a clean handkerchief, which he gave to her. "I'll bring more medicine, to take her pain away. But it's too late, much too late, to do anything else.

Removing all her cancer would be like . . . like trying to remove all the water from Vietnam. It cannot be done. I'm sorry."

The doctor continued to speak, but Qui no longer heard his words. He was nothing but a blur before her. She sobbed quietly, holding on to the handrail, falling to her knees, struggling to breathe. He knelt beside her, but she barely saw him. Instead she saw Tam, saw a time when sickness hadn't found her, saw a perfect baby girl who laughed deliriously as fingers tickled her belly.

Qui gasped, felt herself fading, and then sought to pull herself together, as Tam still needed her. She squeezed the doctor's hand. She didn't pray for strength as she might normally have done. Buddha was no longer a part of her world. She hated him for leaving Tam, for never giving her anything. She hated him for the unfairness of life, for how it brought some such joy and others such misery.

Instead of praying, Qui forced herself to stand. The walls spun about her and she shut her eyes. She moaned, trying to gather her wits. The doctor said something, but a buzz filled her ears. She'd never heard this buzz before, the sound like air escaping from a small hole in a balloon. She wiped her eyes and face, and took several deep breaths. Nodding to whatever the doctor was saying, she turned and wearily climbed the steps.

Tam hadn't moved, and Qui lay beside her,

holding her tight. She kissed Tam's head. More tears threatened to dampen Qui's cheeks, but she wouldn't let them arrive. Instead, she helped her granddaughter roll to her side, so that Tam's eyes couldn't see her own. Qui moved until their bodies curved against each other. "Did you like him?" she asked, her voice calm even while her thoughts spiraled into the darkest of places.

Tam stroked Dung's hair, wondering about the world with all of the happy children. She'd heard about this world so many times, and was ready for its beautiful rivers, its countless gardens. She was tired. She wanted to see her father again and to walk near the ocean. She wanted to listen to him laugh as she told him the story about the small fish.

Hearing Qui cry quietly behind her, Tam handed her Dung. "She'll sleep with you, Little Bird. She loves you . . . just as much as I do."

"She does?"

"I told her how you . . . carry me on your back. How you take me places. She said you must love me very much . . . to do that."

"I do. You know I do."

Tam edged even closer against Qui. "Maybe in the new world . . . I'll carry you."

"Really?"

"I'll try."

"Will you . . . will you promise me to do that, my sweet Tam?"

"Yes."

"Please . . . promise me that. Please."

"You can ride on my back. Dung and I will take you everywhere."

Qui subdued a sob, pressing her face into the pillow. "We'll go there . . . soon. I'll be right beside you. And then you . . . you'll carry me. And we'll see such beautiful things together."

"Like what?"

"Like mountains. And dragons. And a sun that doesn't set."

"I'll carry you, Little Bird. You'll never have to walk."

Qui kissed the back of Tam's head. "We won't ever leave each other." She wiped a tear from her cheek. And though she'd cursed Buddha just a few minutes earlier, she found herself praying once again, praying that Tam would carry her in the new world, that Tam's feet would barely strike the ground. "Would you like me to tell you a story?" she asked, rallying her strength, kissing Tam again.

"Yes."

"About what, my sweet child?"

"About a beautiful place . . . that I'll carry you to. Could you please tell me . . . about that? About a place we'll see together?"

ELEVEN

A Time for Offerings

On the center's roof, the day began like most any other. Geckos sat still until insects moved before them. Patches of black mold and green lichen clung to exposed concrete, glistening with dew. Spiders the size of skipping stones hid in cracks and nooks, aware that birds might drop from the sky. In small puddles, mosquito larvae twisted and grew. The rooftop was its own ecosystem, having been practically untouched for many years.

Yet on this morning the rooftop had changed. Qui, Tam, Thien, Iris, and Noah sat on a tarp that Thien had spread out to create a picnic area on the roof. The tarp was covered with a red tablecloth, several bouquets of tropical flowers, and platters bearing fruits and Chinese dumplings. At the edges of the tarp, Thien had arranged a variety of pillows upon which people now sat. She had placed the tarp so that Tam could rest with her back against the short wall that rose above the edge of the roof. By positioning pillows all around Tam's spot, Thien had made a couch of sorts.

As the residents of the center ate together, Iris tried to hide her sorrow. The previous night, upon

Qui informing her of the doctor's prognosis, Iris had gone to her computer and started researching childhood leukemia. While Noah had also searched on the computer beside her, she'd visited dozens of medical sites and support groups, looking for possible cures to such a late-stage diagnosis. What she'd found, or didn't find, had left her in tears. Unless the blood work revealed some sort of miracle, Tam was going to die.

Never had Iris felt as helpless and frustrated as she did now. She didn't understand how humanity could put a man on the moon and could split the atom, but couldn't solve the horrors of cancer. She was angered that billion-dollar sports stadiums existed when children like Tam were dying all over the world. The priorities of her fellow citizens made her question the sanity of her own species. How, she asked herself, could people own yachts and planes and five-carat rings while Tam was living and dying on the street?

Aware that Tam's eyes had drifted to her, Iris made herself smile. "Do you like it up here?"

Tam nodded. "It beautiful. I lucky to be here."

"We're lucky to have you," Iris replied, nibbling on a slice of star fruit. "You're our first student, Tam. And that's very special."

Thien stood up and reached for her Polaroid. "We should have a picture, Miss Iris," she said. "A picture for our wall. Of the three of you and our first student."

"Of me?" Tam asked, surprised.

"You're the star," Iris said, moving beside Tam, as did Qui and Noah.

Thien waited until Tam lifted up her doll so that Dung would also be in the photo. "Now smile," Thien said, raising the camera's viewfinder to her eye. "Smile like you are listening to Mr. Noah sing."

"Hey," Noah said, aware that Thien was trying to infuse the moment with a happiness that didn't exist. "My voice isn't so bad."

"Oh, really? Then maybe you could sing us a song? Stand up and dance and sing us a song?"

Tam grinned at the thought of Mr. Noah dancing, and as she did, Thien took a photo. A square white sheet rolled out of her camera and she held it carefully, waving it in the air. "I think Tam does not believe you, Mr. Noah," she said, smiling. "I think she believes that elephants could fly better than you could dance and sing."

"For sure," Tam said, still grinning.

"Well, maybe tonight I'll prove you wrong," Noah replied.

Iris nudged him with an elbow. "Do you know that I saw him sing once? In high school? He was in a play and he sang with a pretty girl."

"Really?" Thien asked. "Was he good?"

"Actually, he was."

Thien looked at Tam. "Maybe elephants can fly."

Tam's smile widened. "Maybe."

"Stop it, you two," Noah said, relieved that Tam no longer looked to be in pain.

Thien blew on the photo. "Oh, how beautiful you are," she said, handing the picture to Tam. "Like a piece of the sky that has fallen down to us."

Tam saw herself and she smiled. "Dung look pretty."

"Not as pretty as you," Iris replied, peering at the photo. "We'll have to frame this and hang it in the entryway, so everyone can see our first student."

Qui, who'd barely taken her eyes off of Tam during the entire exchange, squeezed her granddaughter's hand. "You are beautiful," she said in Vietnamese.

"Dung is so happy," Tam replied, still looking at the photo.

"Why?"

"Because she has a family."

"Yes, she does. And so do you."

Tam nodded. A spasm of pain deep in her hips caused her smile to fade. But she didn't moan. "I'm also happy today."

"You are?"

"I like my family."

Qui squeezed Tam's hand again. "And they like you."

"Can I go to sleep here?"

"Of course, my precious child. Close your eyes if you're tired."

Tam nestled into her pillows, pulling Dung to her

chest. A horn sounded somewhere below. Even three stories above the ground, the buzz of traffic persisted, like static from a radio.

Iris saw that Tam was falling asleep. "Thien," she said softly, "maybe you could tell Qui more about our plans for the center. I'm going to talk to Noah for a minute."

"Of course, Miss Iris."

Noah rose awkwardly from his pillow and followed Iris to the far side of the roof. Iris leaned against the hip-high wall, studying the city below. "It makes me sick that we can't help her," she said. "Just sick."

"I know."

"Is there anything we missed? Anything at all?"

Noah absently watched scooters gather at a stoplight, wishing that Tam could be fixed, that her parts were replaceable. "I don't think so. Unless the new blood work gives us a miracle, she's going . . . Tam's going to die." Noah's own words seemed to weigh him down. He remembered carrying her through the rain, remembered how she'd clung to him as if he were her father. "I've got a friend in medical school," he said, "and I e-mailed him about it. But I don't expect good news."

"It's not right," Iris replied, glancing at Tam. "All she needed was treatment. But how could she receive treatment when she lives on the street?" She wiped her eyes. "Damn it, Noah. Why do we live in a world where little girls are allowed to die?

With all our wealth, why does there have to be so much suffering?"

Noah reached into his pocket and removed a flask of whiskey. He took a swallow and grimaced as it burned his insides. He suddenly needed the whiskey as much as he needed air. Without it he'd suffocate.

"I once read Darwin," Iris said, not looking at him. "His laws . . . they shouldn't apply today. It shouldn't be only the fittest who survive."

"Some things never seem to change."

"They should."

He nodded. "And they could. At least, I think so."

"How?" she asked, turning to him.

"It's just my opinion. Something I've thought about since Iraq."

"Tell me, Noah."

He sipped his whiskey, Tam still dominating his thoughts. "Well, try to imagine this. What if the trillion dollars we've spent in Iraq had instead been spent on something else?"

"I'm listening."

"What if that money had been given to the world's poor? If thousands of schools and hospitals had been built around the globe? If millions of people had been fed? Do you think we'd be hated then?"

"I don't know. I suppose not as much."

"That's right. Because we'd be saving little girls

like Tam. And people don't hate a country that's out saving little girls."

She remembered her father saying something similar. "What about the worst of them? Who hate us the most?"

"The worst of the worst . . . we have to destroy. But we'd be better off helping the rest." Noah shifted his weight, trying to get comfortable, glancing at Tam. "Remember that big earthquake in Pakistan? That killed thousands?"

"Sure."

"What do you think would have happened if the U.S. had pledged a billion dollars to help rebuild those cities? If Bush had flown over there and lifted a shovel and started to dig? Do you think so many Pakistanis would hate us today?"

"No."

"Hell, no. They'd love us. We'd be heroes. At least to most of them. And the world would be a much better place. But that didn't happen, because those cowards . . . those pathetic little cowards in Washington would rather drop their goddamn smart bombs than build schools."

Iris studied his face, having never heard him speak so much, or felt such passion in his voice. "You think it's as simple as that?"

"After you open your center, how do you think people around here are going to feel about Americans? They're going to feel good about us. It's as simple as that. And we had the same chance with the tsunami. It killed two hundred and fifty thousand people, many of them Muslims, and we really didn't do that much to help."

Iris remembered seeing images of the tsunami on the television. Noah was right—the story had quickly gone away. "Why isn't there . . . more outrage about what happened in Iraq?"

He shrugged. "I don't know. Maybe because the lies keep coming. And people like me . . . we eat them up."

Iris moved closer to him. "You've got a lot to be proud of, Noah. You didn't—"

"I'm proud of those I served with. Of my friend Wes. I wish he were here . . . right now. He'd help us so much. He'd smile and he'd work. And he shouldn't have died in Iraq. Not in that worthless Humvee."

"Did he believe in what he was doing?"

Noah turned toward her, the scene of traffic below changing to a view of her face. "There's nothing noble about how he died, Iris. He was blown to pieces. And his little boy . . . he'll never hear his father's laugh. He'll grow up without him, never knowing how wonderful he was."

"I'm so sorry."

"You know . . . all those goddamn politicians should see what happens when a smart bomb lands in a neighborhood. I saw that once." Noah took another drink. "Jesus," he muttered, remembering the mayhem, the sirens, the wounded woman frantically digging for her child—a lifeless child whom Noah helped pull from the wreckage. "If they were on the ground to see that . . . their thinking would change. And maybe little girls like Tam wouldn't be left alone to die."

"Please don't say that. About Tam."

He felt the whiskey numbing him but couldn't stop himself from taking another drink. He needed to escape. "But most people don't think like that," he continued, glancing again in Tam's direction, his mind never far from her. "I didn't until I lost my leg. But I do now. And I wish that more people did. Because we're going to bury that sweet little girl. Bury her before she ever had a chance to live."

"I don't . . . I don't want to bury her, Noah," Iris replied, tears welling in her eyes. "Please tell me we won't have to."

He looked skyward, wishing that he believed in miracles. "I think all we can do now is . . . make sure that her last days are good ones. Let's try to give her some joy. Something to smile about."

"I'm so afraid for her."

"I know."

She swayed unsteadily. Her legs trembled. Her chest hurt. "Will you help me do that for her? Give her some joy?"

"Of course."

Iris looked at Tam. "Will you also pray for her? Right now?"

He shook his head. "I don't believe in God. Or I hate him. I'm not sure which."

"Please, Noah. Please pray for her. Do that for me."

He saw the pain in her face, and he wanted to soften it. "I'll pray for her," he said, even though his prayers never seemed to be heard and he no longer asked for anything.

Iris squeezed his arm. "Thank you." She then closed her eyes and started begging for miracles.

THE SLEEK NEW DEPARTMENT STORE WOULD have attracted customers in any city in any country. The white walls glistened as if covered in fresh snow. The mahogany floors were polished and partly covered with Oriental rugs. Piles of carefully folded sheets, blankets, and pillowcases rose like a city of fabric skyscrapers. Neatly dressed salespeople were eager to help hesitant customers. And tumbling from unseen speakers, Christmas music reminded shoppers of the joy of giving.

After making sure that Tam was comfortably resting in the dormitory, Noah and Iris had spent much of the morning at Ben Thanh Market buying bedding for twenty girls. But Iris hadn't liked the pillowcases available, as they were coarse and uncomfortable, so they'd driven to the department store and quickly filled her shopping bag.

Neither Iris nor Noah had spoken much. Both were upset about Tam. Uncharacteristically, Iris didn't smile at passersby. Noah repeatedly reached for his whiskey flask, despite a sense of lethargy that rendered him senseless to nearly everything but misery. At one point Iris snapped at him for bringing the flask, angry that young shopkeepers might see him drinking. Noah had taken a sip after her rebuke.

Iris paid for the pillowcases and stepped from the air-conditioned store into the tropical sun. One world was so different from the other. Beads of sweat appeared almost instantly on Noah's brow. He wiped them away and walked to Iris's scooter, where he lashed her purchases to a rack behind the seat.

"Be careful with those," she said as he pressed down on the pillowcases.

"Do you want them to fly away?"

"No, but I don't want you to ruin them either."

"I'm not ruining anything."

"Really?" she asked, loosening the straps.

"And if money is so short, why'd you buy silk pillowcases?"

"Because I want those girls to get a good night's sleep. Isn't that obvious?"

He leaned down to rub his aching stump. "Obvious? No, it's not. But I'm glad that you've got it all figured out."

Iris was about to respond when a whistle sounded to her right. She glanced toward the store's entrance and saw a security guard who appeared to be holding a boy by his ear. The boy didn't struggle, though he rose to his tiptoes. A girl started yelling at the security guard. As she yelled, a box tumbled from the boy's hand, red and black plastic pieces scattering.

Turning to Noah, Iris said, "Isn't that—"

He saw what she saw, and the sight of Minh in pain caused Noah to hurriedly limp forward. "Stop!" he shouted, reaching out, soon looming over the security guard.

The local looked up and spoke angrily in Vietnamese. He released his grip on Minh, who was pulled from danger by Mai. As the guard continued to rant at Noah, Iris arrived and stood protectively in front of the children. "What happened?" she asked Mai.

"We only ask customer to play game."

"That's it?"

"Sure, sure. Nothing else."

Noah swayed unsteadily on his good leg. "Why did you grab his ear?" he asked the guard, his voice loud, his anger over Tam's illness threatening to overwhelm him.

"You in Vietnam," the guard replied, standing his ground. "You speak Vietnamese!"

"I'll speak whatever I—"

"That's enough, Noah," Iris interrupted. "We need to leave. Now."

Noah glared at the guard, aware of the children's tears. "You don't ever touch them again. You hear me?"

"Next time I call police," the guard replied. He turned toward Mai and Minh and spoke in Vietnamese, his voice much louder than the nearby traffic.

The children lowered their heads, avoiding his eyes. He continued to lecture them, then kicked one of the game pieces into the street. Before Noah could respond, the guard stepped back into the store.

A taxi nearly ran over the piece before Noah managed to retrieve it. Minh stooped to collect the remainder of the pieces while Iris held Mai's hand. "What did he say to you?" Iris asked, wiping a tear from Mai's cheek.

Mai shook her head slowly. "He . . . he say all street children the same. He say . . ."

"What? What, Mai?"

"He say we all garbage. Should be put into a dump forever."

"Oh, Mai, you know that's not true," Iris said, hugging Mai while Noah moved beside Minh.

Mai thought about sleeping next to garbage, about eating garbage. She wondered if the guard was right. "He say what he believe. Not first time we hear this."

Iris dropped to her knees. "You speak two languages, Mai. You're smart and you're beautiful. And just because you've lived on the street doesn't mean that you can't do wonderful things."

"She's right," Noah said. "She's right and he's wrong."

"No, you wrong!" Mai replied, tired of trying to run from the truth. "You say I do wonderful things. What? You think I become doctor or movie star? Or maybe I be president? That man . . . he right. He say only what everyone think."

"We don't think that," Noah said.

"What I care what you think? Maybe you gone tomorrow, go back to America. That man, he here always."

"But—"

"And today we have no games. Minh win nothing. And tonight, how we give five dollar to Loc? If we no give him five dollar, he hurt us." She thought of Loc pressing her face into the water, and her tears increased.

"Who's Loc?" Iris asked, again wiping Mai's face.

"No one. Everyone."

"Who is he, Mai?"

"He big man. We pay him five dollar each day. He protect us. But he also hurt us. I very afraid of him. Sure, sure, I am."

Minh moved to Mai's side, offering her his stump, which she grasped.

"Where do you sleep, Mai?" Iris asked.

"Under bridge. In basket."

Iris stood up, placing her hands on Mai's shoulders. "Would you like to live with us? In our center?"

"But your center only for girls. I never leave Minh."

"But we could find another center for Minh. We could—"

"No!"

"There must be someplace he can—"

"No!"

Noah saw the pain in Mai's face and was reminded of his own sufferings. "Wait," he said, as she turned away. "What if . . . you lived in the center and . . . and Minh lived with me, in a nearby apartment?"

Mai wasn't sure that she'd heard him correctly. "With you?"

"That's right. Maybe he could study with you, but live with me. At least for now."

"But Loc. Sure, sure, he be angry. He look for us."

Iris glanced at Noah, thinking of the man who'd threatened her. She'd told Noah about the man, and wanted to tell the policeman. Now it sounded as if they had two such men to worry about.

"I'll handle Loc," Noah replied.

"You no understand," Mai said, seeming to shrink. "He hurt us if we no pay."

Noah took a step closer to her. "Then we'll pay him. We'll find him and give him enough money to leave you alone."

Mai dropped Minh's stump and took Noah's hands in her own. "You can do this? No lie? You can pay Loc, and I can stay in center, and Minh can stay with you?"

"That's exactly what we'll do," Iris said. "And you can do something for us. Something important."

"What?"

"There's a girl in our center, a very sick girl. You met her. Remember? You can be her friend. You can learn at our school and be her friend."

Mai had never been asked by an adult to do anything other than earn money. At first, she didn't know how to respond. Then she thought of living at the center, of helping the sick girl, of Minh staying with the nice American. And these thoughts, which were gifts almost beyond her ability to imagine, prompted her to smile. "Thank you," she said, squeezing Noah's hands. "Thank you so much." She wiped her face of tears and grinned. "And Minh thank you too. Later you see. He let you win game and then you know how happy he is."

Iris wiped away a tear that Mai had missed. "We need you, Mai. You can help us. You really can."

"Sure, sure?" Mai asked. "We stay with you? We no worry about Loc?"

"Sure, sure," Iris replied, smiling.

Noah looked into the store. "Let's go in there. Let's buy you a pretty dress. We'll show him who you really are."

Mai's grin wavered, but Minh moved toward Noah and nodded, eager to see Mai in such a dress.

"For me?" Mai asked. "But . . . but maybe dress too pretty."

Iris glanced at Noah, surprised and pleased by his idea. "Every girl needs a pretty dress, Mai. Especially if she's going to make a new friend." Iris put her arms around the children. "Let's go find you both something," she said, moving toward the store. "And then we'll take you home."

As Mai answered excitedly, Noah turned about, looking for a man called Loc, wondering if the man could be bought. Most people could be bought. But what if Loc wasn't such a person? What if he came for the children?

Noah reached for his flask and took a small sip. He didn't want a confrontation. But Mai wanted to laugh. And Minh wanted to learn. And Noah was going to take whatever steps necessary to let them do both.

NIGHT HAD NEARLY FALLEN BY THE time Noah and Thien drove toward the bridge, which was in a putrid, rotting part of the city. Squat buildings loomed like old tombstones over the rutted street. Half-dead trees sprouted from planters alongside weeds and lonely flowers. Iron gates protected the wares of filthy shops, enclosing engines, axles, bricks, and vats of oil and diesel fuel.

The unlit street twisted like a serpent, vacant but for occasional scooters. Thien followed this serpent, deft with the handlebars of Iris's scooter, unworried by the darkness. Noah sat behind her, peering ahead. He couldn't believe that Mai and

Minh walked this street and slept nearby. Despite recent rains, the entire area smelled as if it hadn't been cleaned in a thousand years.

"Do you think we'll find him?" Noah asked, his voice rising above the purr of the scooter.

"Do not worry. They have not paid him for today. And so he will be there."

"Will this work?"

"Sometime, Mr. Noah, I hope you can see the beauty of Vietnam. Now all you see is an old street. But Vietnam has green mountains, white beaches, and beautiful temples."

"Tell me about your village."

"My village?" Thien avoided an immense pothole, maneuvering the scooter as if it were a part of her. "My village is in a valley next to a wide river. It often floods, so all of the homes are on stilts. In the shade beneath the homes, women sew, children play. My father's rice field is not far away. It is so lovely, Mr. Noah. Rows of green stalks, water reflecting the blue sky. When I see it, I always sing."

Noah heard the happiness in her voice and experienced a brief pang of jealousy. How lucky she was to love such simple things. "Do you miss it?" he asked, her ponytail flopping against his chin as they hit a bump.

"I miss my family the most. My brothers and my sisters. But I always go home to help my father with the harvest. And then my mother and I talk all

308

night. And she knows that I am not so far away."

The buildings on either side of the road vanished. Noah glanced to his right and saw the silhouette of a river. A bridge appeared before them. "Is this it?" he asked.

"Yes."

"Are you scared?"

"No. But I have heard of this man. This man who wears the baseball shirt and . . . and makes children his slaves. We will have to be careful."

"Is this smart? Maybe we should be going to the police."

"I will tell Sahn of what we have done. And I think he will approve."

Noah studied the bridge. "Please translate for me."

She drove up on a sidewalk that ran alongside the river. Switching the ignition and headlamp off, she used a chain to lock the scooter to a nearby lamppost. "He will not be happy about losing Mai and Minh," she said. "But the money should be enough to change his mind."

"Let's find him."

Thien left the sidewalk. She walked to the end of the bridge and entered a labyrinth of shanties that teemed about the area like flies on a dead bird. The shanties were dark and mostly silent. Somewhere an infant cried.

Staying close to the bridge, Thien moved toward the river. Noah noticed that she walked slowly, allowing him the time to navigate the treacherous footing. To his amazement she started to sing, bringing life to a song that he'd often heard emanate from her lips. If she was afraid, she didn't outwardly show it.

The rutted trail that they followed twisted under the bridge. Something large passed above, for the bridge rumbled ominously. After a few more steps they circumvented a woman asleep on a torn section of carpet. Noah carefully eyed his surroundings, reminded of searching for insurgents in the slums of Baghdad. Those nights he'd held an assault rifle and walked beside men and women whose bravery had often seemed limitless.

Glad that he no longer carried a weapon, but feeling vulnerable without one, Noah looked for a man in a Yankees jersey, a man who shoveled fear into the hearts of Mai and Minh. Discerning anything in the darkness was difficult. The only light came from a fire near the water. Several figures surrounded the flames, talking quietly.

Noah tried to avoid broken glass, splintered wood, trash, and sleeping people. Mostly men seemed present, though a few women and children lay atop makeshift beds. A cat hissed from the nearby shanties. Someone coughed. The scent of decay seemed to be a living creature that permeated each molecule of oxygen.

Thien walked to the river's edge. The fire and those surrounding it were about five paces away.

Noah studied the group, realizing that they were using pointed sticks to roast meat above the flames.

"He isn't here," Noah said, his voice carrying into the distance.

"Then we will wait."

And so they waited. After a few minutes, they walked to the fire. Two men and a woman held long sticks, taking care not to drop their meals into the flames. Their clothes were patched and ragged, but remarkably clean. Thien looked at the oldest man. "Hello," she said in Vietnamese.

The man had never seen a foreigner under the bridge. He guessed from Noah's clothes that he was American. The man remembered the war with fondness, for he'd enjoyed driving Americans around Saigon. Those had been the best days of his life. "Yes?" he finally replied.

"So sorry to interrupt you, but we are looking for someone."

"And who is that?"

"Someone named Loc."

The older man's gaze dropped to the fire. "He's here."

"He is? Where?"

From the shadows stepped a large man, his arms crossed in front of his Yankees jersey, as if he were cold. Thien saw the ugly mole on his chin and raised her eyes to his. She was aware of Noah moving closer to her, of his hand reaching for hers, but she was unresponsive. So this is what a monster looks like, she thought, disgusted by the sight of Loc, but hiding her emotions.

"Where are they?" Loc asked in Vietnamese, his arms unfolding. The grip of opium had left his body several hours before. He'd been searching for Mai and Minh ever since, his anger growing as the day aged.

"Who?" Thien answered.

"Who else? The half boy and the girl."

Thien sensed his breath befouling her. It was the breath of a cobra, full of poisons and death. "Mai and Minh are safe," she replied, hating him.

His nostrils flared. His bloodshot eyes widened. "You think you can steal from me?"

"We—"

"From me?"

"We've come to make a trade."

"What trade?"

"Two hundred and fifty American dollars. We'll give you that if you promise not to come near them. And in six months we'll give you another two hundred and fifty."

Loc glanced at her pockets and then the American's pockets. He thought about robbing them but decided that no need existed. Promises could always be broken. He edged forward at the prospect of so much money. With it he could indulge in high-priced women and light his pipe for days on end. His gaze drifted back to Thien, and for the first time he noticed her beauty. "How much for you?" he asked, wanting to blow smoke on her naked body.

Thien stiffened. "I am not for sale."

"Everything has a price. Everything. Now name yours."

Though she wanted to turn away, to spare herself from further insults, Thien remained still. To turn from him would endanger Mai and Minh. "Do you want the money or not?"

Noah saw Thien's jaw tighten. "What's happening?" he asked, eager to help her but feeling powerless.

She looked at him, wondering how he could be so good when her countryman was so bad. "We are negotiating," she replied, aware that the truth shouldn't be told.

Noah reached into his pocket and removed a stack of bills. "Maybe this will speed things along," he said, flashing the money to Loc.

Having never seen such wealth, Loc stepped toward the American. "Take the girl," he said in Vietnamese.

Thien shook her head. "The deal is for Mai and Minh. Not just one."

"I need him. And he's only a half boy. He's—"

"Both of them. We'll take both of them. You hear me?"

Loc glanced again at the money. "Then have the half boy too."

313

"And you stay away from them," Thien said. "And in six months we'll come back with more."

"You'd better," he replied, reaching for the money, squeezing the thick wad of bills.

"This is a deal between us. But you break it in any way, and we'll go to the police. We'll have you arrested and you'll never see our money again."

Loc hacked and spat. "If the police care about the girl and half boy, why do they sleep here?" He smiled. "Bring three hundred in six months. And next time tell me your price."

Before she could stop herself, Thien wished that he'd die of an overdose. She knew that opium had claimed him, and that he'd trouble them again. Taking Noah's hand, she led him away. While pleased that they'd successfully bartered for Mai's and Minh's freedom, she felt soiled. She'd survived the encounter only because Noah was with her. But children like Mai and Minh had no one. They could be easily manipulated and terrified, and that was the source of Loc's power. That was how the monster lived.

"Can we hurry?" she asked. "Please?"

Noah pushed himself to keep up with her. He slipped once, but she paid him no heed. She needed to flee the monster, to breathe air untainted by his presence. The scooter materialized before her, and she unlocked it, sat down, inserted the key, and pushed the start button.

"Is everything okay?" Noah asked, moving

behind her, pulling his aching leg into position.

She twisted the throttle and the scooter gracefully moved ahead. "Mai and Minh will live with us," she answered. "And this makes me happy."

"But you don't seem happy."

Thien reached behind her and placed her left hand on his knee. "Thank you for asking, Mr. Noah. I am happy. I am looking forward to seeing Mai and Minh when we tell them the good news."

"But?"

"But I do not like the world we just saw. I see it too often. And I feel so powerless when I see it."

"You're very brave."

"I would rather see something beautiful. I would rather take you and Miss Iris and the children to see something beautiful. Like my father's rice field, or my village."

Noah wanted to tell her that she was beautiful, and that her beauty came from her courage and her spirit. He wanted to tell her that he felt stronger with her beside him, that his aches weren't so terrible when he heard her voice. But if there was ever a time for such words, this was not it.

"Can you sing something?" he asked, as they drifted through the empty streets. "Maybe right now you can't show me something beautiful. But you can let me hear something beautiful."

She nodded, reminding herself that while monsters ruled the underworld, dragons reigned above. Dragons were all around her. Some had only one hand. Some were sick and near death. But they were dragons all the same. They were loyal and pure, and would protect the world from darkness. And she would do her best to help them. Even though she was young and small and sometimes scared, she would do her best.

Thinking of these dragons, Thien began to sing. She sang quietly at first, but the rising wind seemed to give her strength. And her voice blossomed. It carried Noah, taking him to places he'd never visited, to realms she'd imagined but he had not.

THOUGH SHE HAD BEEN IN THE dormitory for more than an hour, Mai still gazed about in wonder. She'd been betrayed so many times before that she thought her eyes must also be treacherous. The two rows of bunk beds couldn't be more inviting. The clouds above must be illusions. Even the floor was too clean. Had it been scrubbed for a special visitor?

Mai sat on the edge of a bed. Four beds down, Qui read softly to Tam. In the corner of the room a large fish tank rested on a steel table. While Mai felt the sheet beneath her and asked herself if she'd ever touched something so soft, Minh knelt in front of the fish tank. He'd seen fish in the shallows of the river but had never looked at them through a pane of glass. The fish mesmerized him, moving with such grace that he was sure they had wings instead of fins. He wondered what the fish thought of him. Did they know he was awkward and clumsy? Did they see his stump and realize he couldn't play like other boys? Minh hoped that they didn't care about his stump. He liked the fish. He wanted them to be his friends.

The room was quiet but for Qui's whispers, which lingered like motes in the air until footsteps echoed in the stairwell. Mai listened to the foot-steps, momentarily fearing that Loc had come for them. When she saw Iris appear, she put her hand over her heart and breathed deeply.

Iris carried a tray full of bowls. The bowls each contained two scoops of vanilla ice cream. She smiled and asked Mai and Minh to come to Tam's bed. "How about a treat for everyone?" she asked, trying to hide her worry over Noah and Thien as well as her sadness for Tam. "If you're going to paint a rainbow, you need something to keep you going."

Mai looked up at Iris. "A rainbow?"

"Thien told me. She told me all about your paint-brush."

Reaching into her pocket, Mai produced the paintbrush that Thien had given her. "I always carry it. Sure, sure, I no lose it." She grinned at the thought of a rainbow, Loc vanishing from her mind.

After Qui helped Tam rise to a sitting position, Iris gave her a bowl. "Will you paint with us, Tam?" she asked.

Tam's chest hurt. Her knees and elbows also ached, and she held back a moan. She looked at Mai and Minh, and she wanted them to be happy. Dung and Little Bird were happy. And the new boy and girl also needed to smile. Tam had decided that this room was for smiling only. Such a room must never contain sad faces. "Yes," she finally replied. "I paint."

Iris handed bowls to Tam, Minh, Mai, and Qui. She took the last bowl for herself. She watched Mai and Minh grin as they licked their spoons, and their grins lessened her burdens. Perhaps she'd helped to save them, but their mere presence would repay her a thousand times over. For a reason unknown to her, she thought about Charles Dickens, about how he wrote of sacrifice and nobility in *A Tale of Two Cities*. While Iris didn't begin to compare her deeds to those of Sydney Carton, she understood for the first time why he allowed himself to be guillotined so that his adversary could marry the woman they both loved. Beauty existed in his sacrifice, and beauty existed right before Iris. Three street children were smiling—three children who'd been abandoned by an uncaring world.

Iris finished her dessert, and walked to a chest near the stairwell, removing a paint-splattered canvas sheet. She dragged the sheet a few feet until it rested beneath the room's entrance. "I think we should paint the rainbow here," she said, "so that everyone always walks under it. Let's surprise Thien. She'll be so happy to see it."

As the children gathered about her, Iris positioned a ladder beside the door frame and then opened cans of paint. "Qui, since you've seen the most rainbows, why don't you paint the first color? We'll let your paint dry, and tomorrow we'll add another color."

Qui smiled. She helped Tam to a nearby chair. Closing her eyes, she tried to imagine the last rainbow she'd seen. It hadn't been long ago. She remembered viewing it through the window of their room above the canal. The rainbow had arched over the canal as if it were a colorful bridge that connected two worlds. She'd studied its beauty with Tam, who'd asked if her mother might see it from her home in Thailand. Qui had replied that she most certainly did. She'd then created a story about rainbows, about how they carried love from mothers to daughters, about how that love could be held within hearts.

After contemplating which color to use, Qui dipped her brush in a can of yellow paint. She carefully climbed the ladder, eyeing the spot above the door. She wanted the rainbow to reach each side of the door, the way the rainbow had crossed the canal. And so she started to the left and slowly created a yellow arch. Her hand was surprisingly steady. Her brush left a uniform track of paint. Qui dipped the brush in the paint can again, and worked until her arch was complete. Then she descended the ladder, admiring her creation.

"It's pretty, Little Bird," Tam said in Vietnamese, remembering the story, eager to add her color to the rainbow.

Mai watched the old woman. She saw how the wrinkles in her face deepened as she smiled. Though Mai had never experienced familial love, she felt the bond between Tam and Qui as surely as if it had been made of rope. Because of Minh, Mai didn't feel jealous. Instead she felt a strange combination of joy and sorrow. She was happy that Tam had such a grandmother. But she was sad because she'd seen the grandmother cry, and she feared that this rope might be severed.

Then Mai thought about the rainbow, about painting something beautiful and walking under it each day. And she saw how the old woman continued to smile, as if the yellow arch contained a secret that made her happy. Suddenly Mai didn't want to wait until tomorrow to add the next color. Tomorrow seemed a thousand days away. She left the group and hurried to her bed, grabbing several of her fans. "Let's dry it," she said in Vietnamese to Minh, her words as quick as her feet. "Let's dry it and Tam can paint the next color."

Mai and Minh climbed the ladder together. They waved Mai's fans inches from Qui's arch. Everyone except Tam gathered close to watch as the paint faded slowly, as its fresh brightness gave way to a profound permanence. Mai and Minh continued to work, moving left to right, forcing warm air upon all parts of the arch. Sweat beaded on their skin. A fly threatened to land on the fresh paint and was blown away by Mai.

"I think it's dry," Iris said, unsure what to make of Mai's persistence but pleased by it.

Minh nodded. He knew that Mai was anxious to see the rainbow finished and so he had worked hard. He'd thought about Noah while he worked, wondering if he would really get to live with the kind American. He couldn't imagine such a life. No longer would he have to worry about food and police and Loc. He could play his game just for fun. He could learn to read.

Mai stepped down the ladder, almost knocking Minh from his perch. "Sure, sure, it be dry," she finally replied in English. "Now Tam can paint."

After Minh had descended, Qui and Iris helped Tam move to the paint cans. "What color would you like?" Iris asked, wishing that Tam weren't so light.

Tam studied the colors. She thought of Qui's story, of how rainbows were magical paths that connected mothers and daughters, of how love floated along these paths. What color would best carry love? She wanted her rainbow to bring love to everyone who walked beneath it and so she thought long and hard. Soon her legs trembled. Her chest hurt. Qui asked if she wanted to sit, but

Tam shook her head. This question could not be rushed. It needed thinking.

Finally, Tam decided to dip her brush into the orange paint. Orange was the color closest to yellow, and since Qui had chosen yellow, Tam knew that she must choose orange.

She weakly climbed the ladder, aware of hands supporting her, of Iris behind her. She smiled when her brush touched the wall. She'd never created any work of art, but as she pulled the brush she felt something emerge from within her, something beautiful that would remain on the wall long after she'd traveled to the new world.

⌒ TWELVE

Elephants and Escapes

A rooster woke Noah. Its shrill cry reverberated within his mind as if it were trying to punch holes in his skull. Around midnight he'd gone to the bathroom and had heard Tam's muffled coughs. He had hardly slept since, consumed with thoughts of her suffering. As the night went on he'd grown increasingly agitated, fading into a shallow slumber only after swallowing a sleeping pill.

Normally, Noah might have tried to return to sleep, as its warm darkness was a refuge. But this morning was different. Tam needed him. And he'd give her whatever he could.

After he dressed and put on his prosthesis, he walked quietly downstairs. To his surprise, Thien wasn't in the kitchen. Perhaps she'd also slept poorly, worried about Tam or their encounter with Loc. Noah was used to her presence, and the kitchen seemed desolate without her. Its walls didn't resonate with her voice. Its hollows didn't carry her smell.

Noah passed through the kitchen and into the playground. Slender sprouts of grass had emerged from the soil, and he carefully made his way along the path he'd created. Iris sat on his half-finished seesaw. A notebook lay atop her lap. Her hair, usually held tight behind her head, tumbled below her shoulders. She was wearing a T-shirt and an old skirt that fell to her knees. Her feet were bare.

"You're up early," she said, yawning as if to emphasize her words.

"So are you."

She shrugged. "I thought I'd start a journal. So I won't forget anything."

"You won't forget."

"Why not?"

"Because this place . . . it's a part of you."

Iris smiled. "Where's your whiskey?"

"Not far." He moved closer to the seesaw. Propped against it was a pair of plywood elephant ears that Thien had meticulously painted. "When did she do this?" he asked, his fingers tracing her brushstrokes.

"I'm not sure. Maybe last night, after you got back."

"She's so talented."

"I know. But I don't think she knows."

"I don't think she cares."

"She doesn't."

He lifted one of the ears and awkwardly moved to an end of the seesaw, the extra weight hurting his stump. He'd drilled holes in the plywood so that he could bolt it to the seesaw. "This is going to be nice," he said, pleased with Thien's idea to create the elephant, to make Tam happy.

"It's going to be wonderful. Just wonderful." Iris glanced around the playground. "You're creating something special here, Noah. Your mother, you know, she'd be really proud."

He studied the seesaw and saw her notebook, which she'd put aside. "What about your reviews?"

"I guess they're going to have to wait."

"But your career?"

"The books won't go anywhere," she replied, watching as he slowly bent to his knees and prepared to fit the ear into place. "Do you need help with that?"

"Sure."

She picked up a bolt, and when he nodded, she pushed it through the plywood and then through the reinforced end of the seesaw. She put a large washer and a nut on the end of the bolt, twisting the nut quickly, aware that he was straining. As she reached for another bolt she realized that he was staring at Thien's artwork. "I think she's enamored with you," Iris said, pushing the second bolt into place.

"What?"

"Thien. I think she's falling for you."

"For me? Don't be ridic—"

"I think you know, Noah. Though I don't think you have any idea what to do about it."

He released his grip on the plywood after she'd secured the second bolt. "I can't . . . I can't deal with that right now. It's too much."

"Yes, you can."

"She's too good for me."

"Don't say that."

"Don't say the truth?"

Iris rose from her crouched position. "Stop it. Right now. Just because you've got problems doesn't mean that you can't make someone happy. She's not a fool, you know. She's seen who you are and it's only brought her closer to you."

He shook his head, the seesaw forgotten. "I'm not sure."

"About what?"

"What if I'm afraid?"

"Afraid?"

"Of disappointing her."

She watched as he looked away. "Are you afraid of what that would do to her . . . or to you?"

"Maybe both."

"That's a chance you have to take," she said, putting her hand on his shoulder. "But you haven't disappointed me and I don't think you'll disappoint her."

His eyes found hers. "I don't know what to do. I really don't."

"Take her somewhere."

"What do you mean?"

"Take her somewhere tomorrow. She'll go with you. I know she will. Take her somewhere beautiful."

"And?"

"Just . . . go somewhere. She's told me she wished we could see other parts of Vietnam. Go. Get train tickets or plane tickets and go somewhere beautiful."

"Plane tickets? That sounds like too much."

"You're not fifteen, Noah. Don't worry. She won't be scared off. Just take her somewhere nice and come back. That's all you have to do."

His heartbeat quickened, a nervousness he hadn't felt in years seeping into him. "And I should just ask her?"

"Get the tickets today. And then ask her."

"But we've got so much work to—"

"It's just one day."

"But the seesaw."

"Finish it. Take Tam for a ride. And then go somewhere tomorrow. I can handle things for a day."

Noah glanced toward the kitchen. He hadn't wanted to be close to a woman since he'd lost his leg. He'd been ashamed and afraid, and far too despondent to care for anyone but himself. But somehow Thien had managed to capture his attention or, better yet, his imagination. He wanted to take her somewhere beautiful, to walk beside her—because when he was beside her, his hurts weren't so overwhelming.

"What if she says no?" he asked.

"She won't say no."

"How do you know that?"

"Because I can see."

He looked to her. "You said no."

Iris started to respond but stopped. She remembered him asking her to a movie, remembered how she'd been waiting in vain for her father to pick her up from school. She had turned Noah down, preferring the company of her books. "I didn't date anyone, Noah. Not in high school, and barely in college, and I've had one boyfriend in the last two years. And I certainly didn't . . . I didn't look at you like Thien does. If I'd looked at you like that, my answer would have been different."

Noah tried to think about what he might have done with a woman before he'd been injured. Should he follow such a path, or walk a new one? When no answer arose, he gently squeezed her hand. "Thank you."

"You don't need to thank me."

"That's not true. I wouldn't have had the courage to ask her."

"But you will now?"

He studied her face, wondering how she could give so much and ask for nothing in return. "Are you happy?"

Her brow furrowed. "Me?"

"Yes, you."

She looked at the center, toward the dormitory. "I don't want Tam to die. And I can't be happy with that . . . looming over everything. But I'm glad to be here. I can't imagine being anywhere else."

"Why not?"

"Because it's time for me to do something. And here I'm doing it. Maybe I'm doing it for my father. Maybe for myself. But whatever the case . . . I think we're creating something wonderful."

"You are."

"I like it when you smile, Noah. You have such a great smile."

He gestured toward the other plywood ear. "Can you help me with that?"

She nodded, grabbing another bolt. "Tam's going to love this."

"I know," he replied, lifting the ear into place. The strain of moving the cumbersome object caused pain to race from his stump to his neck. He grimaced, but his thoughts didn't spiral into an unwanted darkness. He pushed the darkness away and, at least for the moment, held it at bay. "You're not the only one who's glad to be here," he said, shifting his position so that she could place the second bolt.

Iris twisted the nut, nodding. "Take her somewhere beautiful, Noah. She's a beautiful person and I think she'll walk with you, if you show her what she wants to see."

SAHN NAVIGATED THE STREETS PARTLY FROM memory, having explored them countless times. Through his damaged eyes he'd seen about all that could be seen—suffering and hope, sorrow and happiness. He'd watched a taxi crash into an elephant, and the procession of a prime minister from another land. Though such sights had been obscured by the dimness of his vision, he had experienced these events with clarity. He'd smelled the elephant's blood and knew that it was doomed. He'd heard the prime minister's minions long before the man himself had arrived.

Sahn didn't take his senses for granted. Nor was he unaware of using them. When his sight failed to give him enough information, he paused to smell, to listen, to touch. Of course, he was surreptitious about how he examined the world. He always pretended to be looking intently, as if he had the eyes of a magpie.

"Good morning, Captain," a shopkeeper said as she swept the cement in front of her store.

Sahn recognized her voice. He might have recognized her face, if given time. But her voice solved the riddle. "Has the street spoken lately?" he asked, for rumors were rarely quiet.

"Some Thais bought all my batteries," she replied casually, as if talking about the weather. "So strange, I thought, to buy fourteen boxes of batteries."

Sahn nodded, his mind churning. A group of Thais buying batteries could mean nothing. Batteries were probably more expensive in Thailand. But certain Thais were also involved in child prostitution and opium smuggling. Could batteries play a role in either operation? "How were they dressed?" he asked.

"Money. They had money. Their clothes were nice and they didn't try to bargain."

"Did they pay in cash?"

"Yes."

He grunted. "Keep listening."

"I will, Captain. And I'll tell you what I hear."

Sahn looked ahead, noting obstacles before starting forward. He continued on his patrol, pausing to speak with people he trusted. He asked about the Thais, but no one knew anything else. At one point a silk merchant produced an American twenty-dollar bill and asked if it was counterfeit. To Sahn, the blurry bill looked like any other. He hadn't heard lately of counterfeit money and said that the man had nothing to worry about.

Turning down an alley, Sahn proceeded toward the new center for street children. He wanted to talk with Thien. She was the only one who could answer his questions, who could tell him if the center was right or wrong. He wondered if they had such centers in America. Didn't everyone there sleep under a golden roof?

After a few minutes the center materialized. When he was about twenty paces away, he paused, listening. He quickly identified the foreign voices, which came from the rear of the building, where the soldier was creating a playground. Good, Sahn thought, moving ahead. He didn't want to talk with the Americans. At least not today.

The gate in front of the center was partly closed. Sahn moved past it. "Hello?" he called out in Vietnamese. No one answered, and he stepped inside. His eyes struggled to adjust to his new environs. He stood still, waiting for objects to take on muted dimensions, for bright halos to darken. When satisfied that he could see no better, he proceeded into the kitchen, which smelled of fresh croissants but was empty.

His feet fell softly as he made his way up the stairs. Again he wondered what had been painted on the wall. Why was everything green? Was it a jungle of some kind?

At the top of the stairs, he turned into the office. To his surprise, Thien spoke to him before he realized she was there.

"Captain?" she asked, stopping whatever she was doing.

He cleared his throat. "You should have told me about what happened under the bridge. Better that I hear about these things from you than from an informer."

Thien set down the bucket that she'd been using to water plants. "But that was just—"

"Last night?"

She nodded. "I was going to tell you."

Sahn seemed not to hear her, his face expression-less. "Do you know who he is?"

"Would you like to sit?"

"Questions and answers do not need chairs."

"Maybe you should speak with Miss Iris."

"But I want to speak with you."

"Two children came to us," Thien said, choosing her words carefully. "They wanted to stay with us. And they warned us about a man."

"A man?"

"A man named Loc. They worked for him. And they were afraid about what he might do if they left him."

Sahn shook his head. "Whose idea was the bribe?"

"Mine," Thien replied, though it was untrue.

"Then you must know the risks. He still might come for them."

"I know."

"What will you do if he does?"

"I'm not sure. We haven't talked about that."

Sahn let his voice carry some of his frustration.

332

"Then you'd better start talking. You've put a scorpion in your pocket."

"We'll talk, Captain. I promise."

"I know this man. And he's dangerous. I'll watch out for him, but I can't be everywhere."

"You—"

"These Americans, they may be good. But they don't know Vietnam. You must be the leader here."

"I know. And I'm trying. We all are."

"Do more than try. They need you." He slapped at a mosquito that had drawn blood from the back of his hand. "What is it like, working with the Americans?"

"They're both very kind. And they work so hard."

"Their country almost destroyed ours."

Thien stiffened. "Time doesn't stand still, Captain. These are wonderful people. We're lucky to have them."

"I hope so."

"Believe me. We are."

"And my fish?"

"Your fish? They're fine. We feed them bugs."

"And they eat them?"

"As fast as we can catch them."

Sahn nodded, pleased to hear that his fish were eating so well. "I watch over four girls," he said, "who sleep in a park. They're fine girls. But they're getting too old to beg. Soon they'll turn to stealing . . . or to other things."

Thien finally understood why he'd sought her

out. His pride wouldn't allow him to ask Iris, but he could ask her. "I'm sorry to hear that, Captain," she said.

"Can they stay here? They won't trouble you. And they'll study hard."

"Well, I'll have to ask, but I think so. We still have a lot of beds to fill."

"I don't have money, but I can do something."

"You don't—"

"What do you need? What's something that you need?"

Thien thought about her response. If she asked for too little, he would be offended. If she asked for too much, he'd try but fail. "We'd like a swing," she said, unconsciously rising to her tip-toes, hoping that she had found a solution.

"A swing?"

"For the playground."

"But isn't the soldier doing all that?"

"He can't do everything."

Sahn grunted, knowing it would be difficult to locate a swing. "A swing for two?"

"That would be perfect. Should I tell Mr. Noah to expect it?"

"Of course," Sahn replied, remembering how he used to swing with his brothers and sisters. How happy his siblings had been. How he longed to have more recent memories of them. "You'll get the swing in a week," he said, still thinking of his siblings.

"Thank you, Captain."

He stared at her, believing that she was smiling. She's never felt the blast of a bomb, he thought. Never heard the screams of her sisters. How lucky for her. "Thank you for taking the girls," he finally said. "They'll work hard. I promise."

"I'm sure."

Sahn nodded. He then turned and walked into the stairwell, into a darker place where his memories unfurled.

THE PLEASURE BOAT ROCKED GENTLY IN the Saigon River. Loc opened his eyes, trying to make sense of the world around him. His mind was still muddled by opium, and the room seemed much larger than was true. The walls and ceiling weren't wood like the outside of the boat but were covered with giant mirrors. The mirror above him seemed to reveal the most. He looked for his pipe and saw that it had fallen to the floor. Was it empty?

Beside Loc lay a high-priced lady. Though she was naked, he couldn't remember all that had happened between them. For sure, they'd smoked his pipe until everything seemed to sway in tandem with the boat. She had asked him where he was born, but he'd thought of being homeless in Nha Trang and told her that she wasn't paid to ask questions. And so they'd smoked more. Soon she had removed her clothes. He'd understood then why she was so special, why she cost so much. He had fallen on her swiftly, needing to dominate her with his size and strength.

To his dismay, Loc could recall nothing more of the night. From the potency of the sunlight streaming through the room's only window, he knew that midday was near. His time with her was over; it was after the hour that she was obligated to be his. He cursed her. He cursed himself. The pleasure boat, the woman, and the perfectly refined opium had cost him most of his money.

He studied the contours of her body and felt himself growing aroused. Could she still be groggy? Could I take her again? He reached for her, his stained fingers squeezing her flesh. He must have squeezed too hard, for she rolled away from him. "Come here," he said, his voice cracking, his mouth dry.

She blinked repeatedly. She reached for her cell phone, which lay on the bed. Her brow furrowed when she saw the time. Putting her hand against a nearby wall to steady herself, she rose.

"I said, come here," Loc repeated.

She pulled on her skirt and high boots, glaring at him. Though her stance was unsteady, she dressed as quickly as possible.

He picked up his pipe. "Let's smoke."

"It's gone. Remember?" She flicked open her cell phone and typed a text message, her fingers moving as if they were independent creatures.

"Don't ever call us again," she said. "I don't sleep with water buffalo."

Loc would have beaten her, but as he started to move toward her, he recalled that she was protected by men who were much more powerful than he. To beat her would prompt his death. "You won't always be with them," he said, knowing that she'd age and would one day be on the street.

"We'll see about that," she replied, putting on her sunglasses. She turned and opened the door. Her high-heeled boots seemed to echo against his skull as she walked to the deck.

Loc rubbed his aching head. He looked for his clothes, the mirrors playing tricks with his mind. Finally locating his pants, he counted what remained of his money. He could find only a handful of nearly worthless dong notes. He threw the bills at his reflection, cursing loudly. He hated himself then, hated the world and everything in it. All that mattered to him was opium and women. And right now he had neither. His pipe was empty, and he'd been scorned by the most beautiful woman he had ever touched. She's laughing at me right now, he thought, wanting to break the mirrors before him, to destroy his reflection.

The boat suddenly shuddered, and Loc fell sideways on the bed. Realizing that the boat had bumped against a pier, he began to gather his belongings. He dressed awkwardly, not ready for such movements. To his surprise and delight, he saw what resembled a small brown rock on the floor. He hurriedly picked it up, inspected it, and then set it in the bowl of his pipe. He held his lighter against the flake of opium and sucked on the pipe. The opium began to glow, releasing its smoke.

Loc felt the drug enter him. It filled his lungs like some sort of magical serpent. This serpent divided itself into a million smaller snakes that sought out other parts of his body. Soon he felt as if he were being lifted off the bed. Floating upward, he was unaware of his extremities, of any sort of pain. He exhaled deeply, air suddenly a gift, something sweet to be savored.

Voices called from above. Loc wasn't sure what had been said, but knew it was time to leave. He finished dressing, hid his pipe in his sock, and gathered his money. The door swung open slowly, pushed by his fingers, which didn't feel the weight of the wood. Nor did his feet sense the stairs beneath him. He was outside his body—a spirit that used a physical form to move but wasn't attached to that form.

Loc soon drifted on the streets. His mind wandered, resting in familiar and undiscovered places. He wondered if this floating world was one of many, longing to stay in it forever. His thoughts and emotions and experiences were magically connected. He heard the voices of his parents and wished they hadn't left him to the streets. He remembered what he'd done with the woman. And he pictured the one-handed boy and knew that he had to steal this boy. With this boy beside him, he'd never be without money, without the means to drift into new worlds.

As Loc drifted, he began to plan, unsure how he would steal the half boy, but sure that he'd do it.

TAM HAD NEVER MUCH CARED FOR sleep, but recently she'd had no choice but to close her eyes and succumb to the profound weariness that dominated her body and mind. She didn't understand why she was so tired. She wanted to talk with Little Bird, to comb Dung's hair, to do so many things. But her body allowed her only short windows of time through which she could pursue her desires. Otherwise, she simply couldn't keep her eyes open. And closing her eyes was also the only sure way to stop her pain. The medicine helped, of course. But it had limits.

And so Tam spent her days and nights drifting in and out of sleep. In that sense she was like the sun when a storm was threatening. Most moments she was engulfed in darkness. Occasionally the clouds parted enough so that she was able to shine her light on the world around her. The fact that most of this world wasn't aware of her light didn't bother her. She needed only her grandmother.

Qui understood how and why Tam drifted between light and dark. When her granddaughter slept, Qui either cleaned the dormitory or lay by Tam's side. She wasn't interested in anything else. Out of courtesy and gratitude she spoke with Iris and Noah, and she was kind to everyone else. But she sought out conversations only with Tam.

As Qui waited patiently for Tam to awaken, she thought about the elephant that Noah and Thien had made. They'd shown it to her an hour before and explained that they wanted Tam to ride it. The sight of the seesaw had filled Qui with warmth. She'd managed to momentarily hold back her tears, touching the painted plywood as if it were some sort of religious relic. Understanding the significance of their gift, Qui had grasped the hands of Noah and Thien, and then her tears had fallen.

Now, as Tam stirred and moaned softly, Qui stroked her granddaughter's brow. She gently pushed her hair out of her face. An eyelash lay next to Tam's nose. Qui carefully picked up the lash. She studied it closely, her gaze sweeping up and down the perfect black curve that had once protected Tam. Qui wished she knew where her daughter was. If she did, she would tape Tam's lash to a card and mail it to Hong. Perhaps then Hong would see the lash, sense the beauty of Tam, and hurry to her. Why, Hong, why don't you come home? Qui silently asked her daughter. Why have you abandoned your precious girl?

"Little Bird?"

Qui glanced up from the lash. "Yes?"

"What are you looking at?"

"I . . . I'm looking at a piece of you."

Tam smiled, not seeing the lash, but happy with the response. "I dreamed again about flowers."

"What kind?"

"I don't know. But they were purple. And I swam in them."

"What a fine dream."

"It was."

Qui's fingers joined with Tam's. "A surprise is waiting for you, my sweet child, my beautiful child."

"A surprise?"

"Can you climb on my back?"

Holding on to her doll, Tam wrapped her arms around Qui's neck and managed to pull herself up. "Where are you taking me, Little Bird? Did Momma come?"

Qui put her arms behind her, so that her hands met beneath Tam's bottom. "No, your mother's still working. She can't do more than send money and her love. But there's something wonderful waiting for you outside. Now, hold on."

"I'm holding."

Glad to have Tam atop her again, Qui grunted as she stood up. How far have I carried her? she wondered. Have we walked enough to circle the world? Qui didn't know much about the world but had heard that there were endless deserts, snow-capped mountains, and vast, gleaming cities. She'd have liked for Tam to see snow. Surely it would have made her laugh.

Reaching the bottom of the stairs, Qui turned toward the playground. Outside, everyone seemed hard at work. Noah was nailing long pieces of wood together. Iris and Thien were planting flowers along the fence. And Mai and Minh held watering cans, giving the grass a drink. Thien was the first to spot Tam and Qui, and stood up and walked toward them.

"Are you ready for a ride?" Thien asked Tam in English.

"What?"

"Come and see what Mr. Noah has built for you."

They all stopped what they were doing and proceeded to the far end of the lot, where the seesaw sat. The side bearing the elephant was heavier and rested against the ground.

"Didn't you want to ride an elephant?" Thien asked, smiling.

At the sight of the seesaw, Tam's eyes widened. She'd ridden a seesaw once and remembered pushing with her feet and sailing into the air. Little Bird had been on the other end, and they'd laughed until their bellies ached. That seesaw had been nothing more than a steel pole with a seat on each end. The seesaw she saw now was so different. The profile of an elephant's head rose almost as high as Mai's shoulders. The elephant had big black eyes and a pair of tusks that were the color of clouds.

"We saved the first ride for you, Tam," Iris said.

Noah saw Tam's smile, and he remembered what it was like to be a boy. He helped Iris lift Tam from Qui's back. Tam held her doll against her. She giggled softly as they placed her within the elephant. Knowing that the elephant was heavy, Noah said, "Mai and Minh, why don't you get on the other end?"

"Sure, sure?" Mai asked, glancing at Qui, thinking that she might like to try.

Qui smiled, a gap in her teeth revealing her pink tongue. She could see that Minh was eager to ride the seesaw, and so she gestured for the two children to climb on. "Please go," she said in Vietnamese. "I'll be so happy to stand and watch."

Minh set down his watering can and straddled the opposite end of the seesaw, which didn't yet have anything attached. He wondered if Noah would create the back of an elephant or the face of another animal. He hoped for another animal. Minh was happy to see the elephant, happy that a man with one leg could build something so wonderful.

"Don't jump too high," Iris said to Mai, worried that Tam would fall.

"No, jump high," Tam replied, giggling softly, trying to push her end up from the ground.

Noah saw that she was struggling and grasped the elephant's ear and lifted. The seesaw rose upward, and Tam laughed. Mai and Minh reached the bottom and kicked against the soft soil. The elephant and Tam plunged down, and she shrieked in delight.

"My stomach dropped!" she said in Vietnamese, pushing with her feet against the ground. Noah lifted and the seesaw swayed in the other direction.

"So did mine!" Mai replied, laughing.

Minh smiled, gripping the bar in front of him and pushing with his feet.

"I didn't know elephants could jump so high," Thien said.

Tam watched the world rise and fall. She'd rarely seen things move so fast, and she urged her elephant onward. Gripping her doll with one hand and the seesaw with the other, she kicked and pushed and laughed.

After a few minutes, Noah stopped the seesaw. "Do you want to ride with Tam?" he asked Qui.

Not needing to be asked twice, Qui moved behind her granddaughter. Instead of holding the bar in front of her, Qui put her arms around Tam's waist. Noah waited until everyone looked secure and then he pulled up on the elephant's ear.

Qui enjoyed the feeling of soaring, of reaching new heights. She watched Mai and Minh propel their side off the ground and laughed as she and Tam dropped. "What an elephant!" she said into Tam's ear.

Tam grinned. She hadn't run since she'd been sick, and she'd missed it. Her elephant ran now, and she giggled. She saw Mai and Minh laughing, and this sight caused her giggles to intensify. Suddenly she couldn't stop laughing. She laughed with each breath, and her bones didn't ache, and she didn't long for her mother. She simply laughed as any child might. And she felt so lucky then. She heard Qui behind her, saw the smiling faces around her, and she knew that she was loved. And more than anything else, Tam wanted to be loved.

Believing that she'd finally found a family, Tam kicked harder. She didn't want to sleep. She wasn't aware of the cancer gnawing at her bones. She'd been saved and nothing else mattered.

THE SUN HAD JUST SET, AND the sky looked like the inside of a giant orange balloon. Noah sat on a plastic chair atop the roof, staring at this balloon, which encircled the bustling, noisy city. Though the city moved in thousands of different ways, the balloon remained still, changing only as it slowly darkened. Even when the balloon had disappeared, having floated off to a different place, the sky didn't completely blacken. The city's infinite lights faintly illuminated the underbelly of the heavens, creating a strange twilight that would remain until dawn.

Noah took a long gulp from a Tiger beer. He savored the taste, licking his lips and listening to the symphony that was the city. Is it ever quiet here? he wondered, the endless beeps of scooters filling his ears. He'd grown accustomed to these beeps. They somehow comforted him, the knowledge that millions of people were nearby making him feel less alone. Noah had listened to Chicago and Kabul and Baghdad. But he couldn't recall any of these cities sounding like this one. The beeps of the scooters resembled the calls of crickets on an autumn night. Only these crickets didn't quiet as the night aged. They chirped until the sun returned to spread its colors, and then they kept on chirping.

The beer can was emptied. Noah reached for another, his pulse beating quicker than usual, his pockets containing a pair of airline tickets to and from Hanoi. Though Iris had enthusiastically approved of his idea of taking Thien to Halong Bay, the most famous of Vietnam's sights, Noah still worried. Was he being too bold? What if she said no?

His back and stump ached, but Noah resisted the lure of a pain pill. He didn't want his senses numbed when he asked her. He took another gulp of beer. The beer wasn't much cooler than the night air, and he wiped sweat from his forehead. Like the noise, sweat always seemed present in the city. If he washed it off, it returned in a matter of minutes.

Noah finished his third beer and exhaled slowly. He wanted to wait longer but couldn't. Thien would soon go to bed. She'd spent the late afternoon looking for an apartment for Minh and him, and had to be exhausted. And so he stood up and moved toward the ladder. Its rungs were stout and warm. He descended slowly, wondering if he'd ever grow comfortable with his prosthesis. Maybe when he was an old man and movement wasn't so important.

He glanced in the dormitory and saw that everyone had gone to bed. Downstairs, Iris typed before a computer. Their eyes met. "What are you working on?" he asked, stepping toward her.

She motioned for him to leave. "Go, Noah. Ask her now. I was just in the kitchen, and she's almost done cleaning up."

"And you're . . . sure about this?"

"Very. Now, get going before it's too late."

He turned and proceeded down the stairwell, moving even slower than usual. Sounds of Thien singing emerged from the kitchen. He stepped into it. Her back was to him, and he watched her scrub dishes at the sink. She wore a red shirt, white pants, and sandals. Her baseball cap was slightly askew, making her ponytail fall crookedly.

"Can I help?" he asked quietly, not wanting to startle her.

She turned and smiled. "Doing dishes? No, thank you, Mr. Noah. I will finish them." She set a glass down. "May I get you another Tiger?"

"That's okay."

"Are you hungry? I could cut up a juicy mango."

His smile was faint, but spontaneous. "Why do you always wear that baseball cap?"

"Because the sun is so bright, you silly man."

"But there's no sun now."

She shrugged. "It is rising somewhere."

"Maybe someday I'll buy you a new one."

"Why? Is this one too old?"

"No, no. It looks great."

"Do women in America not wear caps? What do they do about the sun?"

He stepped closer to her, lifting a dirty plate and setting it next to the sink. "In America, people often stay inside. Women don't usually wear caps."

Thien nodded slowly, as if absorbing the information but unsure what to do with it. She wiped her hands on a towel and proceeded to peel a rambutan fruit, setting aside the hairy red skin. "Your seesaw was wonderful, Mr. Noah. Tam was so happy. What a gift that was."

"You did most of the work."

She offered him the white flesh of the fruit, which he took. "You were happy too," she said. "And it made me happy to see you happy."

"It did?"

"Of course. I want you to be happy."

"Why?"

"Because you are a good man. And good men should be happy."

He looked into her eyes and was again surprised at how large and dark they were. Suddenly he longed to be closer to them, to see his reflection.

"I . . . I wanted to ask you something," he said, his voice softer, his heart thumping quickly.

"About the apartments? I tried so hard, Mr. Noah. Tomorrow I will look again."

"No, not about the apartments."

"No?"

"The other night you said that you want to take me somewhere beautiful."

"I do. You should not see only the ugly parts of Vietnam. Our country is so lovely."

Noah pulled the tickets from his pocket and placed them on the counter. "Can I . . . Would you let me take you instead?"

Thien glanced at the tickets, uncertain what he meant. She stepped closer, her brow furrowing when she saw that they were airline tickets. "Hanoi?" she asked.

He recognized her confusion and wanted to see it vanish as quickly as possible. "Not Hanoi, but Halong Bay," he replied. "I heard it's the most beautiful place in Vietnam, and tomorrow I want to take you there."

"Halong Bay?"

"Is that okay?"

"Really? Really, Mr. Noah?"

"Do you want to go? With me?"

She smiled and stepped to him, hugging him tightly. "Of course. That would be wonderful! I have never visited Halong Bay and would love to see it."

Noah felt all of her against him. Was she hugging him as a friend? As something more? "It's an early flight," he said, looking down at the top of her head. "We'd leave early and get back late. It'll be a long day."

"And our jobs at the center?"

He hoped that she couldn't feel the speed with which his heart raced. "Iris said you haven't taken a day off in weeks. It's just fine with her."

She looked up at him and suddenly her eyes were much closer to his. "I am so excited, Mr. Noah."

"Please call me Noah."

"Is it really true?"

"It is."

"Thank you. Thank you for thinking of me."

"Of course."

Nodding, she moved slightly away from him, though her hands held his. She glanced at the tickets, wishing they were already there, thrilled by the prospect of seeing the dragons, of traveling with Noah. "Do you know the story of the bay?" she asked, griping his hands tightly.

"No."

"Do you want to hear it?"

"Sure."

"Halong Bay means . . . 'Bay of the Descending Dragons.'"

"Why do they call it that?" he wondered, enjoying the link of their hands and not wanting it to end.

"A long, long time ago, Vietnam was at war with China. And the Chinese were sailing across the sea to destroy us. A family of dragons saw our troubles and came to our aid. The dragons started spitting out giant pieces of jade. These pieces struck the sea and turned into thousands of islands, creating a barrier that the Chinese ships could not pass." Thien paused, smiling.

"And what happened?"

"And the Chinese sailed home. And later, when there was peace, the dragons so loved the bay they had created that they flew down and decided to live in the blue waters. They still live there. When the bay is rough they are said to be swimming."

"You believe in them?"

"Most certainly. And I think you will too. After you see what they did."

A scooter passed by on the road near the window. Thien glanced at the window, and then her gaze traveled back to his face. She remembered how he'd smiled at the sight of the children on the seesaw. She had rarely seen him smile and had wanted to do so again. She'd longed to help with his pain. Never had she experienced such pain, and she'd have liked to take some of his suffering and make it hers. One person, she often thought, one good person, shouldn't have to endure such misery.

"Thank you for my gift," she said quietly, feeling the heat of his hand in hers.

"You haven't seen it yet."

"I know. But you are going to show me." She squeezed his hand. "Good night . . . Noah."

He felt her fingers leave his, and suddenly he was alone. "Good night, Thien," he said. He watched her step back to the sink and then he turned. Behind him, he heard her start to sing as she again began to clean. Though he wanted to sit on a step and just listen, he climbed the stairs until he reached the roof, until her voice was but a memory in his head, swirling around and filling him with warmth.

⸺ THIRTEEN

Into the Light

Thien awoke before the roosters. She was making fresh orange juice when she heard them announce the coming of dawn. She knew each of the three roosters—knew where each lived and recognized each distinct cry. Though most city dwellers despised the racket that roosters made, she didn't mind. The noise reminded her of home, brought back memories of lying between her siblings on a thin mattress and moaning at the sound of roosters waking the world.

After Thien had prepared breakfast for everyone, she went outside and swept the stone path in the playground. The children had made a mess the previous day, when they'd enjoyed the seesaw for so long. She was pleased to see the muddied stones, the trampled grass. These sights told her what she wanted to know, that children had played and laughed in a place that she'd helped build.

Thien had already cleaned the playground and first floor of the center when the sun began to gradually illuminate the sky. As she had worked, she'd hummed quietly, her voice mirroring the mood of the morning. She had mused about Noah. So much of him is locked away, she'd thought. That bomb didn't take only his leg. It took his hope, his joy.

Thien had realized that she hoped to discover the parts of him that had been stolen. She didn't know if this longing was because she wanted to see all people happy, or if it was more than that. Did she want him to be happy because he was with her? Because she cared about him? Because she was a source of his joy?

Such questions had echoed in Thien's mind while she'd worked. She had asked herself how she saw him, and what she wanted. She worried about falling for him, as she knew that in all likelihood he'd vanish in a few months. He would leave Vietnam and possibly never return. And when that happened she'd be hurt. The issue was—how much pain was she willing to endure?

Now, as Thien walked upstairs, she pushed thoughts of Noah aside. She wanted to ensure that the center would be fine in her absence. She worried about Iris having to tend to everything. It didn't seem right to leave her without help, no matter how tempting the invitation. What if her American sister needed her and she wasn't there?

Thien stepped into the dormitory. Mai and Minh appeared to have recently awoken. Still in their pajamas, they were playing a game of Connect Four on the floor next to their bed. Mai laughed, trying to remove a game piece that she'd dropped down the wrong slot. Minh blocked her fingers with his stump while attempting to place his own piece and win the game. Managing to slip his piece past Mai, Minh threw his hand up in the air, smiling while Mai giggled.

At the other end of the room, Tam lay in her bed. Qui sat beside her, gently combing her hair. Thien said hello and was surprised when Tam didn't return the greeting. Making conversation with Qui, Thien glanced repeatedly at Tam, not liking the pallor that seemed to have seeped into her face. She looked as if she'd eaten old meat. Worried for her, Thien reached down, picked up Dung, and placed the doll in Tam's hands. "I'm going to be gone for today," Thien said, looking from Qui to Tam. "Will you please rest so tomorrow I can watch you more on the seesaw? No one can make that elephant jump like you. And I want to see him jump."

Tam might have nodded. Thien wasn't sure. Qui continued to comb her granddaughter's hair.

"She'll ride tomorrow," Qui said, doing her best to smile.

"Do you need anything?"

Qui shook her head and held up a postcard. "Do you know what came in the mail yesterday?" she asked. "A postcard from Bangkok. From Tam's mother."

"Really? May I see it?"

"Of course."

Thien held the postcard before her. The card depicted downtown Bangkok and carried a Thai stamp. But Thien was certain that the card had never been mailed from Thailand to Vietnam. It was too clean, too crisp. She glanced at the back and saw barely readable handwriting. Words spoke of a mother's love for her daughter, of how that love was as wide and deep as the sea. Thien didn't have to wonder who'd written the card.

"You're lucky to have such a loving mother," Thien said, tucking the card between Tam's arm and the sheet. "And she's lucky to have you. We're all so lucky to have you, Tam. You're our first student and soon you'll learn so many wonderful things."

"Thank you," Tam whispered, closing her eyes, weariness overcoming her.

Thien realized that Qui was trying to hold back tears. "She's so brave," Thien whispered, gently squeezing Qui's arm. "I don't think I've ever met anyone so brave."

Qui nodded, watching her granddaughter, almost unaware of Thien. Not wanting to intrude, Thien said good-bye and slowly walked away. She felt weak and had to hold the handrail as she descended toward Iris's office. She entered the room and saw Iris working at her computer, typing numbers into small boxes. The windows of the room were shut, and beads of sweat covered the back of Iris's neck.

"Miss Iris, do you want me to open a window?" Thien asked, moving toward the wall.

Iris turned toward her, raising a hand. "No, no. Please don't. I need some silence. I need to think."

"May I help you?"

"Don't you have a plane to catch?"

"Soon. We are leaving soon."

Iris sipped from a glass of orange juice that Thien had brought her earlier. "Are you all right?" she asked. "You look tired."

"I am worried about Tam."

"I know. I'm going to call the doctor just as soon as he gets to work. And I'll have him stop by."

"Will he help her?"

"I don't . . . I'm not sure, Thien. I don't know what can be done. He did more tests, you know. And the results weren't good."

Thien shook her head. "I should not be leaving you today, Miss Iris."

Grasping Thien's hands, Iris rose from her seat.

"Please, Thien. Please don't worry about us. We're going to be fine. You're just going for a day. That's all. Everyone will be here when you get back, and it will be like you never left."

"But there is so much work."

"Please do this for me. For Noah. Go and see something beautiful. Please."

Thien started to speak and then stopped. She felt the strength of Iris's grip. She looked into her eyes. "We will be back tonight. And tomorrow I will work so hard. You can just rest."

"That'll be fine, Thien. Just fine. I'll write a list of things for you to do."

"A big list, Miss Iris. Please."

The sound of a scooter's engine springing to life echoed in the stairwell. "That's him," Iris said, leaning forward to hug Thien. "He's waiting for you."

"Are you sure? I think—"

"Go to him. Go and be happy."

Thien nodded, rising on her tiptoes to kiss Iris's cheek. "See you tonight."

"See you then."

Nodding, Thien moved to a nearby desk and picked up her Polaroid. She said good-bye and hurried to the stairwell, the beat of her heart moving with the speed of her feet. Now that she'd been released by Iris, she felt an unfamiliar sense of anticipation. Though she liked to visit beautiful places, Thien had done very little traveling. She'd walked throughout the valley where her father's farm rested. She had been to the Mekong Delta and seen wondrous sights. But she'd never looked upon the sea, and from what she had heard of Halong Bay, it was a sight not to be forgotten.

Thien soon reached Noah. He sat at the rear of the idling scooter, a small pack on his back. "Are you ready?" he asked, holding out his hand.

She paused for only a second. Then she took his hand and sat in front of him. He reached forward and carefully withdrew the camera from where it hung about her neck. He put it in his pack, moving ahead until his chest touched her back. She felt something thump against her, and she wondered if his heart was beating as fast as hers.

"We'd better catch our plane," he said, gripping the edge of the seat.

Thien saw his reflection in the side mirror and realized that he was looking into it, and at her. "Thank you, Noah," she said, happy that the glass served to connect them. Though the mirror was pointed up too high and she couldn't spot the road, she didn't adjust it. She wanted to see his face.

"Let's go find those dragons," he said, smiling faintly at the glass, at her.

She twisted the throttle and felt him draw nearer to her. As their speed increased, the distance between them vanished. His hands wrapped around her waist, and he clung to her as they weaved around slower traffic.

• • •

To Noah, the flight to Hanoi was like any other. The cramped conditions of the airplane cabin made his back and leg ache. He asked for a Tiger beer as soon as they left Ho Chi Minh City. The beer calmed his nerves—both mental and physical.

Thien had never been on a plane, and even the ancient Russian jetliner caused her smile to widen. She sat in the window seat, her eyes rarely straying from the sights below. She marveled at the shimmering sheets of rice fields, dozens of rivers snaking through lush highlands, and miles of coastline where frothing waves tumbled against deserted shores. Everything was so green, as if it had rained each day for a thousand years. Thien thought the undulating land looked like an emerald sea. At times she wanted the plane to go lower, so that she could more closely inspect this sea. But she also enjoyed the perspective that their great height gave her.

"I feel like I am on my father's shoulders," she said, turning to Noah.

"You do?"

"He used to carry me around our village, and I would feel so high up, like I was a bird."

Noah saw her smile, and for the briefest of moments was jealous of her unburdened mind. "What did you see?" he asked.

"When farmers ride their elephants, they use a

blunt hook to tug at their ears to tell them where to go. This is what I did with my father. I would gently tug on his ears and he would take me places." She smiled at the memory and then reached into her pocket and withdrew a tangerine. "I saw so many things. People, streams, frogs in the rice field."

"Why are you always eating those?"

She shrugged and offered him a slice. "Because I am hungry."

"Why don't you eat something that will actually fill you up?"

"Because then I would not be able to eat so many delicious fruits. And you would not get so many slices."

He bit into her offering. "They are good. Thanks."

The plane rumbled as it bounced through air currents. Thien glanced out the window, surprised to see that clouds surrounded them. "What is happening?" she asked, her tangerine forgotten.

"It's just some turbulence. Nothing to worry about."

"Turbulence?"

"The wind . . . or maybe your dragons . . . are making the plane shake."

She searched the clouds. "If it is dragons, then we have nothing to worry about."

"We don't."

"Do you want children?" she asked, still thinking about her father, about how many of her brothers and sisters he'd carried on his shoulders.

Noah moved his prosthesis so that less pressure was against his stump. "I thought Vietnamese were supposed to be private. And shy."

"Whoever said such a thing?"

"I don't know."

"I do not believe they visited Vietnam."

"Neither do I."

The clouds parted, revealing a stunning shoreline of white beaches and green islands. Thien reached for her camera and took a picture. The camera ejected the photo, which she began to blow on. "Do you want them?"

"Want what?"

"Children."

"Oh. I don't know. Not now. And you?"

"I want many. Maybe five, six, or seven."

"Seven?"

She smiled at his expression. "I want to laugh with them. To watch them grow. To feel the love between a mother and her children."

He nodded, studying her face, knowing it would one day be filled with laugh lines. "You'll be a wonderful mother," he said, wanting to see her hold her child.

"How do you know that?"

"Because you love children. And I've never seen anyone as happy as you."

She took his hand, her small fingers resting in his. "You can be happy, Noah."

"Oh, I'm not so sure about that."

"You were happy yesterday, when Tam was on your seesaw. I saw you smile and I know you were happy."

"But that's . . . that's just one moment."

She continued to hold his hand, her thumb making small circles around his knuckle. "Yes, but maybe yesterday you had one moment. And today . . . maybe today you will have two. And tomorrow three. Maybe that could happen. If your life went from good to bad, why cannot it go from bad to good?"

Noah wanted to hold her, to pull her close against him and let her take away his pain. He knew that she could comfort him, could carry him to a place where life could begin again. He closed his eyes briefly, imagining them together in such a place. "I'll try," he finally replied.

"I will help you."

"I know. I know you will."

A thump sounded from below as the landing gear moved into place. "Is that Hanoi?" she asked, pointing out the window.

"Must be."

"And we will take a bus to the sea?"

"That's the plan."

She squeezed his hand. "I have never been to the sea. Thank you for my wonderful gift."

He wanted to tell her that she was the gift—a gift to the world, a gift to him. But instead he simply sat and let her hold his hand. He didn't want her to pull it away. And when they landed he let her guide him into the light of day.

THE STREET SEEMED QUIETER THAN USUAL, and Sahn wondered if the weather was responsible. Showers the previous night had burdened the air with moisture. There was no breeze to sweep the city's scents inland or to the distant sea. On such days, Sahn's eyes bothered him the most. The blurred objects before him seemed to emanate heat as if from the embers of a fire. He wanted to step from this fire and into a cool and dark place.

Holding a folded newspaper in one hand, Sahn proceeded to a small park near the city's center. Massive trees cast long shadows on the sidewalk, and Sahn felt the touch of the shadows the way someone else might feel the fingers of a lover. He walked to a tree and sat down, resting his back against its trunk. Unfolding the newspaper, he pretended to read.

As he flipped through the pages, he listened carefully. Though the raid on the brothel would occur many blocks away, Sahn hoped he'd be able to detect the sirens. They'd tell him what he wanted to hear—that his fellow police officers were storming a brothel offering the services of young girls. Through his network of informants, Sahn had discovered the existence of the brothel and had notified his superiors. It had taken two days to organize the operation, and Sahn had barely slept those two nights, worrying constantly about a betrayal within his station.

Upon pretending to reach the end of the newspaper, Sahn stood up. He walked to a garbage can and threw away the paper. Where are those sirens? he wondered, once again exposed to the merciless sun. Gripping the handle of his baton, he gathered his will and walked away from the brothel. He didn't want to be seen near it, regardless of what happened with the raid. Better that another officer got the credit, as well as the inevitable offers of bribes. Recognition wasn't in Sahn's best interests.

The owner of a noodle stand said hello as Sahn passed. He had tried the woman's food before and thought it overpriced and bland. But he returned her greeting. Perhaps someday he'd eat again at her stall and ask what occurred in the park after the sun set.

The distant sounds of sirens caused Sahn's feet to hesitate and falter. He listened carefully to the sirens and thought he heard four police cars. Good, he thought. Now show your strength and let everyone see it.

Sahn had asked permission to interview each girl who was taken from the brothel. He wanted to know where they'd come from, how they were forced into such work, and, most important, if any of them could be saved. If he believed one or two of them could be, he'd talk with Thien and ask that they be taken into her center.

He had thought about the center a great deal over the past few days. As he'd suspected, finding a swing set had been difficult. In the end, he had made an agreement with six shopkeepers whose stores were often broken into. The arrangement was simple—Sahn would extend his beat by a block and would look after these stores. He'd do that for a year. In return, the shopkeepers would pool their money and buy a new swing set.

Thinking of the swing set, Sahn walked toward the center. The squat building soon confronted him. Stepping past the gate, he moved inside. No noises came from upstairs. Curious where everyone was, he walked through the kitchen and into the playground.

He heard the American's voice before he saw her outline. She might have glanced up at him as he approached. She sat on the ground while four figures occupied a bench in front of her. One of them appeared to be under a blanket.

Iris paused from reading to look at him. "Hello," she said. "May I help you?"

He shook his head, wondering if she was glad to see him, if she understood how he tried to protect them. "Not now," he replied.

"I just opened a book. I'm going to read a story."

"Good."

"You don't mind waiting?"

"No."

"Well . . . thank you."

Sahn didn't turn away and seek someplace quiet to sit. Instead he studied the four figures, finally recognizing Qui and Tam. He listened to Iris read a story about a British family who lived in India. At first Sahn didn't like the family, for he knew that the British had colonized India in the same way that the French had occupied Vietnam. But as the story unfolded, he was captivated by the tale of a mongoose that fought cobras to protect a young boy. The mongoose was named Rikki-Tikki-Tavi. Sahn had never seen a mongoose, but he'd heard of them, and he grew to admire Rikki-Tikki-Tavi, who risked his life in an epic struggle to rid the family's garden of cobras. The mongoose was cunning and brave and loyal, and his dedication and love for the boy were commendable.

Glancing up as she read, Iris could see that Sahn was listening to her every word. Thien had told her about his promise to deliver the swing set and his desire to save four homeless girls. Though Iris still felt uneasy in his presence, she also was surprisingly pleased to have him listening to the story. As she read, she wondered why her father had been sent to fight such men. She couldn't imagine Sahn killing her father or her father killing him. It just didn't make sense.

Iris continued to read, now watching the children, aware that Mai and Minh were completely mesmerized by her words and that Tam was trying to stay awake but was drifting to sleep. Thinking of Tam's fate, of what the doctor had said earlier that day, Iris felt weariness creep into her voice, even though she tried to keep it at bay. She did her best to inject excitement into her story—a story that she'd loved since childhood.

As Sahn listened, he heard her exhaustion and felt her strength. He saw how she continuously glanced at Tam, how she sought to make the children smile. And her passion, her commitment to the children were suddenly as tangible to him as the sun on his skin. She treated them as if they were her own.

Perhaps she is the mongoose, Sahn thought. She's everything that he is, and she's doing everything that he does. She's saving those girls from snakes, and I've been nothing more than a grasshopper who watches from afar. It's true that her country destroyed my family . . . and . . . I'll never forgive that crime. Never. But she's a mongoose in a world of snakes. In my world. And I think she wants my help. And I need to help her, even though I'm no longer a mongoose like her. I'm old and poor. I can't see. I still have hate in my heart. But I'm not going to blame her. Instead I'm going to help her. Perhaps I can be the bird that warns this . . . Rikki-Tikki-Tavi of the snakes. If she can be the mongoose, I can be the bird. I don't care if she's

American, if her father killed my countrymen. She's doing what's right and I'm going to help her.

THE OLD BUS MOVED CAUTIOUSLY THROUGH Hanoi's crowded streets, as if its driver were afraid that a bump might cause it to spontaneously disintegrate. Sitting at the front of the Russian-built vehicle were Noah and Thien. Her camera on her lap, Thien gazed through a cracked window at the passing sights. The treelined boulevard on which they traveled brimmed with cyclos and scooters. Mothers and children dominated most of the scooters, though soldiers, workers, and monks also darted about like fish competing for a downed fly.

For several minutes, Thien saw the same sights she did in Ho Chi Minh City—block after block that combined century-old French architecture with bland, two-story shops. They passed a giant outdoor market where women sold everything from puppies to prawns, eels to onions. A few minutes later they approached Hoan Kiem Lake. Thien had studied Iris's guidebook before the outing and knew that the lake was one of Hanoi's most famous sights. Massive willow trees surrounded the large body of water. Students and lovers strolled around the lake, often walking hand in hand. At small courtyards men played board games and women practiced tai chi. A curved red bridge led to an island. This bridge was called the Flood of Morning Sunlight, and Thien was impressed by the aptness of these words. Upon the island was the Temple of the Jade Mound. She'd read that the temple had been created to celebrate the masters of literature. Famous writers had searched for their muses there for generations.

The bus turned slowly onto a wide road that led east. The pace of traffic was fast, and the bus gradually sped up, leaving downtown Hanoi's presence behind. Concrete buildings transformed into cinder-block stores and then into stone and wooden structures. Before long they sped over gentle hills and across lazy rivers. Endless rice fields reached out in every direction.

When the road narrowed and was no longer smooth, the bus protested with creaks and groans. The driver tried to avoid potholes but might as well have attempted to steer around the dragonflies that struck the windshield. Beyond the roadside stalls, the land grew wilder, as if they were driving backward into time, away from the hand of humanity.

Soon Thien detected a strange scent in the air. "What do I smell?" she asked, lifting her camera to photograph three boys on the back of a water buffalo.

Noah tried to smile, though the lurching bus caused pain to race up and down his back. "The sea," he replied. "You're smelling the sea."

"The sea? But how?"

"Well, you can't smell the factories, the city. And the sea has its own scent."

Thien breathed as deeply as she could. "When will we reach the water?"

"Soon."

The bus driver increased their speed as they came upon a new road. The land around them blurred. Before long they approached a harbor. Fairly modern fishing boats mingled with listing military craft. Out in the water, solitary fishermen threw nets from large, circular vessels that resembled floating baskets. Thien and Noah absorbed these sights as the bus neared a wooden pier. At its end rose an old sailing ship that had a pair of masts. The ship was wooden and stout, its sides blackened by the sea.

Thien and Noah made their way to the vessel, walking across a wooden bridge to reach its deck. After handing a pair of tickets to a weatherworn sailor, Noah led Thien to the bow.

"How does it float?" she asked, in awe of her surroundings.

He leaned against a railing, watching how the sun struck her face and disappeared beneath her cap. "It's wood, Thien. All wooden things float."

"I know that, you silly man. But it is too big. It must be too big to float."

"Just like you thought our plane was too big to fly."

Thien shook her head in wonder, gazing about as other passengers filled the deck. Before long the ship was unmoored from the pier. An engine came to life and propelled the vessel into deeper waters. Once the shoreline had thinned to a nondescript track of green, the engine went silent and the two sails unfurled. The sails were ribbed and red and angular, resembling the top fin of a fish. A strong wind pressed against the fabric, effortlessly pushing the ship forward.

Now that other passengers were about, Thien moved closer to Noah. "I feel like we are flying," she said.

"Me too," he replied, watching her smile spread.

"I do not know what to expect. A dragon?"

"Just keep looking."

"I am. Everywhere."

Even though the sights around them soon blossomed into something unworldly, Noah rarely took his eyes from Thien's face. He watched her gaze about, saw how she twisted this way and that, how her lips moved as she whispered in wonder. Thien was utterly transfixed by what unfolded before her, for countless limestone islands rose straight from the sea. Many of the islands were larger at the top and appeared as if they might fall to one side or the other. Most were immensely tall, reaching higher into the sky than the buildings of downtown Hanoi. The gray islands—which were topped with lush foliage—tended to rise in lines, as if indeed purposely placed to keep out invading ships. The islands were everywhere, as numerous as worshippers in a temple. The sun was low in the sky, and the islands cast enormous shadows that made Thien think of dragons swimming beneath the surface.

When Thien finally turned to Noah, she took his hand in hers and squeezed it tight. Something stirred deep within her. What do I feel? she asked herself. Magic? Love?

Whatever she felt, something new touched her. "Do you believe in the dragons?" she asked.

"I do," he replied, listening to waves crash against the bow. "But there's a lot of ugliness in the world too."

"I know."

"A lot of ugliness and pain."

"But can you also see the beauty?"

He witnessed the extraordinary magnificence of the land, of her. "I saw beauty in Saigon," he said. "And I see it now. Especially now."

Thien wanted to smile, to hold his hand and run somewhere. But she was afraid of the future, of getting hurt. "When will you leave Vietnam?" she asked, fearful of his answer.

"I don't know."

She glanced away. Islands rose like a stone forest around them. She thought of the dragons spitting out their gemstones, of magical creatures swimming in the blue-green water. She longed to ask Noah to stay but knew that she'd never voice such words. To voice such words would betray him. She wanted him to walk on a path of his choosing, not hers.

The ship turned to the north, passing massive islands that seemed as if they'd topple over with the touch of a finger. Some of the islands had small beaches. Thien had never felt the sand on her feet, or the sea on her face. And though she'd seen beauty, she had never seen a world such as this.

A part of her wished that he'd say what she wanted him to say, just to please her for the moment. He had created the moment for her, and it was nearly perfect. She turned back to him and realized that he was looking at her. She sensed his longing and knew that it was as strong as hers. He needed her. And while she'd never needed anyone, she wanted to know what his love felt like. She sensed that it would take her to a higher place, to a place like what she saw now. Only this place would dwell within her heart.

To her delight, he squeezed her hand. "Thank you," he said.

"For what?"

"For being here . . . with me."

She had a sudden urge to touch the scar on his forehead, to tell him that he wasn't alone. "There is no place I would rather be," she replied, leaning toward him, so that more of their flesh met.

He smiled.

And to her, it was the first time she'd seen him smile without doubt, without fear. "We should look for dragons," she said, her fingers stirring against his.

"The water . . . it's flat. So they must be asleep."

"Maybe. But remember, they can fly. So we should also look above."

"And what if we see one?"

"If we see one . . . then we saw it together. And no matter if you stay . . . or go . . . we can always remember that we saw something magical together."

‿ FOURTEEN

Moonset

Only a few hours after Thien and Noah returned, Tam took a turn for the worse. She had been weaker than usual the previous day, and her pain had also increased. She'd gone to bed without dinner, clinging to Qui and Dung. Sleep had found her but was shallow and full of troubling dreams. The dreams reminded her of dirty streets.

She'd awoken in the dark, and discovered that breathing was difficult. It was as if she were trying to fill her lungs by sucking through a narrow straw. Panicking, she'd squeezed Qui's arm and tried to rise from bed, but was unable to do so. Qui had called out for Iris, who quickly appeared, followed by Thien. Not far behind, Noah had managed to hop up the stairs on his good leg.

Iris had taken one look at Tam and decided that she should be seen at a hospital. Thien, Iris, and

Qui had taken her. Someone had needed to stay with Mai and Minh, and Noah had been the logical choice.

Now, as they sat in a taxi and sped through dark streets, Iris tried to comfort Tam and calm Qui. Thien sat in the front, urging the driver to hurry. Iris was terrified of the way Tam appeared—with her eyes unfocused and her breathing so labored. Tam dropped Dung, and Iris picked up the doll, setting it on Tam's lap. "Are we almost there?" she asked Thien, slapping the door through the open window, as if the taxi were a steed that she could urge onward.

Thien turned, sweat on her brow, her cap nowhere to be seen. "Yes. It is only a few more minutes."

"That's what he said before!"

"I know. I am sorry."

"Please, Thien. Please tell him to hurry. We've just got to get there."

While Thien spoke again with the driver, Iris saw that Tam's head had started to roll with the motion of the car. "Oh, no," she said, reaching over to hold her head in place. Qui, who sat on the opposite side of the taxi, had her arms around Tam and was whispering in Vietnamese. Qui looked shell-shocked. Her shoulders trembled. Her nose bled from when she'd bumped it getting into the taxi.

Still holding Tam's head, Iris began to pray. She couldn't imagine that God was about to take this sweet girl, and she pleaded with him not to. She also tried to speak to her father. Tears on her cheeks, she told him that she'd come to Vietnam to complete his dream, and that it was his turn to help her, to help her save Tam. Please, Father, she begged. Please don't let her go. I've given you all that I can. Now please . . . please give me this.

The hospital—dark and foreboding—suddenly loomed in front of them. Putting her hands beneath Tam's limp form, Iris forgot her father and her prayers. Nothing mattered now but getting Tam inside.

FOR NOAH, AFTER THE WOMEN HAD left with Tam, time ceased to move forward. Once he had gotten Mai and Minh back in their beds and whispered words of encouragement, he'd returned to his cot and put on his prosthesis. He had started to reach for his flask of whiskey but had stopped himself from such an escape. Instead, he'd walked outside and sat on the seesaw that Tam had so enjoyed.

Now, as he watched the moon through a barren sky and thought about Tam, he remembered how she'd clung to him when he had carried her, how she'd looked at him and asked that he be her friend. The memories brought tears. He didn't wipe his eyes. Instead his hands found the handle that Tam had gripped. He recalled how she had smiled and laughed that day. Her pain had been forgotten. Her face had been young again.

Noah touched the edge of the elephant's ear. Squeezing the wood tightly, he thought of the hardships of Tam's life. He saw her begging. He envisioned her home. He closed his eyes when he remembered the little moans she made when her pain was acute.

Suddenly he couldn't bear to be apart from her. Even though Qui, Thien, and Iris were beside her, he knew that she would want everyone near. She'd look for him, and for Mai and Minh.

Moving as quickly as possible, Noah left the playground and stepped inside. He went up the stairs faster than ever. At one point he fell and banged his stump. Though the pain was considerable, he got up and kept going.

Mai was whispering to Minh at the foot of their bunk bed when Noah entered the room. "I think she'd want us there," he said, kneeling beside them.

"Sure, sure," Mai replied. "We go now."

"Do you want to go? And what about you, Minh?"

Minh stood up, nodding vigorously.

"See that?" Mai asked. "Of course he feel the same as me. We must go now. Tam need us."

"Can you tell me how to get to the hospital?"

"It not hard."

"Get dressed, then. I'll meet you at the scooter." Noah glanced around the room, his eyes settling on a bottle that held fresh flowers. "And, Mai, grab a flower for her, will you? I think she'd like that."

"And where Dung?"

"Dung?"

"Her doll. She want her doll."

"Oh, she's got Dung, and her blanket."

"Okay. See you downstair."

Noah nodded and hurried to the stairwell. He proceeded down as fast as he dared, grabbing the scooter's key from where it lay near Iris's computer. Outside, the moon had moved higher. To Noah, it had never seemed so ugly. He started the scooter as Minh got on behind him. Minh put his good arm around Noah's waist, shortening the space between them. Carrying the bottle and flowers, Mai sat at the scooter's rear.

Eyeing her load, Noah asked, "You won't fall off, will you?"

"I never fall from scooter. Impossible."

Noah switched on the headlight and twisted the throttle. As the scooter edged forward, he hardly felt the weight of the children, though he was aware of Minh holding his belt. "Please try to smile at Tam," he said as they gathered speed. "Try to make her happy. She's really sick. And she hurts. And we need to let her know how much we care about her."

Minh pinched Noah's side, telling him that he understood and agreed.

"Will she die?" Mai asked, for she'd seen two of her friends die and she didn't want Tam's eyes to go blank.

"No," Noah replied, increasing their speed. "No one's going to take her from us. Not Tam. Not today."

"And Minh and me?"

"No one's taking you away either."

Minh shook his head, wondering how Noah could say such words. Too many things had already been stolen from them for him to believe that Tam couldn't also be taken. He'd lost his hand, his family. Mai couldn't remember what her mother looked like. And she didn't laugh as much as she once did. For the first time since he'd known Noah, Minh didn't believe him. Anything could be taken from Tam, from Mai, from any of them. Noah should have known that.

Minh had seen Tam earlier that night and knew she had little left to give. Too much already had been stolen from her. Noah could promise no such thing.

THE WALLS, THE CEILING, AND EVEN the bed frame were green. Tam had never seen so much green. She thought the color looked like the water that surrounded islands. Though she hadn't set foot on such a place, she'd seen photos of islands that rose from emerald bays. Maybe whoever painted her room had been born on an island, she thought. Maybe she missed her home.

Tam took a long, shallow breath, using her strength to draw air into her weary and aching lungs. She clutched Dung tightly at the pain that this movement caused, as if her doll could somehow share her burden. Tam knew that Dung would help her if she could. Dung was good at that.

Looking around her bed, Tam saw that Qui, Thien, and Iris were gathered nearby. Qui was the closest, sitting beside her, stroking her face. Iris and Thien were speaking with a woman in a white dress. Why is Miss Iris angry? Tam wondered. Why are she and Thien crying?

Tam watched Iris turn away from the woman in white and lift a blanket from a nearby shelf. Iris must have known that she was cold, because that blanket felt so warm on her legs and body. Tam tried to thank her, but suddenly her pain was so vast that the green walls seemed to fall upon her. Though she felt her mouth move, no words came out. She squeezed Qui's hand. She closed and opened her eyes.

The woman in white stuck a needle in the back of her hand. Tam didn't like the needle, but when she tried to pull it out, Iris and Thien held her still. Attached to the needle was a clear thin tube that ran to a bag. A frightening coldness emerged from the bag, as if liquid ice were being forced into her. Again she struggled. But soon, mercifully soon, the coldness turned to warmth. The aches in her joints and lungs vanished as if a magic man had taken them away. Tam could breathe. She was very tired, but she could breathe.

As she relaxed into her bed, her tattered and beloved blanket tumbled from her grasp. Iris bent down to retrieve it, placing it atop her hand. To Tam's surprise, Noah, Mai, and Minh entered the cramped room. She was so happy to see them. Her friends had come. Her family was gathered close by. Everyone was present except for her mother. "Little Bird?" she asked weakly, pulling on Qui's sleeve.

"Yes, my sweet child?"

"Is this . . . Is it a holiday?"

"What?"

"Everyone . . . is here."

"Yes."

"Why, Little Bird . . . why are you crying?"

"Do you feel better, my sweet? Is that medicine helping?"

"Where's Momma?"

"She's . . . she's on a bus. She's coming, Tam. She told me to tell you how much she loves you. She'll be here . . . she'll be here soon."

"Don't . . . don't cry."

"Do you hurt?"

"I'm fine. Tired is all. So tired. Like that fat cat . . . who always slept near the river."

"Your friends . . . they want to hug you."

Tam watched as Iris leaned close. Iris licked her tears when they reached her lips, but a few still fell on Tam. Iris whispered something as she held her, but Tam didn't understand what was said. She could only understand Vietnamese, the sounds that she'd heard since birth. Noah came next, holding her tight. Tam remembered how he had carried her through the rain. She'd felt so lucky to be in his arms. How strong he had been.

Thien's embrace reminded Tam of flowers. Tam wondered if she'd ever smell like Thien. She hoped so. Next came Mai and Minh. They leaned close and hugged her. Their heads touched hers and Tam saw herself in their eyes. She hoped that their mothers were coming for them too, that they'd all play again on the elephant that went up and down.

As a deeper, more powerful weariness began to grip Tam, she watched everyone but Qui leave the room. Qui sat near her, stroking her cheek.

"Where . . . where did they go?" Tam asked, her voice nothing more than a whisper of wind.

"They'll be back. The doctor wanted to talk with them. And I wanted to be alone with you. Just the two of us . . . like old times."

"Why are you crying?"

"Because I don't want you to leave. Please don't leave."

"But I'm tired. So tired."

"I know."

"I'm going . . . to the new world, remember?"

"I do."

"Father will be waiting. Like you said."

"He's there. Waiting. With his arms held out for you."

Tam glanced at the clear medicine, which no longer seemed to be working. She sought to breathe, pulling what felt like wet, heavy air into her lungs. "Are . . . are you going to take me . . . to him?" she whispered.

Qui repressed a sob, her body shaking as if a leaf in a storm. "I'll carry you, my sweet child. I'll carry you to him."

"You've always . . . carried me."

"Not always. But for a long time."

"Will the sun shine there?"

"Yes."

"Will children laugh?"

"Yes."

"What about . . . me? Will I be able . . . to run?"

"You'll run, my love. Like a girl . . . playing soccer."

"So fast?"

"Even faster."

"Can I bring Dung . . . and my blanket?"

"Of course."

"I'll miss . . . my new family. My soft bed."

"The beds are soft . . . so soft, where we're going."

"Tell me . . . please tell me more. Before we leave. I'm so . . . so tired. But I . . . want to hear."

"Oh, Tam."

"Please . . . please don't cry, Little Bird. Don't cry like that."

"I can't . . . I can't stop."

"Tell me more . . . about where we're going."

"The birds. They . . . always sing."

"Will we . . . ever have to sell books?"

"No. Never again."

"Good."

"Never again, sweet child."

Tam tried to nod, but she couldn't move, couldn't breathe. The room seemed to be filling with water—the green-blue water of island lagoons. "Little Bird?" she asked, trying to stay awake.

"Yes?"

"Thank you . . . thank you . . . for loving me."

"You're so easy to love, Tam. Nothing in my life . . . has been easier. Or better."

"Thank you . . . for carrying me."

"I would carry you anywhere. To the moon. To the stars."

The water rose higher around Tam. "So warm," she whispered.

Qui crawled into bed beside her granddaughter, turning so that her back was against Tam's chest. She gently pulled Tam's arms forward and put them around her own neck, as if she were carrying Tam. "I'm . . . I'm taking you . . . to the new world," she said. "Where . . . you'll ride elephants every day."

"Good."

"It's close . . . my love. Do you see it?"

"Yes."

"What do you see?"

"Streets."

"Streets?"

"Clean streets. And our shadows."

"We're walking?"

"Will you . . . always love me?"

"Always, Tam. Nothing can take that away. I'll love you forever."

"That long?"

"Always, my precious child. You and I . . . we are one."

The water reached Tam's face. It remained warm, even as it filled her mouth, her lungs. Tam tried to speak, but her voice had gone. She felt Qui carrying her, and she squeezed the wrinkled hands that had so lovingly touched her cheeks. Somehow Qui brought her forward, through the water, toward a distant island.

Tam closed her eyes. And a miracle happened then—because she saw her own feet. And they started to move beneath her, bearing her weight, taking her to the new world.

QUI TURNED WHEN SHE FELT TAM go limp, turned so that she could face her granddaughter. She held Tam's hands, trying not to sob, not wanting her to hear such wails. She could feel Tam's hands growing cold, feel her going away. Qui had never been apart from Tam and couldn't imagine or endure such separation.

Reaching into her pocket, she removed a plastic bag that contained all of Tam's pain pills. With trembling hands she stuffed dozens of pills into her mouth. She swallowed some. She chewed others.

Qui edged closer to Tam, kissing her forehead, her eyes. She began to tell her a story, the story of how a young girl brought joy to an old woman, filling the old woman's heart with so much love that it almost burst.

Soon Qui's voice slowed. She felt herself growing tired. "I'm . . . I'm coming for you . . . my love," she whispered, her fingers gently tracing the contours of Tam's lips. "I'm going . . . to find you. Oh, Tam, I'm going to find you. You'll never be alone."

Qui closed her eyes, holding Tam tight, looking for her, peering through haze, through memories. She saw Tam smile. She reached for her.

And then their hands met and Qui was free.

SEVERAL HOURS LATER, IRIS AND NOAH sat on the steps leading to the hospital. Though the sun had risen and cast its red glow across the sky and into the city, Iris didn't want the light. She thought darkness should have prevailed for much longer. Dawn was a time of renewal, of promise. And dawn had no right to come so early, to intrude upon the mourning for Tam and Qui. As far as Iris was concerned, the world should remain black for weeks.

Wiping her eyes with a damp tissue, Iris stared blankly ahead. She was almost unaware of Noah at her side. Thien had left not long ago, returning to the center with Mai and Minh. Iris couldn't go. Someone needed to handle the details that followed the deaths. Besides, Iris wasn't ready to see Tam's bed or slippers or anything to do with her. She couldn't see these sights and remain strong before Mai and Minh.

Iris knew that hospital officials were waiting for her. They wanted to cremate the bodies, and she agreed. But she couldn't move. She couldn't talk about Tam's death, because to Iris, Tam was still alive. She still brushed Dung's hair. She went up and down on the seesaw. She smiled from her bed.

As the sun climbed higher, Iris closed her eyes. In this darkness she swore at God. She hated him. She told him that if he was going to steal little girls from the world she wanted no part of him. What a false world he had created. What a world of lies.

"Tell me . . . please tell me it's all a dream," she said, her throat and voice raw.

Noah turned to her. He'd seen too much death to try to deny what had happened. He knew that Tam was gone, knew that he'd never carry her again. And the weight of this wisdom bore down on him like tons of rock and sand. "You did your best," he said softly.

"It . . . it didn't matter."

"Yes, it did."

"I hate this world."

"I know."

"It's not right . . . what happened to her. What happened to her for her whole life. It's just not right."

"It's—"

"I wanted . . . to save her," Iris said, putting her head in her hands, no longer able to hold back her sobs. As Noah embraced her, she wept and shuddered, tears flowing down her cheeks as if they were pieces of Tam and Qui that Iris was being forced to shed.

"You gave her . . . something," Noah finally replied, his vision blurring as his eyes also filled with water.

"No, I didn't."

"You gave her a family. You gave her joy. You gave it to Qui too."

"It didn't last. Nothing lasts."

"For Mai and Minh . . . it can last."

"I feel sick."

"Just slow down. Breathe. In and out. And here . . . put your head on my shoulder."

Iris did as he asked, wanting to be held, needing to be held. If she wasn't held, she didn't think that she could endure the pain, the knowledge that the world had lost Tam and Qui, a pair of angels who would never be replaced.

FIFTEEN

In the Footsteps of Dragons

The kitchen smelled of roasted garlic and shrimp, but no one seemed interested in the meal. Iris, Noah, Thien, Mai, and Minh sat around a wooden table and poked at their food. A stray shrimp was eaten but not tasted. A pork dumpling was dipped in sauce but then left idle. Several times Iris or Thien tried to start conversations, but words quickly became hollow, meaningless. Thoughts about anything other than Tam and Qui seemed traitorous, and thoughts about Tam and Qui were too painful to bring to life.

Though everyone around the table had experienced death, Noah had suffered its sorrows most often. And events of the previous night reminded him of those sorrows. Tam had been too young to die, just like his friends in Iraq. He'd seen too many of his friends perish—bright and brave soldiers who were young fathers and mothers, who had dreams that would forever go unfulfilled. His best friend, Wesley, had told him about such dreams. And now Wes was gone, just as Tam was—both beautiful souls that should have flourished for decades longer.

While Noah lamented the loss of Tam and Qui, and reflected on the war, Iris thought about the events of the past two weeks, asking herself if she should have done anything differently. Should she have gotten on a plane with Tam and taken her to America? Would someone at home have been able to save her? What if she'd come to Vietnam a year earlier with her father? Maybe she'd have met Tam and been able to rescue her.

Iris assailed herself for what she saw as failings. She had failed her father, and she'd failed Tam and Qui. They were all dead, and she'd done too little to save them. She thought repeatedly about how Qui had held Tam, at the end, and knew that this vision would always remain with her. Her tears came and went as she drifted between misery and self-condemnation.

Iris no longer believed God to be compassionate and caring. Those were lies told over thousands of years. If God existed, he was obviously indifferent to Tam's sufferings. And Iris could never love such a being. Such a being deserved only her scorn.

And yet, her disdain for her fellow man and woman was stronger than her disgust at God. At least, she thought, God didn't walk the Earth. He didn't see and touch horrors and choose to ignore them. He didn't buy massive diamonds or ride in limousines when children were sick and hungry. He didn't watch Tam beg and hurry past without a second glance.

Hating the world, and the lies that were told,

Iris looked up from her food and saw that Thien was also trying to hold back tears. The sight of Thien's misery caused Iris to shudder. At that moment she'd have given anything to hear Thien sing and Tam whisper to Dung. Before Thien could cry, Iris gathered her will and said softly, "I think we should rename the center . . . after Tam."

At first no one responded. To Iris's surprise, Mai was the first to speak. "Sure, sure," she said, holding Dung carefully, cradling the doll as if it contained Tam's spirit. "This good idea. It make Tam happy. And it make other children happy."

"Do we . . . do you know her last name?" Noah asked Iris.

"Tran. It was Tran."

"The Tam Tran Center for Street Children?"

"Yes," Iris replied, wiping her eyes. "That's it."

Thien took Iris's hands in her own. "We could have a sign made with her photo."

Iris nodded, thinking of the picture Thien had taken of Tam. "She'd . . . I'm sure she'd really like that." Iris sniffed several times, the memory of the photo causing her grief to rise up as if the bonds holding it in place had snapped. Before she started to weep, she turned to Mai and Minh. "Why don't you go outside and play? It's such a beautiful day."

Minh pretended not to see Iris's tears. He put his stump in Mai's hand.

"Good idea," Mai replied, letting Minh lead her out of the kitchen. "You come too. Okay, Miss Iris?"

"I will."

"Promise?"

"I'll be there."

Mai and Minh departed, and to Iris the room abruptly seemed empty. Without the children, the kitchen had lost its life, the way colors fade from a fish that has been stolen from the sea. Iris wanted to add life and colors to the room, not to see them taken away. "Do you think . . . What do you think about spreading their ashes beneath the trees you planted?" Iris asked Noah. She wiped her eyes, no longer able to keep her tears at bay. Shudders consumed her—aftershocks from the collapse and departure of beauty.

Thien wrapped her arms around Iris and held her tight. "It is good to cry, my sister," Thien said, even though she hated tears.

Noah moved beside them, searching for their hands, unsure what to say. He couldn't speak, because he understood that some wounds could never be completely closed. To speak of such healing was to lie. And he didn't want to lie to Iris and Thien, any more than he wanted to dishonor Tam and Qui.

And so he simply sat and held Iris and Thien as they cried over a girl and an old woman whom they'd found and lost—stars that had shimmered in their presence for a moment and then disappeared into an uncaring sky.

FOR TWO DAYS, LOC HAD BEEN watching and waiting. Pretending to be a blind beggar, he'd sat near a gate in the fence that surrounded the playground. Staring blankly into the playground, he'd looked for Mai and Minh. He had seen them several times, but they'd always been accompanied by an adult.

Sitting so idle had been a hellacious experience for Loc. It reminded him of his youth, of years spent begging on corners. Even worse, he hadn't been able to light his pipe during the long hours by the playground. And not being able to float between worlds caused aches and memories to torment him the way flies bite at the tender flesh beneath a water buffalo's eyes.

Loc blamed Mai and Minh for his predicament. If they'd stayed loyal to him, he wouldn't be out of money, wouldn't be desperate and sitting against a stone wall. Instead he'd be drifting above the filth that comprised his life. He'd be free of pain. A woman might be beside him, sharing his pipe and soon his bed.

Loc cursed, feeling old and tired without opium within him. Without opium, his rotting tooth assailed him, his once-broken ankle ached. He needed the drug, needed it the way a bicycle needs wheels. Without opium to carry him, he'd end his life. He'd find his mother, kill her, and then step in front of the nearest bus.

Though Loc was unafraid of death, he wanted to live. Opium made this desire possible. With opium he was strong. He could travel to places far and near. He could feel the soft contours of a woman and know that, at least for the moment, she was his.

Mai and Minh's money allowed such realities and fantasies to exist. Above all other needs in his life, he needed the girl and half boy. Without them, nothing else mattered.

Holding a long, rusting nail in one hand and a beggar's bowl in the other, Loc continued to watch the playground. When Mai and Minh suddenly appeared, his aches and bitterness departed, replaced by anger and greed. The children were alone. They moved toward a seesaw and soon started to go up and down.

Loc's rage increased when he realized that the children were wearing new clothes. The money for those clothes could have gone to him, could have bought him a night of pleasure. Gripping the nail like a knife, Loc hurried across the street, moving silently and swiftly, eager to see them cry and to once again hold them in his power.

To Minh, the seesaw didn't seem so extraordinary without Tam on it. When she'd been on it, she had seemed to infuse light and life into the plywood elephant to the point where Minh thought it might charge across the playground and into the city. Now the elephant merely went up and down. It didn't seem real. It didn't make him smile. It simply was a pair of painted boards connected by another board.

Minh wished that he'd been wrong about Noah's promise. But in the end, Tam had been taken all too easily. She hadn't even gone kicking and screaming. She'd simply gone. And in her absence, Minh wondered what would be taken next from him. Maybe he'd get sick and die. Maybe Noah would leave. Most frightening, maybe Mai would make new friends at the center and forget all about him. He was nothing special, he knew. She'd already remained with him far longer than anyone else had. Anyone, that is, but Loc.

"Should we stay here?" Mai asked, pushing against the ground with her sandaled feet.

Minh tapped his finger on the seesaw, wanting her to stay, even though new friends might steal her from him.

"I wish you'd talk," she replied, frowning. "Why won't you ever talk to me, Minh the Silent?"

He shrugged, unwilling to answer.

"I should call you Minh the Stubborn, or maybe Minh the Scared. How can you be so smart at games and so scared to talk?"

He kicked harder against the soil, sending her downward quickly.

"Just for once I wish you'd talk to me," she said, swatting away a bee. "You could tell me anything and I'd listen. You could talk about your toes, your stump. About how I saw you steal that croissant when we were starving. About the Shaq. Or Tam. Just tell me about something or someone and I'll be so much happier."

Minh shook his head.

"That's right. Just sit there. Sit there looking stupid and ignoring me." Mai wiped away a tear, and started to get off the seesaw.

Minh was about to reach for her when to his horror he saw Loc suddenly appear behind her. Loc grabbed her, slamming her against him as if she were made of straw. He held a nail near her eye. Minh looked toward the center, his legs swinging off the seesaw.

"Don't move," Loc said, the nail's point touching Mai's lashes. "Either of you brats move or make a sound, and she loses an eye."

Minh glanced at the nail, and again at the center.

"Don't test me, half boy," Loc snarled, his lips drawn back. "I took your hand and I'll take her eye."

His vision clouding with tears, Minh nodded. He had never known how he'd lost his hand. He had always wanted to believe that he'd injured it as a baby, that no one could have ever intentionally hurt him.

"You'll cry more if I poke out her eye," Loc said,

pulling Mai from the seesaw. "Now, follow me—both of you. And keep your mouth shut, girl, or you'll never see again."

Minh did as asked, struggling to breathe as Loc carried Mai's limp figure from the playground, through the gate, and into the street. Loc headed toward a distant scooter that Minh soon recognized. He tried to reach out to Mai, to touch her hand and tell her that he was sorry. But Loc swatted away his fingers and all he could do was cry.

NOAH TOOK A DRINK FROM THE whiskey lemonade that Thien had made for him. Though alcohol usually soothed him, he didn't feel his aches fading away. Listening to Iris and Thien talk about Tam, he felt helpless and hopeless. Thien's tears made him want to hold her, but he knew that Iris needed her and so he remained still.

He took another sip of his drink and rose awkwardly from his plastic chair. "I'm going to see how Mai and Minh are doing," he said, looking from one set of watery eyes to the other.

Iris nodded. "We should . . . get them out of here for a while. What could we do?"

"We could go to the zoo," Thien suggested. "Or a puppet show."

Iris blew into a tissue. "The zoo. That's a good idea. Noah, why don't you ask them?"

"Sure," Noah replied, moving slowly, his prosthesis giving him more problems than usual. He stepped outside, scanning the playground. To his surprise, Mai and Minh were nowhere to be seen. Though the seesaw was empty, Noah walked over to it, as if it might tell him where they'd gone.

"Mai?" he called out, holding the elephant's ear. He glanced around, noticed the open gate, and stepped through it and into the street. He looked left and then right. And his heart dropped like a stone when he saw Mai and Minh being forced onto a scooter by Loc.

"Hey!" Noah yelled, hurrying ahead. "Let them go!"

Loc turned in his direction and smiled. He then twisted the throttle and the scooter sped away. Minh was at the rear and reached back toward Noah, his stump held out over the back tire.

"Jump!" Noah shouted, still trying to run after them.

Minh shook his head.

"Turn the key, Mai!" Noah screamed. "Turn it!"

The scooter sped around a corner and vanished. Noah swore, hurrying back toward the kitchen, shouting to Iris and Thien as he drew near, "He got them!"

Iris stepped from the doorway. "What?"

"He got them!"

"What are you talking—"

"Loc! He took them!"

"Loc?"

"He took Mai and Minh!"

Thien stepped on a pot and looked above the fence. "Which way did he go?"

Noah spun around. "I don't . . . I started shouting and he . . . he turned toward downtown. They were on a scooter." Noah hit the side of his hip. "Minh reached for me. He wanted me to help. And I tried. I tried but I was too goddamn slow."

Iris struggled to clear her reeling mind. "Where, Thien, where do you think he'll take them?"

"I do not—"

"Answer me!"

Thien raised the brim of her hat, still peering above the fence. "I am not sure. But . . . but I do not believe he will keep them in the city."

"Where would he go?" Iris asked. "For the love of God, how can we catch him?"

Noah turned to Iris. "Are your keys upstairs?"

"Wait, Noah."

"I'm going after them. Right now!"

"Just—"

"Your keys! Where are they?"

"Stop!" Iris shouted, moving between him and the doorway. "You're never going to find him like that! Are you crazy?"

Thien put her hand on Noah's arm. "We should find Sahn. He will know where to look."

"Sahn?"

"The policeman."

Iris nodded. "That's right. He said he'd help us."

She ran her hands through her hair, besieged with dread, trying to think of a plan. "You two, take the scooter. Thien, you know where he walks. Go look for him."

"And you?" Thien asked.

"A police station isn't far. I'll run."

"But you cannot speak Vietnamese."

"That doesn't matter. Someone will speak English and he'll help." Iris glanced at the empty seesaw, struggling to control her emotions, to fight an overwhelming sense of panic the likes of which she'd never known. "Why . . . why is this all happening?" she asked, rubbing her brow, her breath coming too fast and shallow. "It's my fault. I sent them outside. I should have gone with them like Mai asked me to. If only I'd—"

"Stop it," Noah said, shaking his head, squeezing her shoulders.

"But I shouldn't have—"

"We're going to get them back. You hear me? They took Tam and Qui, but they aren't going to take Mai and Minh."

"They can't, Noah. They just can't."

He squeezed her shoulders again. "They won't."

"But how can you say that? How can you know that?"

"Because Loc needs them. He stole them because he needs them. So he's not going to hurt anybody. All we have to do is find them. Find them and bring them back."

"You're sure?"

"That's what we're going to do. Right now."

She reached into her pocket and handed him the keys to her scooter. "Then find them. Please find them."

"Just hurry to that police station."

"I will."

He turned to Thien. "Let's go get Sahn."

THIEN DROVE THE SCOOTER WHILE NOAH scanned their surroundings. She drove with speed and efficiency, weaving around slower traffic, navigating cluttered streets as if she were the wind brushing past leaves. Noah's gaze was much less precise, darting into crowds and shops. Though his time with the marines had taught him how to focus under pressure, he found it difficult to settle his emotions. Mai and Minh were being held against their will, and the thought of Loc mistreating them filled Noah with worry and rage. While he knew that Loc needed them, he also knew that they could be hurt in ways that wouldn't prevent them from sitting on a corner and begging for Loc's money. And this was the knowledge that tore at him, the knowledge that he'd kept secret from Iris.

Painfully aware that each passing minute only gave Loc more time to escape, Noah urged Thien to drive even faster. He often had to hold tightly on to the scooter as she followed the contours of roundabouts or turned abruptly down narrow alleys. People on nearby scooters, usually so polite and understanding, often glared or gestured at Thien for her excessive speed.

"Where else could he be?" Noah asked, wishing they had two scooters.

"We will find him. We just—"

"There!" Noah shouted, pointing toward a uniformed policeman. "Isn't that him?"

Thien didn't answer, instead crossing the busy street, holding up one hand as she drove against the flow of oncoming traffic. The beep of her horn sounded when they neared the curb, and Sahn turned toward them. He looked angered by the intrusion, but before he could speak, Thien said hurriedly in Vietnamese, "Captain, Loc kidnapped Mai and Minh! Just now! He came to our center and took them!"

Sahn grunted. "Kidnapped them? How?"

"We were inside. They were out in the playground."

"You left them—"

"They were only alone for a minute! He must have been watching."

"And you're sure it was Loc?"

"Noah saw him take them."

"Against their will?"

Thien rose above her seat. "He took them, Captain!"

Sahn's fingers tightened around the handle of his baton. "Do you have a photo of the children?"

"I don't think so."

"Yes or no?"

"No. No, we don't. They just started living at the center and we—"

"Silent," Sahn replied, holding up his hand. He thought about calling his superiors, about starting a manhunt. He'd do these things, but they'd take time, and they didn't guarantee the return of the children. "You'll have to go after him."

"Go after him?"

"Without a photo, do you think the police will find them? Who would they look for?"

"But Minh . . . he's easy to describe."

"He's one of thousands of homeless boys. You can't rely on that."

Thien thought about all of the street children in Saigon alone. "Doesn't Loc have a record? Can't you search for him?"

"Of course we'll search for him. But he won't be caught easily. And it will take time for us to move. Do you want to wait?" Sahn turned from the sun, his mind churning. "I know this Loc. A long time ago, I arrested him. His family is from Nha Trang. He has friends there. Go. Go to Nha Trang. Look for them on the beach, where the tourists are."

"Nha Trang? But that's—"

"He can't stay in Ho Chi Minh City. And if he can't stay here, where else would he go but Nha Trang?"

"Will you notify the police there?"

"Right away. But you'd be foolish to count on them. Most will be lazy or corrupt or nothing more than men who sit at desks and kill flies. And they won't move fast enough."

"But they might—"

"Better to count on yourselves than them. Count on yourselves and you'll have no regrets. You or the police will find them, and you'll have no regrets."

Thien thought of Nha Trang. She'd never been there before, and while she agreed that they had to move quickly, she didn't like the thought of being without help in a strange city. "Will you go with us, Captain?" she asked, wincing as her calf bumped up against the hot muffler of the scooter.

Sahn would have liked to do just that—to save the children and break Loc forever. But with his eyes, he'd be more of a liability than a help. "If the children were to somehow escape," he said, "where would Loc go?"

"He'd come back for them. To the center."

"And I'll be waiting for him. With the American woman. I'll protect her and arrest him."

Thien didn't respond, and Noah asked her what was happening. "Just another minute, please," she said in English. "And I will tell you everything."

"Can he move on that leg?" Sahn asked in Vietnamese.

"He does his best."

"But can he move? Because if you find those

children . . . you're going to have to take them. Loc won't give them up. You take them, and if he comes for you, start screaming so loudly that he'll be forced to run away. He won't come after you if people are around. So you take them and make a scene. And then get on the first train back."

"What if he's not in Nha Trang?"

"Then go to the police station there. I'll leave instructions for you. I'll have the police looking everywhere else. And they'll be looking in Nha Trang. I just don't want to count on them there. Not when you two can so easily identify the children."

Thien eyed the oncoming traffic for a break that would allow her to cross the busy street. "Thank you, Captain," she said, her grip tightening on the throttle.

"Is he a good man?" Sahn asked, staring at Noah.

The question caught Thien off guard, but she straightened and said, "As good as anyone."

Sahn noted the defiance in her voice and the speed with which she rushed to defend him. "You protect her," he said in English to Noah. "You understand?"

Noah nodded, wishing that he could speak Vietnamese. "I will."

"Now go," Sahn said, continuing in English. "Go and find them. And take them. With strength."

"Please watch over Miss Iris," Thien replied, and then twisted the throttle and darted into the approaching traffic.

Sahn did his best to watch them go. Even with his crippled eyes, he knew that she was lovely, and that she loved the American. Are they doomed? he asked himself, thinking about the war, about how thousands of American soldiers were forced to run from their Vietnamese lovers. The soldiers had either died or escaped to America. And the women had remained, their fates usually unpleasant.

Will it end for her in tragedy? Sahn wondered, hoping that it wouldn't. She seemed so full of life and promise—a woman who could carry Vietnam into the future.

"Be careful," he whispered, trying to locate her scooter in the chaos, hoping that the past was dead and that this time the American would stay.

MAI HAD NEVER BEEN IN THE back of a pickup truck. Under normal circumstances, she'd have enjoyed the experience. The wind would have caressed her face while the movement of the truck made her smile and laugh.

As it was, she couldn't have been more despondent. She sat next to Minh with her back near the cab, her feet bound together with electrical wire. Loc sat opposite them. He'd already expelled some of his rage, and Mai's stomach still ached from where he'd struck her. She had wet herself immediately afterward and now sat in her damp shorts, wishing that she'd never been born.

Mai no longer bothered to wipe her tears. They

simply ran down her face and fell to her lap. Though she wanted to comfort Minh, she didn't have the strength to even find his eyes. Better to simply sit and watch the landscape pass. She didn't know where they were going, other than that they were headed north. She'd heard this bit of information as Loc spoke with their driver before they left. The men had laughed and smoked from Loc's pipe.

For the first time in her life, Mai wanted to use the pipe. Perhaps it would free her, if even for a moment. To be free for a moment would be worth most any price. She'd tried to find her own freedom by going to the center, tried her hardest, but freedom had again been taken from her. Maybe she'd never even had it. Whatever the case, she was once again a slave to her own fate. Freedom was a myth.

Mai glanced at the swiftly moving cement, wondering what it would feel like to tumble from the truck. Would the bus behind them crush her? Would she drift away as Tam had? Would anyone but Minh cry for her?

Wishing she knew what death felt like, Mai looked at the sky. It seemed to be a deeper shade of blue here, beyond the city. Maybe death was like that—a deeper shade of blue where she could be born again.

AN HOUR INTO THEIR DRIVE, NOAH wished he had his bottle of pain pills. Though Thien was an expert at avoiding potholes and debris, the road was rough, and his back throbbed from the constant jarring. He tried to reposition himself on the thickly padded seat, but nothing helped.

Noah scrutinized his surroundings, hoping that luck would befall him and he'd see Mai and Minh on Loc's scooter. The man's baseball jersey would be hard to miss, even in the midst of the chaos around them. Noah's gaze darted about more haphazardly than he'd have liked, but he found it impossible to remain calm, despite his training. He thought time and time again about how Minh had reached for him, about the fear that must grip the children. And the knowledge of their fear fueled him with a sense of desperation so powerful that he felt more like an animal than a man. His instincts dominated his logic. His adrenaline demanded immediate action. He needed to find and protect Mai and Minh, no matter what the cost to himself.

But finding them seemed impossible. Though Noah had seen many unusual sights over the past few years, he was unprepared for what he saw now. The highway leading north reminded him of some sort of bizarre, postapocalyptic world. Thousands of buses, trucks, cars, and scooters weaved their way forward, trailed by clouds of dust and exhaust. The vehicles carried anything the mind could conceive—water buffalo, streetlamps, teak tree trunks, marble statues of Jesus, and the occasional bundle of old artillery shells. Alongside the highway, endless tin stalls served the needs of travelers. Food vendors were plentiful, as were repair shops, temples, and giant steel drums that served as mobile gas stations. All of the shops and buildings were accessed by scooter rather than by foot. People simply drove up and asked for what they wanted. Occasionally, the stalls vanished and the jungle sprang forward. Hundreds of hammocks hung from serpentine branches and supported weary travelers who'd paid a nominal fee for the pleasure of resting.

The highway was being rebuilt in places and often detoured around projects powered by both modern-era heavy equipment and oxen. To Noah's surprise, Thien didn't follow traffic but drove directly through these undertakings, sometimes weaving in and out of vast earthmoving machines as if their scooter were an ant scurrying among turtles. She took such shortcuts whenever possible— driving on the wrong side of the highway if oncoming traffic was light or moving into the wakes of speeding buses that cast all other vehicles aside.

Noah kept expecting her to stop for a drink, for a moment's respite, but she drove on, stirring only to adjust her cap against the glare of the sun. He wanted to ask her to let him drive but knew that he could never make such rapid progress. Mai and Minh needed her to remain where she was, as she could best close the gap between the two groups.

The scooter might as well have been an extension of Thien's hands and feet. She and it weren't separate entities, but one—an agile creature that he found to be almost magical. Thien slowed and darted and turned a second before obstacles or opportunities presented themselves. She anticipated the behavior of the traffic as if she were a boxer in the ring, constantly jabbing and defending.

"How do you do it?" Noah asked after she held the side of a nearby truck as it moved toward them, threatening to send them careening down an embankment.

"Do what?"

"Drive like this."

"This? This is easy. Just wait until it gets dark. Then the driving will be difficult."

SAHN SAT UNCOMFORTABLY IN THE PLASTIC chair. He'd always preferred to stand, but since the American woman had offered him a seat, he had accepted her gesture. He now sat upright, with his arms crossed upon his chest. He stared at the empty playground, noting the seesaw, wondering where they'd put his swing set. The young grass was taller than when he'd last seen it. In another week it would need to be cut.

He watched the blur of the foreigner emerge from the kitchen. She handed him a bottle of mineral water, which he took but didn't taste. While most of the young people in the city drank filtered water, Sahn had grown up on tap water. Even if it was full of chemicals and parasites, he'd continue drinking it. Water shouldn't come from a plastic bottle, he reasoned, hating how the containers littered the city.

Iris sat beside him. "I feel like we should be doing something else," she said, tapping her foot, her eyes bloodshot. "Isn't there something else we could do?"

Sahn studied her. "I already call police in all major cities," he replied, wishing that they could talk in Vietnamese.

"But you said they can't always be trusted."

"Some can. Some cannot. That is why I tell your friends to go."

She leaned closer to him. "But what about Ho Chi Minh City? Should we be looking here? Maybe they're still here."

Normally Sahn would have been irritated with anyone who asked such questions. But she'd told him about Tam and Qui, and he let her comments pass without rebuke. "Loc no stay here," Sahn replied, carefully setting the bottle on the ground. "But if he do this, then I hear about it. And I catch him."

"You really think he'll take them to Nha Trang?"
"Yes."
"But why? Why are you so sure?"
"As I say before, he from there. He know people

there." Sahn didn't tell her that these people were dangerous—criminals who dwelled in the underworld, growing rich by smuggling opium. Sahn's hope was that they'd stay far away from Loc, understanding that he'd kidnapped the children, and not wanting him to draw attention to themselves.

Watching Sahn intently, Iris wondered where his thoughts lay. She knew he wasn't telling her everything. What's he hiding? she asked herself, trusting him but wishing that he'd tell her more. Is he worried about Noah and Thien as well? Should I be back at the police station? Why in the world am I placing all my faith in him?

Iris ran her hands through her hair, her emotions raw. She still ached from the deaths of Tam and Qui, and now that Mai and Minh had been kidnapped, it took all her remaining strength to try to rally her thoughts around bringing them home. Her only solace was what Noah had told her—that Loc needed them, and therefore he wouldn't hurt them.

"May I ask you something?" she said, still not used to his blank stare.

"Depend on question."

"What's to stop this from happening again? What if another child is taken?" She wiped sweat from her brow, feeling as if she were suffocating beneath her own perspiration. "I came here to house and educate children. Not to protect them. I don't know how to do that."

"Your friend? With the leg? He can no protect them?"

"His name is Noah."

"He no protect them?"

"I don't know if he'll even stay."

"Then you must find someone. Someone strong to protect them."

Iris closed her eyes, unable to imagine searching for a security guard. She had too much to do without the additional burden of hiring another key person. The mere thought of it seemed to worsen her headache. She'd started to rub her brow when an inspiration struck, and she opened her eyes. "What about you?" she asked. "You could be that person."

"Me?"

"Why not? You know the area. People respect you. No one would bother the children with you around."

Sahn wasn't someone who was easily surprised. But Iris's words caused him to bend toward her, as if he needed her to repeat them. He had assumed that she'd want somebody young and strong for the job, perhaps another foreigner whom she could speak with easily. Sahn had always believed that he'd be a policeman until someone discovered the truth about his eyes. And then his career and his life would be over. He'd find a tall bridge and start the search for his family. But now, with the American woman's words lingering in his mind,

413

he wondered if another fate might be possible. Could he watch over these children? Could he stand in the shade and listen to them play? Wouldn't that be a better fate than walking the streets on his aching feet, looking for criminals he couldn't see?

Iris saw that he was torn and pressed home her point. "Please," she said, leaning toward him. "I just . . . I can't do this and worry about their safety. It's too much. And the children deserve to live somewhere safe. They need to have someone watching over them."

"But I old."

"You're not old."

Sahn twisted in his chair, wanting to tell her certain truths, but having never confided in anyone, he didn't know what to say. "This is not . . . It is not good idea."

"Why not? I can pay you. I'll figure out the money. I'll get it from somewhere. Please. Mai and Minh . . . they're out there. All alone. Because I couldn't protect them. Please help me protect them." Iris thought about Mai and Minh being held against their will, and her vision blurred. She turned from him, wiping her eyes.

Sahn allowed her to regain her composure. "You . . . you must understand."

"Understand what?"

"In the war . . . Americans kill my family. And then I kill Americans."

"I'm sorry. I'm so sorry."

"Those are terrible times."

"I know. I've seen what they did."

"Yes."

"But you can still help me. Today. We're talking about today, not something that happened decades ago."

Sahn nodded, glad that she didn't hate him because he'd killed her countrymen. But what about my eyes? he asked himself. I must tell her about my eyes, and when I do she'll no longer want me. Very well. I won't lie to her. If I lied, and a child was hurt, then I'd be no better than the men I've sent away.

"Won't you please help me?" she asked, wanting to reach for his hands but holding back.

"There is more."

"What?"

"My . . . my eyes," he said, his heartbeat speeding up. "They hurt in war. I no see well. No one know this. Only you."

"But you're a policeman. How can you do that and not see?"

He stiffened. "I see a little. And I listen. And people tell me many thing."

Iris ignored a fly that landed on her shoulder. "If you'd been here earlier, would Mai and Minh have been taken?"

Sahn pursed his lips, needing to ask himself the same question. If I'd been on the playground, would Loc have dared to show his face? No, he wouldn't have. He'd have stayed far away, and the children would be safe. "No," Sahn finally responded. "If I here, they safe. If you always keep my eyes secret. If you tell people, then children no safe."

"Then I won't tell anyone. Never. Only you and I will know."

He sighed, still surprised by the conversation, and not knowing what to think. Could he work for an American? Would his parents forgive him? Though he knew that he'd be happier here, protecting and listening to children, he wasn't sure what to say.

"We could get you better glasses, you know," Iris said, still tapping her foot, desperately wanting his help. "You could go to a doctor, in secret, and he could look at your eyes."

"New glasses?"

"Why not try to see better? For the children's sake. Do it for them."

"But I—"

"Don't you want them to be safe? To learn and grow and be safe? Isn't that why you come by here almost every day? Why you're sending those four girls to me? You pretend it's only to take my money, but you're really looking after the children, aren't you? You see them as . . . as the future of your country and you want to help them."

Sahn had never experienced someone looking

inside him with such power. "Yes," he replied, incapable of saying anything else.

"Then help them. Help me. Please. You can work here and you'll be doing such good." Iris saw him hesitate, and when he looked away she couldn't help but cry, "Do you understand . . . that if you'd been here . . . Mai and Minh wouldn't be missing? They'd be safe. With us. Instead they've been taken. And I don't know what's going to happen to them. I just don't. They're gone and I couldn't protect them. And they shouldn't be alone out there. All alone and afraid." Iris took several deep breaths, trying to gather herself, feeling nauseated as she thought of Mai and Minh.

Sahn didn't see her tears but heard them. He heard her sorrow and concern, and he knew that they were real. Though she was American, though her countrymen had killed his brothers and sisters, she cared for his people. She was good and pure, and he realized at that moment that he'd help her for as long as she wanted.

Sahn stood up. "It time to find them," he said, blinking at the sunlight, at the wetness within his eyes. "Together we go find them."

MINH WATCHED THE SUN SET OVER vast rice fields. The sunlight shimmered atop the water, green rows of rice stalks creating lines that separated the golden water into uniform rectangular shapes. Occasionally, marble tombs stretched above the water, surrounded by irises and other flowering perennials. Farther to the east, whitecapped waves rumbled toward an unseen shore. Minh had never seen the sea and wondered about its turbulent nature. What made the waves tumble? Why did they never stop?

He'd have liked to know the answers to such questions. He wished he could read, or that someone, perhaps Noah, would tell him these things. Then someday, maybe he could sit beside the sea and understand why it seemed so impatient.

Minh hoped that Mai would look at the sea, but her eyes remained downcast. He watched her tears drop to her lap. She'd been crying for hours, crying for so long that he wondered how her body had any water left for new tears. The strong, indomitable Mai he'd known for so long was gone. The streets had worn her down as if she were nothing more than the heel of an old shoe.

Throughout the drive, Minh had risked a beating by reaching over to hold her hand. He'd tried to give her strength and hope. But her fingers had been lifeless against his. And she hadn't met his gaze, only continuing to stare at her bound feet.

Minh had wanted to scream at Loc when he'd punched her in the stomach. Mai had doubled over, weeping, her shorts dampening as her bladder emptied. Minh had understood her pain, sorrow, and humiliation. He'd felt those same emotions many times before. He knew what it was like to feel alone and afraid, to sit in the sun and think that you were suffocating—as if you were being held underwater.

Mai and Minh had saved each other often during the previous few years. When he'd felt helpless, her laughter had carried him to brighter places. And when her laughter was absent, his gentle touch had restored a smile to her face. But now, as the sun fell below the treelined horizon, Minh could do nothing to raise her spirits. She seemed beaten, as if she'd fallen to the ground too many times to rise once more.

Looking above, Minh saw clouds gathering in the darkening sky. The clouds appeared more ominous here than they did in the city. The sky was rife with them, and he wondered if it would soon rain. He didn't want rain to fall, as a downpour would only further discourage Mai.

Risking another beating, Minh glanced at Loc, who sat in the middle of a truck tire, his back propped up by an old sofa cushion. Loc's head rolled from side to side with the movement of the pickup, and Minh realized that he'd fallen asleep. Wanting to stop Mai from crying, Minh squeezed her fingers. But she didn't move. More of her tears fell, and Minh desperately wished she'd talk with him. He knew that she needed to talk, to release her frustrations. She couldn't keep them all inside, the way he could.

Minh nudged her, hoping that she'd finally

whisper to him. When she didn't respond, he looked again at Loc, who was now snoring. Certain he was asleep, Minh touched his sandal against Mai's ankle. As she knew, before they'd left for the center, he had cut a slit into the back of this sandal and had wedged their fifteen dollars deep inside. This money represented their future. With it they could escape Loc forever.

When Mai ignored the touch of his sandal, the touch of their money, Minh leaned against her, resting his head on her shoulder. For a reason he didn't understand, she began to cry harder. She shuddered. She turned away from him. The sight, the sensation of Mai looking away wounded Minh. He knew then that she'd lost hope, that in her mind she was doomed. He'd seen other girls and boys crumble the same way, and the thought of her giving up made him tremble. She couldn't give up. Not now. To give up might ease the burden she carried, but ultimately she'd die or, maybe worse, become a girl who walked the streets with nothing to sell but herself. Minh started to cry as he imagined her sitting outside a massage parlor, asking customers to enter. He knew such girls, knew how the money let them eat well and drive shiny new scooters. They danced at clubs and seemed happy. But their happiness didn't last. Somehow, somewhere it was stolen from them.

If Mai would not look at him, he knew that she was leaving him, even now as they sat, their feet bound, in the pickup. She was thinking of it now—how and where she'd leave him. Minh wiped away his tears, trying to keep his misery silent. Loc couldn't awaken now. Minh had to reach out to her this very moment. He had to reach out before she stepped farther away.

For five years, Minh hadn't uttered a word. He'd stopped speaking after Loc had badly beaten him for saying the wrong thing. He had hoped that by not speaking, he wouldn't anger Loc. And his plan had worked—at least for the most part. As the weeks, then months had passed, it became easier not to speak. By not speaking, he could protect himself, from both Loc and an uncaring world. Never again would anyone laugh at something he said. Never again would he sound like a frightened little boy. He'd just be Minh the Mute.

Mai had asked him to talk on many occasions, but he'd never said a word. He'd felt warm in his cocoon of silence, and hadn't wanted to step from it, at least not until Loc was nothing more than a memory. But now, as Mai cried and looked away, Minh felt that she needed him more than he needed himself. Without his voice, she was lost and wouldn't be found. Not by him, not by a fate she deserved. She'd leave him soon—sneak away in the night, never to return.

He leaned even closer to her. "Mai?" he whispered, his voice sounding strange, deeper than he remembered.

421

She turned to him slowly, as if she'd been napping. But her eyes were wide open, her mouth ajar. "You . . . you . . . can talk?" she asked quietly.

He put his lips against her ear. "Please don't leave me," he said, unnerved by the sound of his own voice and the thought of her departure. Tears dropped to his lips and touched her earlobe.

"But . . . but you're talking."

"I can—"

"Talk? You can talk, Minh?"

"Yes."

"But how? Why?"

He sniffed, wiping his nose. "I didn't forget."

"I don't understand."

"Promise me. Promise me you won't leave."

She squeezed his fingers. "I won't. Not ever."

"Really?"

"I swear it. I wouldn't want to."

Minh glanced at Loc and once again pressed his lips against her ear. "Does my voice . . . Does it sound all right?"

"Sure."

"Really? You won't laugh?"

"What do you mean?"

"Laugh at me."

"Not unless you're trying to be funny."

"You won't?"

"Oh, I'd never laugh at you . . . Minh the Talkative."

Minh smiled faintly. The pickup hit a bump and

Loc stirred. Around them the single headlights of scooters appeared like bouncing yellow balls. "We're not alone, Mai," he whispered, watching the traffic behind them.

"Yes, we are. Just like we've always been."

"He's going to come," Minh replied, thinking about how Noah had tried to run after them, how he'd grabbed at the air.

Mai shook her head. "They couldn't help Tam."

"He's coming. I know he is."

"But how will he find us?"

Minh's lips pressed against her ear as the pickup rounded a bend. "We're going to help him."

"How?"

"Everyone, everywhere, will see my stump. And we've got money. We'll call them, Mai. We'll tell them where we are."

"But what if they don't come?"

"Then we'll run into the jungle. We'll escape. And I'll talk with you every day, Mai. I'll talk with you and you'll never be alone."

"You'll talk? Every day?"

"I wanted to talk with you. So much. But I was afraid of Loc hearing. He made me . . . stop talking. And he likes it that way. So I didn't talk. I'm sorry."

"You tricked us all."

"Just Loc. He thinks that I won't speak anymore. To anyone."

"Please don't be quiet again."

"You won't leave me? You promise?"

Her grip on his hand tightened. "You're my brother, Minh. And brothers and sisters don't leave each other. Never. Maybe our parents left us. Maybe they never loved us. But I love you."

"I love you too. I was so afraid . . . just now . . . that you were going to go. Please don't go, Mai. Don't ever leave me."

Mai wiped tears from her cheeks and watched a bus pass them. It was full of sleeping tourists. "I wish we could take a bus," she whispered. "Take one to a new place."

"We will."

"But who'll want us? All I can do is sell fans. You only have one hand."

"We can go to school."

"School?"

"Yes. At the center. After Noah comes for us. You can study English, and later maybe work in a hotel."

She smiled for the first time during their ride. "And you? What will you study?"

"The ocean. I want to study the ocean. What do you think makes the waves, Mai?"

"You're talkative now. Now that you've found your voice. I'll have to think of new nicknames for you."

"We'll have so much to talk about, after he rescues us."

"You're sure?"

"They want us, Mai. Don't ever forget that they want us."

Mai nodded, leaning against him, her body moving in concert with the pickup. Soon the rain began to fall. Loc awoke, cursing. He checked to see that their bonds were tight, and dragged them to opposite ends of the pickup's bed. Loc asked Mai where he might buy another game for Minh to gamble with. While she answered and they looked at him, Minh again pretended that he had no voice, even though he wanted to say so many things, and so much beauty existed in the stories, the questions, and the feelings that he wanted to share.

THE RAIN HAD BEEN WARM AT first, as if Noah and Thien had turned on a shower and been enveloped in comforting wetness. But after the sky had grown dark, the air and rain cooled. The rain seeped through the ponchos they'd bought and chilled their skin. As exhaustion had finally overwhelmed Thien, she'd gotten on back and let Noah drive, edging close enough to him that the touch of their bodies generated welcome heat.

The land around them had changed significantly over the past few hours. The roadside stalls had disappeared once they'd neared the coast, fifty miles beyond Ho Chi Minh City. Now the jungle seemed to encroach upon the highway. Though few hardwood trees remained standing, a wall of bushes and palm trees rose on either side of the road. The behemoth hardwoods that did reach sky-ward looked out of place—awkward reminders of what had once existed, the bones of species that no longer graced the land.

Their scooter passed over countless streams and rivers as the rain fell harder—fortunately driving into their sides and not their faces. To the east, the South China Sea seemed blacker than the night, gatherings of lighted fishing boats occasionally interrupting the darkness. The fishing boats each carried two giant booms that were filled with hun-dreds of lights and could be swung out over the water. The lights attracted fish, and from a distance the bobbing boats resembled fireflies navigating a breezy night. As he drove, Noah glanced at the boats, having never seen anything like them. In the dead blackness of the sea, the brilliantly illumi-nated boats looked surreal. He wondered what it would be like to work within such a contrast of light and dark. How many fishermen had fallen overboard, never to be seen again?

The longer Noah drove, the rougher the road became. No streetlights existed, no distant homes glowing from within. The lone headlight of their scooter seemed laughably insignificant, revealing only a stretch of pavement that ran a hundred feet before them. To the south, west, and east darkness prevailed, so thick and ominous that Noah couldn't tell if his eyes were closed or open when he glanced in those directions.

Few vehicles used the highway, and the drone of billions of insects rose above the splatter of the rain. Frogs croaked. Crickets chirped. Snakes slithered across the pavement. Noah drove with care, knowing that a punctured tire would cost them dearly. His teeth chattered, and he wished they'd each bought two ponchos. He had torn his in several places, and rain penetrated these openings the way water rushes down a drain. He tried to drive with his arms held close together, so that they rested against his sides. The bumpy pavement had long ago conquered his back and stump, which now ached despite the aspirin and beer he'd swallowed at a roadside stand.

Though miserable, Noah drew strength from the presence of Thien so close behind him. He was keenly aware of how she'd eased her arms beneath his poncho and wrapped them around his torso. Her hands felt warm against his belly. Her head rested against his back.

When musings of Thien weren't occupying his mind, Noah thought about Mai and Minh. He pictured them on Loc's scooter, being forcibly taken away. He imagined them on a park bench in Nha Trang, shivering beneath the onslaught of the rain. How frightened were they? Had Loc hurt them? Did they feel abandoned and betrayed?

Such questions rolled about Noah's mind like the waves he occasionally glimpsed. The questions filled him with a mixture of sorrow and misery and rage. Believing that he'd failed Mai and Minh, he did his best to plan for the coming day. He knew that Loc would station the children near places populated by tourists. Along the beach, maybe? Near the train station?

Noah was sure Loc would keep a close eye on his captives. He wouldn't let them out of his sight again. How am I going to get them away from him? Noah wondered, his cold fingers easing off the throttle as he avoided a fallen branch. If Loc confronts me, what should I do? He'll probably have a knife. And I don't want anyone to get hurt. Not even Loc. But I'm sure as hell not going to let him take them, either. That's never going to happen again.

The road dipped and suddenly water covered it completely. Noah braked hard, and the scooter skidded for a few feet on the wet pavement. He peered ahead, but the headlight revealed only more water. "I guess we'll have to drive on and see what happens," he said, trying to gauge where the road went.

"Wait, please," Thien replied, getting off the scooter. "I think it would be best if you followed me."

"Followed you?"

She took off her sandals and held them beside her. "I will see how deep it becomes."

Noah watched her step into the murky water, his

gaze resting on her slender calves. She walked carefully, but with determination. Soon the water was almost to her knees. He followed ten feet behind her, aware that if the water got much deeper it would silence their scooter.

Pausing, Thien turned to her right. "Do not go that way," she said. "That way is only mud."

The rain continued to pelt them, driving inland, as if picked up and thrown from the sea. Noah licked the wetness from his lips, standing to empty the water that had pooled on his lap. His eyes settled again on Thien, and despite his aches and chills, he shook his head in admiration. She adjusted her baseball cap, turning the bill into the wind. Her purple poncho billowed around her, flapping like a kite stuck in a tree.

"I can see the road!" she shouted, hurrying forward.

Noah sped after her, and soon they were on dry land. "You're really something, you know that?" he said as she sat down behind him, wrapping her arms about him once again.

"What do you mean?"

"Why don't you ever complain?"

"Complain? Why would I? I am very lucky."

He shook his head, keeping their speed slow in case more water should appear. "I complain all the time," he replied. "To myself mostly."

"But, Noah, you have lost a leg. You have a great deal of pain. It is all right for you to complain. If you did not complain . . . then you would have given up hope."

"Tam never complained."

Thien shifted behind him. "No. She did not. But Tam was very loved."

A lone scooter passed in the other direction. Noah watched it through the curtain of rain, wondering where the driver was headed. "I'm glad that . . . I'm really glad that you're with me," he said, turning his head slightly so that she could hear him better. "And . . . I like the feel of you against me."

"I know."

Noah wanted to tell her things—hopes and fears that he'd told no one. Normally, he would have simply buried this desire deep within him, but tonight, he felt like only the two of them existed and he needed to speak of truths. "Can I tell you something?" he asked, slowing slightly, so that she wouldn't misunderstand his words.

"Of course you may."

"I want . . . I want to feel all of you against me."

"You—"

"Sorry. I know that's maybe too much to say. But it's the truth."

She tightened her arms around him. "I want this also. But will you stay? Will you stay in Vietnam?"

"Yes."

"Why?"

"Because of you. And Minh and Mai. And Iris. But mostly you."

"But you could be with any girl. Why are you interested in me?"

With his left hand he reached beneath his poncho and felt for her fingers. "I've never met anyone like you," he replied. "You're . . . so pure. You make me feel free."

"Free?"

"The way you sing. How you're always peeling fruit and asking me if I want some. How you pour whiskey into my lemonade. You just . . . you seem to understand me. And I'm not easy to understand."

"Yes, you are."

"I think that . . . I'm falling for you."

Thien rested her head against his back for a moment, repeating his words in her mind. "Do you care for me," she asked, "or the thought of me?"

"What do you mean?"

"You are an American in Vietnam. You are hurt and . . . longing to feel better. Maybe you want to fall for a Vietnamese girl. And so you are."

"But I didn't want to fall for anyone, Thien. I wasn't looking for that. But that's what happened. And it happened because of you."

She rose slightly and kissed his neck. "You are too hard on yourself. Much too hard."

"What do you mean?"

"You are good. And you are brave. And you should not forget these parts of yourself."

"You think?"

"I know."

He squeezed her fingers. "Thanks."

"And once we find Mai and Minh, once they are safe, then we will have time together." She felt him lean back against her, and she wrapped her arms tighter about him. "Please be careful, Noah, once we find them."

"I will."

"I care for you also. And you have been hurt enough already. And when we take Mai and Minh, Loc will want to hurt you."

"I'll be careful. Believe me, I don't want to get hurt either."

"Good." She kissed his neck again, and the rain fell harder.

"I feel like we're swimming."

They crested a hill and saw lights twinkling in the distance. "Nha Trang," she said, wiping her eyes to see better.

"Are you sure?"

"Yes."

Noah increased their speed. Soon the road flattened and broadened, and a median separated flows of traffic. From the middle of the median carefully cultivated hedges created an endless line of green. The city resembled a miniature Saigon. The shops, the signs, and the sights were all the same. But unlike Saigon, Nha Trang seemed to sleep.

The road curved eastward, and soon they drove

only a few dozen feet from the sea. Waves crashed rhythmically, reminding Noah of the sound of distant explosions. He didn't know where to drive and, seeing that no one was out, decided that they should rest for a few hours before daylight. He proceeded to what seemed to be the heart of the city—a line of modern hotels that appeared to almost lean over the beach toward the sea. Opposite the hotels sprawled a park that sparkled from thousands of Christmas lights. Noah drove into the park, stopping at the very edge of the pavement. After turning off the scooter, he took Thien's hand and slowly led her forward, past immense banyan trees that were inundated with lights. His prosthesis was even harder to move than usual, though he paid it less heed than usual. At the beach, large umbrellas had been shut and stuck from the sand like giant needles. Noah opened one as far as it could go.

"Why did you not go to a hotel?" Thien asked, as she sat on the damp sand.

He moved beside her. "Because I knew you'd want to see the ocean. Even in the rain."

Leaning toward him, she kissed his forehead. "Thank you for . . . falling for me," she said, smiling. "It makes me happy."

"I want to make you happy."

She turned toward the silent city. "Are you scared?"

"Of Loc?"

"Of not finding Mai and Minh."

He lay back on the sand to take the burden off his back. Fortunately, the umbrella was big enough to protect him if he bent his knees. "They're here," he said, wiping his eyes. "If this is his hometown . . . like Sahn said . . . then Loc's brought them here."

She moved beside him, her hand seeking his. "And do you think that we can find them?"

"We're going to find them."

"We have to, Noah. We have to bring them back where they belong."

He sighed, turning so that he faced her. "Let's try to get some sleep."

"I agree."

"But one last thing."

"What?"

He thought of her wading through the water, leading him forward. "I was proud . . . really proud of you today. You brought us here. So let me take the risks tomorrow."

"I do not—"

"I'm taking the risks, Thien. And then we'll bring Mai and Minh back to Saigon. And everything's going to be just the way it was meant to be."

SIXTEEN

Reunion, Separation

The unfinished hotel complex had already been overrun by the jungle. Vines, shrubs, and flowering weeds stretched toward the sun from corners and cracks of concrete structures. The abandoned project was massive in scope and size. Villas and restaurants, swimming pools and shops were all unfinished skeletons. It was as if, having poured a trillion pounds of cement, the builders had no materials remaining for walls and amenities.

From the third floor of the main hotel, Mai and Minh looked out at the South China Sea. Waves tumbled upon a deserted beach. Gulls hovered amid a constant breeze. To the north, the jungle stretched, complete with its own green waves and swells. Nha Trang lay a few miles away in the opposite direction—a collection of high-rise hotels and a harbor boasting hundreds of brightly colored fishing boats.

Not far from Mai and Minh, in the center of the unfinished room, Loc and four other men took turns sucking on Loc's pipe. Though Loc wore his stained baseball jersey, his friends were clad in new motorcycle pants and jackets. Their shiny black leather outfits seemed out of place in the ragged room, as did their short, stylishly spiky hair and their perfect white teeth.

Standing at the southern end of the room, a boy kept his eyes on the road leading toward the project from the city. Mai guessed that he was a lookout. The boy had been allowed one drag of the pipe, and Mai had watched as a strange smile had dawned on his face.

Now, as the boy stared toward the distant hotels, Mai listened to Loc tell his friends about how he'd duped Noah into giving him two hundred and fifty dollars to let Minh and her go free. The men chuckled at Loc's tale, smoke escaping their mouths like exhaust from revving engines. Loc spoke about Mai and Minh as if he owned them, as if Noah could no sooner take them away than leave with Loc's jersey and sandals.

As Mai listened to boasting and laughter and opium being smoked, she tried to make herself as inconspicuous as possible. She didn't like how several of the men looked at her, stealing glances in her direction while the others smoked and chuckled. Doing her best to avoid their stares, Mai watched the sea and pretended not to be frightened. She couldn't fool Minh, though, and he gripped her hand, speaking to her with his touch even if he didn't dare use his voice. Minh had once again gone silent, the way trees cease to move when a storm is gone.

Mai tried to stay strong. She didn't want to cry in

front of the men. She sensed that tears would betray her, putting her in even greater danger. And so she imagined that she and Minh were staying in a beautiful new hotel and were looking out from a glistening balcony toward a sea that they'd soon feel. They were going to search for shells, to glue them around the border of a mirror and make something pretty.

She sensed a man behind her, the smoke from his lungs rolling over her. She didn't glance up but gripped Minh's hand tighter. The man loomed over her, his shadow falling onto her lap. She continued to stare at the sea, tears forming even though she tried to keep them in. He spoke to her, but she didn't listen. She didn't turn. She wanted to cry out for help but could only stare at the sea and pretend that she was swimming. The water was warm, and she floated in it like a branch tossed into a canal.

The man put his hand on her shoulder, squeezing it as her tears tumbled to the dusty floor. Mai started to lean away, toward the abyss below. He laughed at her, leaning so close that she could smell the scent of opium on his breath. Where are you, Father? she asked as the man traced the line of her jaw. Why did you leave me so alone? Why? Why? Why?

Though her father didn't answer, Minh did. He stood up swiftly, as if a scorpion had crept beneath his leg. All eyes fell on him. Even Mai's. Minh hurried a few feet away and lifted up a thick piece of wire. After pointing at the men, one by one, he proceeded to etch a grid into the concrete floor. The grid was seven rows across and six rows down. He drew an "x" in the middle square at the bottom, and then handed the wire to the mustached man who'd touched Mai.

"He . . . he wants . . . to play . . . Connect Four with you," she said weakly, wiping away a tear, finally understanding what Minh was doing. "He'll play you for a dollar." She stood up and, improvising, added, "He'll play . . . against everyone. A game for five dollars. All of you against him."

Loc set down his pipe, smiling. "Try to beat the half boy," he said, motioning for his companions to play. "He's good, I warn you. But a half boy shouldn't beat four men."

The mustached man took the wire from Minh. "Make it ten dollars," he said, moving toward the grid.

Unsteady on her feet, Mai held on to a piece of steel that jutted from the concrete. She watched the leather-clad men gather around Minh. Though they'd been smoking opium for an hour and probably couldn't write their own names, Mai worried about Minh. If he lost, Loc would have to pay the men. If he won, they'd be angry and even more dangerous. Mai knew that Minh had no choice but to win, as Loc probably didn't have ten dollars. And Minh would win. But the men would want another game. And when that game was over, or when five games had ended, the men would look back in her direction. The mustached man would come for her.

Desperate to escape him, Mai stepped forward, her legs as weak as if she'd walked twenty miles. "Minh's never . . . he's never been to the beach. If you win, you get ten dollars. If Minh wins, we get five dollars and a trip to the beach. A trip right away."

Loc turned in her direction. "What? Ten dollars against ten dollars! That's the bet! Nothing else—"

The mustached man held up the wire, thrusting it toward Loc's face. "It's not your bet to make!"

"But she's with—"

"Don't come to my city and tell me what to do! Cousin or no cousin, I'll stick this through your tongue. Or have you forgotten what my father wanted to do to you?"

Loc, taller and broader than the other man, stood his ground. "Make it six dollars . . . and a trip to the beach."

"Done." The man hacked. "And next time you visit . . . don't let me smoke your poppy if it's been scraped from the hoof of a Cambodian water buffalo."

Loc stuck his pipe in his sock. "The half boy's waiting. Play him."

Her heart still thumping wildly, Mai watched the men bend over the grid. Loc's cousin was the last to drop his gaze toward the floor. Holding the wire like a dagger, he glanced once more in her direction, hacked again, and pushed Minh aside so that he could eye the markings at their feet.

THE SENSATION OF HEAT WAS WHAT finally woke Noah. Light from the low sun angled under the umbrella and coated his flesh with warmth. He and Thien lay against each other—her chest touching his back. Immediately after opening his eyes, he felt her presence behind him. Moving slowly, he turned, wanting to glimpse her as she slept. He'd never seen her face so close and marveled at what he interpreted as perfection. Her skin was unlined, so smooth he wanted to touch it with the tips of his fingers. Her lips, while cracked from the long journey, were full and seemed to be drawn into a faint smile, as if she were dreaming of something pleasant. As far as Noah could tell, Thien wasn't wearing makeup of any kind. A small blemish on the side of her nose was uncovered. Her eyelashes weren't enhanced with artificial length and thickness.

Noah was studying her long, black-as-night hair when she opened her eyes. She took a deep breath, smiled, and rose slowly to a sitting position. "What . . . what were you looking at?" she asked, shielding her eyes from the sun.

"You."

"Me?"

"I was watching you sleep."

She smiled again. "Was it boring?"

"Not in the least."

"Did you sleep?" she asked, brushing sand from her arms.

"I liked . . . lying with you. Even in the rain. In the cold."

"I know." She touched his knee, remembering how he'd put his arm around her. "Thank you for keeping me warm."

He started to reply but noticed someone approaching from behind Thien. A woman had hung what looked to be pots from either end of a bamboo pole that she balanced on her shoulder. "What does she want?" he asked.

"Breakfast," Thien replied. "I am sure that she is selling breakfast."

"Shouldn't we leave? Mai and Minh might be nearby. We should start looking."

"Yes. In a moment. But better to eat something first. And maybe she has seen them."

The woman walked to their umbrella and knelt to the ground, lowering her wares. She spoke in Vietnamese to Thien, gesturing toward her pots, her smile revealing several missing teeth. She nodded, opening one pot and pointing to dozens of closed shells.

"Do you like scallops?" Thien asked Noah.

"Sure."

Thien spoke to the woman, who smiled and removed a wire lid from the top of the other pot, which contained a metal rack above glowing coals. She put ten of the biggest scallops atop the rack.

"It will just be a minute," Thien said, retying her ponytail and slipping her cap into place.

"Ask her where we should look."

Thien handed the woman twenty-one thousand dong, which was a thousand more than the price of breakfast. "May I ask if you've seen two children?" she said in Vietnamese. "A girl and a boy. They might be here, begging on the beach. The boy is missing a hand. He doesn't talk. The girl does all the talking for him."

The woman used a pair of tongs to turn over the scallops. "Are they running from someone?"

"They were taken by someone. Someone very cruel."

"And they beg? Nothing else?"

"They play games for money."

The tongs continued to poke and prod. "I haven't seen them," replied the scallop seller. "Not that boy and girl. Mind you, there are dozens like them on this beach. If your boy and girl are in Nha Trang, you'll find them here. Stay close to the water and you'll find them."

"Do you—"

"Don't ask around too much, dear. This city is better for answers than questions. And people will talk. Maybe the wrong people. Just open your eyes. And see that boy and girl before whoever took them sees you. That's the trick."

"Thank you."

"Are you from Saigon?"

"I live there now."

"And him?"

"He's American."

The woman smiled, using her tongs to set the opened shells on a folded piece of newspaper. She speared a scallop with a bamboo chopstick and handed the steaming morsel to Thien. "I remember when the Americans came," she said, preparing to give Noah a scallop. "I was a girl. Living in Saigon. They rode in big trucks and they gave me so many sweets."

"Oh, that scallop is delicious."

"It ought to be, dear. My husband brought these in last night. As far as men go, he's not bad. He once found me a pearl. And he finds enough scallops that I've never had to sell it."

"I hope you never have to."

"That would be a nice surprise," the woman replied as she organized her wares. She stood up. "Stay here for two days. If you don't find them in two days, they're not here. I'll also poke around. Come back to this spot tomorrow, at this time, and find me. I may know something."

Thien thanked the woman and watched her walk toward a distant pair of beachgoers. "Here," she said, handing a scallop to Noah.

He ate it quickly, eager to start searching, envisioning Mai and Minh and what they might be enduring. "Do you think . . . they think we've abandoned them?"

"I do not know. They have always been abandoned. They probably think that we are no different."

"We need to find them. Soon."

She nodded. "I will drive. You look. If we see them and can get them to our scooter, let them sit between us. Put Minh on your lap and I will speed away."

"Speed away?"

"You have never seen me drive fast."

"And you could drive fast with four people on the scooter?"

"If we find them, and Loc starts to chase us, I will drive like the wind. So please hold on to them."

Noah ate his last scallop. After she finished hers, he offered her his hand and helped her up. "Do you know something?"

"Do I know . . . what?"

He started to lead her toward the scooter. "In Iraq, we saved some people. Some people worth saving. And that felt good."

"We are going to save Mai and Minh."

"But we also lost some good people. And they're never coming back. And if something goes wrong . . . you run. You get the police. Don't wait for me."

"No, Noah. We are together. We are a team."

Stopping, he turned toward her, raising the bill of her cap so that he could kiss her forehead and then her lips. She put her arms around him and he felt the press of her body against his. "Don't worry, Thien, about leaving me behind. I'll find you."

She traced the scar on his forehead with her fingers. "I do not want you to get hurt. You have been hurt too much already. So I will stay by your side. I will protect you."

"You can't—"

"I will not leave you. I am not afraid."

"Maybe you should be."

"Maybe. But did you see Tam . . . when she was dying?"

"Yes."

"She was so brave. She hurt so much, but she was so brave."

"I know."

Thien watched the waves tumble, wondering if Qui and Tam were still together. "Mai and Minh are brave too. They are alone and they have no one. All they want is to go to school, to be safe, to be children. Is that too much for them to ask?"

"No, it's not."

"They only want to be happy."

"They will be happy."

"Mai wants to paint with me. I promised her that we would paint together."

"Iris showed me the rainbow."

Thien sniffed, her eyes glistening. She thought about painting with Mai, about how a girl who lived in filth wanted to create something beautiful.

445

"Mai and Minh . . . they are the dragons. They are the ones who will look after us, who will make the world a better place. And I will give everything I have to bring them back. Just as I will do anything to protect you."

He kissed her, tasting the salt of her tears. "Then don't get hurt. Your smile, your songs, those are the things that protect me. Do you understand?"

"How . . . how do they protect you?"

"Because they take away some of my pain. Better than any drug. Better than any drink. So don't get hurt. If you care about me, if you want to protect me, then you can't get hurt."

She nodded, rising on her toes to kiss him. "Soon I will sing to you again. Just to you. And then you will see Mai and Minh, playing on the seesaw we built. And there will be other children. And they will laugh, and run, and learn. And we will be so blessed."

His lips touched hers and he pulled her closer, feeling her, adoring her. "You . . . you saved me, Thien. And I think . . . I know I'm falling in love with you."

"Please do not stop."

"I won't."

"Because I feel the same." She glanced at the city. "And now we are going to save Mai and Minh—the dragons who have been stolen from us. No matter what we have to do, we are going to save them and bring them home."

• • •

TO IRIS, THE OFFICE SEEMED LIFELESS, though Sahn sat in the chair next to her. She'd never felt so alone, not even as a little girl, when her father didn't return as promised. At least then she had her mother and her books. Now she had no one, and her books seemed only to tell lies, to fashion worlds and people who suddenly seemed so trite. Had her favorite writers ever really suffered? she wondered. Had they watched a child die? Had they walked the streets and seen people on the cusp of starvation or insanity? Did they have any inkling about the true nature of the sorrows that they brought to life on the page? Maybe, maybe not, she thought. Certainly some novels had made her cry. So maybe those authors had suffered. Maybe they knew about the ache of loss. Or perhaps they were simply good storytellers, able to create emotions and thoughts that they'd never experienced.

Whatever the case, Iris wished that she could find solace in something, whether books or work or memories. But she couldn't. Tam and Qui were dead. Mai and Minh had been kidnapped. Everything that she'd wanted to accomplish was in danger of being destroyed. Her father's wishes, and her own dreams for the center, would be meaningless if Mai and Minh weren't found. Nothing could ever replace the hole that their disappearance would leave in her. She would go on, of course. She'd open the center. But it would always be a hollow place for her, a place of haunting memories and unfulfilled spaces.

Having not slept all night, Iris sipped some strong tea. She pinched her thigh, trying to rouse her sluggish mind. "We should call the station again," she said, turning to Sahn.

He opened his eyes, dragging his thoughts back into the present. "What you say?"

"Can you please call them again? Maybe something's changed."

"I speak with them three time already."

"Please? Please make the call."

Sahn sighed. "Once more. But then we wait for them to call here."

"Thank you." Iris picked up the phone and dialed the number for the Nha Trang police station. She handed the phone to Sahn. She listened to him talk softly but firmly. His face, usually so expressionless, depicted frustration, then anger, then satisfaction. As she often did, Iris wished she could speak Vietnamese. She'd take lessons, she promised herself, as soon as the center was opened.

Sahn handed the phone back to her. She set it in her lap. "Well? What did they say?"

"They are looking."

"Do you believe them?"

He nodded, pleased by the response of his countrymen. "They are trying."

Iris reached between them and took his hands in hers. "Could we call the other cities again? And the smaller towns? Maybe someone saw something."

Sahn tried to remember the last time a woman had held his hands. It must have been my mother, he thought, probably the day before the bombs fell. To his surprise, he didn't mind Iris's hands gripping his. "I call them," he said, wishing he could see her face clearly, if even for a moment.

She squeezed his hands. *"Cam on."*

"You . . . you speak Vietnamese?"

"Only a few phrases. And 'thank you' is one of them."

"You say it just right. Perfect. Who your teacher?"

"No one. I've just been listening. On the street."

"You want learn more?"

"I do. Very much so."

He straightened, proud that she wished to learn the language of his ancestors. "After children are back, I teach you one word every day. Okay?"

"That would be wonderful. Really wonderful. I want to learn. I just haven't had time."

"Vietnamese easy. Not like English. English give me headache. Vietnamese sound like . . . like birds talking in a tree. So nice. You be happier here when you speak Vietnamese. Then you have less problem. Then everyone smile at you."

"Everyone already smiles at me. Except you, of course."

The corners of his mouth rose slightly. "No believe everything you see."

"So your frown is really a smile?"

"Just learn Vietnamese. Then my headache will go. And we can talk as many as you like."

She picked up the piece of paper listing the phone numbers of the police stations in nearby cities. "Are we going to find them, Sahn?" she asked, scanning the long list of numbers. "Please tell me that we're going to find them. I've been praying that we will. Praying so hard. But I just . . . I really don't know."

He sighed, watching the curly mass of her hair float before him. "Yes," he finally replied. Aware that she was seeking encouragement, that she needed it, he added, "Loc is no smart. He should take them far from here. But he is no smart and he is lazy. So he will go to Nha Trang. I know his kind. Their life is like a . . . pattern. They are easy to see, even if my eyes no work. I catch hundreds of these men. These cowards. And we soon catch Loc. And he never see the children again."

"And when we do that . . . will you do something else for me?"

"Do what?"

She leaned closer to him. "Spread the word on the street. Let everyone know what happened to Loc. What he did and what happened to him. Tell them you're with me. And that no one is ever going to hurt another one of our children."

Sahn nodded slowly, thinking again that she was a mongoose. "I tell them this and more."

"Cam on."

"Khong co chi."

Iris nodded. Though still sick with worry over Mai and Minh, she no longer felt so alone. Sahn might be old and nearly blind. He might have once killed Americans. But he was her ally, perhaps even her friend. And he'd protect what she held most dear.

After dialing a number from the top of her list, she handed him the phone. As he began to speak, she patted his knee twice, closed her eyes, and tried to think of anything else she might do to bring Mai and Minh home.

About two hundred miles to the northeast, Mai and Minh walked along the white-sand beach that dominated the shoreline beside Nha Trang. The beach appeared to go on forever—an immense, curving world that housed countless discoveries. Crabs scurried before them. Silverfish darted in the shallows. Palm trees swayed in the breeze. Though the city could be heard and seen, it seemed secondary to the beach. The sea, which stretched into the horizon, was the color of the sapphires that Mai had once seen in a storefront window. She thought the sea looked infinite, in some ways like the sky at night. Only the sky was one-dimensional, whereas she could stick her toe in the sea and look out across waves that never ended.

Though normally the sight and feel of the sea would have prompted Mai to run and play, she knew that Loc was near, and she couldn't forget how the mustached man had put his hand on her shoulder and squeezed it. His touch had made her feel cold and violated. She hadn't wanted his hand on her skin, but he'd touched her all the same. If Minh hadn't jumped to action and distracted the men, Loc's cousin would have touched her more.

Feeling panic rise within her, Mai reached for Minh's stump, holding it tight. "We have to escape," she said. "Today. Tonight might be too late. Please, Minh. Those men are mad at you for winning the game. And Loc's cousin . . . he . . . he scares me. I don't want to see him again."

Minh nodded, studying their surroundings, wondering if they should pay someone to drive them far away.

"Stop it, Minh! Don't stand there and pretend that you can't speak!"

He turned toward the sea. "Loc is on the sidewalk by the street," he whispered. "I could hit him with a stone."

"So?"

"So, I don't want him to see me talking."

"Please, Minh. I can't stay here with him. I'm too scared. Can't we just leave? Get on a bus and leave?"

"He'll see us."

"What if we went to the police?"

"I don't trust the police. He'll bribe them."

"Maybe it's time to take a chance. Maybe they'll help us."

A Westerner walked toward them, and Minh lifted up packets of postcards that Loc had bought for them to sell.

Knowing that Loc was watching, Mai tried to smile at the foreigner. "Good morning," she said in English. "You like postcards? Maybe it time for you to write your mother. I think you away from home for long time. Sure, sure, she want to hear from you."

The man smiled and extended his hands. Minh gave him the packets.

"Please, sir," Mai said. "We hungry. No eat breakfast. Please buy one packet. Only fifteen thousand dong or one U.S. dollar."

Leafing through the postcards, the man shook his head. "These aren't very good."

"Please, sir," Mai replied, "please buy one packet. Maybe you have a wife or girlfriend? Sure, sure, they excited to get postcard from you. You make them so happy. And my brother and me, then we can eat breakfast. Maybe enough rice so we not hungry today."

The foreigner sighed. "I've got ten thousand dong. I'll give you that."

"No. Please, no. That not enough. I buy these packets for ten thousand each. I make no profit if you only give ten thousand. Please. Fifteen thousand. It not much money. So little money to make your mother happy. Please, kind sir. Fifteen thousand dong to make your mother happy. Sure, sure, you is good son. Please make her happy."

He smiled, reaching into a zipped waist pouch. "You're a good saleswoman."

"No. I good saleswoman if you give me twenty thousand dong for one packet. Then I very good. Then I make good money and your mother is so happy."

"Twenty thousand?"

"That great deal for me and you."

He laughed, handing her twenty thousand dong. "You win," he said, and took the packet.

Mai gave the money to Minh. "You is good man," she said. "Sure, sure, your mother happy now. Tell her I say that you are good man. Tell her what you do."

"I will."

"Do you have children?"

"Two. A boy and a girl."

"How old?"

"Five and seven."

"Do they go to school?"

"Yes."

"They must be lucky. Do you bring them something from Vietnam?"

"A couple of dresses. And a stone dragon."

Mai nodded, wishing that the man were her father. Minh's father. He seemed wonderful. She would go anywhere with him, do anything to be his daughter. She bit her lip, holding back sudden tears. "Tell your daughter that Vietnamese girl say hello."

"What's your name?"

"Mai. Tell her Mai say hello."

"Good-bye, Mai. Thank you for making my mother happy."

"You are welcome."

Mai watched the man depart, his footprints deep and long. She wanted to follow him. Maybe he'd hold her hand and take her someplace warm and beautiful. "I don't want to say good-bye to him," she said to Minh, a tear finally tumbling. "Maybe if we told him about Loc, maybe he'd help us."

Minh shook his head. "Stop, Mai. Don't do that."

"But he—"

"He's leaving. And so are we. We're going to leave Loc forever."

She rubbed her eye. "How?"

Minh pointed down the beach toward a series of towers that carried cable cars to an island. An amusement park dominated the near side of the island, the destination of the cable cars. "We're going to walk toward that, and when we get near it, we're going to run. We'll pay for a ride, and we'll go to that island. I don't know if Loc will have enough money for a ride. Probably not, knowing him. So we'll get to the island and use our money to pay someone to take us in a boat to one of those villages we passed. And then we'll take a bus to somewhere he'll never find us."

"Not the center?"

"No. Not now. Later, maybe. When he doesn't expect us to return."

"But where will we go?"

"Somewhere in the mountains. Far from here."

"But what will we do there? Our money will be gone."

Minh shrugged. "We'll help a farmer. We'll plant rice. Or catch fish from a river. Or maybe we . . . we can find flowers in the mountains and sell them at a market. And I'll talk with everyone, Mai. Loc will never hear about a one-handed boy who doesn't talk."

Mai looked at a cable car that glided toward the island. "Have you always been so smart, Minh the Schemer?"

He took her hand. "I wanted to talk with you. But I couldn't."

"You won all those games. So many games. No one ever knew how smart you were. Not even me."

"Will you run with me, Mai? To the cable cars?"

"Now?"

"No. Let's get closer. And then we'll take off our sandals and run."

"He'll chase us."

"I know. But we'll be faster. He won't run well after smoking so much."

She squeezed his fingers. "What if he catches us?"

"He won't."

"Are you sure?"

"I'm sure."

She shook her head. "I'm afraid."

"Don't be. He won't run fast with so much opium in him."

"That's true. Sometimes he can hardly walk. I've seen faster turtles."

"He won't catch us."

Still holding his hand, Mai started to head toward the cable cars. "Thank you, Minh," she said. "Thank you for taking me away from him."

"You're my sister, Mai. Of course I'm going to take you away."

"Do you think we'll be happy? In the mountains?"

"We won't have to beg. And we won't have Loc."

"You're not afraid?"

"I'm afraid. Of course I am. But there must be more good people in the world. People like Mr. Noah and Miss Iris and Thien. People who won't hurt us. I just want to find them. Then we'll be happy forever."

Mai looked ahead, her heart starting to beat more quickly. "When will we run?" she asked, scanning the nearby street for Loc.

"Soon," Minh replied, also looking for Loc, needing to find him. "Remember the day we saw the rainbow over the river?"

"Yes. That gull's droppings almost hit you."

"Remember how later, that man let us sit at his bar and watch basketball next to those Americans?"

"The Shaq was so good that day."

Minh smiled, glad that she hadn't forgotten. "Pretend that you're the Shaq when you're running. He won't catch us if we're two Shaqs."

She tucked the packets of postcards into her shorts. "I won't ever leave you, Minh the Magnificent."

"And I won't leave you. You're my sister. And my best friend."

"Do you want to see how fast I can run?"

"Oh, yes. And when we get to that tree, the one that's leaning toward the water, we'll run. And no matter what he says or does, don't stop running."

"I won't," she replied, her heart thumping, her face and neck damp with perspiration.

"Don't stop, Mai. He'll shout, and frighten us, and you'll want to stop. But don't."

"I won't. I promise."

Minh reached down and removed his sandals. He held them in his good hand and placed his stump against Mai's palm. He turned his head and saw Loc walking beside the water, not more than a hundred paces behind them. "What does he care about the sea?" Minh asked.

Mai scrutinized Loc, studying him, hating him. "His legs . . . they're not working very well. He's still full of opium."

"You're right."

"Let's walk faster. And then we'll run. Run so fast."

"He's never going to hurt us again, Mai."

"You promise?"

"Just run like the Shaq. And don't let go of me."

Mai squeezed his stump. "I want him to see us running together," she said, trying to slow her breathing, to stop her fear from spreading.

"Why?"

"Because I want him to remember how we ran away together. How we never left each other. He laughs . . . He's always laughed at your stump. But he's going to see me holding it. That's the last he's ever going to see of us, Minh the Wonderful. He's going to see me holding your stump, and then we're going to leave him forever."

THE WATER FELT WARM AGAINST LOC'S feet. He walked in the shallows, following Mai and Minh. He didn't care if they saw him. In fact, he wanted them to see him. Though Minh had won six dollars for him in the game against his cousin, Loc was angry that it hadn't been ten dollars. He'd bought the packets of postcards and had said that if they didn't sell them all before lunch, they'd suffer.

Thinking about Mai, Loc remembered how his cousin had looked at her. Loc knew what Vien wanted. But he wouldn't get it until the price was right. And the price would be high.

Loc bent over and splashed some water on his

face. When he stood up, the world seemed to spin. He cursed his eyes and the cloud that the opium had left in him. Too much time had passed since he'd put the pipe to his lips. He needed to be lifted again. Then he'd be content. Then he'd find a woman and she'd please him as he imagined that she was his.

Closing his eyes, Loc felt the sun on his face. He wasn't happy to be back in Nha Trang. His mother had abandoned him here, and he'd had to learn how to live on the streets. He'd been beaten. Kicked like a dog. Later he was put to work by his uncle, growing marijuana in the hills to the west of the city. His power had increased as the years passed, at least until he tried to double-cross his uncle. Then only their shared blood had saved him. He'd been stripped of his money and possessions and sent to Saigon in the back of a truck full of pigs. That was almost ten years before.

Loc opened his eyes and saw the ocean. For a moment, he couldn't recall why he was at the beach. Then he remembered the children and turned in their direction. To his surprise, he realized that they were running. They were holding hands and hurrying toward the far end of the beach. What are those brats doing? he wondered. He saw the half boy glance back at him, and suddenly Loc understood.

Swearing, he kicked off his sandals and began to chase them. At first running in the deep sand was difficult. But then his mind and body started to clear. His strides lengthened. His speed increased.

Loc's rage at their betrayal was what fueled him. They were trying to escape, to abandon him once again to the streets. Without the children, he'd have no money. Opium and women would be beyond his reach. His life would be over.

He clenched his fists, imagining what he'd do to them. He would have to teach them a lesson they'd never forget. He'd take them to a quiet place where no one would hear their screams. And he'd hurt them. Hurt them so terribly that they would never leave him again.

"You're mine!" he shouted, gaining on them with every step. To his delight, the half boy stumbled and the girl had to pull him up. They started to run again, helping each other over the uneven beach.

You'll never hold each other again, Loc thought. Never. I'm going to break your spirits. Break them in such a way that they'll never mend.

MINH HEARD LOC YELL AND HE turned around, realizing that Loc was much closer. "Hurry!" he shouted at Mai, uncaring whether Loc heard his voice.

Mai began to cry, doing her best to run in the deep sand, still holding Minh's stump. She frantically looked for someone who might help them,

461

but this part of the beach was empty. And the cable cars were still far away. "He's . . . so fast," she sobbed, gasping for breath.

"We can make it! Don't stop!"

"But he's . . . too fast!"

"Hurry, Mai! Please!"

"I can't!"

"You can!" Minh shouted, leading her toward drier sand. She stumbled and he did his best to pull her up. Loc wasn't far behind. Minh could see his bared teeth. "Run, Mai!" he screamed. "You've got to run! Faster!"

Mai wiped her brow, and sand fell into her eyes, mixing with her tears, making it hard to see. Still, she did her best to run, terrified of Loc's rage, knowing that she hadn't seen the worst of what he could do to them.

THE STREETS OF NHA TRANG WERE much easier to navigate than those of Ho Chi Minh City. Thien effortlessly drove their scooter up and down the long boulevard that ran parallel to the beach. As she wound in and out of slower traffic, she scanned the sidewalk and beach for Mai and Minh. To her surprise, the wide beach was sparsely populated. Only a few of the countless umbrellas were opened. Several foreigners threw a Frisbee. Vietnamese children played soccer. But vast stretches of sand were vacant.

"Maybe we came too early," she said, turning

her head so that Noah could hear her.

He kept his gaze on the beach. "Where else would tourists be this time of day? Are there temples here? Places to shop?"

"Yes. I think so."

His body aching from the rigors of the previous day, he tried to reposition his prosthesis so that less pressure was on his stump. "Maybe we should go to those and come back here later."

"But the woman. She said to look here."

"I know. It's just so empty. I didn't expect that. And we've already been up and down this road four times." He peered into a market that they passed. "Goddamn it. Where the hell could they be? How are we ever going to find them? What if Sahn was wrong? They could be hundreds of miles from here. We should stop and—"

"Noah!"

"What?"

"There!" she said, pointing. "Look there!"

He followed her finger, his heart seeming to stop when he saw Loc running along the beach. "What's he running—"

"There they are! Look ahead!"

"Holy shit! Pull over!"

"Right next—"

"No, no! Go ahead! Get ahead of them!"

Thien twisted the throttle, speeding forward. She pulled in front of Mai and Minh. "Here? Should I stop here?"

"Not yet, not yet! Wait . . . just a bit more. Now! Now, Thien, now!"

She swerved onto a ramp that led to the sidewalk. As soon as they were clear of traffic, Noah awkwardly leapt off the scooter and began to run. His stump throbbed with every jarring step. His gait was unsteady. But soon he was on the beach. "Mai! Minh! Over here! Look over here!"

They didn't notice him. So consumed were they with escaping Loc that they ran with their eyes to the sand. The beach was wide, and Noah struggled toward them, his prosthesis difficult to plant and lift in the sand. Loc saw Noah and seemed to double his efforts. He was gaining on Mai and Minh—sixty feet behind, forty feet behind.

"Mai!" Noah screamed repeatedly, waving his arms. She finally spotted him, pausing and then turning in his direction. Noah stumbled forward. He reached out as Loc neared them. His hands found theirs and he yanked them behind him. Loc took a few more steps, and Noah raised his arms, his fists clenched. Though his lungs heaved, he didn't bend down. Coughing, Loc tried to circle him and come at Mai and Minh from behind, but Noah spun, keeping himself between Loc and the children. Thien arrived and started yelling at Loc in Vietnamese. He lunged forward, and Noah moved quickly, stepping ahead, jabbing his fist at Loc's nose, missing his nose, but splitting open his lips in a burst of blood. Though Loc staggered and could have easily been overwhelmed, Noah stepped back protectively in front of the children. Thien continued to shout at Loc. His hands against his mangled lips, Loc turned away. He began to run. He fell, stumbled forward a few more feet, and fell again. Finally he made it to the bushes that marked the border between the sand and street, vanishing into a crowd of onlookers.

Noah turned to Mai and Minh. He dropped to his knees and they leapt into his arms. He hugged them tight against him. They were weeping, and he kissed their foreheads, the sight of their tears making him cry. As he kissed them, he promised that they'd never be alone again, that he'd take care of them. They were going to go to school, sleep in soft beds, be surrounded by people who loved them. Also on her knees, Thien echoed his words, her arms around Mai and Minh.

"We're going to take you home," Noah said.

Mai looked up at him, her bloodshot eyes glistening, her body still shuddering. "You promise?" she asked, hugging him tight. "Please, Mr. Noah. Please promise me. Promise Minh."

"I do, I do. We're taking you home. Where you're loved. Where you'll never . . . never feel alone again."

They held Noah tighter, crying together while waves crashed, and then, as breezes stirred and the sun strengthened, they each began to smile, and laugh, and all that seemed to exist was the four of them huddled on the sand.

Two hours later, Loc sat in the back room of an electronics store. The store was one of the many fronts that allowed his uncle's illegal drug trade to flourish and sold everything from the latest flat-screen televisions to iPods to karaoke machines. Music and talk shows blared all day from a variety of speakers. Visitors shopped, haggled, and made purchases, never knowing that drug money was counted and distributed behind closed doors.

Within this room, Loc held a wet cloth to his swollen and split lips. They'd finally stopped bleeding, though they still ached considerably. He lowered the cloth, held the stem of a whiskey bottle above his mouth, and poured the whiskey into the back of his throat. He passed the bottle to his cousin Vien who made himself a drink and raised his glass before a light, inspecting the clarity of the whiskey. Three other men were present—the same men who'd smoked opium with the cousins earlier that morning.

"Help me find them," Loc said, gently touching his lower lip, which was in the worst shape.

"Why?" Vien asked.

"Because my mother and your father are—"

"That's not enough," Vien replied. He started to drink his whiskey, but his cell phone beeped. After reading the text message in his in-box, he quickly typed a response and again faced Loc. "Your mother left my father. Just like she left you."

"That doesn't mean—"

"It means whatever I think it means. You want my help? You pay me for it. You pay my father for it. He's not pleased you're here, by the way. You'd have been smarter to go somewhere else."

Loc licked his battered lips and tried not to wince. He thought about the man who'd hurt him, thought about putting a knife to his stump. "The American has money. A lot of it. You can take it."

"I can rob anyone I want. That's not what I do."

"But he's—"

"Give me the girl and I'll help."

"No. She's not available. At least not for free."

Loc's cousin twisted the hairs at the corner of his mustache. "Are you going to kill the American?"

"Slowly."

"Then I want the girl. If you won't give her to me, get out of my building."

Loc drank more whiskey. "Fine. Take her."

"And his money. I get it all. You just get the children . . . after I'm done with her."

"How will we find them?"

Vien laughed. "You think anything happens in my city without me knowing? Don't act as stupid as you look." He opened his phone and began to push buttons. "I'm sending out the word. We'll have them in an hour."

• • •

AFTER RESCUING MAI AND MINH, THIEN and Noah decided to drive directly to the Nha Trang airport. They'd been told on the street that Vietnam Airlines operated almost hourly fights to Ho Chi Minh City, and there might be seats still available for a trip in the afternoon. Aware that Loc would likely find help and look for them, Thien had driven as fast as possible to the airport, which was located over a series of low mountains to the west of the city. The drive hadn't been easy, as the airport road was under construction, and Thien was forced to weave in and out of earthmoving machines.

They'd arrived in time to secure three tickets on the next flight. They'd thought about buying four, but Noah wouldn't abandon the scooter. It was too valuable to the center, and they didn't have enough money for another. Though Thien had disagreed with him, Noah promised to leave for Ho Chi Minh City just as soon as their plane departed. The plan was for him to drive a few hours to a safe place, check into a hotel, and then finish the trip in the morning.

The airport at Nha Trang wasn't much more than a large, two-story building that overlooked an immense stretch of concrete and several runways. A waiting room on the second floor was filled with plastic chairs facing a wide expanse of windows that allowed people to watch planes arrive, passengers disembark, and vehicles speed about. Many of those present were foreigners, and the air echoed with the conversations of French, German, Israeli, Swiss, American, and Vietnamese travelers. The room wasn't air-conditioned, and ceiling fans spun above, hopelessly overwhelmed by the heat and humidity.

Mai and Minh were still traumatized by their escape from Loc and sat between Noah and Thien. Though Noah tried to explain how safe airports were, both children often glanced at the doorway, looking for Loc. Noah still couldn't believe that Minh could talk, and asked him a variety of questions, enjoying the sound of his voice.

Aware that Mai and Minh must be hungry, Noah got up and shuffled to the gift shop, which was nothing more than a table covered with candy bars, magazines, cheap souvenirs, bags of dried fish, medicine, and canned drinks. Noah bought everyone a snack and returned to them with some haste, as he could tell by their worried glances that they didn't like him to be away.

"Here you go," Noah said, handing everyone a candy bar and a drink.

Mai took her snack and looked out the windows. "I hear planes fall from the sky," she said in English. "Sure, sure, scooter is better. Maybe we all take scooter."

Thien smiled. "Planes are safe," she replied. "Much safer than scooters. Mr. Noah just took me on one a few days ago. And it was wonderful."

"Why?" Minh asked, holding his candy bar between his stump and his thigh so that he could open it.

"Because you can fly," Thien said. "Like you are on the back of a big bird. And you can see rivers. And mountains. And the ocean."

Minh cocked his head toward her. "The ocean? Do you see fish? Or whales? Or dragons? Do the water end or go on forever?"

Thien put her hand on his knee. "You will see for yourself. Soon enough. And you really will think that you are flying."

Minh nodded and took a bite of his candy bar.

Noah leaned closer to him, so that other passengers wouldn't hear their conversation. "I always thought," he whispered, "that if you ever spoke, you'd be really quiet. You'd say a word here and there, but that would be all. It never occurred to me that you'd be able to speak English so well."

Minh shrugged. "But I always listen. Even in game, I listen." He smiled and took another bite of his candy bar. "Sometime, in game, the people talk in English about what to do. They think I no understand. And then I beat them. And they so surprised. They never know I speak English."

"Even I no know," Mai replied, helping herself to his candy bar. "All this time, I no know. Same, same, every game. I do all speaking for him."

"I can't believe you never figured it out," Minh

said in Vietnamese. "All those games that I won. I listened to everything that you said, that they said."

"You're too smart for me, Minh the Trickster," she replied, pushing her knee against his, smiling as she finished his candy bar. "I told you all those stories. You're going to have to tell me so much."

"Are you going to eat all my food?"

"Yes. As your punishment. For not talking to me. I'll get fat, and you'll weigh nothing more than a dragonfly, and I'll blow you away whenever you bother me."

"I'll come back, looking for you."

"I know," Mai said. "And I'll let you stay. But you'll have to tell me so many stories. You'll have to fly around and look for them. And if you don't come back with enough I'll squash you with my foot."

Thien smiled as Mai stepped on Minh's toes. He playfully hit her in response, and as they teased each other, Thien stood up, walked past them, and sat beside Noah. She took his hand in hers and moved close to him, so that her mouth was near his ear. "I wish you would come with us," she whispered. "Will you please come with us?"

"I want to," he replied, twisting toward her, remaining close to her. "But Iris needs the scooter. And there's no money for another. I'm broke."

"Then sell it here and buy another when you get back."

"There isn't time for that. You're going to leave any minute. And I'd never get what it's worth. It's almost brand-new." He glanced out the windows toward an idle plane. "Iris depends on it. She's told me how it's made her life easier. And she's done so much for me. I just can't let her down."

Thien pulled away from him slightly. "What about Loc? He could find you."

"He's not going to find me. I'll leave as soon as you get on the plane, and head straight for Saigon."

"He could wait somewhere for you . . . ahead on the road."

"Thien, he isn't going to find me. He doesn't have any idea where we are. And just to be safe, I'll take some back roads out of Nha Trang."

"But I do not want to go without you. It will be such a long ride back for you. Please come with us . . . with me."

Noah kissed her on the forehead. He wanted to kiss her lips, but with so many people about, he turned and watched a plane race down the runway. It rose awkwardly above the shimmering cement, in no way resembling a bird. "When I was a boy," he said, "I used to collect things."

"What?"

"We would go to the beach for a week every winter. And I'd collect shells. I'd spend all day looking for them. I'd come back to the room sun-burned and tired, but I'd have a basket of beautiful shells."

Her brow furrowed. "Why are you telling me this now, Noah? When I am about to leave?"

"Because I still have those shells. And I saw them once . . . after I got back from Iraq. I wanted to throw them away, because it hurt me to look at them. I was jealous of the boy who found them. I wanted to be him again. More than anything in my life, I wanted to be him again. I still do."

"Why have you kept them?"

"I'm not sure. But I have my shells, my coins, and my fossils. As much as I wanted to throw them away . . . I couldn't. They meant too much. And I couldn't walk away from them, even though I sometimes hated them."

"I would like to see them."

"I'm not going to walk away from you," he said, whispering into her ear.

"Why not?"

"Because I love you."

She squeezed his hands. "Do you know why I sing so much when you are near?"

"Tell me."

"Because you make me want to sing. And that is why I know I love you."

At the front of the room, a man announced in Vietnamese and then in English that boarding for the flight to Ho Chi Minh City would soon begin. As people started to stir, Noah kissed the side of Thien's head. "I'll see you tomorrow," he said, watching her fingers move against his. "Please do me a favor and show Mai and Minh the rivers, the ocean. Tell them what they're seeing. Maybe you can get them each a window seat."

"I will."

"I love you, Thien. I didn't know I was capable of such love. I thought that part of me was dead."

"It is not dead."

"Only because of you."

Despite the crowd around them, Thien leaned even closer to him, kissing his cheek, wiping away her tears. "Please hurry back to me."

"I will. I promise."

"We need you."

"I'll be back soon. Before you go to sleep tomorrow I'll be back, and you can sing something for me. And I'll just lie there and listen."

"And then?"

He thought for a moment, his fingers curling around hers. "And then everywhere we go, we'll go together."

TO LOC, THE ROOM IN THE rear of the electronics store seemed to get smaller by the minute. Though whiskey had helped to dull his pain, his need for revenge was overwhelming. The sooner he found the American and hurt him, the sooner he could think of things beyond the humiliation that he had suffered. He'd beat the American in front of the half boy and the girl. And then he'd beat them.

Loc's sense of humiliation was compounded by

the presence of his cousin and his reliance on him to help capture the American. He knew that Vien would take advantage of his misfortunes and, in fact, already had. The talk about Mai was only the beginning.

A woman entered the room and whispered in Vien's ear. She was dressed in a short skirt and a formfitting tank top. Her face could have graced the cover of any magazine. Loc looked away as she kissed his cousin. He didn't want to see her touch Vien, not when Loc craved to touch her.

Loc tried to ignore her faint murmurs and moans. Regardless of whether they were fake or real, they weren't for his benefit. They fueled his rage, a rage that he released by imagining what he would do to the American. He'd start with the half leg. He'd see how much it could still bleed.

A shrill beep penetrated the room, and Loc turned toward Vien, who moved the woman aside and opened his cell phone. He pushed a button, and his brow furrowed. "Leave," he said to her. After she'd gone, he turned to Loc. "They're getting on a plane," he reported, rising from his chair.

Loc swore. "Then we're too late. We can't—"

"The American didn't go."

"What?"

"He didn't get on the plane."

"Why not?"

"He's a fool, obviously. And he doesn't know who I am." Vien began to type a message into his phone. "I want his money, his credit cards, his passport. Everything."

"What do I get?"

"You get him. Or would you rather I let him go?"

Loc glanced at the bloody cloth that he'd been holding against his lips. As of that moment, the American had won. He'd humiliated Loc and stolen the half boy and the girl. "I want him . . . and his scooter," he said, shoving the cloth into his pocket.

"A scooter? You didn't tell me about—"

"I want it."

"You want to sell it."

"What's the difference?"

"I'll sell it, and I'll give you half."

Loc nodded. "And I want something else."

"Remember your place, cousin," Vien replied, shutting his phone.

"Bring a camera."

"Why?"

"Because I want those brats to see what I did to him. When they see that, they'll never smile again, never hold hands again. They'll be as good as dead."

Vien saw the look in Loc's eyes, and suddenly the room seemed small to him. "We'll catch him in the hills," he said, picking up his sunglasses. "But we'd better go now, before he reaches the city."

BUOYED BY THEIR RESCUE OF MAI and Minh, Noah drove the scooter as he might have as a boy.

The road through the low mountains was almost barren, and he weaved along the fresh blacktop, swooping to and fro the way a kite navigated the sky. The sun and wind were invigorating, and he felt freer than he had in many years. He and Thien had done what he'd secretly feared was impossible—they'd saved Mai and Minh, returning them to a place they could call home. And tomorrow, Noah would be able to watch them play and laugh, and later he'd hold Thien in his arms and tell her about his love for her. She would sing to him. He'd gently touch her face. He'd kiss her lips, her neck. And if her desires were the same as his, he would undress her slowly, marveling at the beauty that lay hidden beneath her cap and paint-stained clothes, delighting in discoveries. And perhaps best of all, he knew that she wouldn't mind his own nakedness. The ugly scar on his forehead, the stump of his leg—to her these would be only parts of him, no different from his hands or his eyes.

Noah shifted atop the seat. Though his back ached from all of the riding, he was too happy to pay it much heed. Instead, he studied the scene around him. To his left, a lush mountain rose about a thousand feet high. To his right, several hundred feet below, waves crashed against a white-sand beach. Several seemingly uninhabited islands interrupted the view of the horizon. Otherwise, the bright blue waters of the South China Sea dominated the distance. To his surprise, only a few fishing boats prowled the swells. Unlike the beach at Nha Trang, which was heavily developed, the sand below was free of humanity's embrace. No hotels or homes or roads existed. "It's only a matter of time," he said quietly, wondering if the huge hotel chains had already bought chunks of the pristine land, dividing them up like chips on a poker table.

He eased back on the throttle, decreasing his speed so that he could better enjoy the view. Another scooter passed him, a woman driving with two small children straddling the seat before her. One of the children waved, and Noah returned the greeting. He loved Vietnam. Parts of it were troubling, of course. The poverty, the exploitation of the young and weak—these were sorrows that he didn't like seeing. But balancing out such misery appeared to be a genuine happiness that dwelled within most Vietnamese. They seemed to realize that their country was moving in the right direction, that better days lay ahead. Not for them necessarily, but for their children. And what a place to be a child, Noah thought—at least, a child of some means. With mountains, lakes, and thousands of miles of coastline, Vietnam was far more beautiful than he'd have ever guessed, with endless places to explore.

Noah gazed at the distant islands, wishing that Iris could see them. They'd called her from the airport, and her relief at Mai's and Minh's safety had overwhelmed her. She hadn't been able to speak. Instead she'd tapped the phone against something, tapped it until her voice finally returned. She'd asked to talk with Mai, and Noah had watched Mai's face as she smiled and grew teary eyed from whatever Iris said. After a few minutes Mai had given the phone back to Noah, and he'd listened while Iris told him about hiring Sahn as a security guard, about how Loc would never again step foot in their center.

I owe her everything, Noah thought. Every little piece of who I am right now is because of her. She brought me here. She brought me back to life. And I need to do something for her. Something wonderful. Maybe I could send her away, to a beach like the one below. I've seen a lot more of this country than she has, and that's not right. That needs to change.

He approached a hill, continuing to think about what he might do to help her. Suddenly two motorcycles and a van appeared, driving in the opposite direction. The motorcycles skidded, wheeling around to follow him. Noah's heart dropped. Instinctively he twisted his throttle as far back as possible. His scooter darted forward, the wind tugging at his hair and loose clothes. The motorcycles were much more powerful and quickly caught him. He glanced at each and saw that they were driven by men in black leather. Noah tried to ease over so they could pass. But the drivers had no interest in overtaking him. Instead they used their larger vehicles to push him toward the guardrail. He squeezed the brake lever, and the motorcycles sped ahead. But then the van came at him. Noah looked behind and saw Loc in the passenger seat, clapping his hands, screaming like a madman. Able to do no more than twist the throttle and race ahead, Noah sought to control his panic. He knew that panic could kill as easily as a bullet, and he tried to remember what he'd passed going up the mountains. The construction crews weren't too far below. Maybe another mile. Maybe two.

A month earlier, Noah had wanted to die. But not now. Not with Thien and Mai and Minh and Iris in his life. He swerved to the other lane, driving fast the wrong way down the new road. He hoped that a truck would come in the opposite direction. He'd be able to maneuver around a truck, while the much bigger motorcycles would have a harder time doing so and might be forced off the road. And the driver of the van would never risk such an encounter.

"Come on!" Noah shouted, knowing that he didn't have to go much farther before he reached the construction crews.

A taxi abruptly appeared, its horn sounding. Noah swerved around it, narrowly missing the opposite guardrail. The motorcycles darted toward the other lane, one of them hitting the van, seeming to rebound against it, falling sideways, the driver trapped beneath steel, sliding hundreds of feet down the fresh blacktop.

Noah thought the van might stop and attend to the injured or dying man. But the vehicle didn't alter its course. The driver opened his window, and a handgun appeared. The gunman gestured for Noah to stop, but he rushed ahead, his scooter rocking dangerously as he hit a fallen branch. The gun sounded, and the seat behind him burst into shreds. A second bullet shattered his side mirror. Noah squeezed the brake lever as hard as possible and was almost thrown off the scooter. The van flew past, but the remaining motorcycle, much more agile, slowed alongside him, its driver producing another handgun. Only a car's length separated them, and, desperate to increase that distance, Noah swerved to the right, toward a dirt road that headed to the sea. A bullet struck a nearby fence post. He lowered his head and went bouncing full speed down the primitive road. Coconuts and palm fronds littered the way. He dodged most of these obstacles, though several struck his scooter and almost toppled it. For a moment he heard the crashing of waves. Then the roar of the motorcycle filled his ears. He looked for a trail to turn onto, but the road just stretched ahead, ending in sand. Noah swore, reduced his speed, and frantically tried to drive down the beach. He managed to for a few seconds, but the deep sand proved impossible to navigate. His scooter started to fall and he leapt to the side. Without pausing, he half ran, half skipped toward the water. Believing he could dive beneath the waves and somehow outswim his pursuers, he continued on. He didn't look back. He only ran, eyeing the water, his feet finally hitting damp sand.

The sea was up to his knees when he was tackled from behind. A massive weight pressed his face into the water, but he slammed his elbow into the man atop him, and the weight abruptly lessened. He could breathe again. Two men faced him, with two others approaching. He stepped toward the larger of the two, striking the side of his head. The other man came at Noah even as his companion fell. Noah grunted from a blow to his belly, but he brought his good knee up swiftly, ramming it into his adversary's groin.

Noah dove toward the deeper water. He swam with every last reserve of his strength, pulling at the sea with his hands, kicking with his good leg and his prosthesis. He had always been a strong swimmer, and for a moment it seemed that he'd either escape or be shot at. But then someone grabbed onto his prosthesis, pulling it from his stump. He tried to dive beneath a swell, to escape within the sea that Thien believed was full of dragons. For a moment, he saw their world, saw swirling bubbles and what almost looked like the windswept sand of a faraway desert. Then hands dragged him toward the surface. Something hard struck him on the back of the head, and the white sand turned to black.

THE SOUNDS CAME FIRST—MEN TALKING in a language he didn't understand. The words seemed to echo inside him, so foreign, so unknown. Visions danced next. In a dark world that glittered with pinpricks of light, he saw vague forms appear. Thien materialized, peeling a tangerine. She set a slice in his hand and departed, even though he reached for her. His mother took Thien's place, telling him to look both ways before crossing the street. He saw himself selling lemonade. Cars passed and he called out, waving his sign. A few cars stopped, but most sped onward. He collected quarters as the sun burned his flesh pink.

Cold water striking his face finally awoke him, causing him to try to stand up as his eyes opened. His arms and legs didn't respond, and he blinked repeatedly. He couldn't remember what had happened and was surprised to see that his wrists were bound to the arms of a chair. His prosthesis lay on the floor. He wanted to rub the back of his aching head but could only roll it in a circle as he tried to drive away his pain. He blinked again and sought to bring the shadows around him into focus. Four men stood nearby. He recognized Loc by his baseball jersey. Next to Loc, a mustached man held a handgun. The other men were dressed as he was—in black leather pants and jackets. Aware that they were watching him, Noah glanced at his surroundings and saw that a handful of fishing boats were in various stages of construction. One was almost finished—painted red with blue trim. Most were mere hulls. The building that they occupied was a large metal structure, curved from top to bottom, as if it were a giant can that had been cut down the middle and set on the ground. At the far end of the building—directly in front of Noah—a pair of tracks went straight into the sea. This side of the building had been partly opened, and Noah saw waves crashing against the shore. He studied the simple beauty of the waves, fearing that he'd never see them again.

Loc picked up a wooden oar and stepped toward him. "Where is they?" he asked in broken English, his swollen lips slurring his words.

Noah looked back to the waves. "Who?"

The flat part of the oar swung through the air, striking Noah's stump with immense force. He screamed, writhing in his bonds. He'd felt plenty of pain before, but nothing like the agony that now consumed him. He choked back a sob, keeping his eyes on the waves, trying to pick out one and follow it to the shore.

"They go Saigon?" Loc asked, his puffy lips forming a smile.

"They're . . . safe," Noah replied, closing his eyes as the oar swung forward. His stump exploded in pain and he thrashed in his chair, almost knocking it over. Clenching his teeth together, he tried to think about Halong Bay, about how he'd touched Thien as she leaned against him. Through the haze of his agony, he listened to her voice. Nothing was as beautiful as the sound of her voice. Not the sea. Not the wind. Her voice transcended everything.

Someone must have moved behind him, for fingers forced open his eyelids. He saw Loc raise the oar to a striking position. Again he thought of Thien. Loc swung the oar. Noah shrieked as it slammed into his stump. He struggled against his bonds, suddenly wanting to kill Loc with his bare hands, heedless of the promise he'd made to himself to never kill again.

"I find them," Loc said, taking a practice swing. "I find them soon."

Noah took a deep breath and sought to steady himself. He imagined Mai and Minh riding on the seesaw. He saw Tam smiling from her bed. Thien had been right—they were all dragons, beautiful creatures that had flown into his life and now would never leave, no matter what Loc did with him. "She . . . she was . . . right," he whispered, moaning, his stump swollen and bleeding.

"Who?"

"You can't . . . hurt me," Noah replied, thinking about Wesley, wondering if they'd soon meet again. "You're nothing."

Loc swore, twisting his body, swinging the oar with all his might. The pain was like a bomb detonating within Noah. He couldn't think or breathe or curse. The agony was too absolute, too overwhelming. He fought against the ropes that held him, writhing like a worm that had been chopped in half. As he fought, someone hit him repeatedly on the side of the head.

The oar started to swing again, but this time two men pulled Loc back, and the wood passed inches from Noah's stump. He managed to open his eyes and saw that five or six newcomers were present. As he shuddered and groaned, he watched an older man speak to Loc. The older man was dressed in green pants and a white T-shirt. He seemed to be angry, pointing at Loc and then Noah.

Noah tried to follow what was happening between them, but his pain was too vast, and he began to black out. Again he saw the faces of those he loved. Past conversations reverberated within. He lost track of time and location. His Humvee had been blown up, he remembered. Where was Wes? He shouted out to his friend, but no answer was given. Oh, Wes, he thought, what have they done to you? Where are you? Is Thien with you? She is? Good. Tell her something. . . . Tell her . . . tell her I love her. Tell her . . . I'm sorry. She'll have to watch the children alone. With Iris. You and Thien and Iris can watch them. Be their friend. Protect them. They're so wonderful. But they don't know it. They've been told they're bad, they're worthless. Tell them the truth, Wes. Tell them the truth until they believe it. You'll be so amazed . . . at what you see . . . at what you feel. You'll never forget it. Never. And remember . . . to tell her I love her . . . and that I heard her sing . . . one last time . . . at the end.

Noah felt someone shaking him. "Wes?" he asked, trying to focus his eyes. Someone was kneeling on the floor, untying his hands. "Thank you," he whispered. "Thank you . . . my friend . . . for coming back to me."

Water was poured into Noah's mouth and splashed against his face. He gulped, pulling the liquid into his aching body. He coughed up the water, holding his sides, aware of foreign words again in his ears. Gritting his teeth against the pain, he tried to understand the scene before him. To his surprise, he saw that Loc was still talking to the older man, who seemed as angry as ever. The man pressed his finger against Loc's chest and then turned to Noah.

"Leave them . . . alone," Noah whispered, thinking of Mai and Minh.

The older man stepped toward him, his open mouth revealing a golden tooth. "My nephew has told me about these children," he said in clear, precise English. "Did you take them from him?"

"Take them?"

"Take them from him?"

"No. They . . . they came to me. To us."

"Why?"

"To live . . . with us. At . . . our center."

"And you paid him? Two hundred and fifty dollars for their freedom?"

"It didn't work. But we tried."

The older man stooped closer to Noah. "Tell me about this center. Why would children go there?"

"To leave."

"To leave where?"

"The streets. To leave them. To escape. And . . . and to learn."

"You take care of them? You teach them?"

"Me? I just . . . I built a playground. We made a seesaw . . . for sweet Tam."

The man raised and dipped his fingers and wrist. "A seesaw? Like this?"

"Yes."

"And did these children play on your seesaw?"

Noah shook his head, weakly spitting blood. "They tried. But . . . but he took them. He took them from it."

The man rose to his full height, grunting. "My nephew," he replied, "is weak. As weak as a blade of grass." He turned to Loc and in Vietnamese said, "Your mother and I, we were left on the streets. We had nowhere to go. Nowhere! And do you know what became of us? Do you?"

"You—"

"We became thieves! We stole to survive, and

she was only a child herself when she had you! And then she left us both because her shame was so great. She left us and now I'm sure she's dead."

"She didn't—"

"Shut your mouth, nephew, or I'll feed your tongue to the crabs!" The older man cleared his throat. "Maybe your mother could have been saved by something like this foreigner is doing. Did you ever think about that? Did you think about how I had to crawl through the gutter to get where I am? Through piss and piles of human waste! Do you have fish guts for brains? Where's the money the foreigner gave you? Did you spend it all on opium?"

"It's—"

"And you have the impudence to come here, having kidnapped those two children? You bring them to my city! Do you know how many police are looking for them? And you bring them here! And now the foreigner is in my factory! Half-dead? You dare to endanger me? My family? My wife and daughters? My son is no better than the ass of an elephant for bringing you here. His offenses are almost as great as yours."

Vien stepped toward his father with his hands outstretched, his palms up. "Father, I didn't mean to—"

"Silence! If I want to hear your pathetic voice, I'll tell you to speak!" The older man turned again to Loc. "You put me in jeopardy for what? A pair of children? Have you sunk so low? You steal from me, a decade ago, and then you return. And when you return, police swarm about me like bees around their queen! Were you going to kill this foreigner in my factory? Without my knowledge or consent?"

Loc bowed his head. "No, Uncle. Only a beating."

"I don't believe you! You spew lies, as always. Well, I'll never hear your lies again. You'll never foul my city again." He turned to two men behind him. "Take him out to sea. Far, far out. Let him smoke his precious opium. Bowl after bowl of it. Then see if he can swim to shore."

"Please, Uncle!" Loc said, falling to his knees. "We have the same blood! My mother—"

"Take him!"

"She wouldn't—"

"Take him now, damn you!"

The two men moved toward Loc. He tried to fight them, but both were highly trained bodyguards, and they beat him into submission in a matter of seconds. He moaned as they dragged him away, begging for mercy. His uncle didn't look at him, didn't even seem to hear him. Instead the older man stepped toward Noah, motioning for one of his other bodyguards to pick up Noah's prosthesis. The man put it on Noah's lap.

"Can you understand me?" Loc's uncle said in English.

Noah tried to bring him into focus. He still wasn't sure why Loc had been beaten and dragged away. "Yes," he finally whispered, spitting out more blood.

"Tell no one what happened here today and you will live."

"What?"

"You understand? No police. Never. You found the children and you went back to Saigon. You never saw me or my son or this place."

Noah silently repeated the older man's words, trying to understand. "You . . . you're going to . . . let me go?"

"If you promise to say nothing."

"I . . . I promise."

"If I hear of anything . . . anything at all told to the police, you will die."

"I understand. I won't . . . say anything. Ever."

Loc's uncle bent lower. "Go. Build your center. Build it well, and teach the children well. You have nothing to fear from me."

"Thank you."

"You can save the children. Before they give up. Before they become . . . men like me."

"I'll try."

"Go, then."

Noah nodded, his head pulsing with pain, his heartbeat in his ears. He reached for his prosthesis and, grimacing in agony, reattached it to his swollen and bleeding stump. He tried to stand but couldn't put any weight on his stump and started to fall sideways. Two men grabbed his arms before he toppled. They carried him from the warehouse. Outside, Noah had to close his eyes. He'd never seen such bright light. It temporarily blinded him.

The men opened the back of a van and pulled out his scooter. They helped him onto the seat. One of them took the key, inserted it, and pressed the start button. They then left him alone. Mustering his strength and his will, Noah gently twisted the throttle. The scooter accelerated effortlessly, and, squinting, Noah eyed the road as he drove slowly up a hill.

Before long he was on the main highway that led away from the airport. No other traffic existed. He looked for Nha Trang but didn't see it. There were only mountains and the expanse of blue water.

The scooter wobbled when Noah closed his eyes, but he managed to bring himself back into the present. He thought about Thien and he wanted to be near her. He'd never wanted anything so much. Spitting out more blood, he increased his speed. The wind began to tug at his hair. The pavement blurred beneath him. Though pain continued to almost overwhelm him, he didn't dwell on his misery. He was alive. He would see Thien again. Tomorrow he'd touch her face. He'd feel his lips against hers. And he wouldn't be alone.

His love for her was what kept him going. He should have pulled over to the side of the road and passed out. But he didn't, because that would only increase the time he was away from her.

As he crested a hill and saw Nha Trang, he envisioned those he loved. Through some sort of miracle, they hadn't been taken away. The stranger had given him life, handing Thien back to him just as he'd been saying good-bye to her, when the thought of their separation was like a sword piercing his soul.

"Why . . . why did he save me?" Noah whispered, trying to remember the older man's words.

Though the words escaped him, Noah believed that a miracle had happened. In Baghdad, a part of him had been killed, and that part would never fully return. But in a warehouse outside Nha Trang, he had been given the chance to live. He'd seen his death looming and suddenly realized that his life did matter. And the story of his life hadn't yet been written. Yes, the future would contain pain, a pain that would test him again and again. But he was no longer afraid of such misery. It was a part of his life, but would be outweighed by the good. Thien would stand beside him, as would Iris and the children and his family back home. And one day, when he was old and again facing death, he wouldn't think about the pain, the suffering, the black parts of his life. He'd think about the good parts, about those he loved, about what he'd done. These things would define his life, things that had been given to him, not things had that been taken away.

Noah felt the wind draw tears from his eyes, pulling them back into his hair. Reaching the highway that led south, he turned into heavy traffic, not slowing his pace. He got behind a fast bus, dodging potholes, remembering how Thien had done the same. The sun warmed him. The sea was beautiful and endless.

He twisted the throttle back, passing the bus, moving closer to home.

— EPILOGUE

And Night Turned to Day

Three weeks later, Iris stood in a corner of the playground and chatted with a high-ranking city official. The man was kind, his words welcome. But Iris wasn't really listening. Instead her eyes feasted on the scene before her. The playground was filled with twenty girls who had moved into the Tam Tran Center for Street Children. The girls, ranging in age from seven to twelve, cautiously explored the grounds before them, taking turns on the seesaw, rising and falling on Sahn's swing set, and climbing to the top of a wooden fort that Noah had built.

Iris nodded to the man, smiling when appropriate, thanking him for his support. She wished him well and turned away, pretending that she had something important to oversee. As she walked to the back entrance of the center, she continued to gaze in wonder at the playground, thinking about the bare lot that Noah had so painstakingly transformed. Where there were once only dirt and cement chips, grass and tree saplings now rose. Where trash had once collected, a swing set brought smiles and laughter.

Standing not far from the swing set was Sahn. He no longer wore his police attire, though Iris had bought him a green uniform so that he might look official. With his back to the fence, he appeared to watch the scene before him. Of course, Iris was aware that even with his new glasses, he couldn't see much of the activity, but she could tell by his faint smile that he was listening to everything. She'd come to understand him well and knew that he was proud to watch over the children and delighted in doing so. He might not talk about such pleasures, but she knew he felt them. He was easier to read than he realized.

At the base of the fort stood Thien and Noah. They'd been nearly inseparable since Noah's return. He had been badly beaten, and she'd spent several days at his side, tending to his battered stump and listening to his ideas for the playground. Since then, they had often worked together after she finished her duties in the kitchen. She'd painted his fort, singing softly, peeling her tangerines. Almost every day they'd gone on errands together, taking the scooter to bring back fresh fish and produce. Though the trips had lasted longer than they once had, Iris was pleased by the delays. Thien and Noah deserved time alone with each other. Their love was obvious and beautiful, and Iris felt lucky to witness it.

Guiding several of the newcomers around the playground were Mai and Minh. As she often did, Iris marveled at how much they'd recovered from their ordeal with Loc. Minh talked as much as Mai, studying with the girls, often teaching them how to play games. He lived with Noah in an apartment near the center. Each night they'd depart together, often dribbling a basketball that Noah had bought. Sometimes Thien accompanied them, but usually it was just the two of them. They spoke while one of them bounced the ball. Iris knew Noah was teaching Minh about the ocean. Minh's fascination with it seemed endless. In the short time since his return, he'd become a bit of an expert on the sea and the creatures that dwelled within it.

As Iris watched Mai and Minh help the other girls, she smiled, stepping inside the center. She still couldn't believe it was complete. Though they'd missed their Christmas deadline, no one seemed to care. More than thirty adults were present for the grand opening, and Iris had spoken to all of them. Many had made donations of money, time, or materials; and expressions of support and encouragement were unanimous and abundant. These people were helping her plan for the center's future, providing her with the expertise and resources that she'd once dreamed of possessing.

Iris moved into the kitchen, wanting to see the entire center, to revel in what had been accomplished. Tables seemed to sag beneath the weight of the food that Thien had prepared. There was nothing extravagant, just piles of fruit and croissants that rose between bouquets of fresh flowers. Music played from a small radio that Thien had purchased with her own money.

The stairwell had been completely painted, and images of colorful parrots on tree limbs graced the walls. Iris climbed higher into the tree, noting patches of sky above. She entered the classroom next, surprised at how quickly it had come together. A painted map of the world dominated the largest wall. Tables and chairs were abundant. In the far corner, a pair of tall bookshelves comprised her library. She'd gathered almost five hundred books, many purchased by the sale of her signed first-edition novels. Several publishing companies where Iris had friends had also made donations. The books were new and written in either Vietnamese or English. The children had opened them with what Iris believed to be awe. For their whole lives, they had seen other children go to school. They'd dreamed of going, of being normal. But they'd never had the chance until now.

The dormitory looked as she would always remember it. The clouds that she and Thien had painted were as wondrous as ever. Qui and Tam's rainbow brought tears to her eyes, as did the sight of Tam's bed, which Mai now used. The previous night was the girls' first in the room, and Iris had been surprised to find several sleeping on the floor. Apparently their beds were too soft.

Iris climbed the ladder leading to the roof. She smiled at the sight of the garden that Noah and Thien were building. Noah, Sahn, and several volunteers had tied a chain to a wooden rowboat and, standing at the side of the roof, had pulled the boat to the top of the building. Noah and Sahn had filled it with dirt, and Thien had planted row upon row of seeds. Tender sprouts now emerged from the dark soil. Thien planned on teaching the children how to nurture the young plants.

Moving to the edge of the roof, to where she could see the playground, Iris watched the scene below. As the children hurried about, she recalled scattering her father's ashes around the playground and, later, repeating the process alongside Noah, Thien, Sahn, Mai, and Minh as they spread the ashes of Qui and Tam beneath the banyan tree that Noah had planted. Tears had been plentiful at that moment, just as they'd been when a portrait of Tam had been hung beneath her name on the front of the building.

A child laughed below, and Iris smiled. She realized then that she had never felt as fulfilled as she did at that very moment—not when she'd graduated from college, or when she first fell in love, or when she'd seen her byline in major newspapers. Of course, those were important moments, moments she'd cherish. But they were nothing like what she felt now. The laughter that found her ears, the sights that she so readily consumed, were gifts piled at her feet.

Footsteps sounded from behind her and Iris turned. Mai stood alone, smiling. "Why you here?" Mai asked, lifting up her foot to pluck a small stone from between her toes and her sandal.

"Oh, I just . . . I needed to see it all," Iris replied.

"Me think you just tired of talking with so many people."

"Well, that's true too."

"Why do big people just stand and talk, while children play? Sure, sure, big people have more fun if they play too."

Iris shook her head. "We can play too, Mai. Just wait. We'll rent a bus, and we'll all go to the beach. Then you'll see us play."

Mai smiled. "Do you know what I call you? When I speak with Minh?"

"I have no idea. What?"

"Iris the Great."

"Oh, I'm not great. Just ask my old boyfriend. He'd tell you a story or two."

"He must be so foolish, Miss Iris. Like an elephant who worries about a fly. But I glad that you no go with him. Because then you come to us."

Iris took Mai's hand. "I'm glad too."

Noah's voice rose from below. Mai and Iris watched as he pushed a girl high on a swing. She laughed and shrieked, and some of the other children paused to see her soar. Iris noticed that most of the adults had also turned in the girl's direction. Many seemed to be momentarily entranced by her glee, perhaps reminded of their own childhoods.

Next to the fence, not too far from the swing, Iris saw a girl sitting by herself. "Mai," she asked, "is that Long?"

"Yes, I think so."

"How is she doing?"

"Just okay."

"That's all?"

Mai took Iris's hand. "We go down and cheer her up. Sure, sure?"

Iris smiled. "Sure, sure. Let's do that."

And so Mai and Iris descended the many stairs. Soon they were outside. Several other city officials complimented Iris on the center. She also passed Sahn and greeted him in Vietnamese, pronouncing the words just right, as he'd taught her. He nodded and said something that she didn't understand. But I'll learn, she thought, moving ahead.

The girl—eight years old, if Iris remembered correctly—sat next to the fence and looked at her feet. Iris and Mai moved to each side of her.

"Would you mind if we sat down?" Iris asked, speaking slowly, trying to recall how well Long understood English.

"No."

"Do you want to play with the other children?"

"No."

Iris nodded. "That's all right. Maybe Mai can tell you about what we do here. She's lived here almost a month."

Mai edged closer to the smaller girl and began to speak in Vietnamese. Iris listened to her, proud that she wanted to help Long. Iris knew that Mai had been saved. Just as Minh had been. Not all the children would be successfully rescued. Iris had already resigned herself to that. But Mai and Minh had been saved from the streets, from where fate had so cruelly cast them. And if they could be saved, so could others.

Iris leaned against the fence. She looked around the playground and knew without doubt or reluctance that this place had become her home. She loved its sounds, its sights. And she felt a beauty here, something she'd never sensed before. She wondered if what she felt was what the great writers had tried to portray. She'd read their words and been moved to tears by them. But what she felt now wasn't what had been described to her. It wasn't just happiness, or love, or contentment. It was a sense that the human spirit wanted to soar. Despite all the suffering, pain, betrayal, and ugliness of life, the human spirit couldn't be easily beaten, easily caged. That was why Minh was laughing with Noah, why Mai spoke to the little girl as if they were lifelong friends. That was why Tam and Qui had gone forward together, holding hands, loving each other even as their hearts slowed and ceased to beat. And that was why her father had returned to a land that had once tormented him.

Iris understood. She glanced at Mai. She smiled. And then she closed her eyes and listened.

Dear Reader,

I've been lucky enough to do a lot of traveling. A time existed, after I graduated from college, when I taught English in Japan and then backpacked around Asia. I had little money and tended to stay in rooms that cost a few dollars a night. With nothing more than a couple sets of T-shirts and shorts in my backpack, I visited places such as Vietnam, Thailand, Nepal, India, Indonesia, Hong Kong, and Korea. Some of these countries I grew to know quite well. I'd find a cheap room, rent a scooter, and explore as much of an area as possible. Sometimes my future wife or my friends were with me, though I was often alone.

I saw so many beautiful things throughout these adventures, sights such as the Taj Mahal, the Himalayan peaks, and white-sand beaches unspoiled by humanity's touch. But I think that I witnessed the most beauty within the street children I encountered. These children seemed so similar, country to country. They were out at all times of day and night, selling their postcards, their fans, their flowers. For many nights in Thailand, I played Connect Four with a boy who wasn't older than seven or eight. Some travelers told me not to play with him, convinced that his parents were nearby and were sending him out at night to work. But I never saw his parents, and one night I spied him sleeping on a sidewalk, a piece of cardboard his bed. I don't think I ever beat him in a game.

Throughout these travels I met hundreds, if not thousands, of children who lived on the street. Sometimes they were sick or had a physical deformity. But most of them were simply homeless—abandoned into extreme poverty. Bright, eager, and unafraid to laugh with a stranger, they taught me so much. I owe them so much.

It is my hope that *Dragon House* will be a success, and out of that success something good can happen. I plan on donating some of the funds generated from my book to an organization called Blue Dragon Children's Foundation. This group works with children in crisis throughout Vietnam. Blue Dragon offers disadvantaged children a wide range of services and support to help them break out of poverty, forever, by getting them back to school and helping them achieve their best.

To my delight, officials at Blue Dragon want to someday open a center for street children in Ho Chi Minh City. I know the immense good that such a center would provide, and in some small way I hope to be a part of this movement. So, thank you, dear reader, for supporting me. Your support allows me to aid this wonderful organization, an organization that sits quite close to my heart.

Of course, there are also massive numbers of street children in my home country, America. In fact, it's estimated that one out of every four homeless individuals in the United States is a child. Groups like StandUp For Kids are helping these children. I am attempting to assist this national organization, which is run by volunteers and serves more than a thousand children every week.

The future of Vietnam, America, and the world depends on children, and I hope that we can all do something to ensure that we don't leave children on the streets. That abandonment needs to be a thing of the past. It should have no presence on earth.

As always, I thank you so much for your support. Feel free to send me a note at shors@aol.com.

My very best wishes to you,
John

ACKNOWLEDGMENTS

I COULD NOT HAVE WRITTEN *Dragon House* without the support and love of my family. Allison, thank you for your belief in this novel, and for your patience. You've worked every bit as hard as I have during this process and are deserving of at least as much credit. I'm blessed to have you as my wife, my partner, and my friend. Sophie and Jack, you're our two little dragons, and I can't wait to take you to Vietnam, and to watch you explore a world that you will only make better. To Mom and Dad, and my brothers, Tom, Matt, and Luke, I love you all and wouldn't be who I am without each of you.

My wonderful editor, Kara Cesare, has always given me the support, encouragement, and feedback that I've needed. And I continue to be impressed by everyone I meet at Penguin. To my agent, Laura Dail, thank you for your guidance, kindness, and hard work. I always enjoy opening your e-mails, which seem to almost magically appear in my in-box.

I also am grateful for the help of Mary and Doug Barakat, Bruce McPherson, Amy Tan, David Axe, Allon Almougy, Shoshana Woo,

Dustin O'Regan, Michael Brosowski, Robert Olen Butler, Karen Joy Fowler, Elizabeth Flock, Gregory David Roberts, David Oliver Relin, and M. J. Rose. To my brother-in-law, Jon Craine, thank you for drawing such a splendid map of Vietnam.

And of course, thank you, readers, librarians, and booksellers, for supporting me and all of my endeavors. Without you, my stories would not exist.

QUESTIONS FOR DISCUSSION

1. What compelled you to read *Dragon House*?

2. What did you enjoy most about the novel?

3. Were you aware that so many children around the world are homeless?

4. Which character did you like the most? Why?

5. Do you think John Shors tried to draw comparisons between the Vietnam War and the Iraq War? If so, why?

6. If you have read John Shors's earlier novels (*Beneath a Marble Sky* and *Beside a Burning Sea*), how do you think he has changed as a writer, if at all?

7. What did you think of Loc? Why do you think the author chose to make him a former street child?

8. Could you tell that John Shors had traveled extensively in Vietnam? Do think it's important for writers to visit the places that they bring to life?

9. The author talks a lot about "dragons" in his novel. What do you think dragons symbolize in the story?

10. Did you enjoy Minh's character more when he was silent or when he spoke? Why?

11. Would you like to read a sequel to *Dragon House*? If a sequel were written, what do you think would happen in it?

12. What do you enjoy most about John Shors's writing style?

After graduating from Colorado College, **John Shors** lived for several years in Kyoto, Japan, where he taught English. On a shoestring budget, he later trekked across Asia, visiting ten countries and climbing the Himalayas. After returning to the United States, he became a newspaper reporter in his hometown, Des Moines, Iowa, winning several statewide awards in journalism. John then moved to Boulder, Colorado, and helped launch GroundFloor Media, now one of the state's largest public relations firms.

John has been lucky enough to spend much of his life abroad, traveling in Asia, the South Pacific, Europe, Africa, and North America. Now a full-time novelist, John spends his days writing and going on family outings with his wife, Allison, and their two young children, Sophie and Jack.

John's first two novels, *Beneath a Marble Sky* and *Beside a Burning Sea*, have been translated into more than twenty languages.

Center Point Publishing

600 Brooks Road ● PO Box 1
Thorndike ME 04986-0001 USA

(207) 568-3717

US & Canada:
1 800 929-9108
www.centerpointlargeprint.com